When the Numbers Don't Add Up

Clare Evans

When the Numbers Don't Add Up
© 2025 Clare Evans
First published in 2025 by Axe River Books
axeriverbooks.co.uk

All rights reserved. No part of this publication may be reproduced, stored in a retrieval system, or transmitted in any form or by any means—electronic, mechanical, photocopying, recording, or otherwise—without the prior written permission of the publisher, except in the case of brief quotations embodied in critical articles or reviews.

This is a work of fiction. Names, characters, places, and incidents are the product of the author's imagination or are used fictitiously. Any resemblance to actual persons, living or dead, events, or locales is entirely coincidental.

Cover design by Jimi Rae www.jimirae.com

This book is produced using print-on-demand technology. It is printed and bound as orders are placed, helping reduce waste and environmental impact.
For information about rights, licensing, or permissions, please contact axeriverbooks.co.uk.

ISBN: 978-1-0369-2608-3

In a London just like ours, disease is eradicated, and everyone is born with 100 years of life, tracked by an implanted Life Counter. Break the rules, and time is deducted. Fairs fair. Until it isn't.

When a new law punishes babies for their parents' mistakes, Cooper and Lexie's newborn is already running out of time.

Determined to fight the system, Cooper is forced to confront his estranged father. As their battle intensifies, so does the public outcry, fuelled by a rebellious neighbour, an insider with a conscience, and the unstoppable power of social media.

With the clock ticking, Cooper and Lexie must risk everything to save their child's future. But in a world where time is currency, some will do anything to keep control.

For fans of Black Mirror and The Handmaid's Tale, this gripping dystopian thriller will keep you turning the pages long after lights out.

To Keith
Always and forever

1.

Lexie

It's a short drive to West Middlesex Hospital, but too far to walk today. Lexie runs a hand over her enormous bump, drawing Cooper's gaze from the road. He smiles, looking calm but probably faking it.

Concentrating on driving again, he cranes his head forward to peer through the grubby windscreen. The fraying wipers she keeps reminding him to replace are struggling with worsening drizzle. He hits the brakes as two women step off the kerb and glare.

'Sorry,' he says, glancing across at Lexie's hands, cradling her stomach.

'Not your fault, Coops. I'm fine. We're early. What can go wrong? Let's just get in there and get the operation over with. We can start the clock again with the baby.' She strokes his arm, feeling the wiry muscles through his shirt. 'We're going to do everything right.' The warmth of his skin is reassuring. She hopes he doesn't notice her hand shake.

It could be the changing light, but Cooper looks a bit grey. He's not good with anything that involves blood.

As they're pulling into St Mary's Maternity Unit the Ten o'clock news comes on the car radio. The first item covers further news on the Mexican earthquake. Lexie squirms in her seat, thinking of children buried in the rubble.

The newsreader continues, 'The latest update to the Crime Survey for England and Wales has been published by the Office for National Statistics today. It shows an acceleration in the steady fall in crime in all major categories, covering murder, physical and sexual assault, burglary and street robbery. The Home Secretary, when approached for comment, gave the following statement:

"Today's figures are a welcome vindication of the

Government's Life Counter Programme, encouraging those tempted to commit serious crimes to think first of the likely effect on their own life expectancy. It is a good day for all law-abiding citizens."

'Load of bollocks,' Cooper says, drumming his fingers on the steering wheel as he gives way to someone reversing out of a parking space.

'Shh,' Lexie replies, stroking her bump. 'It's a good thing, isn't it?'

'Huh,' is his only reply.

"In related news," the bulletin continues. "A New Directive for the Life Counter Programme went live this morning in maternity units throughout the UK. We have unconfirmed reports of anomalies occurring."

Cooper kills the radio.

Lexie moves her hand from her bump in an attempt to grab Cooper's wrist.

Too late.

'I was listening to that,' she says, conscious that she needs to stay calm.

'It'll be more rubbish. Let's get parked and get this baby out.' He turns and gives her the radiant smile that convinced her to have his baby.

It was all so easy then.

*

The lights in the operating theatre are dazzling. Lexie doesn't want to miss a thing, but can't stop herself from squinting. The dominant colour is brilliant white, as if she's in one of those dream sequences where everything is bright and harsh, fading to a blur at the edges. The light is so intense that she imagines the ceiling parting and blazing sunlight pouring in.

She'd like to relax and enjoy the experience, but her brain can't ignore the stench of disinfectant. Apart from making her nose itch, it's reminding her of scary things like injections and childhood illnesses. She wants to move her leaden limbs, but the epidural makes this impossible. Ridiculously, she longs for a bacon bap, oozing with tomato ketchup, butter dripping over her fingers.

She doesn't even like bacon.

'Try counting down from one hundred, Lexie,' the anaesthetist says. 'It might distract you. If I couldn't see you in front of me, I'd think you were running for a bus. The monitor's going crazy.'

She looks down at her hands and stops herself from drumming her fingers on the side of the bed.

'There's nothing to be afraid of,' he continues. 'You'll soon have a beautiful baby. Try to relax.'

Three deep breaths. 'Relax,' Lexie repeats. She tries a little laugh; it comes out squeaky, not like her own voice at all.

'100…99…98…97…' It's awkward talking to him. He's behind her, his warm coffee breath the strongest indication of his presence.

Going through a few numbers isn't going to make a difference. She rolls her shoulders and forgets to count.

One hundred years of life expectancy at birth.

It's guaranteed. That's what the Programme promises.

Lexie massages the heel of her palm, being careful not to dislodge the cannula on her wrist.

What were they saying on the news earlier? She glances at Cooper, but he's scrolling through his phone, head down, brow knotted into baby wrinkles.

It's fine. She checked her Life Counter before they wheeled her in, and it still showed a reassuring ninety-seven years expectancy. Those three missing years really piss her off but nothing she can do now will get them back. Three damn years for one little experiment with E when she was sixteen.

Cooper doesn't get it that the lack of that perfect number incenses her even though she has much more time left than everyone she knows.

'Keep trying to settle,' the man says.

He's persistent. Firm fingers press either side of her neck, pushing out towards her shoulders. 'Don't worry. We're here to look after you.'

Feeling the fingers without seeing the man is creepy, but she's sure he means well.

So rare to be touched by a stranger.

She takes a slow breath. It won't be long now. 'I'm not afraid,' she says. 'Not really. It's excitement that's making me jittery. You're the professionals. I've got nothing to do till the baby arrives. She'll get her hundred years, and I'll…we'll make sure she keeps them. I can't wait.'

The man doesn't reply, but his shoes squeak on the operating theatre floor. He must be doing something important, like adjusting the epidural.

Lexie tries to catch Cooper's eye. Her husband is pushing back his cuticles with his fingernail. Oh, Cooper, how gross. As the father in a mother-centred operation, no one except her is paying him any attention.

Someone hands Lexie a tissue. She swats her dripping face.

She's scared.

They might be hopeless parents. The child could be a nightmare, a reckless type who throws away her precious years.

Like her father.

No, don't think that. It's not fair.

Lexie wants to shift position, to haul herself up to get a partial view. It's not an option. The white screen over her tummy protects her from seeing the gore, but also takes away the excitement. The sensation of being awake but incapacitated is odd, as if her insides are a saucepan of stew and someone is scraping the bottom to stop the food catching.

Beads of sweat trickle into the deep furrows between the surgeon's eyebrows.

Cooper is standing to the side now, as far from the gruesome scene as possible. At least he's stopped looking at his phone, but she catches him examining his palm to check his Life Counter, although he's trying to do so on the quiet. Lexie would be checking hers every minute if she were down to forty-seven years like him. Even with ninety-seven years of life expectancy, it's difficult to avoid looking at your hand in case of unexpected changes.

Sweat drips inside her gown.

Unless Cooper can claw some years back, she will be a single mother by the time this child is fifteen.

Poor Cooper. That beautiful face, gentle features, soft curly hair. A good man, in a bad situation.

She knows him so well. Cooper will be weighing up looking bad by not paying attention against the embarrassment of looking too closely and passing out or throwing up. His usually warm skin colouring has developed a greenish tinge. A soft sheen of sweat is spread over his face like a slick of butter on a slice of bread. Like the time on holiday when he ate a bad oyster and had to camp out in the bathroom for two days.

Lexie concentrates on her breathing, slow and even.

80-79-78-77.

Cooper. Enthusiastic. Idealistic. Charming. Great boyfriend. Thoughtful lover. Lexie's best friend.

She wants to hug him, feel the strength of his arms around her. She can only watch him wipe the sweat from his upper lip and clench his jaw.

76-75-74-73.

The baby! Something's happening.

The scraping sensation has been replaced by a strange lightness and a feeling of air around her middle. The surgeon is smiling, lifting something up, her baby, their baby.

Lexie's mouth falls open. She can't concentrate on anything except her child, being lifted above the screen, red and wrinkled, streaked with blood and grease. A halo of red light softens the outline of her body.

Cooper's pallor has been replaced, as if a switch has flicked, with a child's healthy pink flush. His mouth is working, grinning, words falling out. His arms are out, ready to grab the baby.

The nurse brings her to Lexie.

The precious bundle, checked and draped with a white blanket, descends towards her. Lexie holds her gently without squeezing, astonished by the perfection of this tiny creature with bright, unfocused eyes. She pushes the fabric away. Skin to skin, heart to heart, they remake the connection lost during the process of birth.

The baby is tiny, fragile in her arms. She expected chubbiness, given how enormous her bump felt, but these limbs, although solid, are elegant. Considering Cooper is skinny and she is fit but lean when she isn't pregnant, this isn't surprising. Strange that her thoughts have all been directed to the birth and the baby's life potential, not her appearance. Now she can't drag her eyes away from this miniature human with more hair than she expected, a round, slightly squashed and reddened face and the dinkiest ears she's ever seen. Her eyes are huge. Are they Cooper's? Possibly. Lexie searches for her own face in her daughter's features, but at that moment the baby clamps her eyes shut, making the process harder.

What Lexie does know is that she has performed a miracle in growing this incomparable little creature. Who knew how instant maternal love could be, how trivial work and the wider world could become in the first minute of becoming a parent?

Cooper is at her side, gazing at the two of them, moving his hands hesitantly to touch the baby.

He is disturbed by a cough at her elbow. A faint whiff of stale garlic. A middle-aged woman appears beside them, her eyes pouchy in the unrelenting glare of the theatre lights. Cooper's shoulders move, drawing attention to his laboured breathing. His arm, touching Lexie's, becomes rigid as he clenches his fist.

It's stupid bureaucracy, but it's the same for everyone. Cooper will want to barge the idiotic woman out of the way, as far as possible from their new family.

Don't do it, Cooper.

Don't let that forty-seven become forty-five.

The woman is implacable. She's wearing scrubs, but it doesn't make her a medic. Her job is to hold the gun that will shoot the Life Counter chip under the perfect skin of their tiny baby. Her fingers, ready with the trigger, are dry and cracked.

A deep moan breaks the breathtaking silence in the room. Lexie's unintentional response. What an assault, to interrupt a new life like this. It happens to everyone, to register the birth, keep the child safe by alerting parents to vaccinations, and ensure that the infant becomes integrated into society.

It's not so simple when it happens to you.

The woman stands, obdurate in her determination to perform her duty. A dated floral shirt peeps out from under her scrubs. Tight lips and hooded eyes give little evidence of humanity or kindness. She looks bored at best, possibly exhausted and not in a fit state to mutilate their child. This momentous event for them is an everyday occurrence for her.

Pure hate gleams from Lexie's eyes, but it makes no difference.

Lexie holds the baby a little tighter. In response to the official's unfriendly stare, she loosens the blanket and gently draws her daughter's soft arm out of the covers. She flinches as the woman twists the newborn arm to expose the baby's hand and uses what is effectively a staple gun to punch a hole in her pristine palm. Little eyes fly open. The rosebud mouth forms a perfect 'O'. She begins to bawl, fierce, insistent cries.

The woman's mouth twitches in a parody of a smile. 'See. It wasn't so difficult, was it? They say it's a good sign if the baby cries.' Lexie glares at her. 'It's quite a metaphor, isn't it? We've given her a new lifeline. Much more reliable than palm reading used to be. She's a lucky girl, being born in this day and age.'

If she is expecting gratitude, she's out of luck.

'All official now', the woman continues. 'I'll leave you to it.' Her sensible rubber-soled shoes squeak as she turns away. 'Congratulations, by the way,' she says, twisting her head around for a final look. 'The first one's always the hardest.'

Heat rushes to Lexie's head. The room is swimming. As she

turns to be sick, a cardboard kidney dish appears at her side.

'How did you know?' Lexie asks, once she's recovered. Despite retching, she's kept a firm but gentle grip on the baby, still crying but less violently.

'It tends to happen with the first,' an older nurse says. Her gentle eyes hardened as they glanced up at the CCTV before regaining contact with Lexie. 'I believe it's something to do … with the anaesthetic.' She fusses with the blanket, pulling it round the baby's shoulders and hiding the offending hand.

'What are we calling baby, then?'

'Tash,' Lexie and Cooper say together.

'Lovely. Pretty little thing isn't she?' The nurse continues. 'Absolutely perfect. Let's get everything cleaned up, and we can get you back on the ward.' She's entering Tash's name and details onto a computer keyboard covered with a splash guard.

Lexie draws Tash a little closer. She forgets everything as she smiles at her darling baby. Her eyes are blue. They seem to lock on Lexie.

She will protect this child, whatever the cost.

2.

Cooper

Cooper tries to keep his breathing even. The only way he can calm his agitated lungs is by clamping his mouth shut and stopping his breath mid-movement. It feels like a pre-teen way to cause a fainting thrill and it's making him dizzy but the result is more effective than the exercises for expectant fathers he found on the internet.

At least he's stopped feeling that he's going to throw up.

Lexie's been uptight recently, anxious about the birth. She's so well-organised that the medical process will be clear in her mind so her concerns are bound to be centred on him and his shortcomings, real or imagined.

Of course, he's ashamed that he's beginning his journey as a father with only forty-seven years life expectancy, but it's impossible to explain that it's not his fault. He should have started the conversation about how he became estranged from his parents when he first met her. He remembers opening his mouth to offload the pain, then looking into those eyes that had never known loss, and spinning her a line about falling out with his father over their differing values. He failed the test then, and it is probably too late now.

So he hasn't tried.

It's been hard enough coping with the change in Lexie during her pregnancy. He read all the books, demonstrated more empathy than he thought possible to find within himself and stepped up to do some of the jobs around the house that he's always known he should do more of but managed to wriggle out of before.

It's only fair.

FFS, the hormones were a shock. He can't be responsible for everything that goes wrong. He knows from pub chats with his friends who have already become parents that there are tricky days ahead, but he's prepared.

*

It was unbearable, watching them cut into Lexie. His fault. He put the baby in there and caused her pain. Then, the miracle of birth. A human being he couldn't imagine until the moment he saw her. His baby was suddenly real after being an abstract idea for nine months.

Cooper experienced a moment of pure joy as the baby arrived. Real limbs moving, new skin glistening. The baby's face was so red and covered in gunk, but he knew he loved her straight away. He still can't believe it, one minute not there, the next a fully formed, if tiny, human being. Now he understands what all the fuss is about. It's frightening in some ways to think of the responsibility and the shifting sands of the family relationships, but he's excited, if apprehensive.

That woman wrecked it, with her bureaucratic idiocy, her refusal to let them enjoy the birth undisturbed as a family.

Cooper is proud of his self-control. He doubts if he's fooling Lexie. She has seen him ranting and flailing his arms in disgust every time he sees or hears a negative story about the Life Counter Programme.

Now there's this New Directive to worry about as well. He hopes Lexie has forgotten about that news bulletin.

He hasn't. During the operation, his Life Counter beeped a few times. It was hard to check it unobserved, but the number forty-six flashed up, and it was all he could do not to swear out loud. There is no opportunity to misbehave in an operating theatre. Either the New Directive has retrospectively docked him some months of life or, as he's always believed, someone is out to get him.

Lexie doesn't know who that is, but Cooper does.

Stay calm. Count as you breathe.

1-2-3-4.
Think before you speak.
5-6-7-8.
Concentrate on the baby.
9-10-11-12.
Change the habits of a lifetime. Leave nothing to chance.

'Do you want to hold her?' Cooper jumps, startled by Lexie's voice. He nods, his words frozen somewhere inside. He's desperate to feel her in his arms, but has visions of dropping her on the hard floor or getting her arm caught up in something and twisting it the wrong way.

'Remember to support her head.' She knows what to do already.

He angles his hands under his daughter and gently edges her into the crook of his arm. She's so light, and yet heavy, her head warm and damp against the inside of his elbow. She has opened her eyes, is looking at him, staring in fact.

How astonishing it all is.

She has hair, which surprises him, with a reddish tint. He remembers the way his mum's hair glinted in the sun. A childhood beach scene comes to his mind, from when they were all together. His mother, sitting on the sand, setting the picnic out. His father, lying nearby, exhausted from building sandcastles. Bruce used to smile then, connect with his children.

They were happy once.

No remaining siblings after his sister died, and parental attention was all on him.

The baby's hands have dimples. Was he like that? He thinks back to his parents' living room, photos in silver frames of him as a baby. He can't quite see them. It's been too long.

It's hard to drag his attention back from this little face that engages and unsettles him, but feels the need to say something. His lips fall open, gaping uselessly until he's able to say, 'I can't believe she's finally here.'

It sounds banal, emerging in a voice that is thick and hoarse.

He means it, though. She's astonishing, unique and wonderful. Well, other people would say she's red and wrinkled, but to him, she's exquisite now that she's here. He loves the feel of her, the weight, the warmth, the way her eyes seem to be examining him, although he knows that she can't focus yet. He wonders if she feels a connection yet with him, her Daddy. He hopes so. How clever they have been to produce her. He wants to hold her forever. On the other hand, he's afraid she might start crying and he'll feel it's his fault. He glances at the surgeon, who is head down, concentrating, stitching up poor Lexie. She seems oblivious as she stares at her new daughter, her eyes hungry to take her back. Cooper obliges. His shoulders relax.

The whole thing is quite alarming.

Lexie looks so calm. Perhaps he does, too.

Unlikely.

Cooper feels eyes on his back. Turning, he sees the anaesthetist checking the raw spot on Tash's palm where the Life Counter has been implanted. 'It will heal in no time,' he says, unsmiling. 'It's clever the way the implant grows with the baby.'

Cooper chooses to take his comment as a conversation opener. 'So,' he says, wondering how to start, 'how is it working out, with the babies?' He's left the question deliberately open and keeps his voice calm. His pulse is racing, pounding in his ears.

The man clears his throat, avoiding Cooper's eyes. 'Let's see, shall we? Her Life Counter will be synching now,' he says. 'The details will appear on the monitor any minute.'

Cooper glances at Lexie. She is already watching the screen, while every now and then smiling at the baby. She looks a lot calmer than he feels. Cooper puts an arm loosely around his wife's shoulders so they can experience this as a family. He longs to see that perfect one hundred figure, uncompromised, unsullied. His mind keeps darting back to the news bulletin.

Anomalies is not a comfortable word.

He rubs his palm, expecting another warning buzz. Nothing untoward is happening.

He takes a few deep breaths. It will be fine.

Tash will get her hundred years and will take after her mother, not picking up life endorsements for no reason, like her father. A stab of anger catches Cooper between the ribs at the thought that he is making himself feel inadequate when he's done nothing wrong. All he's ever tried to do is stand up for what's right, expose those who abuse power, and protect those who need help.

Shit. They'll hear his heart pounding.

Breathe.

The operating theatre is quiet. An instrument clatters in a metal dish as the surgeon straightens up, rubbing his lower back. 'All done. Time for the show.' He's sweating profusely. Cooper looks away.

The screen comes to life. Huge red numbers count down from twenty. Music blares from hidden speakers. The globally recognisable Happy Birthday song. Cooper's mouth twitches in a momentary grimace at the cheesiness. He forces a smile as the loud but tinny rendition of the familiar tune continues. Who designs this stuff? The least they could do would be to insert the individual's name into the song, but no such luck.

The countdown stops at 1. Colours flash across the screen, bright, garish, cheerful. A star, sending a trail of glitter from left to right. The music quietens.

'Congratulations,' flashes across the monitor. 'A star is born. Welcome to Tash Box, our newest citizen.'

There we go. She is officially named.

Cooper is disgusted by the razzmatazz, but strangely fascinated. His journalistic mind is already forming paragraphs to describe the show. How clever to make control look fun, a viewing opportunity for the masses.

In how many operating theatres across the country is this same charade being acted out? By the time he's blinked, Tash's arrival will have been superseded many times over.

The magic number flashes up.

100.

Cooper sighs with relief. It's there at last. They got away with it. He blinks. His eyes are so dry. When he looks again, it says 99, 98, 97. It's counting down. What's happening? His fists are clenching, even though his mind has barely had time to connect. He moves towards the anaesthetist. Cooper is yelling. He hears the voice as if it belongs to someone else.

"Anomalies."

"Theft of life."

He must know the final number. He looks again.

80.

It seems to have stopped.

'What the fuck?' he says, moving closer still. 'It's a mistake. Do something.' Cooper is face-to-face with the man. The anaesthetist is backing away. He can't go far without ducking around his equipment. 'She hasn't had time to do anything wrong.' Cooper is aware that he's shouting, but it doesn't make him sound strong, even to himself.

Petulant is a better description.

'I don't understand,' Lexie says. She's holding the baby a little tighter. As if that will make a difference. 'We can put this right,' she adds. She frowns at Cooper. It feels like a rebuke. He envies her naivety. Now it's happened, he realises it was always going to be this way, New Directive or not.

The curse of Cooper has travelled down the generations.

He's put himself in the wrong. Stupid, as usual. The anaesthetist, with nowhere to go, holds his hands up, palms facing Cooper. 'Hold up, fella. It's not my fault.'

Cooper swallows. He takes some slow breaths, but still wants to hit him. 'Uh, Um, I'm sorry. Nothing to do with you, I know. But somebody needs to explain. This isn't what we were promised.'

There are several people in the room, but no one rushes to fill them in.

'She scarpered, didn't she?' the anaesthetist says, once it's clear no one else is going to help him out. 'It was her job to tell you, but I guess it's not her favourite part of the job.' He looks from Cooper to Lexie. 'There's been a New Directive. You've probably heard about it. They issued an update to the software this morning.'

Lexie opens her mouth to speak, but Cooper is one step ahead of her. 'Yes, yes. We know about that. It's been widely trailed in the media. It's supposed to encourage prospective parents to go to parenting classes and eat the right food. All that stuff. We did that. We've always tried to do that. We're not the bad guys here.'

'We try so hard to get it right,' Lexie adds, her voice little more than a whisper.

The anaesthetist licks his lips. He holds both palms up, facing Cooper, and fixes his gaze intently on him, waiting for eye contact. Reluctantly, Cooper looks at him but refuses to blink. The other man swallows. 'That's the Government line, isn't it?' he continues. 'They slipped it through at the end of the last session when all the MPs were desperate to get off on holiday. And they've got that big majority, haven't they, and fearsome Government Whips. The Opposition didn't have a chance. I haven't read the bill, obviously, but I knew the gist of it. It seemed innocuous at the time.'

'Until today,' adds the senior surgeon.

Cooper and Lexie swivel their heads, refocusing their attention. Cooper steps back a couple of paces. 'We've only had one issue so far today in this Theatre, before yours, that is. A little boy lost two years. It was a straightforward birth, so I wasn't involved, but the news spread through the unit, as you'd expect. So we looked up the guidance we'd received,' He nods to the anaesthetist, who moves over to the computer, navigates a couple of screens and begins to read aloud.'

"The New Directive seeks to build on the success of the Life Counter Programme in nudging the Public into more favourable behaviour that will benefit everyone." Blah blah blah. So far, as we've come to expect. It goes on like that, talking about behaviours it is seeking to address, eating well, avoiding alcohol and drugs, taking exercise, getting enough sleep, all that sort of stuff.'

'Like I said, we've been doing all that.' Cooper's heartbeat has settled. His hands are still clenched.

'That's what we thought when we heard about the two-year loss, so we looked at the small print. There's this little footnote that takes you to a buried appendix. You have to access it through several links. Very shifty. When you get to that, you find, and I quote, "In exceptional circumstances, the inability of individuals to follow the best path for their future offspring may result in a minor correction to the life years available to their babies."'

Cooper steps closer to Lexie. Her tears are dropping onto the baby's arm. He gives her shoulder a gentle squeeze and blows air out through his teeth. 'I feel a lot better now. They've admitted that there's an issue. It's in print. We can sue them.'

The surgeon holds his hand up. His face seems more wrinkled than it did an hour ago. 'That's what we thought. Cut and dried. We took immediate advice from the NHS legal team because we didn't want to get sued ourselves. There's an extra paragraph in that footnote that basically says...'

'I'll read it,' the anaesthetist says. ' "Parents considering taking legal action should pause to wonder if it is their behaviour that has caused the shortfall, and they risk having their children taken into care on the grounds of child neglect."'

Cooper feels Lexie flinch and realises he's been clutching her too tightly. He relaxes his hold. 'Shit,' he says.

The surgeon comes closer. He puts an arm round Cooper's shoulder and places his gloved finger on Tash's tiny, reddened hand. Chubby fingers grasp the colourful latex. 'I'm sorry. This has been a shock to you. No one here...' He hesitates, and his focus slides to the left. He lets out a long, slow breath. 'I wouldn't like to speculate about why it has happened. Perhaps the two of you will have an inkling.' He looks from Cooper to Lexie and back again. 'The thing to hold onto is that you have a healthy baby, perfect in every way. Be the best parents you can be from now on. There is a way back from this.'

Fine words. They bring no comfort.

If the odds are fixed from the start, what hope is there?

Twenty years lost.

No hope of getting them back.

Cooper can't bear to look at Lexie. He doesn't need to. Her rhythmic sobbing tells him all he needs to know. Her eyes will hold that despairing look he has seen too often when discussing his Life Counter total. Those lips he loves to kiss will be pursed into a disapproving line, her forehead clenching into tension lines.

In her eyes, this will be his fault – as usual. Damned for a shortened Life Counter, and with no explanation.

Why didn't he tell her when he had the chance?

He must get out of here before he makes a bad situation worse. He heard the warning in the surgeon's voice. Rage rises from somewhere in his solar plexus, building, building. No breathing exercise can control this. He clenches his bony fists, nails digging into his palm, wanting to crush his own Life Counter, relishing the pain, longing to take out the surgeon, nurse, anyone. He wants to kill the messenger. Cooper grabs at his surgical cap, ready to pull it off and storm out. A nurse's gasp stops him in the process of grasping the fabric. He adjusts the gesture, as if he were scratching an itchy scalp.

He's not fooling anyone.

'Mr Box, please. You're in an operating theatre. Your wife and child are at risk of infection. Think about how you conduct yourself, if you don't mind.' The speaker is the second surgeon, a woman with painted-on eyebrows, their dark chiselled shape too strong for her pale skin. They look like snakes, ready to strike, startling and shaming him into submission.

Think about how you conduct yourself.

Cooper drops his hand to his side and takes a deep, slow breath.

Think about how you conduct yourself.

This will be his new mantra.

Hide your feelings. Hide the truth. Get them off their guard. Think about someone other than yourself.

The system has tied you up in knots. You need to think of a solution, and that will take time.

The two surgeons, with their assistants, stand down. Cooper realises how close he has come to being escorted out by security. A young nurse, his hands shaking, wipes the baby's eyes and face as she lies in Lexie's arms. Cooper risks a look at his partner. Contrary to his expectations, she is no longer glaring at him.

Lexie isn't looking at him at all.

Her entire concentration is given to the baby in her arms, a source of fascination and the fulfilment of a long-held dream. Lexie's eyelashes flutter as she gazes into Tash's unfocussed eyes. Strange cooing sounds emerge from Lexie's mouth. Words of love that used to be reserved for him fall readily from her lips. She smiles, but fat tears drip down her full cheeks.

Are they his fault?

Partly, at least.

If only he could redirect his anger into love for their newborn child. That approach seems to work for Lexie. For him, the fury intensifies with every thought of the implications for their baby.

The only thing that helps is knowing that everyone in the room is on his side, even if they can't solve the problem.

Relieved that attention is no longer focused on him, Cooper tries, inconspicuously, to scan the room for the location of the cameras. Of course, there are several. They'll have audio and video of his outburst. He stops himself from checking his Life Counter yet again. He felt a tell-tale buzz under his skin a few seconds ago. It would be his luck to be further penalised himself for speaking out for his daughter.

What does it even matter now? Everything is fucked.

His nerves are fried, even as he fixes a pained smile on his face.

'I apologise. I lost it there, and there's no excuse. It must have been the emotion of the situation. I hope you understand.'

It takes every ounce of his strength to sound calm again.

He receives a sad nod from the senior surgeon.

13-14-15-16

'I know it's not the fault of anyone in this room. I promise I will remain calm. And thank you for your efforts. Can I hold her again?'

Phew.

Lexie looks up at him, raising the baby a little while trying to brush away tears with the shoulder of her gown. 'Here, take her.' There's tension in her voice. She pulls the baby up a little more. 'Remember she's quite heavy.'

'Is it painful? Is the feeling coming back?'

'I can't feel a thing,' Lexie says. Her smile is sweet now. Is she faking it, too, or has she accepted that their daughter has already lost part of her life?

Cooper bends down to pick up the little creature, who is already transforming their existence. It's awkward, more difficult than the first time. Lexie loosens her arms as he tries to pick the baby up.

'Support her head,' Lexie reminds him.

There is too much to remember after such a shock. He edges his right elbow under the baby's head and half rolls her into his arms. It feels wrong, strange. He wishes she were on the other side. Cooper takes a few paces, jiggling the baby in his arms. He finds himself automatically swaying, rocking her. What a miracle life is. Such a responsibility to bring a child into the world.

He finds himself singing 'Rock a Bye Baby,' as his mother did to his younger sister. Lexie's eyes are shut. The medical team is engrossed. Cooper continues singing and rocking, but moves a little further away and turns his back to block the cameras. With the slightest movement possible, he touches the baby's palm, examining the display shining through the semi-transparency of her skin.

Still 80.

Twenty years lost on the day of her birth.

It could be worse. It should be better.

He's not going to accept it.

Think about how you conduct yourself.

How he deals with this is going to take a lot of thought, but, one thing is sure, he's going to fight for his daughter's life. He can't change the past. The future, however, is up for grabs. If he's careful.

'She's beautiful,' he says, handing her back to Lexie, who's sitting up as straight as the epidural allows and has her arms outstretched, desperate to be reunited with her daughter. 'I can't believe we made her.'

'Are you pleased,' she says, 'despite….?'

'Delighted,' Cooper says. He tries to warn her off with his eyes, keeping his face expressionless.

Lexie blinks. Her eyebrows tense, and a little furrow appears between them. She looks down again at the baby, and it's clear that any thoughts of Cooper are gone. It's better that way. He has been displaced, a painful thought.

Is it the same for all men?

One of the nurses catches Cooper's elbow. 'Dad. Why don't you go and get some air? We'll be here a while.'

Cooper feels his mouth lift into a smile at the first use of his new name. Something is salvaged. 'Is that OK with you, Lex? I could do with some fresh air, and you'll all be glad to see the back of me, I'm sure.'

Lexie smiles. 'Sure. I'm in good hands. Go and sit down with a coffee. I'll see you in a bit.'

Truth be told, she seems happy to see the back of him.

'You'll be needing a rest.' He leans down and kisses the top of her head, stroking Tash's fuzzy cranium at the same time. Soft hair tickles his palm. 'I won't be long.'

Cooper counts to himself as he pushes through the operating theatre doors. He takes his time removing his gown and cap and placing them in the bin provided. Striding down the hospital corridor, his jeans flapping against his legs, he feels a little freer, even though he knows he's been dismissed. Confinement in the stark and over-lit theatre has numbed his brain.

Life has changed. As a father, everything he does will affect the next generation in ways he hadn't anticipated. He's already done untold damage, without meaning to.

Wherever he goes, whatever he does, he will be watched. His words will be heard and noted. It's always been this way, but today is the first time he has really understood the weight of surveillance, of his responsibility to others. For his daughter's sake, he must take care.

But he's not going to let it stand.

3.

Lexie

It is so quiet.

They've moved her out of the theatre and into a single room because of the Caesar. For a few minutes, she revels in the tranquillity and privacy, but before long, she's scanning the soulless space, longing for familiarity. Lexie has no experience of being a mother. She only understands the highs and lows of making things happen at work. The buzz she gets from marketing a product effectively and being rewarded for it. The happiness that comes from being with a group of colleagues who admire her talent. There is nothing to see or think of here apart from little Tash, who is sleeping soundly, her eyes screwed shut and her lips closed into an adorable pout. She will wake soon and need feeding and changing. Lexie doesn't feel equipped to deal with this double challenge, especially after the ordeal of the operation.

She didn't expect to be spending this time alone and she doesn't like it. It was a relief when Cooper left the operating theatre and took his anger with him. Lexie can still see the sympathetic looks as the medics fussed over Tash and congratulated her. They must have breathed more freely once he went.

So did she, initially. When Cooper's in a room, everyone knows it. That is part of his charm, but it can be too much. It was, just after the birth. Now, his absence is like a black hole, sucking her joy towards its gravitational field. She wants to see his gangly body bending over the cot, his goofy smile showing that he's as proud of their achievement as she is.

Lexie wants him here, his arms around her.

She needs to talk to him.

Her mind is exploding with the activity of the birth, the medical staff tending to her needs, the joy of Tash's appearance and the horror of the theft of part of her daughter's life. Images flash through her brain, some good, others traumatic.

Lexie's hands shake as her finger hovers over her red button. Tash is still sleeping, her little eyes screwed shut as if she isn't ready to join the world. Rubbery squeaks penetrate Lexie's thoughts as a nurse hurries down the corridor. A giggle of laughter, but also the sound of crying. Suddenly, Lexie wishes she were in one of the crowded bays in the ward nearby. How can she justify calling for help when the baby is sleeping peacefully?

She hasn't told her parents! This is something Lexie imagined they would do together, beaming as they Facetimed the new grandparents with the wonderful news. It hasn't worked out like that. Cooper might have filled them in. Hardly likely, judging by the look on his face as he left the theatre. He gave the impression of someone with murder on his mind.

How long is it since the birth? Lexie picks up her phone, which, thankfully, is sitting on the bed beside her, although she has no memory of how it arrived there. The last few hours are a blur. It is nearly 4pm and Tash was born just after 2.

The screen is a jumble of messages. How could they have made their families wait this long to hear the news?

Family, she should say. Cooper has no one to tell.

Within a few seconds, Mum's and Dad's faces fill the screen, their heads close together. Marika's blonde hair is newly washed and straightened, but her eyes are bruised with tiredness. Joe's round face is wreathed with its habitual smile, but for some reason, he has a couple of butterfly stitches on one eyebrow.

Nobody says anything for a second. Lexie can hear them breathing.

'Well, come on then,' Dad says, and it breaks the tension. 'What's the news? Am I a grandad yet?'

'Let her speak, Joe!' Mum bashes Dad on the arm.

There is so much Lexie wants to say, but only one thing matters at this moment. It's hard to form the words. 'Yes.' She can feel the tightness in her face as the excitement builds and her mouth stretches into a grin. 'Tash has been born and I can't wait to show her off. She's the best baby that's ever existed. When can you come and see her?'

'Straight away. Straight away.' Dad is out of his chair already. Mum is jumping up and down and whooping. She's usually more restrained.

'How fantastic for you both. I'm so excited and relieved. How do you feel? Were they kind to you? What does Cooper think? I bet he's ecstatic. The waiting is awful for the men. I can't see him there.' The words come out fast and furious, each sentence squashing the last without Lexie having an opportunity to reply. Can Mum sense something is wrong?

Lexie fidgets with the bedsheet with one hand. 'Cooper's gone out for some air. It was a bit stressful. You know how squeamish he is.' Lexie's voice wobbles on the final sentence, and she feels tears pouring down her cheeks. 'Please come quickly. I need you both. Now.'

*

They're there in ten minutes, by which time Lexie has wiped her face on the sheet. Excitement at the thought of seeing them and showing them Tash has pushed her anxiety out of the way.

'You were in the café downstairs, weren't you?' Lexie feels her face splitting into a massive grin. Their presence fills the room, bringing the familiarity she craves.

'Couldn't concentrate on anything at home,' Dad says, his eyes swivelling, taking in every detail of the room, leaving the hospital crib beside the bed till last, as if he's afraid to jinx something. Tiny snuffling sounds emanate from inside; Lexie knows that Tash is fast asleep because she has been checking about every thirty seconds.

Although Joe seems embarrassed to give his daughter, who has just endured such an ordeal, a squeeze, Marika shows no such hesitation. Rushing straight up to Lexie, she envelops her in strong arms. Lexie winces in anticipation of pain as she experiences the sensory overload of her mother's complicated mix of fragrances -

cheese and onion crisps on her breath, a new and unfamiliar perfume, hair conditioner and the chemical undertone of aerosol antiperspirant. The combination is heavenly, being so Mum-like and comforting, and makes Lexie want to cry again.

'Oh Mum, Dad, I'm so glad you're here.' Lexie wipes her cheek, knocking it with the cannula that is still, alarmingly, taped to her wrist.

'Well?' Marika says, 'Let's see her then.'

'I can't believe you've been so patient. You've been more desperate for the birth than I have.' The clinical setting drifts away as Lexie looks from the parents she loves so much and into the little plastic crib holding her daughter. Thankfully, she's stirring. 'Do you want to lift her out?' she says to Marika. 'I don't know if I can yet, because of the operation. I'm sure they told me, but I don't remember. I'm in a bit of a fog.' Tears she doesn't want to shed leak from the outer edges of her eyes.

Her mum looks so strong and solid, it makes Lexie feel safer. Already, with only an hour or so of being a mother, she's watching Marika carefully, checking that she's supporting the baby's neck. She doesn't need to worry.

She's never been so desperate for the reassurance of having her parents near.

'Oh, look at her. Isn't she adorable.' Marika jiggles Tash, who has opened her eyes and fixed them on Lexie's mum in a way that looks more deliberate than it probably is. Joe is gazing at the baby, an un-Joe-like soft look on his face as he tips his head to one side.

'Looks like my little sister,' he says.

'Nonsense,' his wife replies. 'She's the spitting image of me when I was a baby. Mum was always showing me the picture when Lexie was born. Now, little one,' she says, letting Tash's hand clamp on her finger, 'whatever anyone tries to tell you, remember you have Polish blood.'

'And British,' Joe says, tickling her under the chin.

'D'you know, that's weird,' Lexie says, her gaze flitting between her mum and dad and Tash. 'I haven't thought much about who she looks like. I see her, only her, and she's perfect.' Marika and Joe say nothing. They're too engrossed in staring at Tash with beatific smiles.

Lexie wants some attention on herself again. She's been so clever in having this baby. Her gift to the world. 'Hey Dad,' she says. 'What's with the stitches? Has Mum been beating you up?' The impossibility of this scenario makes her laugh. She feels high now, elated; her cheeks are burning from the adrenaline.

Joe replies without taking his eyes off his new granddaughter. 'It was those overgrown bushes in your garden. While we were waiting, I decided to cut them back for you. One whipped back in my face. It's nothing.'

'Oh, Dad, thanks.' He's always so kind. 'Wait a minute. While you were waiting? I know I've been out of it, but it was raining as we came in. Surely you weren't pruning in the wet?'

Joe shrugs, still intent on Tash. 'I couldn't do nothing, could I, not when my baby was in danger?'

Lexie floats on a cloud of euphoria. She's so lucky. The best baby and parents who always look out for her. Then, she wonders.

'Dad, when you say your baby, are you talking about me or Tash?'

Marika answers before Joe has a chance. 'Oh darling, it's all about this little one now. That's a brutal lesson you'll learn soon enough.' She's smiling, but there is steel in her words. She edges onto the bed, sitting carefully next to her daughter while still holding the baby. 'Now, tell us how it went.'

This is the moment when Lexie bursts into tears, leaving her mother looking torn between holding the baby and hugging her own daughter.

It's hard to get the words out. Sobs keep jumping up and interrupting as she tries to get the message across. 'The birth was fine.' She swallows. 'Cooper was so happy, like a different person, reborn almost.' Another sob blocks her windpipe. 'Then this woman came to put the Life Counter in. We both hated that.' Mum has put the baby back in the cot, and she's wriggling but not crying yet. Marika strokes Lexie's hand.

'Of course. It's horrible, but it's all for the best, for her protection. You'll forget it soon.'

'No, you don't understand.' Lexie pulls her hand away. 'It's all changed now. When they pressed the button, it went to 100 years, like you'd expect, then it started going backwards.' Lexie puts her face in her hands. She's reliving it, this attack on her baby.

Joe jumps up. 'What? That can't be right. We need to talk to someone; get it put right. It must be some kind of computer glitch.'

Marika is quiet and still, almost as if she hasn't heard, but Lexie knows her mind is active, thinking through the implications. 'I heard something on the News,' she says, 'while your dad was doing his pruning. I never dreamt it would mean this.' She strokes her chin. 'What did it go down to?' Her voice is low; Lexie wouldn't want to be the person to cross her in this steely mood.

'Eighty.' Lexie checked after Cooper disappeared. He might not know the final figure himself.

Joe splutters.

Marika continues. 'Did they say why?'

This is the hardest thing to explain because it's so obvious who the finger will be pointed at. 'There's been a New Directive. It's what you heard, but it didn't sound like it would be a problem. The Government's messaging must have been very effective because it didn't make a splash. It soon will, though. It turns out that if you do something wrong, your baby gets the blame.'

Joe turns towards the window, but Lexie can see him wiping his eyes. 'It's not going to be anything you've done, is it? What did Cooper have to say about it then?'

Lexie remembers Cooper going crazy in Theatre. She doesn't want to tell them, but there's no other way. 'That's the awful thing, Dad,' she says. 'He started to make a scene. It was so wrong – he made it even worse.'

'And?' Marika is still showing icy calm.

What does she say now? She never used to hesitate in telling her parents anything.

'It was like he reset. He cooled down and said the right things, but I know him, he's boiling inside. I'm so scared about what he's going to do, Mum. You know what he's like. When things go wrong, and he can't control them, it's as if he becomes a different person, someone I don't recognise. It makes me scared.'

Marika's eyes connect with Joe's. She looks back at Lexie, stroking her hair, rearranging the ponytail she'd tied it into to stop it getting sweaty.

'Shush now. It will be alright. We'll work something out.'

Joe swivels to face Lexie. 'Where's Cooper now?'

This brings new tears. 'I don't know, Dad. He said he was going out for some air. It seemed reasonable, but he's been gone ages. I need him.'

Joe has started pacing, never a good sign.

'He needs to man up. Strikes me that he's part of the problem.'

A picture of Cooper's look of wonder when Tash was born flashes through Lexie's mind. She knows how good he is. She worries that she's damned him in her parents' eyes. 'He is who he is, Dad, and I don't even know why he's lost so many years. He's a good person.' She waits for his reply, but none comes. She can't bear the silence. 'Then I find myself thinking,' she continues, 'why couldn't he just be, I don't know, more like everyone else?'

'We thought we saw –' Dad begins to say, but a sharp dig in the ribs from Mum stops him.

Marika stands, jabbing her finger at the CCTV. 'Don't blame Cooper. He's a normal human being, with the failings we all have. Well, maybe a few more. But he's a decent man. I can see that. And he loves you to bits. If he doesn't want to tell you why he's lost years, that is his right ... although I wish he would. But you're too good. You've never been in any trouble, even in your teens. You didn't get that from me.' She glances at Joe, who is looking at his feet. 'Or your father, for that matter. You don't understand that other people can't reach your standards. That makes it tough for you, and him.' She takes a long breath and bangs her hand against her chest. 'This is the system. Those faceless bureaucrats, messing with people's lives.'

Joe nudges her arm. 'Not the time or place, love. We might make things worse. Let's see what we can do, go through the proper channels. Get it reversed. Make it tidy.'

'Huh.' Marika pulls away from his touch. 'Your faith in the system amazes me.' She looks straight at the screen, her jabbing finger acting as a weapon. 'I know what it is to suffer discrimination, coming to this country as a child, seeing people look down on us, as if we didn't know how to behave, as if we were some kind of threat. I haven't worked hard all my life to have this happen. We're going to fight this. I don't care who hears.'

Lexie lifts her hand to examine the palm.

'Don't look at that stupid Life Counter,' her mother says, pulling at Lexie's arm. It only does harm. If your generation weren't so obsessed with staying connected, none of this would have happened.'

'That's not fair, Mum.' She's fed up with this same old refrain. 'You can't blame our generation for everything. You're addicted to your phones too. And social media.'

Marika sighs. 'I know. That's the thing. We're all obsessed with information. The corporations are addicted to the data they mine from us. The algorithms are literally there to stir up our emotions. Once the Government understood the power of the data, they couldn't let go of the control it gave them.'

'Yes, I get that,' Lexie says. 'But there's been such an upside, hasn't there? Look at the benefits.'

'True.' Marika isn't looking convinced. 'So, it started with nudge politics. That was fair enough. They said it was all to help the NHS, and we believed them. Next thing we know, they've claimed to knock out disease and we can all live to one hundred!'

Here we go again. 'That's what I mean. It was a huge achievement, Mum!'

'Sure it was. But now we have these monstrosities imposed on us.' She holds out the palm of her hand and points to the red glow of a notification shining through the upper layer of skin. 'And now look where we are.'

    Joe glances at the CCTV monitor high on the wall.

    Marika says no more.

4.

Cooper

A father. He's a father.

The word brings painful thoughts about Cooper's own father and the distance they have put between themselves. He doesn't want to see one atom of Bruce in Tash. The familiar anger, asserting itself whenever thoughts of his father come to mind, rises and swirls, adding accelerant to the blaze caused by that jobsworth bureaucrat with the Life Counter implant.

Cooper is barely aware that he is moving, but after a while, he finds himself somewhere unfamiliar within the hospital. He has been floating around the busy corridors like a ball of fluff pushed by the breeze, always there but unnoticed. What can he do? Where can he go?

He needs a coffee, if only to calm his frantic imaginings.

Cooper follows the signs to the hospital café, and even the thought of food and drink brings his agitation down to such a level that he feels able to unclench his hands as they swing at his sides. He can do this, can be a sensible and grown-up human being. He has no choice.

As he turns the corner, already inhaling the tantalising scent of coffee and frying bacon, his feet come to an abrupt halt at the sight of his in-laws sitting at a table nearby, clasping disposable cups and holding an urgent, whispered conversation. Fortunately, they are engrossed. Cooper remains immobile, and a middle-aged woman, texting as she walks, crashes into him. They both say sorry, and Cooper moves out of the way. Obviously, he should run straight up to Joe and Marika, a huge smile on his face, give them a hug and tell them the wonderful news.

Equally obviously, he isn't going to do that.

He tells himself this is because the news should come from him and Lexie together, not him alone. He knows this isn't the truth. It is abhorrent to think of exposing his raw emotions to these wonderful people, who seem so together and uncomplicated. Cooper sees the way it would go. He would rush up to them, give them an awkward hug and tell them the news. Joe would see the anger behind his smile and interrogate him. Cooper would be unable to stop himself from blurting out the whole terrible story. Joe's feeling that Cooper is not a good enough man for his precious daughter would be confirmed. Marika, understanding more of his pain at the estrangement from his parents, would want to mother him.

No way is he going to tell them at this moment, however much he knows he should.

His second failure as a parent and an adult.

Cooper pulls out his phone, trying to look occupied while he considers his alternatives. A little girl grazes his shin with an upended doll she's swinging by the leg. A man is holding her other hand and pulling her firmly along. The child is snuffling and gives the doll another vicious swing, making it crash into a nearby chair leg.

'Hayley, if I have to tell you one more time…No wonder your toys are always breaking.'

'It's not my fault. I want Mummy.'

The girl grabs the chair leg and holds tight as her father tries to keep her moving. The rubber on the soles of her shoes connects with the hard floor and produces a drawn-out, strident scrape that lifts Cooper's hair out of its follicles and causes a few heads to turn.

Cooper turns his back on the café in case Joe and Marika notice the disturbance.

'Come on,' the man says. His jaw is clenched. The words come out as if expelled by pistons.

Is this what fatherhood is all about?

'We can't see Mummy for another half an hour. Let's go sit in the garden and I'll buy you an ice cream after.'

The magic words have the desired effect, and the little girl's tears disappear. Cooper makes a mental note.

A garden is just the place he needs to be right now. Quiet and solitary. As the man disappears through the double doors of the café, Cooper has a hunch that there's something off about this individual. His behaviour with his daughter is sub-optimal, for a start. Feeling that this particular dad might have a story to tell, he follows, while trying to look as if he is purposefully striding somewhere else entirely. It's difficult to look intentional when following a man with a small child who alternately hurries and dawdles. Cooper finds himself concentrating on the little girl's socks, white with a flower motif. Unfortunately, the left leg has a pink flower and the right leg a yellow one. An indeterminate splodge, hopefully chocolate, mars the pristine white around the yellow flower.

After turning several corners, the man in front picks the child up and rests her on his hip, increasing his pace until he comes to a set of glass doors opening onto a courtyard garden. Cooper follows him out, trying to look inconspicuous. Non-threatening. The airless, over-wiped antiseptic smell of the hallways is blown away in a gust of wind, replaced by something woody and damp. Peat? Cooper's not much of a gardener.

Now he feels as if he's snooping. Instead of a large open space where he could wander, he finds a pleasant but boxed-in garden, viewable from glass-fronted corridors on all sides. Wooden benches, darkened and wet from recent rain, are set between brick planters and drifts of the type of shrubs often found in supermarket car parks. Valiant attempts have been made to keep it tidy, but dandelions and the odd daisy tangle the legs of the benches. Their flowers add a little joy that the official plants, buffeted by the elements, fail to do. Colourful tiles, clearly painted by children, are set into the various planters and run right around the garden. It is charming in a slightly institutional way.

Cooper sits on one of the benches and pulls out his phone. More than ever, he knows he should be upstairs on the ward with Lexie.

'Waiting for visiting time?' The other man is nearby and sits on the bench next to Cooper. His daughter is in a sandpit that forms a centrepiece in the garden. Cooper hadn't noticed it. She's taken her sandals off and is burying them. That may not go down well when her father notices.

'Um...' Whatever he says now isn't going to sound good. 'My wife's just given birth.'

'Congratulations.'

'Yes. Thank you.' He pauses for a moment and looks away. Further words are required. He knows that much. 'It's great. It's blown us away.' He pauses. The man is staring at him. He can't have been convincing. 'It's just, well, they were stitching her up and stuff and I thought I'd come out for some air.'

The man studies him carefully. It's uncomfortable, as if he's reading every negative emotion on Cooper's face. 'This your first?'

'Yes.' Cooper swallows. He feels his Adam's apple stretching the skin on his neck.

'Tough, with the first, when they bring out the staple gun, isn't it?'

Cooper nods and looks at his feet. He wants to cry, something he rarely does, especially since falling out with his father. Anger comes to him more readily than tears.

'I'm Clive, by the way.'

'Cooper. Hi.' He wonders if he should shake hands, but he's still clasping his phone, and Clive is rubbing both his hands together as if he's trying to brush mud from their surfaces.

'It gets easier, you know, as long as everything goes OK.'

The scrutiny is uncomfortable. It sets off Cooper's uncontrollable blinking that tends to happen when he's under stress. He scratches his head to distract himself. 'Goes OK? Sorry, what do you mean?'

'Your baby was born today, you say?'

'Yeah. An hour or so ago.'

'So.' Clive hesitates. He pulls his own phone out, glancing around before swiping a few times until loud music with a heavy beat emerges from it. He puts it on the arm of the bench. 'A bit of music, yeah?'

'Yeah, sure.' Cooper thinks that it's a bit weird to look for conversation and then drown it out with music when Clive clears his throat in a meaningful way.

Cooper looks at Clive and recognises the warning glare he gave Lexie so recently. He keeps shtum.

'You're new to this game, given the way you're looking.' Clive is speaking like a ventriloquist, with little movement of his lips. The words come out muffled. He picks up a pebble from the ground at his feet and studies it intently. 'Look down when you're speaking. It's harder for the CCTV to read your lips. The music stops, picking up the words. Got me?'

Cooper nods. He feels as if he's entered a parallel universe. He wishes he'd had a coffee after all. The adrenaline from the birth has subsided, leaving him shaky and tired. Now, he's scared as well, stuck with a man who appeared to be a normal guy but is turning out to be some kind of weirdo. He'll be talking about getting messages from the plants soon.

Clive carries on playing with the stone, not looking at Cooper but continuing to speak in a muffled monotone. 'Your wife gave birth today. The New Directive's come in. Maybe you're both straight and narrow types and it's made no difference....'

A chill whips through Cooper's insides. He raises his head, enabling him to glare at the man. 'No,' he says. 'It has affected us.'

'Look down, remember,' Clive reminds him. 'Tell me about it, quietly.'

Cooper reaches down and re-ties the lace on his trainers. 'The birth was fine. We were stoked for the announcement of the hundred years, then the counter started going backwards.'

Clive nods. 'What did it go down to?'

Cooper chucks a pebble at the leg of the bench. 'Eighty,' he says. A hard ball of shame sits in his gullet.

Clive plays with a pebble. The man is infuriating. 'Could be worse,' he says. 'Must have been a shock though.'

Cooper wants to kick the ground, the bench, even Clive. Sympathy is something he can't cope with right now. He grinds the rough earth at his feet with the toe of his trainer. 'Yes. It was.'

'Do you know the reason? It's all a bit obscure, their calculations, that is.' A low chuckle rumbles out of Clive's throat.

'It's me. Always me. My wife is perfect, always has been. The Government doesn't like me.' Cooper feels his fists clenching again. 'I've done nothing', he continues, moving his feet backwards and forwards over the ground, 'to be ashamed of. It's complicated.'

'No need to tell me anything. No one's perfect, are they? They're getting more prescriptive now. Strangling us all into submission, by the looks of things. No one really knows if it's because they're becoming more powerful or losing control. Could be either.'

'If it was just me, I'd understand, but my daughter, she's only just been born. She's done nothing. It makes me so angry. I know we've got a crap Government but no way did I expect this.'

Clive makes a strange noise in his throat that comes out as a sort of 'Hmm,' then says, 'you've got a lot to learn, mate.'

Patronising pillock.

'I'm not stupid,' Cooper continues, wishing he were still in the cafe, away from this jaded man with a high opinion of himself. 'I'm a journalist. I want to fight this, any way I can. Get my baby's life back.'

'Of course you do, and you should. Everyone should. It's not that simple though.'

'Who are you, anyway? Cooper has an unpleasant sensation in the pit of his stomach. He doesn't even like this man but has been telling him stuff he should have kept to himself. 'I don't know you. You could be anyone.'

'Anyone, eh. Bit late to think that. I'm not the sort of person who could damage you. You've done that to yourself. I'm someone suffering in the same way. It's up to you if you believe me.' Clive shrugs and drops his pebble. 'Listen. We can't talk for long. It will look suspicious. My advice to you is to interact with people, carefully, without giving too much away. You'll find not as many people are so onboard with the way things are going as you might think. Stay off social media. Feel your way. Look for allies.'

Cooper feels his shoulders slump. 'That's not going to be easy.'

'You'll learn. Start with the older people, the ones who know what life used to be like. Talk to your parents, for a start. They'll have your back.'

Heat builds up behind his eyeballs, and he forces back the tears. 'I'm estranged from my parents. I upset my father, and he kicked me out. I've had no contact with them since. It would be quite the job to reverse that.'

Clive casts a sideways look at him. 'I'm sorry to hear it. If you can, repair the bond. You'll need support.'

Cooper knows how hard that would be. 'So, what's the story with you?'

Clive says nothing for a minute. His eyes are pouched; a hard line runs from his nose to the edge of his mouth. 'Second baby born yesterday afternoon. A boy. Eighty-six years remaining. I used to have some time for the Government. Not anymore.'

This is puzzling.

'I'm sorry. I thought it only started this morning. Do you know why it happened?'

Clive makes a strange gurgling sound in his throat. 'Maybe we got caught by the Beta testing stage. Anyway, it is what it is. It's my partner, not me. It's usually the man, isn't it? She's had some addiction problems over the years. She'd been clean since Hayley was born but she's slipped up a few times recently. It's caused problems in our relationship, that's for sure. Tough on Hayley too.' He nods towards the child. 'She made the mistake of going to AA and NA. Tried to do the right thing but then they hang you for it. The worst thing is, I made her go to the meetings, so, basically, I turned her in and took years off the baby's life.' Clive scrapes his nail along the side of the bench. 'I'm fit to burst, I can tell you.'

Cooper doesn't know what to say. Strangely, he feels better, knowing that someone else is also suffering. 'I'm sorry.' He drums his fingers on the arm of the bench.

'Not your problem, mate. Sounds like you've got some thinking to do yourself. You'll come to your own conclusions, I'm sure. Hayley, what the hell are you doing? I've told you before not to take your shoes off in the sandpit.' Clive jumps up and picks the little girl up, brushing sand off her dress and rescuing her sandals from their submerged position. As he holds Hayley up, hiding his mouth behind her head, he offers some final advice. 'Watch your phone. We all know they're tracking our every move, don't we, but it's easier to put it to the back of your mind. It all started with the pandemic, I reckon. Get yourself a burner phone. Change the SIM as often as you can. Only take your normal phone when you don't mind them tracking you. You need to let them most of the time or they'll know you're up to no good. Best advice you'll ever get.'

Cooper spots the edge of an old-fashioned Nokia peeping out of the man's pocket. 'Yeah. I keep meaning to. I've been thinking about that for a while.'

'Don't just think. Do it now,' Clive says. 'Good luck. And best go and see your wife now. It's a bit wrong being down here, in the circumstances.' Clive walks briskly out of the garden, back into the hospital. Hayley is crying again.

Cooper takes a final look at his phone. He knows they are the immediate and most basic method of data harvesting for the Life Counter Programme. There isn't an easy way round that. Each individual's device is logged with a Government Agency. It's part of the Digital ID that citizens need to access services. It's supposed to make them think twice before they commit an offence or misdemeanour. What will be the effect of getting a burner phone and effectively going offline? It is something he has considered on many occasions. Will it be effective or merely flag to the authorities that he is definitely, rather than probably, up to no good? This Clive man may not have thought through the ramifications. Cooper's a journalist, FFS. He should be giving him advice, not the other way around. Having said that, what Cooper's been doing up to now is definitely not working.

He stands up.

Snap out of it.

The feeling of shame for being down here away from Lexie is overwhelming, pushing out for the time being the random thoughts left behind by his meeting with the disgruntled Clive.

How sophisticated is this surveillance? It tracks all his online activity, for sure, but is the CCTV picking up his every physical move as well? Do they really have enough people or AI capacity to analyse the movements of seventy million people?

The thought is chilling.

Will Tash get more time docked because he isn't up there with them? Now he's being ridiculous. He needs to get his head back into gear.

Cooper pushes his way through the double doors and heads back to the café, picking up a flat white for himself and a soya cappuccino for Lexie. It makes his absence seem a little less appalling. It takes him a while to find Lexie since they've put her in a single room, not where he was expecting. As he enters, Lexie and her parents are all there, gathered around the baby. The silence as he arrives is hard to ignore. Lexie's smile is guarded, but she does appear pleased to see him. Joe raises an eyebrow and turns away, while Marika gives him a quick glance, nods her head infinitesimally and strokes Lexie's hair.

Cooper licks his lips. He has some explaining to do.

5.

Lexie

It's great to be home, away from the artificial hospital environment, filled with noise and bustle and no familiarity. Needing help, Lexie was afraid to ask, seeing how busy the nurses were.

Home belongs to her. Home will be better.

It doesn't feel the same, though. As they drove up to the house, it looked different. The plantation shutters on the front windows were perfect for a couple, demonstrating their modern tastes. Will little fingers, not to mention dust, get trapped in the hinges?

The front door is so much narrower than she remembered, now she is struggling with a baby in a carrier. The stairs are steeper. How will she manoeuvre a pram through the tiny gate in the front wall? The front garden has morphed from compact and manageable to miniscule and awkward.

'Cup of tea, darling?' Marika calls upstairs from her current station in the open plan kitchen. Thanks to having a dad who's a builder, they've managed to fill in the side return and reconfigure the kitchen and diner into a large open space relatively cheaply. They wouldn't have managed to buy this house without the bank of Mum and Dad.

'Not right now, thanks,' Lexie replies, poking her head out of the door of the nursery. 'I'm having a few minutes to myself while Tash sleeps.' She feels guilty for hinting that Marika is making too much noise, but she will be oblivious. Silence and reticence are foreign lands to her mother.

'No worries,' Marika shouts back.

Lexie smiles to herself. Tash doesn't stir.

The nursery is pretty, decorated in powder blue as a gender neutral statement. Lexie remembers her arm aching as she wielded the roller when heavily pregnant.

Cooper helped.

They thought it through so carefully.

The back bedroom so she wouldn't be woken by street noise.

Near their front bedroom so they would hear her easily.

Pretty mobiles hanging from the ceiling.

Soft carpet with a charming rug on top.

Nothing could prepare them for the reality of becoming parents.

The old trolley she repurposed with chalk paint as a changing table seems ridiculous now. Why would she risk the baby falling to the floor? The changing mat is on the carpet, the trolley redundant. She trips constantly on the charming rug when running to the cot. The room, which seemed large enough before the birth, is now stuffed with bags of nappies, furry toy gifts and baby clothes that are still too large. Everywhere she looks, Lexie sees danger. Tash is so fragile, tiny. Every speck of dust on the windowsill might enter her lungs, damaging her brand-new airways. Each sound of a nearby car or police siren could wake her, even in the back bedroom, setting off the nerve-racking and insistent crying that only new-borns make. Lexie might get something wrong, will make mistakes, however careful she is. There is so much she doesn't know. She folds some baby clothes that are sitting in her lap. It's hard to make them neat and the flapping cotton arms offend her. How she wants life to be tidy again.

She is grateful that Marika is here so often, smoothing her path. Lexie dreads being left to cope without her, but is Marika's presence causing a fracture in her relationship with Cooper? Is she a splinter causing inflammation and pain or are they managing that all on their own. Perhaps Marika's cheerful help is reminding Cooper of the family he has lost.

Lexie sits, tense from the pain of her Caesarean wound, in the new ergonomically designed nursing chair they have bought and placed in here. So pretty now. Before, the room was a messy home office. Now it is cleaner than an operating theatre. The window is open to disperse the clinging smell of fresh paint, bringing her worries about particulates from vehicles on the Twickenham Road.

Lexie can appreciate the aesthetics of the room. Tash, of course, is not in it. Her carry crib has taken up residence in their bedroom, as close to Lexie's side of the bed as possible and, of course, exposed to all the traffic noise they were keen to avoid.

She's so tired.

Sometimes she's angry.

During the sleepless nights when she's endlessly feeding Tash, Lexie can't help thinking about those years her daughter has lost before she's had a chance to live. She tries to tell herself that it's not Cooper's fault. The Government has moved the goalposts. How was he to know? When she sees Cooper holding their baby in his arms, with a look of unconditional adoration she has never seen on his face before, she is overwhelmed with love for him. He has grown so much, has become gentle, loving and responsible with his daughter, just as she hoped he might. More than that, he has given her the perfect treasure of an incomparable child.

In the cold hours of night, when he is sleeping contentedly while she is up with the hungry baby, her resentment builds.

This is his fault.

Sitting in the nursery now, on her own for a few precious minutes while Tash sleeps, hearing the comforting clatter of kitchen crockery, courtesy of Marika and her muted but tuneful rendition of *Morning Has Broken*, Lexie considers their options. She must bring Cooper round to the right way of thinking. If only her head were clearer.

Lexie stands up. Her stitches pull. Her back aches. Her hamstrings scream. How can this hurt so much? She creeps out of the door and tiptoes down the stairs. Cooper is in the kitchen, his laptop open on the white painted dining table to the side of the island. He usually sits at the breakfast bar but it looks as if Marika is in the middle of concocting some elaborate meal. The worktop is littered with pots and utensils. Cooper closes the screen and looks at her, his smile coming a fraction too late.

'Where's Mum?' she asks, confused by Marika's sudden absence.

Cooper nods towards the bifold doors at the back of the room. His mother-in-law is sitting in the garden, eyes closed, with her face to the sky, cradling a cup of tea. Lexie nods, thankful they are on their own for once.

'Tash is sleeping,' she says, unnecessarily. 'What are you up to?'

'Oh, you know,' Cooper says, scratching his head. 'Checking out a few things. Coffee?' Cooper gets up as Lexie levers herself into a chair.

'I'll have chamomile. Don't want to keep her awake.'

Is he rolling his eyes? It's alright for him. He can't breastfeed.

'Sure,' he says. 'I'll get it.'

When did they become so careful in their conversations?

'I've been thinking...' they both say simultaneously, then laugh.

'Dangerous, that,' Cooper says, a teabag in his hand, 'in your fragile condition.' He strokes her hair.

Lexie instinctively shakes her head, dislodging his hand. 'There's nothing wrong with my mind,' she says, and is immediately ashamed of her shrill tone. What have they become?

Now he really is rolling his eyes.

'I didn't mean anything. I was joking.' His tone is harsh.

'I know.' Lexie says, resting her head in her hands and raking her fingers through her hair. When was the last time she had time to wash it? 'I didn't mean it to come out like that. Sorry. My head is all over the place. What were you going to say?'

He jumps in, almost before the words are out of her mouth. 'Nothing. You go first.'

'Ok.' Lexie calms her breathing. In fast, out slow. 'I'll try to get this across right, but my brain is so foggy. I can't find the words.' She pauses. Cooper picks the teabag out with a spoon and jettisons it in the bin. Is he listening, really?

'Go ahead.' He brings the tea over and gives her the sweetest smile, which makes it worse. This is so hard.

'We haven't talked much about what happened in the hospital.'

'No.' Cooper fiddles with the edges of his laptop. He has that closed look on his face she sees whenever she asks about his father.

'We need to talk about how we're going to approach this.'

'Yes.' He makes it sound like a question.

'What do you think?'

'That's not fair,' he says. 'You're supposed to be going first. What do *you* think?'

Lexie sighs. 'I think we need to look at what we've been doing wrong and try not to do it again. Consider what we can do to get Tash's timeline back on track.'

'Damage limitation, you mean,' he says. His fingers are tightening into fists, never a good sign.

Lexie shifts in the chair, trying to ease the pain from her stitches.

'I wouldn't put it like that. More a question of putting a positive face on life.'

'Virtue signalling, in other words.'

Lexie glances into the garden, where her mother has fallen asleep, mug dangling from her hand. Cooper is twisting her perfectly reasonable suggestion. He is the one who got them into this mess, after all. She forces herself to wait before answering. Usually, she finds the way Cooper bats back a quick reply to whatever she says endearing, like a good return of serve. Right now, it makes her want to grind her teeth till there's nothing left but a pile of powder in her mouth. She is usually known for her calmness. Lexie wants to pull his hair out and stab him in the eye with a fork. When she does speak, it is slowly and with an artificially produced softness. 'I don't want to fight about this. Tash is asleep and I'm exhausted. Neither of us is thinking straight.'

Cooper sits down, facing her. He leans back and crosses his arms. 'Don't forget your tea.' There's a hard edge to his voice. And his face. Glare from the sunlight pouring through the lantern roof glints on the edge of his glasses, making him look even more explosive.

'You're not wearing your contacts.' She's only just noticed. Cooper hates wearing his glasses.

'Didn't seem much point. It's not like we're going anywhere.'

It feels as if he's slapped her.

'Actually, my eyes are sore. It must be the lack of sleep.' Highlighting this, he takes his glasses off and rubs his fists in his eyes, as if he wants to beat them into submission.

She hates the way men do that.

'Seriously, do drink your tea. You know you need lots of fluid at the moment, for feeding Tash. It might help with the tiredness, too.' His voice becomes softer as he speaks, and the glimpse of normal Cooper is too much for her. Tears stream down her cheeks and, as she tries to brush them away, the ends of her hair dangle in the cup of chamomile tea.

Cooper jumps up and rushes over. Standing behind her, he envelops her in a bear hug and rests his chin on her shoulder. It makes her feel a little safer, the strength of his arms, the male smell of yesterday's tee shirt, coffee and unbrushed teeth. His bristles make her shiver as he kisses her neck. She eases herself up from her chair and puts her arms around his neck. They are both struggling with this, a new baby and now the knowledge that she's been robbed of years of her life. It's impossible to keep thinking of him as the problem when he's suffering as much as she is with the fallout. More, in fact, when she considers his reduced Life Count.

'I love you Coops.'

'Love you too Lex.' She can see his eyes crinkling at the edges through the lenses of his glasses.

'We need to work together on this, as parents. Let's not fight.' She holds eye contact, anxious that he doesn't pull away.

'I know.' He does loosen his arms, but only to hold her out in front of him and examine her face. 'You're as beautiful as ever, Lex, but you do look tired. You need to try to rest when Tash is sleeping.'

'I try, but my mind is racing. I need us to talk about this and work on a strategy. Then I can sleep. You know how much I like to find solutions to problems.'

Cooper eases his hands from her arms and points to her chair. She feels weaker, as if he has pulled her scaffolding away. 'Sit down and hit me with the details. And drink your bloody tea while you're doing it.' The words are abrupt, but at least he is smiling.

Lexie debates with herself the wisdom of being honest here, but she's so tired and needs to get this off her chest. 'OK. So, I've got a list of things we could do to make things better.'

Cooper's elbows are on the table. He rests the weight of his head in his hands. It's hard to tell if he's in despair or just tired. Cooper always seems to find his head too heavy to carry around. 'Of course you have a list. When do you not have a list?' He looks up. 'Go on then, tell me what's on it.'

Lexie knows her lists are legendary. It's her way of trying to control the world around her. She waits for a sigh, but none appears. Cooper does seem to be listening. She wonders whether to hit him with the whole list or merely a subset. She'll feel her way. 'Right, the way I see it is,' she says, before pausing when she notices how much he's blinking. No, she has to say it, however difficult it is. 'We're in the dark about their reasons for punishing us, but we've got to do something to make things better.'

'It's hard to disagree with that.'

It's a start.

Lexie feels hopeful until Cooper jumps up, starts pacing the kitchen and cracks his knuckles with each step.

Lexie gulps down some tea. It's not making her feel any calmer. It's tepid already.

'Let's get one thing clear though, Lex. We're talking about me here, aren't we? No point in pretending this is something we should both be doing.'

Lexie takes another sip. 'Some of the things on my list are ones we can both do.'

'Yeah. Right. Tell me what you think I need to do. I bet you're already on track.'

'OK.' She's going to have to be careful here. 'The first thing is to sign up for every course available to show our commitment to being parents and to getting things right. Virtue signalling, as you say, but worthwhile and we might actually learn something helpful.'

Cooper opens his mouth, but, instead of speaking, he strides to the worktop and yanks a plug out of the socket.

'Why have you turned the smart speaker off?'

He puts his head on one side and eyeballs her in the way he does when she says something stupid. 'The walls have ears.'

'Oh my God, Cooper, you're turning paranoid. You love it.'

'Loved. Past tense. It listens to everything we say, takes note of what we watch, things we buy, everything.'

'It's not the Government.'

'As good as. Don't you even find it slightly spooky that when you look on one website, or buy something online, adverts for similar products pop up everywhere you look, even when you're on completely different sites. I've been telling you about this for years.'

'I suppose. But sometimes it's useful. That targeted advertising on social media is really helpful. I get lots of stuff that way.'

'Point made. That's why they get away with it.' Cooper slaps his foot down on the pedal of the kitchen bin and dangles the smart speaker over the opening. Lexie can't stop her hands flying to her face. The device lands on the worktop instead with a loud clunk. 'Listen,' he says, 'I'm going to take note of your list, but in return, I want you to think, really think, about the covert surveillance that we're subject to all the time. How do you think they have all this bad stuff on me? Not that I accept that I've done anything to merit it, mind.' He's staring at her again, and his eyes have lost their former softness. 'Ditch it, right, or at least turn it off whenever we're having a conversation. You know it makes sense.'

Lexie nods, slowly, and takes another sip. He's obviously not getting enough sleep, and she loves the smart speaker. So useful in her everyday life. It talks to her more than Cooper does these days, for a start.

Cooper stands beside her and leans on the edge of the table. 'Do you have the list of classes?'

Lexie pulls a folded piece of paper out of her track pants pocket. As she opens it out, she notices how spidery her writing is. Normally it is neat and perfect.

Cooper leans over her and reads aloud: 'Healthy Eating, Eat the Rainbow, what the hell's that? Fitness First, Say No to Drugs, Vitamins for Vitality, Lose weight, Live longer. Bloody hell, Lexie. What a load of rubbish. I do most of those things anyway.'

'Those are all e-learning,' she says, and hears the defensive tone in her voice. 'I've done them all already. They won't take too long.'

'Yes, but…'

'It's not what you learn, it's the fact that you've done them. It will show on the system. You'll get brownie points.'

'Whoop-de-doo. OK, if I have to.' He blows out an elongated sigh. 'It might make a difference, but I'm skinny, I eat reasonably healthily and go to the gym. And when did you last see me doing drugs or getting rat-arsed?'

'I know. Do it for the smart speaker then!' Lexie allows herself a little smile and Cooper reciprocates but spoils it by scratching his head, something he does when particularly stressed.

'I'm still not sure about these courses. Knowing my luck, I'll lose even more years for doing the courses, because it shows I think I need them.'

'Cooper.' Lexie feels her shoulders slump.

'OK,' he says. 'What's next? I can't believe I'm going to get away that easily.'

'Do you see the two in the second section of the list? Those two are weekly group classes we go to together. They're at the hospital.'

Cooper has another look. 'Proper Parenting and Ten Ways to be a Better Parent. For fuck's sake.' He screws his eyes tight and rakes his hands through his hair, leaving it standing on end. 'I can imagine how painful those will be, full of dads with scrubby beards, skinny chests, sandals and earnest expressions. Are you trying to punish me?'

The image makes her smile, although his body language isn't encouraging.

Tread carefully.

Lexie reaches up to smooth his hair down and rests her head

against his chest. 'I know it's ridiculous. It's not because you need it, but we must be seen to be trying to do the right thing.'

Cooper sighs and blows out a long slow breath through her hair. 'I know where you're going with this, Lex. You're trying to repackage me, like I'm one of your products where the branding has been messed up.'

Lexie's head is still on his chest. She strokes his shoulder, hoping he can't see the creeping smile that validates his words. 'You're a unique product. You market yourself, but everyone needs a little guidance sometimes.'

Cooper pushes her gently away from him but she knows he is calming down. 'Anyway, no sandals, please, but you can produce the earnest expression without any help from me.' She hazards a grin. She never used to have to overthink her words with him.

'Watch it now. I can go off people,' he says, scratching his chin, rubbing at an imaginary beard.

Lexie strokes his arm. It's hard to judge if he's accepting this or merely tolerating it for the time being. 'Thank you.'

'Is that it then?'

The next bit is going to be harder.

'I thought, maybe, you could look back over the last few years and try to work out what has upset the authorities. You know, see if there is anything you can claw back. I know you've been good as gold for eight years, since we've been together, but there must have been something, in the past, that's caused the damage. If it's drugs, there's NA, or AA for alcohol. I'm not sure how it works with criminality but I'm sure you could get some time back by volunteering for one of the ex-offenders charities. Cooper, are you listening?'

Cooper is standing in front of her with his mouth hanging open. He is listening but he sure as hell isn't liking what he hears.

'Who the hell do you think you married? Shouldn't you have asked some of these questions earlier, like years ago, like before we had a baby? He turns from her towards the doors at the back and yanks at the handle.

Before he can open the bifold doors, Lexie grabs his elbow and gently disengages his hand from the door handle. 'I'm sorry.' She rests her head on his shoulder blade. Managing male ego is exhausting. 'I know you're a good person, but someone up there doesn't think so. We need to manage the situation. Try to think of it as PR.'

'I suppose.' Cooper turns towards her and starts chewing his nail. At least he's thinking about it.

'And we can try not to do anything to make it worse?'

He's laughing now, in a slightly hysterical manner. There's no warmth in it. 'I've told you before, I'm blameless in this. Hard to know how I can stop doing what I've never done.'

Little breathy noises are starting upstairs, easily heard through the baby monitor. The baby monitor? Is that listening to them too? She won't mention it, in case it makes things worse.

They don't have much time before the crying builds up to a piercing yell that pushes all other thoughts out of their minds.

'Shall I get her?' Cooper asks, rather more enthusiastically than usual.

'Before you go, there are two more things.'

He inflates his cheeks and blows air out through his mouth. 'Yes?'

'Your job. Does it put you under too much scrutiny?'

'Being a journalist is non-negotiable.'

'I know. But perhaps you could cover some less contentious subjects.'

All she gets is a 'Humph.'

'Or just do some articles that aren't hostile to the Government?'

'Like they'd believe me.' Cooper is moving towards the door. 'Anyway, I use a fictitious byline. They shouldn't know who I am.'

Lexie ploughs on. 'There's one final thing.'

He turns towards her. He has that blankness in his eyes she's seen before, as if he's moving away from her.

'You've never really told me how you became estranged from your parents.'

Cooper turns his back on her. 'Not now Lexie. I'm going to get Tash. I'll change her and bring her down for a feed. Perhaps that will get me some brownie points. What do you think?'

He's gone without waiting for an answer. The silence in the room contrasts with the rising cries upstairs.

Lexie wishes she'd kept her list to the simple things. With every sentence she has uttered, Cooper has moved further away from her. What is the point of increasing Tash's years if it destroys her parents' relationship?

6.

Cooper

Cooper's thoughts swirl as he takes the stairs two at a time to reach Tash in her cot. He squeezes through the tight space between Lexie's side of the bed and the door to the wardrobe. He doesn't resent the baby being in their bedroom. It's the only way to ensure that Lexie stays in the same room as him. What does infuriate him is her insistence that she knows best about improving their situation.

He is only too aware of his shortcomings. There is no need to point them out.

He also knows that the life penalties have been unjust and politically motivated. How could he ever explain this to Lexie?

Tash's insistent crying drives the painful thoughts away.

She is the one this is all about.

She is the one they should be thinking about.

She is the one they *are* thinking about.

Unfortunately, they are not thinking the same thoughts.

Cooper holds Tash against his shoulder. She nestles her little head into his neck, and her cries calm a little. He loves the feel of her hot breath against his skin. Dampness from her mouth, rooting insistently for a nipple, soaks into his T-shirt. She's so fragile. He desperately wants to make it right, for her, for all of them.

He imagines the cameras watching as he walks through to the nursery and gently lays her on the changing mat, supporting her neck in the way he's been shown. Her little legs flail as he tries, inexpertly and too slowly, to clean her and replace her nappy. His hands feel too large and clumsy, her limbs so frail. As if aware of his inexperience and incompetence, she cries louder and faster, her face puce and wrinkled.

Cooper redresses Tash and carries her tentatively down the stairs, cooing at her as Lexie does, but feeling self-conscious in doing so. It is both a relief and a loss when he places Tash carefully in her mother's arms. Cooper realises he's been holding his breath.

Leaving Tash with her mother, Cooper picks up his laptop and climbs the stairs again. He needs thinking space. Above all, he needs to do something. Pain builds in his chest. Not physical pain, more tension growing from somewhere near his diaphragm. As if someone who is out to get him, his father perhaps, is treading repeatedly on a foot pump, filling his body cavity with pressurised gas that will explode if he can't do something to deflate it. Cooper sits on the edge of his bed, pressing a hand against his chest. Is this feeling real?

He slips his laptop onto his knee and pulls up Google. He begins typing 'Pay as you go ph....' His finger hovers, afraid to complete the search and announce his intention to anyone who might be watching. Is it considered legitimate to search for untraceable devices? Is he signalling bad intentions by doing so? As a journalist, he does online searches all the time. He's never censored himself. Perhaps he should have. His understanding of the world has undergone a seismic change, and his confidence slips away.

Clive, the strange man at the hospital, told him to get a phone. He didn't say be careful how you do it. Hesitation isn't Cooper's way. What was that quote from Mao Zedong - 'The longest journey begins with a single step'?

Cooper jiggles his laptop on his knees. He always goes into incognito mode for work.

This is work. How incognito is it, really?

After a few keystrokes, he is into private browsing and feels a little safer. He carries on typing and soon has a page full of links. As Cooper scrolls through the options, he still half expects a warning buzz from his Life Counter. There is none. He feels emboldened. Within minutes, he is the proud owner of a new untraceable phone – he hopes. It will arrive tomorrow.

It doesn't escape his notice that he's left a very clear audit trail if anyone who is interested can get past his minimal attempts at secrecy.

Too late to worry about that.

Cooper pushes the laptop onto the bed and wipes his palms on the legs of his jeans. This should be easy for him. Because of his work, he is used to investigating, discovering, pushing his nose into corners where it might not be welcome. When did he become so timid?

The answer is obvious. When he realised that his deeds had damaged those he loves most, the ones he is meant to protect. When it became clear to him that someone or something had been watching his every move, probably for years.

Even knowing this, it's clear to him that timidity is no way to put the situation right, whatever Lexie might think.

This situation calls for bravery. He needs to find courage.

For better or worse, he has started. This will not impress Lexie, so he won't tell her.

Lexie. A perfect person, from a happy family. The pressure in his chest increases. Lexie wants him to reconnect with his parents, but she doesn't know anything about his family. A flashback hits him. His father, face contorted in anger, shouting at him. She wouldn't understand. Clive told him the same thing, though. It would look good to the authorities, wouldn't it? And Lexie would be so pleased.

Cooper stands up, hands on hips. He can do this. Can he? He walks round the room, rests his forehead on the wall, pulls it back a bit and bangs it hard, repeatedly, on the plaster. It takes his mind off the pressure on his chest. Trinkets rattle on the bank of drawers by the wall.

'What are you doing up there?' Lexie calls from downstairs. 'Have you hurt yourself?'

'I'm fine. Just banged my head,' he calls down. 'It's OK.' This is true, if not accurate.

'You're distracting Tash from feeding.'

'Sorry.' He's got it wrong again. Is he allowed to pace? Tough if he isn't. But something stills his feet. They remain planted on the floor as he stares out of the front window, through the fancy white venetian blinds he wouldn't have chosen for himself, where their neighbour opposite is performing a complicated manoeuvre, trying to reverse into a small space outside his house, between two unhelpfully parked cars. Cooper can almost smell the burning rubber as the tyre hits and mounts the kerb.

His parents. How long has it been? Too long. Long enough for redemption? His father's face fills Cooper's mind again, and he feels sick. Heavy glasses and a permanent frown of disappointment. Cooper's not the son he imagined. Never was. The frown morphs to an angry scowl in Cooper's mental tableau. Again, he sees his last sight of his father, that solemn face contorted with rage. *Get out of my house. I never want to see you again. You are not my son.* Cooper can't imagine what his own face looked like, but who could forget the sight of his mother, standing aside, distraught at the rupture in her family, dabbing at the tears pouring down her face with a damp tea towel?

He misses her so much, especially now. He'll contact his mother.

But she let him go, chose father over son.

Hard to forgive, harder to forget.

They might not even live in the same house. She could have changed her phone number. The heartbreaking years of no communication flash through his mind and leave an empty ache. His parents don't even know they have become grandparents. Their only child and he has disappeared from their lives as if he had never been born.

Cooper swipes through the numbers on his phone and finds that sad and neglected little name, Mum. How often he has stared at those three letters, longing to hear her nagging him to come out of his bedroom or having a go at him for leaving dirty cups and plates around. He'd settle for a hug and the knowledge that she doesn't blame him.

So many times, Lexie has urged him to get in touch. She's tried suggestion, instruction and even shame. *How could you lose contact with the people who love you most? They must be devastated.* So easy, when you come from a happy family, to imagine you understand the emotions within a dysfunctional one. Are they devastated or relieved that the son they think brought shame on them has disappeared from their view? Bruce is probably thankful that the stain on his reputation has been hidden beneath the carpet. Mum? She'll have kept his things as they were, in the hope that he might reappear. If she's been allowed to.

Why hasn't she searched for him?

Lexie probably imagines that Cooper's shortened life expectancy is the result of drug and drink excesses in the past, although she's never said that out loud. Perhaps she thinks he indulged in petty crime and spent some time locked up. Something like that would be so much easier for his parents to forgive.

The truth is worse, from their point of view. Cooper still believes he did the right thing. Would he do it again, knowing how much pain he caused?

Yes. In a heartbeat. This is bigger than Cooper and his family. Doing the right thing isn't beneficial for everyone but it's the only way to go.

There's no sound from downstairs. The silence sounds empty, like the absence of life. A fly buzzes against the bedroom window, bashing its body repeatedly against the glass before negotiating the slats of the blinds and flying off towards the light fitting. The repetitive noise reminds him of boring childhood afternoons, barricaded in his bedroom after he'd offended his father's high moral code in some way. The memories keep coming back. Always, that forbidding, disappointed face, peering down at him as if he found it hard to believe he'd fathered this inferior specimen.

Today is not a good day. Today is full of pain and regret. He usually tries to block out thoughts of his parents but when he fails his mood plummets. Whatever the cost, he must contact his mother.

He needs her.

Cooper still has her number on the phone in his hand. Before he has a chance to procrastinate further, he presses the call button and hears the tone.

A pulse beats hard in his ear.

'Hello?' Her voice is so familiar, yet distant. Diminished and tremulous.

Saliva builds in Cooper's mouth, collecting under his tongue. He swallows.

'Mum?'

The faint sound of a television theme tune in the background disguises the lack of reply. Cooper can hear laboured breathing.

'Cooper?' Faintly. 'Is that you?' So quiet, he wonders if he's imagining her voice.

'Yes, Mum. It's me.'

Her soft voice brings back memories of childhood hugs, the smell of chocolate muffins in the oven and bedtime stories. Not teenage years, surprisingly.

A muffled noise. Has she dropped the phone? The sound of quiet but sustained crying.

'Mum. Can you hear me?'

He remembers getting her into trouble with Dad on the frequent occasions when Cooper had done something wrong. She often cried, rather than standing up for her son.

A rustling as she picks up the phone. Swallowed sobs. 'I thought I'd never hear from you again.'

'Did you want to?'

'What do you think?' He imagines her wiping her eyes with a tissue, holding the paper still to absorb the moisture. 'Of course, I did. Do. You're my son, my only child for so many years. Where have you been all this time? Did you never think of me, of us?'

'Oh, Mum.' The words catch in his throat. 'Of course I did.'

'But you never....'

'There was no way back from what Dad said.'

'Oh, darling. Your father misses you, too. Only, he doesn't know how to talk about it.'

'He hides it well.'

'You could have contacted me.' She's turned the TV up.

'It's hard to hear you with the noise in the background.' The extra sound makes him edgy. He cracks the knuckles of his left hand.

The signal wavers. Her feet sound heavy on the wooden floor. He can see it now, too shiny from her obsessive polishing. Hinges squeak. She must be walking into the garden. 'Can you hear me now?'

'Yes. You, and the birdsong.'

Tyres on gravel. 'Your father's just leaving the house.'

'So, he misses me so much that you're afraid to tell him I've phoned.'

'It's complicated, Cooper. He's a proud man, with a position to consider.'

So, nothing's changed.

'Mum. I have so much to tell you.'

'Are you well? Are you safe?' She pauses. 'Have you got plenty of years left?'

That question was bound to come. He rests his head on the edge of the blind, takes a slow breath. 'Yes, I'm well. Yes, I'm safe. Years? That's complicated.'

She doesn't reply for so long that he wonders if the phone has cut out. Finally, she says, 'Are you happy, Cooper? That's all I care about.'

What can he say to this? Yes, he was happy, until the moment Tash's Life Counter was launched and the structure of his life collapsed.

'Can we meet, Mum?'

She is silent.

'Just for a chat.'

Still no words.

'And a hug. I need a hug, Mum.'

He can hear her breathing. Her mouth is so close to the phone, he imagines her lips brushing it. 'Oh, Cooper darling. So do I.

Every day I think of you. But, your father...'

'Don't tell him, Mum. Not yet. Let's meet somewhere neutral. How about that big garden centre near you that does lots of garden furniture? We can meet there and walk and chat. What do you say?'

A car alarm goes off outside. Cooper looks out. A cat wanders nonchalantly away from the flashing car, not his own, fortunately.

'You in a garden centre?' She says. 'That's hard to imagine.'

'I've changed. More than you'd believe. I'm a grown man, Mum, and I have so much to tell you. I'd love to meet.'

'When, darling? Now I'm talking to you, I can't wait.' There's a different tone to her voice, lighter, brighter.

'Tomorrow? Afternoon is best. Maybe 3 o'clock? I'm getting a delivery in the morning.'

'I'll be counting the minutes.'

'Remember, don't tell Dad. Oh, and leave your phone at home.'

'My phone. Why?'

'Just do, please. I'll explain tomorrow.'

'Perhaps you're more like your father than you realise. He's secretive too.'

'Never. I couldn't be more different.' The comparison angers him.

Lexie is on the stairs.

'Got to go.'

He kills the call. He wanted to say *I love you,* until she compared Cooper with his father. Lexie might have heard, anyway. He wants to be clearer on how things stand before he lets his jittery postpartum wife know what he's up to.

He needs to forgive his mother before he can express words of love.

7.

Lexie

Lexie has a knot in her stomach. Who was Cooper talking to, locked away in their bedroom with his phone? It's so unlike him. Was it a conscious decision to have a secret conversation while she was busy feeding Tash?

He stopped talking when he heard her footsteps on the stairs.

The tone of his voice was soft and intimate, the way he used to speak to her.

There's no doubt about it: he's behaving strangely.

More strangely than usual.

But so is she, to be honest.

The more Lexie thinks about it, the more she wonders if she went overboard with her endless list of things to improve. It would have been transparent to him that the necessary work was all on his side.

She trusts Cooper completely, but everything is so messed up. She knows she isn't thinking straight and doesn't want to believe that he's having an affair, but it's classic, isn't it? The woman has a baby; the man feels pushed out. Reaches out to some sympathetic, single female from his past. Damn. Surely Cooper wouldn't do that? He's as infatuated with Tash as she is.

But is he still infatuated with his wife?

She wants to say yes, knowing she's being ridiculous.

Tash is sleeping. Somehow, this makes Lexie's worries grow. When she's busy looking after the baby, it's hard to think of anything else. Now the house is empty of Cooper. Mum has gone home, and it has never felt so quiet. Lexie's pushed him out. She knows she has. She wants nothing more now than a big hug and some reassuring words. Why is becoming a parent so damn hard when it's all she has wanted for so long?

Last night, Cooper was quiet. He kept checking his laptop. This morning, he hovered near the door, constantly looking out of the window. When a delivery man came, Cooper blocked her view with his back, signed for whatever it was and shot up the stairs.

Now he's out. Wouldn't tell her where he was going.

Left his phone behind.

Cooper is addicted to his phone.

Lexie's so fidgety. She jumps up from the sofa and decides to make a cup of tea. Bloody chamomile again. What she'd give for a good, strong espresso. Her life hasn't been her own since she became pregnant.

As she flicks the switch on the kettle, the tears start. She tries to hold them back. Lovely Len must have been watering his window box next door. From the kitchen, she sees him brandishing his watering can at their front window. She walks through to the front of the house and opens the door.

'Can I water anything for you, Lexie?' He smiles.

'I'm not sure there's anything much growing out front,' she says, feeling her inadequacy. 'Would you like a cuppa, Len? The baby's asleep.' Her voice wobbles.

'Wouldn't say no, love.'

'Come on in. We'll sit in the garden.'

Len comes through, leaving a trail of damp earth on the wooden floorboards in the living room.

At least he missed the rug.

His polo shirt is crumpled and has a questionable stain on the front. His arms are wiry and brown from spending so much time outside. The gardens are small around here, but his is crammed with colour. As he walks past, Lexie catches a waft of earth and not-quite-clean clothes. There's something so comforting about him. He makes her feel safe. He's been around so long and has seen it all. She won't tell him anything, but his presence will help.

She's never felt so lonely.

Lexie stirs the teabag round and round to produce the treacly brew Len likes. The soggy bag drips on the floor while she's dropping it in the bin, but Lexie's too tired to wipe it up. On a whim, she tips her chamomile into the sink and makes another, slightly less strong cup of caffeine-fuelled builder's tea. She'll worry about the effect on her milk later. The mugs slop onto the engineered wood on the kitchen floor as she carries them through to the garden at the back. Nothing is going right today.

There's a noticeably blackened nail on Len's thumb as she hands him his cup. Normally, she would ask him about the injury. He seems to pick up quite a few during his daily garden potterings. Today, there is no space for anyone else's pain. Lexie sits down heavily in the aluminium chair, automatically checking for new bird droppings on the arms. The day is brightening, a light breeze driving the clouds away, bringing cotton wool drifts in their place. The air touching her cheek is fresh. She will hear Tash through the bedroom window if she cries.

The weather is better, good for sitting in the garden with a drink. Perfect time for a chat. Cooper should be here. With her. Not absent without leave.

He always used to be here when she needed him.

Len is looking at her expectantly. He'll be waiting for enquiries about his health. Lexie forces herself to be polite. 'How are you?'

'Mustn't grumble. Sciatica's playing me up as usual. Sylvia used to massage my back. Always made it better.' Len runs his other thumb around his damaged nail. 'Hit my stupid thumb with the hammer the other day, too.'

'It looks painful,' Lexie manages, wishing she hadn't asked him in. She has an overwhelming urge to run into the house, hurtle upstairs and bury herself under the duvet.

The silence is filled by the distant jingle of an ice-cream van and the thud of a ball against a fence nearby.

'Enough about me,' Len says, which is unusual. 'How are you two and the little one?'

'Oh,' Lexie says, intending to follow on with a generic reply about how lovely it is being parents. Instead, a howl emerges from somewhere deep inside. It is as if she is a shell encasing a ball of pulsating misery, and it has made its way out. Before she knows it, her head is in her hands, elbows pressed to her bare knees, and tears are dripping onto the paving slabs. She is no longer in control of her body or emotions.

She hears a cough. Looking out through her tumbling hair, she sees Len, frozen, staring at her. His eyes dart away and fix themselves on his untouched cup of tea.

'I'm sorry,' Lexie says, straightening up. 'I don't know what happened there.' Her cheeks and forehead are burning, hot and damp. Her breasts ache as the milk lets down, even in the absence of any cries from Tash.

Len presses hard on the arms of his chair, beginning to lever himself up. Appearing to think better of it, he flops heavily down again. She is relieved. Sympathy is hard to take.

'The baby blues,' he says. 'That's what they used to call it, back in our day. One minute the mum is fine, then floods of tears. Comes from nowhere. My Sylvia was like that for weeks.' He stops abruptly and takes a gulp of tea. The white cup is grimy from his earthy hands. 'What I mean to say is, she was fine most of the time, just had the odd off moment, if you know what I mean. You'll soon feel better.' He clatters his cup down hard on the patio slab.

'Oh Len, I wish it were that simple. Tash is wonderful, and I love being a mum. There's something else. Something we weren't expecting.'

She won't tell him. She can't let him know what has happened.

She tells him everything.

The New Directive.

Cooper's loss of life expectancy.

The theft of Tash's future.

Cooper's odd behaviour, the paranoia about being overheard and watched, the secretive comings and goings and this afternoon's disappearance.

She feels better.

Len's jaw is hanging open. His eyebrows are tensed, almost meeting in the middle. If a member of the Government were in the garden now, Lexie wouldn't fancy their chances of getting out alive.

He always seems such a gentle old man, but there is a seam of steel inside. He's had a tough life, and she knows he was not one to get on the wrong side of in earlier years.

'I'm sorry. I shouldn't have burdened you.'

Len picks at the dirt under his nails. His face has settled into calmer lines. 'It makes a change, though, doesn't it? You always listen to me.' He takes his glasses off and rubs the skin under his eyes. He looks older and more defenceless without his protective frames. 'Did I ever tell you about when our Graham got that terrible fever when he was a toddler?'

Len has told her many times, particularly when he's had a drink and is missing Sylvia badly.

'The encephalitis?'

'That's it. I never remember the proper names. Sylvia did all that, talked to the doctors and that. I was down on my knees in the bathroom at night, praying that he'd be spared. That's how I dealt with it. It worked, though. We got him back. Those tubes. I'll never forget all those puncturing his little chubby body.' Len removes his glasses again and concentrates on rubbing them on the bottom of his shirt. It's doubtful that they will get any cleaner.

'It must have been a terrible time.' Lexie has met Graham, but he rarely visits his dad. Only when he wants money, funds that Len can't easily spare. He always hands it out, though. Lexie suppresses a sigh. She wants to wrap herself in her mother's arms, not listen to her neighbour's reminiscences.

'What I'm trying to get at,' Len says, a hint of impatience in his voice, 'is that, back then, we didn't know how long we had to look forward to. You were born. If you were lucky, you got through childhood. One of my brothers didn't. We lost him to whooping cough at three. We expected loss, because it happened, so we valued every day. It's no good the way it is now, counting the years like they're money in the bank. That's not life. Checking before you do anything in case it loses you time. God, you young ones. You need to live a bit, take some risks.'

This isn't what Lexie needs to hear. She certainly doesn't want

Len sounding off to Cooper like this. It will only encourage him. 'I do understand what you mean,' she says, grateful that she can now speak without a wobble in her voice, 'but life's different now. We've got to live in the world as it is.'

'Hmm,' Len says. He stares for some time at a bumble bee that is so full of pollen as it negotiates a heavy head of buddleia that it is struggling to stay in the air.

'I mean, Len. You've done really well, and you're still going strong, so you must have been following the rules.'

Len chuckles from deep in his throat, and it sounds slightly phlegmy. 'You don't know the half of it, young lady. The thing is, we were able to have our fun before they started watching and counting.' He taps his nose. 'Not Sylvia, mind. She was a good girl, and look what happened to her. Taken in a puff of smoke before her time. Bugger them all, I say.'

'It's not fair, is it?' Lexie has seen Len's much-folded photograph of a young Sylvia, extracted from his wallet at every opportunity, but they moved to their house a few years after her sudden death. She can only imagine Sylvia's older self.

'And now I'm left here, with years to go, and I don't even want it.'

'Don't say that, Len.' Lexie feels guilty that they do too little to keep the old man happy in his solitude.

'I've got an idea,' he says, sitting up a little straighter.

'What sort of an idea?' Lexie can't imagine what he might suggest, that they be as bad as possible and see what happens?

Len points upstairs. 'The baby's very quiet. Do you have one of those listening things?'

'The baby monitor? Yes. I rely on it. You can't be too careful in the early months. Even when she's sleeping soundly, I keep checking on her. Having the listener there makes me a little less worried. Without it, I'd probably never leave her room.' She laughs, afraid that Len will think she's ridiculous. They probably didn't have such things in his day. Anyway, part of her is always wanting Tash to cry out, to need her, only her.

'Is it switched on?'

Lexie snaps back to attention. 'Yes. It's always on.'

Len begins to gesticulate, puts a finger to his lips, and mimes the action of pulling a plug out of the wall. 'I'm thinking of what you said Cooper was talking about,' he says. 'Just for a few minutes. Tash will be fine.'

Lexie nods and jumps out of her chair. Creeping upstairs to avoid waking Tash, she tiptoes into the bedroom and quietly presses the rocker switch to turn it off. Tash snuffles and shifts in the cot but doesn't wake. Lexie realises that she's been holding her breath. Surely they aren't tracking them through the baby monitor. She's never heard of such a thing, but it's not like Len to be paranoid. Whatever his idea is, it won't work, but she does want to hear it.

When she goes back, Len is muttering to himself, and Lexie wonders if he is consulting Sylvia.

'I was small when World War II was on,' he says, when he sees Lexie. 'You had to be so careful what you said then, so it comes easily to me. My parents drummed it into me.' He has a twinkle in his eye. Whatever his secret plans are, he's enjoying them.

Len leans forward, clasping his hands together. 'What I'm thinking is….' His voice is quieter than usual. 'Cooper's in trouble, and they're watching him, so he needs to be good. You're Miss Goody Two Shoes, but you have to stay that way or Tash will lose more time. I have all these years left and I'm miserable half the time.'

Lexie opens her mouth to say something reassuring.

Len holds up his hand. 'Let me finish now. I've had my life. I'm living in the past now. I'd be happy to pop off and join Sylvia. Whatever I do, it doesn't seem to make any difference. They don't think I'm worth watching. So, if you want to do anything you shouldn't, find out stuff they don't want you to know, let me do it for you. They don't suspect me.'

Lexie sits up tall. 'It sounds like something out of a spy movie.'

'It does, doesn't it? Sounds like fun to me.'

'Yes, but Len, lots of this would be researching stuff on the internet and things. Do you use the internet much?'

'Ah. Yes. Susan - that's my daughter, if you remember - did give me her old computer a year ago. Was always complaining that I was behind the times and would get left behind. She said she wanted to skip with me or something.'

'Skype?'

'That's it. Skype. But I don't know how to use it.'

'I can show you that. It's easy. Skype's gone now, anyway. But most people use Zoom or Google Meet now anyway. That's even easier.'

Len rubs his forehead with his grubby fingers. 'Zoom, eh. It's hard enough to remember the Skype one.'

Lexie sinks down into her seat. This is never going to work.

'Perhaps you could teach me. I've always wanted to learn.'

'OK, Len. We can try. If nothing else, you'll be able to talk to your daughter more easily.'

'And I can help you.'

'Thank you, Len. You know what, I feel better.'

And she does.

Lexie can't see much merit in Len's idea, but at least she can feel better about herself by helping him to keep in touch with his family.

It might even get her some credit with the Life Counter Programme.

After he's gone, it strikes her that he said his Life Counter never deducts time from him. Of course, he has no online footprint. He's a ghost, as far as the authorities are concerned.

8.

Cooper

Cooper is early. His mouth twitches in a secret smile. Is he becoming a new version of the disorganised but determined embryonic journalist his mother will remember? He is a man now, a father. More likely he hasn't changed at all but excitement at the chance of a reunion with his mother, more richly loved in her absence, has put a bomb under him.

It's hard to forgive her, though, for letting her son go so easily, and not searching for him.

Being in a garden centre voluntarily is also a novel experience. He doesn't notice much among the overwhelming display of green surrounding him. Too late, he realises that he should have specified where in this cavernous space to meet her. Despite the urge to escape the plants, he stays in the outdoor area, rather than moving into the network of rooms inside, offering furniture, tacky ornaments and pet food. He distinctly remembers, as a child, curling up and hiding in one of the dog beds on display. Bored with trailing around looking at plants, he thought it was a great thing to do but she was hopping mad. Now that he is a parent himself, he understands about stranger danger. Then, he thought she was overreacting. The memory brings sadness with it.

Cooper runs a hand through his hair. A snag on his nail catches in a curl. He puts the finger in his mouth and bites down hard, sending a shiver through him. His nails are raw since he called his mum yesterday. So many questions, so much uncertainty.

'Excuse me?'

Cooper swivels. His mouth is dry. He clears his throat in anticipation of his excuses.

'You're in the way.' A florid woman in a motorised wheelchair, a wire basket in her lap, is glaring at him. 'Can I get past?'

'Sorry. Sorry. Of course.' Cooper presses himself backwards, allowing her to pass, in the process becoming engulfed in a large plant with huge leaves that snake themselves around him, forcing him to concentrate hard on balancing to avoid complete capture.

'Cooper?' He jumps out. The plant falls, scattering wet earth on the gravel floor. Not the way he planned to meet his mother after all this time.

She has her hand over her mouth. Is she overcome with emotion? No, she is sniggering, the action showing deep wrinkles around her eyes that he doesn't remember. He wants to feel affronted. Surely there should be tears, recriminations, and emotion?

'Mum!' He finds himself laughing too, the sound deep, rocking his chest. Tears roll down his cheeks, and it's hard to work out what brings them there, positive or negative feelings.

It doesn't matter. They're here, together, after all this time. Cooper runs up, stretches his arms around her and feels the warmth as she buries her head in his chest. She seems smaller, increasingly frail, her bones closer to the surface. He loosens his grip, afraid that he might crush her. She stays where she is, breathing deeply into his sternum.

Gradually, gently, he moves her away, ostensibly to look at her, partially to release the tension he feels at her touch after such a long time. 'I've missed you, Mum.'

Understatement of the century.

She is staring at his face, taking him in. Cooper wonders what she sees. 'I was smelling you just then,' she says, her smile growing broader.

'Smelling me? Do I stink?' Cooper resists the urge to sniff his armpits, instead straightening the offending plant, scooping up fallen soil and depositing it in the tub. When he looks up again, she is still smiling.

'Of course not, silly. We all have our own scent. Breathing in yours took me back through all the years of childhood, the happy times.' Her smile falters a little at the edges.

'I'm sorry. I had to go. You know that.'

'Sometimes I sit in your old room. It's easier to think about you when I'm near where you used to be. I swear I can smell your essence there, even after all this time.'

Cooper swallows and avoids her eyes. He's aware that he's shifting his feet, as if he's still a child, caught out in a lie. 'I said I was sorry. Can we not go there right now? I have things I have to tell you.'

'Of course,' she says, and takes him by the arm. 'But you can't deny me a moment of reconnection. Let's go inside to the café and have a coffee. We can talk there.' He can feel the imprint of her fingers through his clothes.

'No, not inside,' he says, squeezing her arm as it links with his. 'We need to be discreet. Did you leave your phone behind, as I asked?'

'Yes, I did, although I don't know what I'll do if I break down on the way home.'

'You'll be fine. Let's walk as we talk. And make a show of looking at the plants. I don't want to draw attention to us.'

'Are you afraid Dad will find you?' There's a long pause as he fails to answer. 'He longs to see you, you know?'

Cooper can't stand the anguished look on her face. 'I don't believe that, and nor do you. I'm not specifically worried about Dad finding out, although it would be unhelpful. But I have things to tell you and they're for you alone.'

He is having to pull her along. It's as if she's so busy looking at him, she finds it too much effort to put one foot in front of the other. He knows it's been a long time since he's seen her, but there's something indefinably different about her that breaks his heart. She's older, yes, somehow less strong. Defeated? That's his fault, at least partially. He hasn't been there to stand up for her. Looking down at the top of her head, he notices that her hair seems less glossy, thinner. All these changes attack him with a sharp pain. He tries to remember if he used to notice things like that. Probably not. He always took her love and presence in his life for granted. The visible signs that she is ageing are unpleasant reminders of his lack of contact.

And yet she's smiling as if it's all fine again now that he's here.

His heart hurts. Nestled with the joy of seeing her lie thorns of resentment that she failed to protect him, nurture him, choose him over his father. How can she show unalloyed happiness after all that has happened?

Cooper picks up a trailing plant with pink flowers and pulls out the descriptive tag, giving every sign that he is reading it avidly. '"Fuchsia, trailing, excellent for hanging baskets and patio containers." We have a garden now, you know.'

Amy stops abruptly. 'A garden? I can't imagine that. It sounds very grown up.'

'I'm thirty-two, Mum.'

She brushes a stray lock of hair from her face. Her earlier happiness is tempered now by waves of expressions that cross her features as if she's trying them on for size. 'I know,' she says, 'but you weren't when you left, love. Give me a moment to catch up with the new you.' She takes the plant away from him and replaces it on the stand, picking up a similar one of a more delicate pink, with a purple inner flower. 'I prefer this one. Did you say we?' She bites her lip.

'I did.' Cooper can't stop himself grinning, despite his attempts at caution. He wants to hang on to his resentment, but it's hard. He pulls the pot out of her hand and twists it around to look at it. 'I have a beautiful wife called Lexie.' Cooper feels a momentary pang that he's kept this meeting secret from her.

She has a beatific smile on her face, and it takes years off her. The pain has gone. 'A wife. Oh, that's wonderful, darling. Someone to care about you. And you look well. I worry all the time, never knowing how you are. You wouldn't believe the pictures I get in my mind. I imagine you sitting in a corner, on your own, miserable, crying even. Sometimes I think you might be shooting up in some drug den, committing suicide, or at least thinking about it.'

Cooper jams the pot down into the space between two other plants, accidentally breaking a flower off its neighbour. 'Well, thanks for having such confidence in me. Did you never think of me doing well?' He feels irritation rising, just as he did when he lived at home.

'I'm sorry.' She opens her bag, takes out a tissue and dabs her eyes. 'But think back to how you were when you left.'

'Was kicked out.'

'However you want to put it. You disappeared from our lives, and it was such a terrible time. It was hard to imagine things working out well. Then we didn't hear from you for years. I kept reading all the papers and googling you, hoping to see some of your writing, but I never did. What was I supposed to think?'

Try looking for me, he thinks. Your only remaining child. He doesn't want to let his anger show.

'I'm sorry. Let's move on a bit, shall we?' He thinks fast. In all the time they've been out of contact, has he really considered how it must look to her? Any mother would miss her son, but it has never occurred to Cooper that she would imagine him falling apart.

Pride can be selfish. He's kept that thought at the back of his mind. It pops up now.

They walk between the rows, moving towards an area at the end displaying garden pots and ornaments. He lowers his voice. 'My journalistic career is going well. Has been, anyway. I write for various papers and periodicals, and even do research for TV. I'm still doing mainly investigative work, seeking out corruption and fraud, like I always did. I use a different by-line, a fake name, if you like. That will be why you haven't seen my work. I thought it was best to stay under the radar. It gave me a better chance of not being found. Not to mention that Dad got me blacklisted from working under my own name.' Amy shrinks under the intensity of his glare. He isn't ready to feel sorry for her. 'It would have been quite easy to find out, I'd have thought, if you'd tried.'

He's gone too far. Amy pulls herself up to her full height, which isn't as tall as she would like. He knows this much. 'I don't know how these things work.' There are tears at the corners of her eyes. 'I was scared to push it in case you didn't want to see me. I thought it was better to leave you to get in touch. It didn't occur to me that you would never make contact. I wish you could have at least done that.'

Cooper doesn't know what to say. He didn't expect to be on the defensive so soon into their reunion.

'That's the only reason I imagined the worst. I couldn't cope with your silence.'

Shame is a new emotion in his relationship with his family. He has always felt that the fault was all on their side. 'I didn't dare,' he says. 'Couldn't trust you not to tell Dad. Sorry.' Cooper reaches down to look at a large, glazed pot with an embossed design running around the rim. His mother picks up a smaller version and turns it in her hands. Her jaw is set tight around pursed lips. This is her classic tactic to hold back sobs. 'We've no time for recriminations now. You know I love you, always did, always will. I did what I had to.' He touches her arm again. 'I've got in touch now because I have some other news that I want you to know.'

'Yes?' She raises her head.

'We have a baby, Tash, born a couple of weeks ago. You're a granny.'

The small pot crashes to the ground, breaking into shards and slivers that fall on their shoes. An assistant turns her head at the noise and picks up a broom.

'Let's move on.' Cooper grimaces at the woman, who is now quite close. 'They weren't stacked properly,' he tells her. 'It slipped off as we stood there.'

'Don't worry,' the woman replies, grabbing a broom. 'It happens. If you move aside, I'll clear it up.'

As they walk away, Cooper hears muttering. 'Slipped off? Like hell it did.'

'You always used to believe in telling the truth, Cooper. I thought that was why you became a journalist.' He feels a flush rising to his cheeks.

'I still do, Mum, just didn't want to leave a trail today. It's for a greater cause.'

'Hmm. I've heard that one before. Don't forget that saying about the road to hell being paved with good intentions.' She plants her feet and refuses to move any further. 'Anyway, you said I'm a granny. That's what I want to talk about.' She sounds like a little girl who's just been given a puppy for her birthday, and her smile is back. 'A baby. I can't believe it. That's the best news I've heard in such a long time.' She's pulling at his sleeve. 'I'm so excited for you. Does she look like you or your wife? Does she have that big bump you have on the back of your head? What colour's her hair?'

'Hold on, Mum. All in good time. Perhaps you can see her. Soon. But I need to tell you one thing now, and it's the reason I've got in touch. Apart from the fact I wanted to, of course.' He hopes he got away with that one. 'You know what I was investigating, just before I left?'

'The Life Counters?' She raises her eyes to the ceiling, causing the reflection of the lights above to flash a warning from her eyes.

'Yes. And you know what I found out about the fraud that was going on?'

'How could I forget, when I saw what it led to?'

'Well, how was I to know that my own father would be implicated and throw me out of the house when he found out what I was doing?'

'He did offer to let you stay if you dropped the investigation.'

Now it is Cooper's turn to cast his eyes upwards. 'That was not a choice, and you know it. Anyway, what I'm trying to get to is that it's happening all over again, or something like it. Only it's worse now. Tash lost twenty years of her life as soon as she was born. Do you think I should take that lying down?'

His mother clasps her face with both hands. He notices for the first time that she isn't wearing her wedding ring.

'I remember hearing something on the News, but they played it down. What are you going to do?'

'Investigate, of course.' It's so hard. He wants to trust her. Seeing his mother has brought the love back and silenced the anger. But she is Bruce's wife. Where do her loyalties lie? Emboldened by her empty finger, he adds, 'And I'd like you to help me, if you will.'

'Help you? How can I?' She wipes her nose. 'What about your father?'

Cooper touches her ring finger. 'Your ring's gone.'

'Oh, that.' Colour drains from her face. She looks down at her hand. The naked skin is paler, slightly puckered, where the ring must have been so recently. 'It's at the jewellers, being adjusted. My knuckles have grown. It was getting hard to take it off to make pastry.'

Cooper feels his shoulders slump. The sight of that bare finger was so hopeful. He feels his plans falling into disarray like a line of skittles hit by a well-aimed bowling ball.

His mother pauses, pursing her lips, then licking them. She puts the tissue away. 'We're not getting on very well. He's become harder and harder since you left. He's either angry with me or dismissive. Mostly dismissive these days.' She stops and strokes the leaves of a delicate fern, absent-mindedly pulling off a withered stem.

A phone goes off, and Cooper looks around, alarmed that someone is nearby. He realises that it's his burner phone, but can't think who would be calling him.

Amy is oblivious. Finally, she looks up. 'I need to think about it. I'm caught in the middle between the two of you.' She pulls away for a moment, looking away from him and delving into her handbag.

Cooper checks his phone. What's it going to take to convince her?

'No, I've thought about it. I will help you, especially now I know I have a granddaughter. It makes all the difference. I should have done it before. I know that now. My future lies with the next generation, and you. Bruce has lost my trust.'

Relief washes through Cooper. He has made the first step. Lexie and that odd man, Clive, were right that he needs to reconnect with family.

Lexie is often right, guiding him in the best direction with her gentle persuasion. She asks so little but achieves so much.

Game on. His plan is in operation.

But can he trust his mother?

9.

Lexie

Lexie sits at the breakfast bar, cradling her empty cup and staring vacantly into the garden. Tash is still asleep, and the house feels painfully empty. Len's presence facilitated Lexie's meltdown, which was unhelpful, but his absence leaves a hole.

She needs Cooper, and he isn't here.

Len is a concern. While he is excited about the idea of becoming computer literate and engaging in a little light subterfuge, Lexie isn't so sure. What seemed like a good idea when they were sitting in the garden in the sunshine now presents itself as an impossible task. She continues to ponder as Tash wakes up and her cries lead Lexie wearily up the stairs to pick her up. Her thoughts are still tormenting her as she plonks herself down on the velvet sofa in the living room, feeds Tash and lets her eyes run over the abstract painting above the fireplace. Its fluid lines help to calm her brain. Once the baby is sated, Lexie sits with Tash over her shoulder, trying to get her wind up, regretting her choice of furnishing fabric now there's a baby in the family.

Cooper is a natural at burping and soothing the baby when she's fretful.

It's very annoying when Lexie works so hard at getting it right.

And where is he? Still not back from his mysterious meeting. Notifications have been coming in for him all afternoon, as his phone sits, lonely and neglected, on the kitchen counter. Lexie has picked it up several times and moved it into the living room, desperate to find out what's going on but reluctant to cross that line. If he is out cheating on her, the woman is hardly likely to be texting him.

What is she thinking? Why would Cooper choose this moment to betray her, with everything else that is going on?

Whatever this is, Lexie's going to have it out with him when he gets home. She's scared of what she might discover and worried she doesn't have the energy for a confrontation.

A part of her knows she is being ridiculous. It's the hormones driving her crazy.

Lexie hears the key in the lock. Here's her chance.

She stands up, rocking gently, with Tash against her shoulder. Cooper pokes his head around the door.

'Shall I take her?' he asks, holding his arms out. 'Is she windy?' He's beaming, apparently delighted to see them. Is this the sign of a man desperate to escape?

Lexie hands over the baby and a muslin to protect his shoulder. 'She was great earlier, but I've fed her and she's still restless.'

Cooper does a little dance around the living room, bouncing up and down and rubbing Tash's back. A resounding burp comes up, along with some partially digested milk, bearing an uncomfortable similarity to the cottage cheese Lexie had for lunch. It drips over his shoulder and down his back, completely missing the muslin. Tash settles.

'See. I've got the knack,' he says, pressing his smiling face against Tash's head and stroking her back.

It's very hard to stay angry with him, but Lexie knows the bad thoughts won't go away if they don't talk about this. 'Maybe. Where have you been? You left your phone behind.'

'I know. That was deliberate.'

Brazen.

'What have you been up to? Can't you imagine what's been running through my mind?'

Cooper looks at her properly for the first time since he came in. 'Really? What do you mean?' His jaw literally drops. Lexie had thought it was just an expression. 'You didn't think I was up to something I shouldn't, did you?' He tries to draw her into a hug while still holding the baby.

Lexie moves away.

'I didn't know what to think. It's been a difficult day. You've been so secretive, and then you didn't tell me where you were going.'

Damn. She sounds pathetic, and tears aren't far away. Her lip is trembling. She bites it so hard that she can taste the blood in her mouth. It doesn't work. Before she knows it, the sobs build and rack her chest. Within seconds, she is beside herself, for the second time today. She is ashamed by her lack of control. It makes no difference. Emotion has taken over, and it is exhausting.

Oh, to be able to lie on the ground and push the world away.

Cooper's feet are rigid. His body, usually in constant motion, is as still as a person playing musical statues when the music stops. Tash is in his arms, and now his wife has turned to jelly. He looks as he did when they went ice skating for the first time, and an elderly lady fell in front of them when he was using all his concentration on keeping Lexie upright. She knows he wants to help, but doesn't know what to do for the best. Seeing his dilemma and the gentleness that he cannot hide, she feels a little better.

This is Cooper.

He isn't a cheater.

The tears subside. Lexie's face feels hot. Her limbs are weak, longing to fold. 'Here, let me take her. I'm an idiot. I didn't mean to doubt you.' She reaches out to extract Tash from Cooper's shoulder, giving the cheesy deposits on his back a quick dab with the muslin.

'Oh, Lex,' he says, 'I wasn't trying to be mysterious. I was feeling my way and wanted to see where it went before I told you.'

This doesn't tell her much. She rocks gently while cooing at Tash. Tears are dripping onto the baby's head.

'I've got so much to tell you. It's not what you think.'

They always say that, don't they?

Cooper opens the door to the hall. 'Put Tash in the pram. Let's go for a walk, and I'll fill you in. It's better to talk outside.' He pushes up his glasses and rubs the red indentations they've left on the side of his nose. 'I've been following your instructions and it's been a tough day for me too.' He blinks. 'In a good way, in the end.' He pulls the back of his shirt away where it's sticking to his back. 'I might just change my shirt. Back in a minute.'

Lexie watches his gangly limbs as he runs up the stairs. It's strange. Even when she's so angry she wants to hit him, the sight of him and the way his body moves sends a torrent of love through her.

Lexie lowers Tash into the pram parked in the living room because the hall is too narrow. It used to be a calm, minimalist space. Now it is a mess of breast pumps, infant manuals and other baby paraphernalia.

Within seconds, Cooper runs back down, pulling a fresh T-shirt over his pale, hairy chest. 'Let's go. Just need to check my home phone.' He wanders into the kitchen.

'It's in here. I moved it.'

'Oh,' he says.

Lexie wonders what this means. Cooper finds the device on the low coffee table, flicks through his notifications quickly and takes it back into the kitchen, chucking it down on the worktop.

Once they're walking, Lexie is desperate to know what he has to say, but he is thoughtful and quiet. 'I'll push. You talk,' Lexie says, determined to give him a kick-start. 'You said you'd been following my instructions.' She likes the idea that her guidance is working.

'Yes.' Cooper side-steps an already squashed dog turd on the pavement. 'Watch the wheels,' he says.

'Come on. I'm dying to know what you've been up to.'

Cooper scans the housing estate they're walking through, as if looking for government agents hiding behind the wheelie bins. 'OK, so the delivery was a pay-as-you-go phone.'

'Right,' Lexie says. 'I get that. Untraceable. So why hide it from me?' The wind is getting up, sending a damp, peaty smell towards them, and blowing the edge of Tash's blanket. Lexie puts the hood of the pram up.

Cooper scratches the back of his neck. 'I don't know. I suppose I thought you might worry that I was up to something.'

'You were, and I did.'

He wrinkles his nose. 'It was for a good cause.' Spits and spots of rain have appeared from nowhere. Cooper's shoulders start to look damp. Changing his shirt was a pointless exercise.

Lexie stops the pram and faces him. 'Come on. Tell me. I want to know what you've been doing. You've caused me no end of anxiety.'

Cooper stands still as well. He looks straight at her. His eyes are watery. 'That wasn't my intention.' He pauses. 'I went to see my mother.' Before Lexie can absorb the impact of his words, he has walked on. She pushes the pram hard to catch up.

By the time she reaches him, she's out of breath. Her Caesarean wound is pulling. It makes her feel a little sick. 'That's great.' She touches his arm, feeling the hairs shiver a little in the breeze. 'It's fantastic news. I'm so pleased. It's what I wanted, for you, for all of us.' She keeps her fingers resting lightly on his skin. 'Don't stop talking now.'

They reach the gates of the park. The rain is slanting, hitting her in the face. Unpleasant as it is, it's kept others away so there is plenty of space to walk and talk.

They might need it.

It's always a struggle to get Cooper to talk about difficult things. His breath is coming out hard and ragged. His shoes scrape as he hurries along the damp path. He pauses to give a wayward football a resounding kick in the general direction of a group of boys. 'I don't know what to think. It was good to see her, after such a long time.'

'Did you go to their house?' Lexie asks gently. She doesn't even know where his parents live.

'No. I didn't want to risk seeing him.'

'Your father?'

'He doesn't regard himself as my father now, apparently.'

Lexie swallows. It seemed such a good idea to persuade Cooper to reconnect with his parents, but she might have made things worse. He was fragile already.

'So where did you go?'

'A garden centre.' Cooper laughs, but there is no humour in his words. 'I know, not really my scene. I thought it would be neutral.'

'And how did it go?' Getting Cooper to open up is like trying to get a confession out of a career criminal.

The rain is intensifying and beginning to slant horizontally. Lexie pulls the rain cover down over the pram. Sadly, she has nothing to shelter herself and Cooper.

'We talked. I told her about you and the baby. That made her deliriously happy. Apparently, she didn't have much faith in my ability to make a go of my life. She saw me shooting up in a dingy squat.'

Lexie still feels sick and knows it isn't her wound that is causing the issue now. This isn't an image she'd ever have associated with her husband. It crosses her mind that his mother might know him better.

Is this the reason for his lost years?

Cooper has been staring into the distance; now he looks at Lexie. 'Oh, for god's sake. That's not me. It never has been. How could you think that?'

'I wasn't.'

Cooper raises his eyebrows. 'Yes, you were. I'd better explain, or we'll never get past this. The last time I saw my mother, I had a horrendous row with my father. He basically threw me out and said he no longer regarded me as his son. I have been their only child since my sister died. They haven't heard from me since. Given the circumstances, and my mother's nature, she imagined the worst. That isn't because I was the worst. You have to believe me.'

Lexie wants to, so much. Her knowledge of Cooper's past is a blank. There's no going back now. She takes a deep and slow breath.

'You need to tell me everything. You've been so secretive, and secrets lead to lies. Secrets destroy relationships. You know that better than anyone.'

Cooper nods. He's studying her face with great concentration, as if he's suddenly learned something new about her. As if she's more perceptive than he's given her credit for. There's a drip on the end of his nose. At some stage, he's removed his glasses, which gives her a better handle on his expression. He's holding them, absent-mindedly twisting them in his fingers, smearing the rain-spattered lenses even more.

'You're right. I know it's raining but it's time you heard the truth, out here, where no one is listening. You might understand me better once you know.'

Lexie feels relief, but her heart beats faster. If it was simple, he would have told her earlier. 'What about this bench?' she says. 'We can angle Tash away from the rain. She's sleeping soundly.'

Cooper nods. He sits down heavily, as if his body is having trouble holding him up. Lexie joins him, lining the pram up to protect Tash and tucking her in a little tighter.

Lexie tries not to hold her breath. Another couple walks past their bench, heads down and hoods up against the rain. A wet tendril of dirty blonde hair is escaping from under the girl's hood. Lexie hears 'You're always making excuses,' as the partner tips the dregs of his takeaway drink over the grass, leaving an unhappy scent of stale coffee. We are happier than that, Lexie thinks.

At the moment.

'It's like this,' Cooper says.

Lexie gently extracts his glasses and puts them in her pocket. 'You don't need these, and you'll break them if you keep fidgeting like that.'

Cooper is rigid. Lexie raises her hand to his back, massaging gently the tight part where his neck muscles run down towards his shoulder. 'Just tell me. Once you start, it will be easier.'

'Not necessarily,' he says.

She would expect a wry smile to accompany his comment, but there is nothing. He is somewhere else.

Lexie shivers. 'Tell me about your father. He's obviously central to this.'

Cooper nods. 'My father. Yes. Where do I start? God, I could do with a coffee right now.' He blows air through his cheeks and seems to be forcing himself to turn and look at her. 'My father is a Grade A shit. I was never good enough for him and he lost no opportunity to point that out to me and everyone else.'

Although the rain is no worse, a cold wind drives the damp towards them. The sky is crying.

He frowns and holds his chin with one hand.

'I hate him. I want to hate him. When I look back and try to be fair, I recollect that he wasn't always like that. There are vague memories of days out, me and my sister, stories, rides on his back, the things kids are supposed to remember from their childhoods.

'It changed when my sister died. He was driving, you see, when it happened. He probably blamed himself, although it wasn't his fault.

'It turned him. He became bitter. She was always his favourite, Daddy's little girl. From that time on, he seemed to take everything out on me. He became obsessed with the Life Counter thing. It must be connected, although I've never thought that before. It's a mental illness, isn't it?'

Lexie wants to say something reassuring, but she's struggling to process this sudden dump of information, after being starved of any details in the past. She opens her mouth to speak without knowing what to say. Cooper turns his face towards her and she takes his hand in hers.

'How were you able to keep this to yourself all these years? It must have been torture.' It is an inadequate reply.

He shrugs.

'My mother is lovely, though' he continues. 'She tried to make up for what I was lacking from him, but she was always under his thumb. He's become a bully and a controlling bastard.'

'Don't hold back,' Lexie says, wondering if trying to inject humour into the situation will make any difference. As soon as the words are out, she realises it was the wrong thing to do.

Cooper tries to laugh but the smile freezes on his face. 'I've barely started,' he says. 'So, when he laid into me over the *incident*, she was unable to stand up for me. She had to support him. What do you think about that?' Suddenly, his eyes are piercing, frightening, as his gaze holds hers. 'Don't you think a mother should put her child first?'

Lexie keeps her hand loosely in his. The rain is finally easing off, but drips still fall from her arm onto Cooper's back. She picks her words. 'I've only just become a mother. Sometimes I can't believe I am. I know I love you with my whole heart, but what I feel for Tash is different, stronger in some ways, weaker in others. I will always stand by you and do what I can to help and support you, but for Tash I would lie down in front of a tank if it would save her life.'

'Exactly.' He is becoming more animated. The slump has gone from his shoulders, making him more upright. Lexie can no longer reach him comfortably and she lets her arm drop. 'She should have stood up for me.'

Lexie looks away, into the distance, noticing a tree with a broken branch swaying dangerously in the wind. 'I'm sure she feels that every day of her life,' she says, 'having lost you, but I expect it was complicated. She would be so wound up in her relationship with your father, and finances might have played a part. Perhaps she wasn't free to leave. Maybe she couldn't think that fast.' Lexie is struggling to keep up with Cooper's thoughts. How much harder must it have been for his mother, in the heat of an unbridgeable family row? 'Why don't you tell me about *the incident*, as you call it. I've no idea what we're dealing with here.'

'Sorry. You're so wise. I forgot for a moment that you're in the dark. I'll give you some context. My father is a senior civil servant. When I say senior, I mean senior. He was, and probably still is, one of the top people running the Life Counter Programme.'

'Oh.' Lexie's hand flies to her mouth. 'I wondered what you meant by that earlier.' Her mind begins to turn somersaults. Impossible things are beginning to make sense.

'Exactly. Pretty well-connected and a fully paid-up member of the establishment.'

Lexie's breath is coming faster, but Cooper seems to be calming down a little. She's still no closer to the meat of the problem. 'And he wasn't impressed with how you were earning your living?'

'Too right. He wanted me to take the Civil Service exams when I was at uni. Kept hinting at how he could smooth my way. That's what drove me mad. It showed that he didn't believe I could make it on my own, when that would be the only way I would consider it, but also, and this was the bit that really got me, it made it clear that he had no idea of the sort of person I was, that he could think I would want to follow him into being a civil servant, someone who tries to make everyone run along their little tramlines.'

'I can't see that working for you.' This sounds like a classic father and son conflict to Lexie, but it doesn't account for such a massive bust up, even if he didn't value Cooper as he should.

'That's putting it mildly. You know what I'm like. One hundred percent unsuited to sitting in an office and studying spreadsheets, ordering people around, making everything uniform.'

'Is that what caused the fallout?'

'Well, it started it. I knew I wanted to be a journalist, make a difference, be a bit of a disruptor. He hated it but couldn't do much about it. I could tell that Mum liked the idea, apart from the conflict it caused, so I went ahead. Got a job as a journalist, did well, had a few lucky breaks, and got a job at The Times. Perfect job. I was very junior but they let me join the Insight Team. Obviously, I was pretty much making the tea but hey, it was a start. My dream job. Investigative journalism. Undercover. Maybe a bit underhand. Exciting. I loved it.'

'And he accepted it?' The damp is working its way through Lexie's top and she begins to shiver again. It's great to hear some of Cooper's hidden history but the knowledge only makes her sadder.

'He seemed to, for a while. Didn't speak to me any more than he had to. I was still living at home at the time, which made that difficult.'

Cooper pauses. He's rolling his shoulders, looking around. 'I could murder a coffee.'

'We'll go home soon,' Lexie says. Her throat is dry. Tash will need a feed before long. It's a miracle she hasn't woken. 'Let's finish the story first.'

Cooper puts his head in his hands and rubs his temples. Is he ever going to spit it out?

'It all came to a head when I started working on an investigation into the Life Counter Programme.' He's speeding up. His words become a fast jumble. 'We had an idea that there was some dirty dealing going on somewhere, that the data was being manipulated to favour some people over others. That somehow people were buying themselves extra time, hiding indiscretions. We didn't know who was doing it or how. I thought it was happening somewhere at the lower levels, in the IT department, people selling favours and raking in the profits. Something like that.'

'And is that what you found?'

'No. It wasn't like that at all.' Cooper raises his head and looks her full in the eyes. 'What we discovered was that my father was at the heart of the corruption.'

Lexie's chest constricts.

'I still don't know why he was doing it. We had enough money. He was well connected. My guess is that he was trying to cover up something he'd done in the past and buy more time for himself, and then he got caught up in the web he'd made. One thing led to another. Who knows? He wasn't about to tell me.'

'But you didn't print your story?'

'We couldn't, could we? I confronted him with the evidence, said we were going to go to press, but I wanted to give him an opportunity to explain himself. I was giving him a chance, for fuck's sake, before a few senior journalists blew up his life. He didn't see it like that. He went ballistic, as you might expect, given what I've told you about his character. But he said he would forgive me if we pulled the story.'

Lexie nods. 'You would never do that. You're like a terrier once you're working on something.'

'Correct. It wasn't my call anyway. I'd been doing the digging, but I was the most junior member of the team. I refused. I did think long and hard about it because this was my father, after all. But I knew it was so wrong, what he was doing. The world needed to know. Plus the fact that it wouldn't be me making the decision. I hadn't told the rest of the team that I was going to speak to him. I doubt if they even knew he was my father.'

'But you must have realised he wouldn't accept that.'

'I was in a no-win situation. I said I stood by my story. He shouted *Get out*. And for good measure he pulled strings and had me sacked from my job and forced them to pull the story. The people who run things hold all the cards. I didn't have a chance. But he couldn't forgive me for standing up to him, so I was out. Out of their house, out of their lives. That's the story. I've had to pick myself up and build a new life.'

'But you wouldn't give up journalism?'

'No. I never got to work on The Times again, obviously. That's why I work freelance now, under a different by-line. Half the time, no-one knows who you are anyway.'

The final sentence bounces around Lexie's brain. She's had no idea of the problems Cooper has faced. Not an inkling. He's a bigger man than she ever realised.

'So, you weren't doing drugs or anything, losing your years that way?'

'No, they were docked by my very own father. How's that for a story?'

Lexie wants to feel sad, but instead she is angry. What kind of parents were they? Are they? She realises Cooper was something of a challenge in his earlier years, but so are most people.

Lexie rests her head against Cooper's, feeling the warmth and the pulse at his temple. 'I'm sorry. Knowing this makes me love you even more.' A thought occurs to her. Lifting her head so she can look into his eyes, she says 'It can't have been long after this that we met.'

'Not long at all. I went to the marketing conference to pick up ideas on reverse marketing, if you like. I wanted tips on becoming a journalist without a profile so I could remain under the radar. Someone was looking out for me the day I met you there, although it sure as hell wasn't my parents.'

'It was my lucky day too,' she says, believing it.

He squeezes her hand. The memory brings a watery smile to his face. 'Let's go home. I'm exhausted.'

'I'm glad I know.'

'You had a right to,' Cooper says. 'Sorry it's taken so long. I was ashamed.'

'No need. There's one thing I don't understand.'

'Yes?' He sounds guarded again.

'If he's so powerful and well connected, he must have been able to track your movements since then.'

'For sure.'

'So, he will know everything about your life, where you live, about me, and Tash.'

Cooper hesitates. 'Probably. I've always suspected it but it's hard to know for certain. I guess it depends on whether he wants to forget I exist or not.'

'But he hasn't told your mother where you are?'

'No, her surprise was genuine. I'm sure about that.'

'So, what's he up to? Is he responsible for what's happened to Tash? Is this your punishment?'

There is no reply.

'Cooper, I'm scared.'

Cooper puts his arm around her. 'Me too. It makes me feel like he's been watching me all this time. I haven't got the first idea what this is leading to, but I bet he doesn't either. The thing is, Lex, he's a bastard, and a powerful one, but he isn't invincible. He's arrogant, and that means he'll slip up and, when he does, I'll be there to hold him down.'

Lexie stands up. 'Let's go home. You're getting upset. Don't let hostility drive you.' She pushes damp straggles of hair off her face.

Cooper jumps to his feet. His jaw is rigid as he looks at her, without answering her comment. She wishes she could unsay her last sentence. Together, they move the pram. 'I've had years to think about this, Lex. I'm not rushing to judgement. We can exploit his weakness. Mum wasn't wearing her wedding ring. With a bit of luck, he'll have a double agent in his own house.'

This doesn't give Lexie much comfort.

She has stepped into a different world.

10.

Marilyn

Dense grey cloud hovers over Marilyn's Monday morning. Exhaust fumes drift towards her on the damp breeze, as she weaves her way through countless commuters, some hurtling, others dragging their feet, many scrolling through the other world displayed on their mobile phones. She can out walk them all. Mondays, for her, are a release, a supercharge of energy, a wish to get stuck into the workload that awaits her.

A longing to see him again.

No, park that for now.

Dropping into Pret near the office, she's second in the queue. The young barista holds up a cup, already writing her name on it.

'Skinny soya flat white?'

'Yes please. Oh, and a regular flat white too.' She tries to look cool, unaffected by the recognition. She keeps her smile inside.

He's the first person to speak to her today, and the only one to give her a smile since before the weekend. How rude she must seem. Now she smiles, and is about to start a conversation but his back is turned as he wipes the machine and tamps the coffee in. When he faces the front again, his eyes are on the next customer.

Marilyn stares at the counter, her smile frozen.

Heat burns through the cups into her fingers as she travels up in the lift. It's something to savour, the anticipation of sitting down, enjoying her coffee before the madness begins. Marilyn breathes easily, sniffs the aromatherapy essence she's rolled onto the pulse points on her wrist. Today's going to be a good day. Another senior civil servant she knows by sight enters the lift; she gives him a winning smile. Engrossed in something on his phone, he fails to respond, or even acknowledge the gesture. Behind him comes another woman, younger than Marilyn, smarter, more attractive, fashionable in a way Marilyn aims for but never quite manages.

Now he looks up.

The coffee holds a little less promise.

Marilyn blinks. It doesn't matter. Life is not a popularity contest. Success does not equal desirability. Stepping out of the lift onto the softer, deeper carpet on the top floor, Marilyn feels her shoe sink into the pile with a satisfying pressure. She is here. That is enough. She knows she is good, better at her job than those aggravating men with high opinions of themselves, their loud voices drowning out the sense spoken by quieter women.

Softly, softly.

Marilyn is close to power. She has an impressive pair of coat tails to hang onto.

She's where she needs to be.

It's almost a shame the carpet is so deep. She longs to hear her heels click on a hard floor as she strides towards her office. She feels her calf muscles tense. She is strong. She is here. She is needed.

Marilyn opens the door to her office and relishes the feel of her chest expanding into a deeper, more relaxed breath as she enters. Her eyes take in the important points. Wastepaper basket – empty. Desk – clear and wiped. Plants? She touches a finger to the soil of her precious money tree. The perfect consistency. Not wet but not over-dry either. Windowsill – clean and dry. Windows – sparkling. Fragrance? A slight dusty staleness from the air conditioning system with a gentle back-note of L'Air du Temps from the impregnated embroidered handkerchief, inherited from her mother, carefully draped over the top vent on the radiator.

It will do. It is hers. Her sanctuary from the world. She's so pleased that the Ministry for Population Affairs, a sub-department of the Home Office, has allowed senior civil servants to opt out of open plan offices. Marilyn pushes away a thought that she might be weird for preferring work to her non-existent home life.

Marilyn brushes her hand over the immaculate surface of her desk and gently places her coffee cup down, putting the second one off to one side. Shrugging her shoulders out of her coat, damp from the humidity but with no likelihood of dripping, she drapes it on the hook behind her door, which she wedges open.

It is a pleasure to sit down. Marilyn twists experimentally in her revolving chair, liking the tightening in her sides as her waist muscles engage. She returns her knees to the centre and moves them and her feet out, determinedly, and plants them firmly on the floor.

Manspreading. It feels peculiar. Why do they do that?

She returns her feet to a more elegant position and sits up straight. Ready for action. As she reaches for her coffee and pulls the top off the paper cup, she hears a beep from the handbag at her feet.

She forgot to put her phone on the desk ready for all comers before her first sip of coffee. With an uncomfortable feeling that she has already slipped up, Marilyn struggles to open the awkward clasp on her bag, trying to ignore the acceleration in her heartbeat, and closes her fingers over the cool metal as the phone judders with another beep.

Bruce.

Always impatient on a Monday morning.

Marilyn's eyes prickle as she scans the screen.

I need you in here now.
Where are you?
Bring me a coffee. My head is pounding.

Marilyn's mouth is closed but a tiny 'Hmm' manages to escape via her nostrils.

He's not in the best of moods. This is not unusual.

Marilyn stands up, clicks the top carefully back on her coffee cup and picks up the one she presciently bought for her demanding boss. With a wistful look back at the sanctuary of her office, she takes a deep breath and walks out of the door. She learnt some time ago to put her superior's needs before her own.

The air is chilly in Bruce's cavernous office. He's turned the aircon onto max again. Marilyn glances hopefully at the soft grey sofa. Bruce is standing, holding his phone to his ear, massaging the earlobe on the other side with fretful fingers.

'I know. I know. I'm working on it. Believe me. Yes, Amanda, I'm aware that there have been some hiccups with the New Directive, but I'm confident it will….'

Marilyn hears the strident tones of the Home Secretary. There is never a need to put her on loudspeaker. Bruce's left hand is clenching and unclenching. He opens his mouth but the furious monologue on the other end of the phone is not to be interrupted. Eventually, Bruce slumps onto the seat behind his desk.

'Yes. Point taken. I'm working on it.' He hurls the phone onto the desk, from where it skids, teeters on the edge, and falls to the floor. Marilyn bends to pick it up, but Bruce waves her away.

'Bloody woman,' is his only response. His elbows are on the desk now, his head tilted down, resting in his hands, revealing the small bald spot in his salt and pepper hair. He's massaging his temples with stubby fingers.

Marilyn hovers.

Bruce looks up, his brow furrowed, his dark eyes glinting.

Releasing one hand, he points at the desk. She puts the coffee in front of him. He flashes her a smile with a hint of warmth and nods. She knows he appreciates her ministrations that ease his days in the office, but usually he is more liberal with his positive gestures and thanks. These little crumbs keep her going and her fire kindled but they are scant this morning.

Marilyn eases her weight from one foot to another. He's often difficult on Mondays, but not this bad.

Through the thick plate glass window, she hears the distant wail of a police siren.

The finger points again, at the chair beside her. 'Sit down, for God's sake. You're making my headache worse, standing there like a vagrant wanting money.'

Marilyn sits carefully on the front of the chair. Experience has taught her to stay silent until he asks a question. The rebuke is unwarranted, but that's Bruce. His bark is worse than his bite. He's probably embarrassed that she has heard him being treated like a schoolboy with missing homework.

Knowing how much he prefers to be brought solutions than problems, she reaches into her bag and pulls out a strip of paracetamol, breaking out two and putting them gently beside his coffee cup. She remembers her own, steaming pointlessly in her abandoned office. Marilyn swallows. Her mouth is dry, and she has a tickle in her throat.

Bruce is still frowning as he pulls the top off the coffee, slams the tablets into his mouth and takes a large gulp of liquid.

Marilyn twists her hands in her lap. He grimaces.

'Ugh. It isn't even hot.'

'I'm so sorry.' She's half out of her chair. 'Shall I get you a fresh cup?'

Bruce tugs at his collar, scratching the skin on his neck with his knuckles. 'No. Don't bother. It will do.'

He cups the paper container in both hands. His nails are bitten down so hard that the skin underneath is red and raw. He's started on the sides too, she can see.

It's going to be a tough week.

Emboldened by his uncharacteristic silence, and his more familiar moroseness, Marilyn clears her throat.

'Is there anything I can do to help? Do you think you're going down with something?'

'Me? No. There's nothing wrong with me. Just a headache, that's all.'

Can she detect a softness in his voice? Vulnerability perhaps.

'You wanted to see me?'

'Yes.' Bruce stands up. His shoulders are hunched. He walks over to the window and stands with his back to her. His trousers are hanging looser on his tall frame. The back of his shirt is crumpled. The heels of his shoes are muddy and scuffed. This is so unlike Bruce.

It's that bitch of a wife of his. Has to be. Marilyn's hands clench.

That's why he's been so bad-tempered recently. To think she'd been worrying that he wasn't happy with her performance.

Marilyn's thoughts drift for a second. How strange it must be to spend a weekend in a spider's web of mutual commitments, interactions, arguments even. She can't imagine arriving at the office exhausted from the stresses of the weekend.

She jerks back to attention as Bruce squares his shoulders and turns towards her.

'Marilyn. I need you to find me a private detective.'

Something is failing to compute in her brain. She feels cogs whirring, synapses snapping, but her mind is in a fog. A private detective. This sounds like something out of a novel.

So not Bruce.

Marilyn bites the inside of her lip. 'A private detective?'

'That's what I said. What's the matter with you this morning?'

'I'm sorry, but I don't quite understand. If something needs to be investigated….' She searches for the right way of saying this, '….surely we can do it through our usual channels? That is what we do, after all, control, manage and investigate non-compliance.'

Bruce turns away again and stares out of the window. He's trying to hide it but he's chewing the side of his finger. He's quiet for so long that Marilyn feels embarrassed for him. Usually, her nerves are in a permanent state of anxiety in his presence.

No. This is different. He's unsure himself.

'Of course, I'm not questioning what you're asking. At all. But I need a little more information before I set anything in motion. I'm not sure where you find a private detective, in any case.'

Bruce turns, not towards her, but in response to a knock on the door behind her. A man she doesn't recognise is hovering in the entrance.

'Not now. I'm busy. Speak to the assistant outside,' Bruce says, making no attempt to moderate his voice. The man closes the door quietly and slopes away.

'Come and sit down over here,' Bruce says, and drops himself heavily onto one end of the sofa.

Marilyn perches on the edge. Such a compliment to be asked to sit down with him, but he's behaving so weirdly that it doesn't give her the boost she would normally expect.

'Marilyn.' His voice is softer and he's leaning towards her. Dark circles are noticeable under his eyes, made worse by a yellowing and pouching of the skin she hasn't noticed before. 'I've always known I could trust you. That you'd have my interests at heart and would be…discreet.'

Bingo. He needs her. After all these years of taking his right-hand woman for granted. The realisation sends a current of electricity through her body. Is this what power feels like? Imagine if she refused to help.

Marilyn quietly swallows the saliva that is pooling in her mouth. She will remain loyal. That is what she does. But her mind is racing. What is this about? His son. It must be. The bad penny. Not his wife after all. She suppresses a sigh.

'Of course, Bruce. You can always rely on me. I have never let you down, have I?' She risks a long, direct look into his eyes, and is rewarded with a lowering of his lashes. He does, at least, understand the extent to which she has compromised her valued integrity in his greater cause. 'Is this something to do with your son again? I thought we'd wrapped that up.' It makes it easier that she doesn't have children herself. It enabled her to stitch somebody else's child up without thinking about it more than she had to. She isn't proud of some of her deeds. If someone had asked her several years ago, she would have said that she would die rather than do something dishonest like that. It's funny how complicated life becomes when higher goals and individual desires become entangled. This son has been an ungrateful waste of space, from what she can see. So what if he loses some years? He deserves it. She's seen the pain in Bruce's eyes at the knowledge that his only child threw the chance of following him into the department back in his face. To turn down an opportunity like that and, even worse, to investigate his own father. What did he expect?

'No, it isn't Cooper this time. I hope we've taught him his lesson.

Especially now.'

'With the baby?'

'Yes. The baby. I hope it, she, I should say, will keep him on the straight and narrow.' His voice is troubled. There is misery there. Bruce is not a bad man. He's been pushed too far and what powerful man can tolerate such a thing? He must long to see the baby, but has made it impossible, has effectively pushed her away, pushed all of them away. Marilyn disregards the thought that a decent man would not do this. She is invested in the success of Bruce's project.

'So, if it isn't Cooper?'

Bruce rests his face in his hands. Through his fingers, Marilyn hears the words, 'It's my wife, it's Amy.'

Of course it is. How could she have been so stupid? The bad temper, exhaustion, crumpled clothes. Perhaps the patient care and attention Marilyn has devoted to Bruce over the years might begin to pay dividends. She's always had the suspicion that his wife doesn't appreciate him as she should. And yet he's upset. He hasn't noticed the arms that long to wrap themselves around him. This is going to take some time. Marilyn glances at her watch. 'Excuse me a minute, Bruce, while I rearrange something.' Her assistant answers on the second ring. 'Could you postpone my 9 o'clock and bring two coffees? Leave them outside the door. Thanks.' Turning to Bruce, she continues, in what she hopes is an authoritative tone. 'I'm all yours. Tell me about it and we can work on a strategy.' The 'we' makes her feel ten feet tall.

Bruce is silent. Marilyn stands and walks aimlessly around the office, listening to the muffled sounds of activity in the rooms around them, calls, phone messages, footsteps. Life. The air inside this office is still and stale.

Suffocating.

Eventually, there is a discreet knock on the door, and, by the time she turns to look, her assistant is walking away. Marilyn opens the door and retrieves the coffee with relief.

She places the two cups, china this time, on the table in front of them and sits down, smoothing her skirt underneath her. 'Now, tell me all about it.'

Bruce twists the cup in the saucer but doesn't pick it up. 'Amy's been behaving strangely recently. I think she's having an affair.'

Marilyn nods. It seems unlikely, but a welcome development if true. 'Do you have evidence of any kind?'

Bruce looks up. His fidgeting has resulted in some coffee slopping into his saucer, and Marilyn longs to mop it up but doesn't want to break the flow.

'No evidence as such. That's why I want a private detective. She's not herself.'

'In what way?'

'Well, she's been sullen for some time. She hasn't been the same since Cooper left. She blames me, you see. She's always been blind to his faults. But recently, her attitude has changed. She's started standing up to me.'

Now, that is novel.

'Where she used to give me the silent treatment if she was unhappy, now she's begun to question everything I do, throwing Cooper's absence in my face, asking more about my work. She was never interested before.'

'Does she know about the baby?'

'God, no.' Bruce stands up, picks up his cup and drains it in one. 'That would cause no end of trouble. The funny thing is, though, although a month or so ago she was on at me all the time about Cooper, now she's suddenly stopped talking about him. It's as if she's not bothered anymore.'

Bruce stares at his empty cup, swirling the dregs with a flick of his wrist.

'Anything else?'

He looks up, startled. 'She's started taking more care over her appearance, going out more. She seems more confident. It's disconcerting. Not what I'm used to.'

Marilyn opens her mouth to say something, but doesn't get the chance.

'And the other day, I caught her without her wedding ring. When I asked her about it, she smiled, in a weird way, and said nothing. I asked her again and she told me it was at the jeweller's, being cleaned. I don't believe her. That's why I want someone to check her out.'

Marilyn is silent for a while. Where the hell will she find a private detective that they can trust? A thought occurs to her. 'Bruce, I quite understand your concerns. This is very delicate for you and your family. You don't know what they will discover, do you? Could such a detective be trusted not to sell the story to the media? You don't want your son to get wind of this.'

Bruce's mouth gurns. He's chewing his cheek.

'I have an idea,' she continues.

'Yes?'

Marilyn notices that his hair needs washing. Men like Bruce can't cope with marital disharmony. Their lives are made so easy for them, with other people doing all the hard work. If one of the wheels falls off, they're incapable of coping. 'Why don't I do it? We can call it a special project. The New Directive is up and running. I know the Home Secretary is on your back, but we'll get past that. It's teething problems, I'm sure. I can help you keep on top of that and discreetly find out what Amy is up to, without alerting her to my presence. If she's having an affair, it should be easy to find out. What do you think?'

Bruce shrugs, but she's got through. He's been hugging his cup but now puts it down. 'Let's give it a go, shall we?'

Marilyn hasn't touched her own coffee. But she has persuaded Bruce to follow her direction. She feels her lungs swell as she breathes in.

Bruce is examining her carefully, scrutinising her face, letting his eyes travel over her body. 'You're wasted in your current position, Marilyn. Come and work entirely with me. It would make life easier.'

'Oh. I'm flattered by the suggestion, Bruce.' The words are out before she has time to think. She takes a slow breath before letting herself say more. 'It would be wonderful, I'm sure.' Part of her would love to accede to his request. But it's too dangerous. She would be his creature, compromised even more than she already is, and would lose the independence she has been tenaciously holding on to. Politicians come and go, as can civil servants who become too closely linked to controversial projects. 'But I think it works very well the way it is now, don't you?'

Before he has a chance to answer, she scoops up both of their cups and saucers and leaves the room.

11.

Len

The house is silent. Len enjoyed being next door with Lexie, even though she was upset. They've made their house so fancy, with their extensions and wooden shutters and what have you. It was good to see the baby bringing some human clutter to their lives. He's not tempted to modernise. As it is, his home has memories of Sylvia in every dusty, untidy corner.

He likes to keep the TV for company, but something about the inane chatter of the youthful presenter on the morning programme enrages him. What do they know, these young people with everything to live for and no sense of loss? He could teach them about that hollow feeling inside, the echoing cave within his body that reverberates with the memory of his missing wife. She was such a chatty person, talking to anyone and everyone, inviting every Tom, Dick and Harry into the house, telling her life story to the meter reader. He used to long for a bit of peace and quiet sometimes. Now he wishes he could take that thought back.

Peace and quiet is a never-ending curse.

Len shuffles across the sitting room, catching his slipper on the folded newspaper still on the floor from his attempts at the crossword. Damn it. Awkwardly, he reaches to pick it up, hoping his back won't go again. Newspaper in hand, he reaches the armchair, bearing the permanent imprint of his back and bottom, and eases himself down, gripping the arms of the chair so hard his hands shake. After a few minutes of staring at the one remaining clue and searching for an answer in the view from the window, he gives up.

Restlessness surges through his limbs. The less able he is to move freely, the more desperate he is to get out and about, to see people, do things, achieve a little in his pointless existence. The open computer on the dining table, inherited from Sylvia's parents, catches his eye, the light from the screen casting a harsh glare across the room. He's afraid to turn it off in case he can't get it working again, knowing he needs to practise what he and Lexie went through yesterday.

Even the sight of the computer fills him with further gloom. When Lexie is here, with her ever-patient and kind instruction, he can make some progress. It's not as if he understands what it all means, or why it needs to be done in a particular way, but he can at least produce a few lines of words. Very slowly. With plenty of mistakes. He can even correct the errors if she is with him and can guide him through the procedure.

When she's gone, it's all gibberish again.

Len knows he isn't stupid. He writes a beautiful letter, with perfect script. Why is it so hard to translate his literacy into modern skills? When he was younger, he would have jumped headfirst into computer learning. Seeing the children and teenagers with their gadgets, he envies them their ease in the world of today.

He's too old to learn now.

But he must try.

Annoyed that he's wasted effort by sitting down in the wrong place, Len levers himself up and shuffles over to the table. He lets himself down onto the hard chair with a grunt.

He will master this, however long it takes.

Len opens Word. The document they were working on earlier is still on the screen. He can see some howler typing errors but can't for the life of him remember the best way of making corrections. He sits back for a minute, with his hands resting on his knees. He's worried about Lexie. She's fragile. Anyone can see that. The baby's good, as babies go, but it's a demanding time, even if the rest of their life were going swimmingly.

Which it isn't.

Lexie is constantly worrying about Cooper and what he is up to. Not to mention being in anguish that her baby has been docked so many years. There's no justice in the world, that's a fact. Len wants to help, and it seemed such a good idea to volunteer his services, but what will it achieve? It's clear from Lexie's exaggerated patience, and the occasional suggestion of tears in her eyes when she's instructing him, that this will take years, and they don't have years. Not if they want to put it right. He's a fool, and an old fool at that, for suggesting something so impractical. These lessons might be a benefit for him in the long run, but they won't make any difference for Lexie and Cooper.

Len is not one to give up. Sylvia always used to say that he was like a dog with a bone when he had something on his mind. There is an injustice here, and he is determined to right it. Len feels himself going into the heavy, trance-like state that often delivers ideas. In the distance, he hears the cheerful jingle of an ice cream van. He can't see it from where he's sitting, or the children who will be racing towards it. Sound without vision makes it seem as if he's in a parallel universe. This makes him think. He's living a different experience from younger generations, almost in another world where life is slower. He feels an idea coming. Politicians live in a different world. They make rules and laws for other people, but they live in their own privileged cocoon, protected from the worries of normal, everyday folk, the ones who suffer.

That's the answer. He needs to contact the ones who make the rules. What's the name of that woman? The Home Secretary. She's always spouting on TV about improving the lives of UK citizens. He'll contact her.

Len wonders if he should ask Lexie about this. Perhaps they could draft something together. Lexie is very cautious. She might not want to risk it. He's noticed that she likes to be the one in the background, carefully making connections and giving advice. She wants to influence events without being in the limelight herself.

He can surprise her.

This is it. This is the idea that could make a difference.

For the first time, Len feels confident in his fingers as he raises them to the keyboard.

How does he start a new document? He can't remember. Damn it. Is his new idea going to go up in flames?

No, the hell it won't. What's wrong with using a pen to put your thoughts in motion? He's going to write the Home Secretary a letter, in fountain pen. He writes a very good letter; everyone says so.

Easing open the drawer in the table, Len takes out a sheet of pale blue writing paper and a matching envelope. A surge of energy pulses through him as he bends over and begins to write:

Dear Home Secretary,

That will have to do. He can't remember her name for the life of him.

I have watched with interest the development of your policies to improve the lives of us all in the United Kingdom and have very much enjoyed your recent interviews on television.

Nothing like a bit of flattery to make her read on. Len takes his time before continuing.

However, I am very distressed by recent changes, because I have seen for myself the effects they have had on my friends and cannot understand how these new policies can be justified. I am talking about the new rules under which babies have their life expectancy reduced automatically if their parents are considered to have misbehaved. How can this possibly be justified?

Although there has been some mention of this on the news, I don't think many people understand the full implications of what is happening in our country. I only became aware of it myself because my friends recently had a baby and became victims of the new rules.

Many babies are being born every day, and some of these will be affected like my friends. You will be aware that several celebrities are vocal critics of the entire Life Counter Programme. These people are very persuasive. Yesterday, I saw some people with placards on the street.'

This is an invention, but she's not to know that. In fact, Len is astonished that such opposition as there is has been so muted to date. He can only imagine that the small number of people affected so far are in a state of shock.

He continues:

'Soon, there will be an outcry. I strongly believe that you should reconsider these rules before this happens.

Yours sincerely,

Len is about to sign his name. He hesitates. That might get Lexie and Cooper into trouble. After much consideration, he signs the letter with 'from a well-wisher.' It's not true. He hates all politicians, but it seems like a good idea to pretend.

Len rereads the letter. He's rather pleased with the result. It sounds as if it has been written by someone much cleverer than him. He feels a flush of pride but suppresses it. He reads the letter yet again and can't spot any mistakes, but decides to copy it out to make it as neat as possible. He leaves his original on the table and folds and seals the copy into an envelope, addressing it to The Home Secretary, The Home Office, London. His pen hovers. He's not sure of the exact address, but his brain serves up SW1, so he puts this down.

Done. Slapping a stamp on the envelope, Len decides to post his missive immediately. Some fresh air will do him good. He can stop at the coffee shop and have a chat with whoever is there.

Len puts on his light windcheater jacket and places the envelope carefully in the pocket, displacing a couple of sweet wrappers, which drift to the ground. He ignores them. There are more important things to do, like catching the post. After checking carefully for his keys in the other pocket – there was no end of trouble when he locked himself out a couple of months ago –- Len shuts his door with a satisfying slam and walks up his front path to the kerb, ignoring for once the colourful begonias in his window box. With his increased sense of purpose, he feels his feet moving better, his joints connecting and pushing him forward in a more efficient motion. The niggling pain he feels with every step is less noticeable. He has a job to do.

Len arrives at the shops without noticing the length of the journey. The coffee shop looks inviting, full but there are spaces and the hint of condensation on the inside of the windows suggests a convivial fug. He can't wait to be in there, in a place where he is known and welcomed, but he must post his letter first. With a sense of the momentous nature of his action, he drops the letter into the post box outside the newsagent and pops in to buy a paper. By the time he returns to the coffee shop, he is tired. The effervescence is leaving him, making his legs shaky.

Kathy, behind the counter, gives him a cheery wave.

'You sit down, Len, love. Your favourite seat is free.' She points to a small table in the window where he can catch people's eyes as they come in. Everyone knows him now, and many are happy to talk. He tells good stories to those who have the time to listen. 'Your usual?'

'Yes, please, Kathy.' Len waves back. The action puts him off balance, and he performs a quick shuffle and a grab of a nearby chair before anyone notices. It's such a nuisance getting old, especially when people see your frailty.

Len opens his paper and turns straight to the crossword page for the one clue he couldn't manage yesterday. The answer is 'coercive control.' What the hell is that? Words used to mean something years ago, but now they're wrapped in subterfuge. Before he has time to ponder this further, Kathy slaps down his latte and a flapjack.

'The flapjack's on the house, Len, a little present for a regular customer on a gloomy day. You're looking sad, old friend.'

Len looks up. 'Thank you. You always make me feel better. Don't ever leave, will you?'

'Not unless business turns down. You keep on coming now,

won't you?'

Len chuckles. 'I will, especially if you keep giving me flapjacks.'

'Cheeky so and so. Might be a slapjack next time.' They always banter like this, and it brings a smile to Len's face. Kathy has the look of someone who's about to turn and leave.

'Actually, I'm feeling good today. I've just done something about a matter that's been troubling me.'

'Well done, you.' Kathy sits down, which is exactly what Len intended. 'Have you heard about this new government thing where babies lose years, like adults?

'No.' Kathy's shoulders tense beneath her blouse. 'What's that all about then? It's bloody ridiculous, if you ask me. What's a baby supposed to have done wrong? Kids get a chance till they get older, so babies should. It stands to reason.'

'I know. I couldn't believe it, but it happened to my friends.' Len is about to name Lexie and Cooper, but stops himself in time.

'Look, Len, there's people waiting. I've got to go, but you should talk to Steve here,' she says, pointing to a tall man coming through the door, traces of wood shavings on his faded jeans. 'His lady has a baby on the way.'

Len meets his eyes and smiles. 'Steve. Good to see you.'

'All right, Len? How's it going?'

Steve powers up to the counter, and Len fears that he will be in too much of a hurry to talk. He smiles to himself as he hears Kathy's whisper, 'Sit down with Len for a minute, will you? I'm too busy, but I think he needs a chat.'

'Sure thing,' Steve replies, picking up his takeaway coffee cup and a paper bag. By the time he sits down next to Len, with a mumbled 'OK if I park myself here for a bit?', the grease from his sausage roll is seeping into the paper, and Len is tempted by the tantalising smell of hot pork and flaky pastry.

'Help yourself,' Len says, as if this wasn't the outcome he was fervently hoping for. 'Is that lunch already?' He points at the contents of Steve's hand.

'Tracy made me some healthy thing. I'll have that later. I need some calories for now.' Steve pushes the sausage roll out of the top of the bag and takes a big bite, leaving pastry crumbs sticking to his stubble. 'Kathy thought you had something on your mind.'

It's difficult to know how to start. If Steve's about to become a dad, will he want to start worrying about what he's done in the past? Len decides he can't hide his knowledge.

'Have you heard about these new Life Counter rules, where babies have their years docked if their parents have done something wrong?'

Steve stops chewing. There is a lump sticking out of his cheek where his sausage roll is stuck. After a while, he starts again and swallows fast. 'You're joking?'

'No. I wish I was. It's just happened to some friends of mine and I'm hopping mad.' Len demonstrates his anger by banging his fist on the table, making Steve's coffee bounce alarmingly on the surface.

Steve puts his roll down on the table, rescues the cup and levers the plastic top off. He takes a few gulps, his Adam's apple rippling as he swallows. 'Tracy will go ape when she hears about this. I'll get the blame, that's for sure. What sort of things do they mean?'

'I don't really know, but I'm not going to take it lying down. I want to do what I can to help.'

Steve runs his fingers up and down his stubble. 'What can you do, though, once they've made up their minds? Bastards.' He rests his hands on the table as if he's about to stand up.

'I've just written to the Home Secretary, registering my disapproval.'

Steve is standing now, picking up his purchases. His mouth is half turned up, in an attempt at a smile that lacks any sign of happiness. 'Good luck with that. I don't rate your chances. They don't listen, do they?' He starts walking backwards but pauses. 'I don't suppose she'll even read it. Whoever opens the post will put it straight in the shredder. You need to get what you want to say out there where it matters. No way am I telling Tracy about this. She's bat-shit crazy at the moment anyway with her hormones and what not, but if you can do anything, do. Shame the sods into a U-turn for all our sakes.' Steve's hand is on the door, leaving a greasy imprint on the glass.

Len has spoiled Steve's day, and to what effect? He sips his coffee and nibbles at the flapjack, which brings a welcome sugar burst to his mind and limbs. Make it public. What can he do? His eyes fall on the copy of the Daily Mail on the table. He hates the paper. Likes the crossword. He still has a copy of his letter on the table at home. With a few changes, he could send it as a letter to the Editor. If it gets published, they might launch a crusade about the New Directive. Newspapers love to make people angry and cause a stir. That's what he'll do. He's much more likely to get some publicity with a letter in the paper.

The flapjack continues to speed his limbs once he's home and inside the door. It's astonishing how much more limber he feels than earlier in the day. Len sits at the dining table and picks up his copy of the original letter. He'll need to make some changes. Thinking back to the letters page, he remembers that the ones that get published tend to be punchy, relatively short and to the point.

In his new spirit of positivity, the words come easily. He writes carefully, but fast:

Dear Sirs,

The New Directive on baby Life Counters is daylight robbery.

He likes this. Daylight robbery is the sort of phrase that will appeal to Daily Mail readers. He underlines it with the ruler he keeps in the table drawer.

How can it be right that babies can be born one minute and have years of their intended life stolen the next?

Under a New Directive recently issued by the Government, mistakes made by parents are deducted at birth from the Life Counters of their babies. Not many people know this at the moment, but it will soon become public knowledge.

There will be an outcry, and I trust that the Government will have the sense to reverse this decision before any more children suffer.

Yours faithfully,

Len is about to add his name, but again wonders if this is a good idea. The last thing he wants to do is make life worse for Cooper and Lexie. Instead, he puts *name supplied* at the bottom of the letter, even though he has not offered this information. He has often seen this written at the bottom of letters to the editor, and it seems appropriate.

Len scans the words and places the letter in an envelope before he has a chance to change his mind. With less difficulty than earlier, he stoops to pick up yesterday's paper and copies the address given onto his missive. While he's at it, he fills in the final answer, 'coercive control' and throws the paper down with a flourish. Despite knowing that a second walk will tire him, Len repeats his earlier set of checks that he has his keys, redons his coat, and heads, with a spring in his step, to the post box.

*

The next day, Len is up early, as usual, and busies himself with some chores around the garden. Today is drier and he spends some time watering his window planter and pots and tidying up their foliage. He can't wait to stroll to the coffee shop for his morning drink and chat.

As he walks through the door, Kathy is on the phone. Her hair is falling out of her habitual ponytail, and wispy strands frame her reddened face. As she listens, she looks upward at a wayward curl and blows it off her face. 'Like I said,' she almost shouts, 'if the milk arrives that late again, I'm moving my contract. I have a business to run here.' She spots Len, drops the phone and relaxes her frown. 'Hello, Len, love. Your usual?' She starts to make it without waiting for his reply. She doesn't look in the mood for a chat, so Len wanders over and picks the Daily Mail from the rack. He knows it's too soon for the letter to appear, but can't stop himself from looking at the letters page. He's right. It's not there.

*

The following day, he proceeds with the same routine. He feels a little less optimistic, and a man is sitting at his favourite table, reading what Len considers to be 'his' copy of the newspaper. Len's previously good mood evaporates. This same person is still in possession of his table and paper when Len has finished his coffee. Frustrated, he leaves the café and decides to buy his own copy. Outside the newsagents, he opens the paper at the Letters page and is delighted to see that his letter is there, in pride of place, as the first one on the page. Not only that, but they've put a border around it.

Len feels such a sense of pride that he absolutely needs to return to the coffee shop to let Kathy know.

'That's great, love,' she says, giving the letter a cursory read. 'Short and to the point. I hope it does some good.' Her tone is flat. It's unlike Kathy to remain in a bad mood, and Len finds himself worrying about her on the way home. Her gloom is contagious. It was an achievement to have the letter published, but really, what good can it do, unless the newspaper itself begins a crusade? Now he is restless. Outside, he fidgets with his pots and window trough for such a long time that Lexie comes out of her house next door.

'Is there anything I can help with, Len? It looks as if you're having trouble.'

'No, not a bit of it. I'm fine. At a loose end, that's all.'

'Would you like another lesson now? Tash is sleeping. We could run through some things at my house.' Lexie's kind expression and the tiredness under her eyes give Len a pang of guilt. Is there a risk he could have made things worse for her? He feels his skin flush, something that hasn't happened to him for years, if not decades.

'Not today, thanks. Maybe tomorrow? I'd better go back inside.

I've left something on the stove.' He shuffles indoors, leaving her standing on her path.

As the day continues, his sense of foreboding increases. That night, he tosses and turns, failing to fall asleep until the early hours, at which point he dreams that a white van comes to take Cooper, Lexie and Tash away, dragging them out of their front door, as Len cowers behind the curtains of his own house. It seems so real that it is a surprise to pull open his window in the morning, stick his head out and observe his neighbours' house, which looks exactly as normal. Cooper emerges from the door with Tash in a baby carrier, singing to her as he heads off for a walk.

Thank goodness.

Len is still a little jittery on his way to the coffee shop. He wonders if his letter to the Home Office has arrived and what, if anything, they will do about it. It all seems rather pointless.

As he enters, Kathy is huddled at the counter with Steve. They're examining a newspaper, while Steve holds up his phone, as if he's comparing something. Both their heads turn at his arrival. Kathy's hair is tidier today, and she looks less frazzled. She gives him a big smile. 'Just the man. You'll never guess what, Len?'

It is true. He won't. 'You'd better tell me, hadn't you?'

It is Steve who replies. 'You're a right one, aren't you?'

Len shuffles over to where he's standing. 'What do you mean?'

'Your letter's only trending on X, isn't it?'

Len doesn't have a clue if this is a good or a bad thing. 'I think you'd better explain.'

Steve holds up his phone. 'Look. It's on social media, isn't it?'

Len squints at the screen. He sees his letter filling the space. 'I don't understand how it got there.'

'Apparently, this lady, Shelley, is grieving after having a late miscarriage, and she happened to read your letter in yesterday's paper. She was so angry that she took a photo of it and put it on social media. Let's have a look.' Steve types and swipes on his phone until he comes up with a photo of a smiling woman with long, extremely curly red-gold hair. She has large glasses that match her hair colour and a round, freckled face. She looks so happy in her photo. Steve is whooping. 'Look. She has twenty thousand followers. Works in PR, so she knows what she's doing. It's been retweeted thousands of times already.' Steve claps Len on the back. 'Well done, you old dog. You've made a splash.'

Len grins, but he's struggling to make sense of what Steve is saying. 'But what difference does it make?'

'It's been noticed. It could fizzle out or it could get taken up by others. My guess is this will fly, especially if the paper takes it up. You're in business, mate!'

Len takes the coffee that Kathy has made him. His hands are shaking. What has he started?

12.

Marilyn

Marilyn's coffee goes cold as she stares at the handwritten letter in front of her. It is rare to receive communications of this sort, painstakingly produced by hand and delivered in the post. It has been passed to her as an oddity that no one at a lower level knows what to do with.

Her first instinct is to put it through the shredder immediately. The writer couldn't even be bothered to find out the name of the Home Secretary. It's a wonder it has made it this far, although, since the stamp on the first page shows it has been logged and redirected, it clearly has. The Home Secretary does *not* need to see this. Bruce's political boss must not learn that the so-called teething problems with the Life Counter Programme are making larger waves with the general populace than he has led her to believe. She's already been on his case about issues the media has been highlighting. There's only so far he can push the line that dissent is coming from no-hoper recidivists. Their lives increasingly isolated from the individuals they serve, from fear of attack, politicians rarely need to face up to angry voters except at election time. They believe what they want to believe, mainly their own perfection.

Marilyn has a duty to protect Bruce's reputation, she thinks, kicking her shoes off and wriggling her newly liberated toes. The second-last thing Bruce needs is to see the letter himself.

Marilyn stands, the letter in her hand, and stares out of the window at an unappealing vista of flat roof and air conditioning units. Pools of water are collecting on the tarry surface, new drips plinking depressingly into the existing puddles.

What the hell should she make of this feeble little letter?

Discussions on how to roll out the New Directive were endless. Focus group feedback was sought on reactions to a hypothetical implementation of this policy, as well as many other possible ways of ensuring compliance with nudge policies. The responses were not positive, but the Home Secretary was so invested in the idea, which, to be fair, Bruce had fed to her over a period of months, that the policy was approved to go ahead. Foolishly, it now seems, it was decided to introduce it quietly and without fanfare, without any announcement at all, in fact. It was thought that the effect for the vast majority of families would be so small that it would become popular. Law-abiding people, who might be more likely to vote anyway, would probably have their potential years reinstated. The numerically tiny number who would be badly impacted could be managed. Fear of losing further years would stifle dissent. That had been such a powerful driver for the Life Counter Programme, although this motivation was never overtly stated. Successive governments had become weary of the uphill struggle involved in trying to push through any necessary changes against the vocal opposition of recalcitrant sections of the public. Fear of losing years clipped the wings of those who liked to join any rent-a-mob.

This would be a vote winner with those who wanted a quiet life.

So the Government thought at the time.

She should ignore the letter. Someone communicating in this way is unlikely to have much reach with the people who matter. Marilyn taps the piece of paper on the top of the radiator. One sentence still concerns her. *'Once this is widely known, there will be an outcry.'* That sounds like a threat. She puts the letter down and squeezes her bottom lip between finger and thumb until she's formed a large pleat in the flesh and pulls it up and down, enjoying the strange popping sound her lips make.

This New Directive is making waves and is being noticed – bad.

There has been nothing too untoward in the media yet that she is aware of – good.

This person is probably old, given the method of communication, and less likely to make a big fuss – good.

He or she is making an overt threat – not so good.

This person's friends are probably criminals – perhaps it will be preferable if their progeny have shorter lives.

Marilyn gasps, her rapid intake of breath catching her in the bottom of the ribs. Where did that thought come from? This is not the person she is.

She came into the Civil Service to make a difference, but professional life brings difficult decisions. It changes a person.

She's not ready to be transformed into someone who has a thought like that. Has she worked for Bruce too long or is she becoming a bitter old bat all on her own?

Marilyn decides to file the letter in her 'not important enough to deal with now but potentially too important to ignore' file, picking a small silver key out of the saucer underneath one of her plants, wiping it discreetly on a tissue and opening a small drawer in her desk, where she deposits the letter.

She's allocated today to investigating the activities of Bruce's wife, Amy. With each day that passes, Bruce has become increasingly irascible. He is restless, bad-tempered, short of attention span and, Marilyn fears, more liable to make mistakes and bad decisions. He is no longer the man she has admired for so long. There is not a moment to lose.

Slipping her feet back into her shoes, she reaches for the large gym bag stowed under her desk and extracts a well-used backpack, which she picked up from the charity shop near her home. It is surprisingly heavy, weighed down by the pair of Doc Martens she managed to purchase in the same establishment. Marilyn is excited by the freedom that a change of identity will give her. She can be another very different person for a day.

Only for a day.

As a precaution, Marilyn calls up her online calendar and types in 'Policy research meeting – out of office, do not disturb.'

Some of this is true.

The gym bag will stay under her desk. She glances at her coat, on the back of the door, and the leaden sky. The rain, at least, has eased off. Leaving the coat where it is, she holds the rucksack at her side and leaves the building. How she will account for returning in a few hours with a tatty bag full of clothes which are not the sort she would ever wear is a question for later. Marilyn walks to the Tube station with a secret smile sitting behind her actual features. Now she's out of the office her earlier anxieties have gone.

This is going to be fun.

She likes the sound of her shoes tapping on the pavement, feels surprised by the ease with which she gets a seat on the train because it's the middle of the day, and enjoys mounting the steps of another station, in the knowledge that she's about to disguise herself. Marilyn looks around. Several pigeons peck at some half-squashed chips that have scattered from a discarded McDonald's bag. She knows the location of some of the CCTV cameras at this station, but not all. It doesn't matter. She will be picked up by the cameras for sure, but she will soon be a different person. Marilyn crosses the busy road, weaving between taxis, rangy cyclists and impatient motorists, and ducks into a branch of Costa. She lowers her head as she ambles to the rear and into the Disabled toilet.

Marilyn doesn't think anyone noticed her coming in. She's not someone people remember at the best of times. For once, this is in her favour. As soon as she's inside, she strips off her sensible office suit, cream blouse and neutral tights, folds the garments neatly and stuffs the tights into the front of one shoe. Standing in her underwear, Marilyn begins to shiver. Giving herself a mental kick up the backside, she bends down to unzip the backpack, trying not to look at her reflection in the mirror, or her back view which is visible from another one on the wall behind her. The first garment out of the bag is a pair of faded jeans, baggier than Marilyn would usually wear and with an impressive tear in one knee. Lifting them to her nose, she is thankful that she gave them a precautionary boil wash. The fragrance is her normal fabric conditioner, rather than anything less pleasant that might make her speculate about the previous owner. Marilyn pulls them over her hips and zips them up. She threads her own black leather belt through the fraying loops. The hems are a little short, but that's fine, perhaps even a good idea. Next out of her lucky dip is a T-shirt that has once been shocking pink but is now of a gentler tone with a tinge of grey, with the remains of a slogan, announcing 'Fuck the rich.' Marilyn pulls it over her larger than average breasts, realising that all that is now visible is 'uck the ric'. She suspects that people will get the message. She tucks the T-shirt in and is, so far, pleased with the result.

This is so freeing.

Next, she puts her arms through the sleeves of an ancient leather bomber jacket, scuffed on the elbows and cracked on the inner arms. Marilyn glances at her reflection and can't fail to notice the curl of distaste on her lips at the noticeable stench, a mixture of years of cigarette smoke, underarm sweat and general lack of hygiene. She wants to pull it off and risk freezing, rather than be seen as one of the great unwashed. No, it's good. It will make her more authentic. Marilyn forces herself to settle her shoulders inside her new second skin. Finally, she pulls the Doc Martens out of the bottom of the bag and, after pulling out and putting on a pair of socks of indeterminate colour, yanks them onto her feet and laces them up.

Marilyn squares up in front of the mirror. The effect is startling.

She is no longer her.

Still more to do though.

Marilyn dips into her handbag and extracts a scrunchy from a side pocket. Pulling her hair into it, she twists it round and round, resulting in a high ponytail that stretches the skin over her cheekbones. Her earrings, simple silver hoops she thought carefully about when dressing this morning, work well. All she needs now is the baseball cap, hers but unremarkable and unbranded. She pulls it low over her eyes and sticks her ponytail through the size adjuster at the back.

She is happy. In fact, she's ecstatic. No-one would look at this mismatched, scruffy person and recognise her as the senior civil servant who walked into this small room a few minutes earlier.

Marilyn practises scowling and rather enjoys the experience. Standing sideways, she adjusts her posture away from the standing tall, assertive shoulders back stance she favours to something closer to a slouch, head a little forward, shoulders slumped in a suggestion of defeat at all that life throws at those less lucky in life. She likes the effect. It perplexes her that dressing like a vagrant is a pleasant experience given her usual views on clothes and deportment.

Interesting.

Marilyn is good to go.

She asks herself when she last felt this energised and can't think of an answer. Now all she needs to do is discover, for Bruce's and her own satisfaction, what is going on with Amy.

Bruce had been sceptical about her plan. This made her more determined to prove him wrong. She takes her phone out of her handbag, stuffs the now quite empty bag into her backpack, and heaves the latter onto her back. She looks around the toilet, satisfies herself that she hasn't left any clues, and checks the details of her plan in the notes section on her phone before deleting the file. She opens the door, is pleased that the few people seated nearby are fully engaged with talking or eating, and slips through the café and out into the street. A final waft of coffee, with a back-note of chocolate and sugar, leaves her with a whisper of regret, but she is unwilling to risk drawing attention to herself by lingering.

Marilyn enjoys the heavy clump of her boots as they hit the pavement and is surprised at how roomy and comfortable they are. She keeps the peak of her cap low and her eyes trained on the ground. Although the streets are busy, everyone seems caught up in their own concerns and journeys, failing to notice those around them. Marilyn heads back down onto the tube and checks the route. After a couple of changes she emerges from Bruce's nearest station and follows her mental map to reach the leafy West London road of Victorian villas where he lives. Counting down the house numbers, she deliberately overshoots his house, checking out the building and front garden with a sly side look. There is no one around. She's a few minutes early - there would have been time to stop for coffee after all. There is a bus stop on the other side of the road, only a couple of doors down. She'd worked this out with the help of Google Street View during the planning stage. When she's been to Bruce's house in the past, she's arrived, laden with documents, in an official car or an Uber, and has been hurried into his study. She has only seen Amy as a vague presence, drifting around the house with a supercilious half-smile, or as a reluctant plus one at office functions, dressed in clothes slightly too formal for the occasion.

Marilyn crosses the road and plants herself near the bus-stop. It's convenient and allows her to loiter without drawing attention to herself. She pulls her phone out again, something to be engrossed in if anyone notices her interest in the nearby house. She checks her watch.

Almost time.

As if she's called them with the power of thought alone, an unmarked, dark blue transit van pulls up at the house. Two men in white plastic coveralls approach the front door and speak to whoever has answered their knock. It should be Amy, if all is going to plan, but Marilyn can't see because there are bushes in the way.

This is already Plan B. A few days ago, she arranged for a surveillance van to park outside, while students from a nearby acting school dug up the road unnecessarily and then filled it in again. Two nosy neighbours called the Council. Fortunately, Marilyn had anticipated this and had fed the officials who answered the calls with a line to take with callers. Sadly, Amy didn't move from the house all the time they were there.

Marilyn hasn't consulted Bruce about the latest plan, apart from asking that he should be away from home. Since it's a weekday, this is guaranteed. Is this a stupid way to get Amy out of the house? There's no guarantee she will go anywhere that will bring answers to Bruce's worries. Marilyn begins to doubt herself. There is no Plan C. She's not cut out to be a private detective, but she could hardly have employed someone and risked them going to the media if they found anything juicy. The anxiety causes a knot in her stomach; she feels an urgent need to wee. She was so busy disguising herself earlier that she forgot to use the facilities for their intended purpose.

Yes! Amy is crossing the road and approaching Marilyn. She has her phone to her ear. Marilyn drops her head lower and pretends to examine her own. Her heart is pounding at the thought that Amy might see through her disguise.

'I'm leaving the house now,' Amy says. 'Can you be at the park in twenty minutes?' There's a welcome lull in the traffic, enabling Marilyn to catch Amy's words.

'Yes, I did ask. You're so suspicious. It's something to do with security. Bruce has had some weird messages apparently, and they think our computers might have been hacked. They're checking all the settings and examining the CCTV while they're at it. They wanted me out of the house. It gives us an opportunity to meet up.'

Amy is passing now, still on the phone, listening intently. Marilyn doesn't dare look up. She has an urgent need to clear her throat but manages to suppress it. A teenager passes between her and Amy, white earbuds sprouting from dark brown ears like an emerging flower. The delicate scent of a floral perfume drifts Marilyn's way and she curses inwardly that her view is blocked. Surely the grungy young person is not the source of this delicate feminine fragrance? Perhaps Bruce is right about the affair after all.

'No, it's fine, not a scam,' Amy continues. 'I'm telling you. It's come straight from the office of that sour-faced woman who works with Bruce. What's her name? Marilyn. The one who looks like she folds herself into a cupboard in the office over the weekend.' Amy titters, a gentle tinkling sound that makes Marilyn want to smash her in the face. She can't stop herself raising her eyes. Amy is wearing make-up and looks annoyingly pretty. A diaphanous scarf lifts gently off her shoulder in the light breeze. Fortunately, she's engrossed in her conversation and fails to notice the sour-faced woman scowling at her. 'I shouldn't say that, should I? It's unkind. I'm sure she's very good at her job. I'll see you shortly. Love you.'

Amy is well past Marilyn now, pocketing her phone. Time to get moving. Marilyn tries to bury her intense irritation at Amy's nasty comment and focuses on the 'Love you.' The evidence to back up

Bruce's belief is getting stronger. Amy is walking fast, so Marilyn tries to speed up her deliberately slouchy walk to keep her in sight without her presence becoming obvious. She concentrates on analysing Amy's appearance. She's wearing red trousers, not quite chinos, longer than pedal pushers. They look good. Amy has kept her figure. Marilyn wasn't able to see her top before she passed, but she has a little navy jacket and a small bag slung over her shoulder. The floaty scarf is drifting, in danger of becoming caught in the strap. Amy looks good, damn her. She might dress like this for a secret date. But would she wear trainers? Marilyn certainly wouldn't, but when was the last time she was asked on a date?

Marilyn looks down at the charity shop clothes that gave her so much pleasure a few minutes ago. She feels deflated. Pathetic. Unattractive. A sour-faced woman, no less.

It's difficult to know which way it will go. If Marilyn brings news of Amy's affair, will Bruce fall into his assistant's arms or shoot the messenger? The way he's been acting recently, Marilyn isn't sure if she wants him now. Perhaps his attraction has lain in being unavailable.

She does want his good opinion, if nothing else.

Amy turns a corner. Marilyn accelerates and is forced to pull up sharply when she almost runs into her prey. Amy has stopped at a flower stall and is taking her time deciding what to buy. Marilyn ducks into the doorway of a shop and bends down to adjust her laces. This is harder than she thought it would be. Eventually, Amy is satisfied with her purchase and moves off again, carrying a bunch of brightly coloured flowers.

This isn't what Marilyn was expecting. Each deviation from the expected trajectory causes her anxiety level to rise. She is used to being in control and is way out of her comfort zone.

Amy crosses the road and Marilyn follows at a distance as her stalkee enters a park through a set of wrought iron gates. She walks purposefully, down a path, turning abruptly to cut across some longer, rough grass and ending up in a wilder space. She's approaching a small lake shrouded with willows and other trees Marilyn can't identify. She scans the scene, trying to imagine she's a real detective. This location makes sense. Most vantage points are broken up. There is shadow, some areas are hidden. Anyone trying to take a photo or overhear a conversation would find it difficult. Conversely, there are trees for Marilyn to lurk behind.

Of course, Amy may not be trying to hide anything if she doesn't know she's being followed. Perhaps she likes being near trees and water.

Marilyn's knowledge of surveillance techniques is gleaned entirely from TV and movies. The limitations of her experience are becoming obvious.

Amy has slowed down, casting her gaze around. Trainee detective Marilyn examines, from a distance, each individual she spots and tries to fit them into her theory of a secret romantic meeting. An old man sits on a bench, occasionally taking a bite out of a sandwich, while staring vacantly into the distance. He drops a few crumbs at his feet, where an intrepid squirrel scoots up and steals them away. Clearly not him.

There is a man walking nearby, moving in Amy's direction. He is smart, a silver fox, with a face much younger than his grey hair might suggest. He's dressed for the office, popping out for an unscheduled break with his lover. Marilyn is so engaged with checking out this likely contender that she loses sight of Amy.

Oh no. Where has she gone? All this effort for nothing.

There she is. Marilyn breathes again. Amy has run away from the path, behind a tree and is now emerging from her hiding place and is racing towards a couple pushing a pram. Marilyn refocuses on the young pair, close together as they push the baby. The man is smiling broadly, the woman a little more hesitant. Their pace is measured but Amy has accelerated, almost tripping over her feet in her urgency. She smooths her windswept hair and pulls her scarf into place.

Marilyn finds herself tightening her own ponytail. Much as she dislikes Amy, she feels, as a fellow woman, her anxiety, notices her own sweaty palms, catches her uneven breath.

This is not what she was expecting.

No way.

It is Cooper, with his wife and compromised baby. What she is seeing is a family reunion. Marilyn has seen grainy photos, from his early years and, more frequently, from CCTV captures. It's like comparing a curated Facebook photo with a police mugshot.

This man doesn't look like the petulant, sharp nosed and pasty-faced individual that Marilyn carries in her head from Bruce's descriptions and a few grainy CCTV pictures from years ago.

What will she tell Bruce?

Amy and Cooper are embracing. Her head is buried in his shoulder. They are locked together so long Marilyn becomes aware of her own heartbeat. She wants to prise them apart, knowing the danger in this rapprochement. She tries to imagine the feel of a lost son in her arms, the almost forgotten scent of a child turned man, the warmth of fabric against fabric, skin against skin.

Matching heartbeats.

Marilyn leans against a tree, trying to look inconspicuous while endeavouring to see what's going on. Cooper is gently extricating himself from his mother's hug. He is introducing his wife. Amy brushes away tears. She hesitates in front of the young woman. This must be their first meeting. She goes for the hug. Marilyn wouldn't have done that. Marilyn would never hug a stranger, especially one who had replaced her in a son's affections.

It's hard to imagine what goes through the minds of mothers.

The wife is taller than Amy. They embrace briefly and Amy pulls away to examine her face. The flowers must be squashed by now, but Amy passes them to the young woman anyway. Amy is beaming.

She brushes away more tears, bending to peer into the pram. Her head almost disappears inside the hood. Cooper takes the baby out and hands the child over, his head close to his mother's as they pass the bundled baby between their arms. Amy's lips are moving; a small chubby arm reaches up to touch her mouth. She is swaying, singing perhaps. She pushes the baby up to her shoulder, nestling the little face into her neck. It is a beautiful tableau of a happy family, the way it should be.

If only it didn't give Marilyn a sharp pain in her heart.

Layers are falling away from her. She completely forgets she is dressed in a ridiculous disguise, that she is supposed to be hiding from the people she is watching, that what she is seeing is a bad thing according to Bruce's strictures. What she sees is that she has been wrong.

So very wrong.

What does it all mean?

Marilyn crouches, hugging her legs, pulling herself into the smallest shape possible. Her knee pushes itself through the hole in her jeans. Before she has time to stop herself, she has clamped her teeth on the exposed flesh, biting down hard, yelping at the pain it brings. A woman comes up behind her.

'Are you OK? Can I help?'

Marilyn waves her away. 'Please. I'm fine. Go away.' She forgets for a minute who she is supposed to be.

The good Samaritan hesitates. Marilyn remembers her adopted persona. 'Just fuck off, why don't you?' Marilyn gives her the middle finger. It doesn't make her feel any better.

The woman backs away. She's seen the expression in Marilyn's eyes.

Marilyn collapses onto the grass, her trembling legs giving way beneath her.

13.

Len

Weak sunshine filters through Len's sitting room window. He moves around his house constantly, unable to settle anywhere, but feels an unusual reluctance to go outside and an even stronger wish to avoid the coffee shop. Each time he ventures there, Kathy and Steve regale him with tales of the success of his letter. Not only is the X storm, whatever that is, continuing, but more importantly, as far as he's concerned, The Daily Mail has started a campaign with an online petition, to force the government to change their policy.

As he makes himself a cup of tea, another one that will end up half-drunk, littering his sitting room and staining the mug, Len reflects that he *has* made a difference. The success is far greater than he ever imagined. The trouble is, this isn't the way he wanted it to happen. His intention was to reach the ear of the Home Secretary and make her consider the unintended consequences of a new policy that, he assumed, had been carefully thought through.

It hasn't worked out like that.

Len finds himself constantly swallowing, so much so that it feels as if he's carrying a rock in his gullet. His mouth floods with saliva, making it hard to concentrate on normal life. This online world seems so unreal to him. He wants to see what people are saying but, without signing up to X, he can't find out, beyond the titbits that Steve and Kathy have shown him. It might be effective, but surely this mass campaign will make the Government angry and determined to dig in? Will they find out who started it? Len isn't afraid of getting into trouble himself. If he could, he would donate the unwanted lonely years stretching out in front of him to Cooper and his baby.

Len's real worry is how this notoriety will impact Cooper and Lexie. They are bound to have heard about the campaign and it's his guess that they will soon realise this is his doing. Len wants to amble out into his front garden and check on the plants, but he doesn't dare.

While he's peeping out of his sitting room window, a police car pulls into the road. Len swallows again. It swings past his house and stops next door. Len's hands, holding the edge of the curtain, are shaking.

This is it. It's impossible to think about anything else. He hides his body behind the fabric, trying to peer out unobserved at the two police officers, one man and one woman, who are ambling, in their rubber soled shoes, from the pavement to the front door. They are both on the solid side and don't look as if they'd be much good in a chase if Cooper decided to leg it over the back fence. Len has a vision of Bodie and Doyle vaulting over hedges in pursuit of a suspect in The Professionals. He used to love that programme. His mind is running away with him, so much so that he misses the moment when they enter the house. At least they didn't break the door down.

Len pushes the curtain back into place. He wipes his sweaty forehead with the back of his hand. Lexie and Cooper are in deep trouble because he's shot first and asked questions afterwards. Len wanders out through his front door, trying to look calm and unconcerned, holding his secateurs. He flits from one end of the window box to another, examining each plant, and carries out some scarcely necessary dead-heading of the couple of shrubs in the tiny space. He has only a handful of shrivelled blooms clutched in his hand when the police officers emerge. It's too late for him to disappear inside but they barely look at him as they walk up the short path, speaking quietly to each other.

It's not like The Professionals at all.

They take their time settling into the squad car. The man picks up a takeaway coffee cup and the woman starts eating a sandwich. Now the man winds the window down and lights a cigarette. Len's illusions are shattered. What he does find heartening is that they have emerged without dragging Cooper out in handcuffs.

Imagining his neighbours' shame at being visited by the police,

Len sneaks back into the house and decides to heat up the remains of yesterday's casserole for lunch. It is difficult to summon much enthusiasm. He's shovelling the congealed remains of the stew into the bin when the doorbell goes. Leaving the plate on the worktop, he hurries, insofar as he is able, to the front door. If it's the postman with a parcel, he might not wait long enough for Len's slow progress and then the delivery will end up back at the post office. As Len turns the latch and opens the door, he's astonished to see Lexie standing in front of him. Without intending to, he looks down at his feet, then forces himself to meet her eyes.

'Hello Lexie,' he says, adopting a light tone. 'How are you?'

'All good,' she says. 'I was worrying about you. We haven't seen you out and about so much recently.'

Len's heart is leading him on a merry dance. 'Oh, I'm fine. You mustn't worry about me. I've been a bit busy.' Len wonders if he's mumbling. Does he appear as guilty as he feels?

'Could I come in for a minute?"

'Of course.' Len stands aside and ushers Lexie into the hall.

Here it comes.

'Something smells nice. I'm not interrupting your lunch, am I?'

'No, don't you worry. I just heated up some leftovers. I've finished now. Come on through.'

Len leads the way through to the living room, noticing too late that his writing pad is still out on the dining table.

'I was wondering if you were ready for another lesson?' Lexie glances at the table. 'Cooper's home this afternoon and Tash is having her sleep.'

'Oh, I don't know. I think I'm too stupid to take it all in.' Len scratches the soft spot behind his ear. 'I'm not sure there's a point in continuing.' Much as he likes Lexie, in normal circumstances, and wants to know the reason for their visit from the police, right now Len wants her out of the house before he blurts out what he's done. He's desperate for her not to know and equally aching to tell her everything.

'That's nonsense, Len, and you know it. We need more time,

that's all. We need to put the effort into it, and then you'll be flying.'

'How is everything going with you two?' Len leans a hand on the edge of his armchair to stop himself toppling over.

'We're fine. Plodding on, you know.'

'I couldn't help noticing…'

'The police?'

'Yes. Sorry. I was worried about you both.' Len hopes he's successfully changed the subject.

'It's nothing to worry about.' Lexie sits down at the dining table and has a look at his computer. She turns to him and smiles. There is no guile in Lexie and her smile looks genuine. 'We made a complaint because we thought we'd been followed. Cooper thinks his dad has put a tail on him, but we turned it round to say we were worried I had a stalker. It sounded better.'

'Oh, I see.' Len sinks into his armchair. The sciatica in his leg has made standing any longer impossible. 'I was afraid….'

'That we were in trouble? No. No more than before anyway.' Lexie's eyes cloud over. 'We're trying to stand up for what rights we still have, put the powers that be under a little pressure. I don't know if it will work. I think they're all conniving with each other, to be honest. It's one of Cooper's ideas to deflect attention.'

Lexie has to shout the last few words, because Len must have sat on the TV remote and the lunchtime news has suddenly come on full volume.

'That's a relief. I was thinking all sorts.'

'I thought you might be.'

Len is desperate to think of something else to say, but the TV is drowning out everything else and he can't reach the remote. He hears the presenter proclaim 'A petition launched recently by The Mail online about the new Life Counter Directive has reached 300,000 signatures. The Government will now be forced to debate the issue in Parliament. The original letter that inspired the campaign was anonymous and efforts are being made to trace the author.'

Len looks at the floor as he tries to pull the controller out from under his bottom.

'Len?'

'Yes. It was me. I'm sorry.' Len almost jumps out of his seat, brandishing the remote and turning off the TV. He's astonished at how fast he has been able to move. 'It was a terrible mistake and I wish I'd never done it. Are you ever going to forgive me?'

Lexie is laughing. 'I was only going to ask if I could help find the remote.' Her eyes are on Len's face; he feels a blush rising from chin to hairline. For some reason that escapes him, her smile hasn't been replaced by anything more threatening. 'That was you?' She gives a slight nod. 'Aah, I see. Are you telling me you're the anonymous person behind the campaign?' Her tone is light.

'Yes.' Len has shocked himself. He's let the information out unnecessarily. Having said that, it's a relief to end the secrecy. 'I didn't think it through. It never occurred to me that it would take off like this.'

Len hangs his head, so doesn't see Lexie moving towards him until she scoops him up in a big bear hug. Her swinging hair tickles his chin. 'Why would you think we'd be angry? Look what you've done. You've single handedly managed what we haven't been able to, despite all our efforts. It's a great achievement.'

Len extricates himself from her arms. 'Really? You aren't annoyed?'

Lexie shakes her head vigorously. 'No, of course not. You've done a fantastic thing. You're so clever.'

Len can't believe what he's hearing. 'I've been so worried.'

'Oh Len. Why didn't you talk to us? Wait till I tell Cooper. He's been digging and investigating, like he always does, and he keeps coming up against a brick wall. It's as if they're one step ahead of him.' Lexie raises her eyebrows and puts a finger to her lips. Her dimpled smile suggests she's joking but the wartime poster of 'Careless talk costs lives' jumps into Len's mind. His brain is jumbled but through the fog her voice continues. 'One letter from you, and everything springs into action. You realise that the Police were so responsive because of the fuss you've stirred up. New babies are big news. They're afraid of the publicity. We wouldn't have got anywhere otherwise.'

Her words help the mists of confusion lift. 'Ah. I feel a lot better now,' he says, and he means it. Len lets himself slip back into the chair. His body drops like an ancient lift that has had its wires snapped. He tries to suppress his usual sigh at the relief of being seated. 'Just so you know,' he continues, 'it was two letters, not one.'

'Two letters?' Lexie rocks on her heels, taking a little step towards him.

'Yes. I wrote to the Home Secretary first. Then someone mentioned to me that it would never reach her, so I wrote again to The Mail.'

'Right. The Home Secretary? I see.' Lexie's smile has disappeared. 'Oh well, I expect your friend is right. It probably never reached her.'

Len's sense of disquiet returns.

'Was that a worse thing to do than the newspaper?' This doesn't make sense to him. His original letter probably went straight in the bin, so did no damage. The fuss from the Mail campaign seems much more problematic.

Lexie is twisting a lock of her hair around her finger. The last time he saw her doing this was when she told him about the Life Counter debacle in the first place. 'I'm sure it will be fine. It will probably have been ignored, like most complaints that reach the Home Office. It's just that... I'm not sure how much I've told you about this. Cooper is estranged from his father, for quite complicated reasons. His father works at a high level in the Life Counter Programme. He works with the Home Secretary.'

'Oh. I think I see the issue.'

'Well. Who knows? It could help. We get the feeling the Police know we're the couple referred to in the letter. Cooper thinks that's why he's being tailed. I can't believe we didn't realise the letter was from you.'

Len shifts in his seat.

'What we don't know,' Lexie continues, 'is how much the Home Secretary knows about Cooper's relationship with his father. If she does know, it could look like we're waging a vendetta. That wouldn't be good for us. If she doesn't know, it could help our cause.'

'I'm so sorry if I've made things worse. I should have talked to you before I did anything. But I was so frustrated with this computer learning stuff and something came over me. I wanted to help.'

Lexie leans down and pats his hand. 'You did help. You've brought it all out into the open. That was a big achievement. Let's wait and see. For now, I'll go over and tell Cooper the news. He's got all sorts of plans about what to do next.'

'No fool like an old fool.' Len tries to guffaw but it comes out raw and croaky. Whatever Lexie says, he still feels guilty that he's set something in motion that he doesn't understand and can't control.

Lexie has her head on one side. 'Don't underestimate yourself, Len. I'd turn it around to "age brings wisdom." We think we're so tech-savvy and clever, but we don't see what's right in front of us. Everything is automated. We're watched, examined, tracked and we accept it, by and large. We're told what to think, basically. It doesn't occur to us that there's any other way to live because we know nothing else. You've come along, thought in a different way, and you've blasted through. Makes us look kind of stupid. We owe you a lot.'

'Oh, I don't know about that.'

'But perhaps we should work together on the next steps.'

'Definitely. I've frightened myself, to tell the truth.' Len fishes in his pocket for a handkerchief and cleans his glasses. 'You know, Lexie,' he continues. 'You have a rare skill.'

'Really?'

She looks taken aback.

'Yes. You don't push yourself forwards but you guide everyone, line everything up, make the right things happen. I wouldn't have done what I've done if you hadn't set the scene. You're a facilitator, that's what you are.'

Lexie smiles. 'That's all I've ever wanted, to achieve the result but not be too prominent myself. That's what marketing is all about really, you produce the right product, gear up the forms of promotion, put the best people in place, then get out of the way.'

'You miss it, don't you?'

'A little. Tash is wonderful, don't get me wrong, but little babies don't give much back. I'm looking forward to getting back to work, but not yet, not for a while. I want to make the most of this time with my baby.'

The way Len sees it, women are torn these days, racked by guilt whatever they do. Maybe it was simpler for him and Sylvia. 'You're doing a great job, love. Don't let yourself think otherwise. And you're helping me.'

She taps his hand again. 'I'll go over and talk to Cooper. You look after yourself now.'

It's a strange thought, that he's achieved something that they couldn't. There aren't many people left now who remember a world before computers. Is it too late to help people see the trap that this complicated world has set for them?

14.

Cooper

Cooper's laptop is open on the kitchen table. He's been trying to research statistics on the history of the Life Counter Programme. He wants to analyse life potential shortfalls across different demographic groups. Specifically, he is interested in discovering if younger age profiles are disproportionately affected. Similarly, he suspects that privileged individuals are extending their life potentials while those lower down the social and economic scale are suffering. Statistics of this sort used to be readily available to those who knew where to look. Now, his searches are futile.

Are these figures no longer available, or are they only hidden from him?

Recently, his laptop seems to exert a malignant force, obstructing his investigations, sending him up blind alleys, laughing at his increasingly desperate endeavours. Has his father nobbled his personal technology, as well as corrupting the systems under which they are all forced to live?

Of course he has.

A cold clench of understanding grips his alimentary canal, sending his intestines into spasm. How stupid can he be? He's taken precautions with his phone, using a cheap burner for expeditions he doesn't want to be logged, worn out his legs and shoe leather taking elaborate diversions to avoid being followed, put a sticky note over his laptop camera and taken great lengths to delete his browsing history. Clearly, that is not enough. Knowing his father as he does, it now occurs to him, as something he should have known all along, that Bruce will have taken steps to control his laptop long ago. Just because Cooper's father is not himself technologically astute, it doesn't mean that he can't use the services of those who are.

Idiot.

He's paying the price for underestimating Bruce, now and in the past. A brutal man, not an intellectual, but cunning.

Carefully, Cooper sits down. He places his palms on the cool, metallic surface of his laptop, allowing his fingertips to caress the keys. He circles his hands over the raised plastic letters, as if he is preparing to practise his scales on a piano. He allows his wrists to guide his fingers to the edges of the raised screen, pressing hard with the pads to gently lower the lid.

You, my friend, are no longer on my side, he thinks, as he strokes the unresisting surface.

He is surprised by his self-control.

Palms on the table. He feels the pressure on his feet as his legs hinge and his quads ache as he rises.

Standing now, looking down.

Who's looking?

Does he care?

His breathing is slow, but, as he thinks of all the trails he has unwittingly laid, the information he has given out willingly, thinking he was safe inside his personal space, his diaphragm tightens, his breath catches in his chest. Unbidden, his right hand travels, as if in slow motion. He watches as it catches the side of the computer and sweeps it off the edge of the table. It crashes to the floor, knocking off a glass of orange juice left precariously on the corner.. The combined cacophony of metal hitting the wooden floor and glass shattering is strangely satisfying. Looking down, as Tash, woken by the din, begins to cry, slowly at first but with increasing pace, he sees the glint of broken glass and sticky fibres of orange flesh spreading across his precious computer. If he'd managed to control his anger long enough to move the glass, he wouldn't now be looking at random orange splashes on the stools at the breakfast bar and wet patches beside them.

That is the moment the click of the key in the lock makes him aware that Lexie is back.

'You'll never guess what.'

Cooper turns to face her.

Lexie is smiling as she enters the kitchen. Not for long.

'Yeah. I've made a mess.' He scratches his scalp with the ends of his fingernails. It makes a crunchy noise as if he's walking across shingle. 'I'll clear it up.'

Lexie beats him to it. Her arm moves so fast she creates a breeze as she grabs the kitchen roll and bends down. 'You go to Tash. I hope she hasn't been crying long.'

Once again, as so often over the last few weeks, Cooper feels judged. He caused this problem, Tash's life shortfall. Having been the instrument of her potential downfall, he has failed to improve the situation. He has tried, so hard. At least they now have an ally and a friend in his mother, for so long absent from his life. His attempts to unravel the causes of their problems have been ultimately unsuccessful and he now knows why. As he moves towards the door, his anger at his own short-comings fizzes, spitting out of him, spreading, moving towards his wife, who always gets things right.

'She's only just started,' he says, his voice a little too loud and without warmth. 'The noise of the laptop falling must have woken her.'

Lexie's hair has fallen over her face, but not enough for him to miss the raising of her eyebrows. Why does she never believe him? Even if she is right. He often wishes she'd yell rather than look disapproving and long-suffering.

'Don't cut yourself,' he says. 'You'd left your orange juice right on the edge. That's how it happened.' He hates himself for saying this, but it's too late to take it back. He scoots up the stairs. The knowledge that he's been untruthful, unkind and unfair, makes him feel even angrier at Lexie. Why can't she be a little less competent sometimes? Give him a chance to shine.

Tash's little face is red from crying, but he loves the way her limbs flail as she sees him bending over the cot. Through her distress, he sees a decent attempt at a smile as she recognises his features. The smiles are quite new and never fail to make his heart jump. The hands that reach down to lift his daughter are not the same ones that pushed the laptop to the floor. He is two different people, it seems. His love and patience for this little creature are limitless, while his nerves, when faced with what's going on, are apt to shatter.

Cooper lifts Tash's body towards him, pressing her face against his. Their hot breath mingles. Her little heartbeat is fast, her skin warm. She presses her cheek tighter to his, as if she wants to be a part of him. He is good at this, he knows. The connection he feels with this child is visceral, strong. In his heart, he's aware she bends to him more easily than to her mother, the one who is so competent but perhaps a little too business-like in her dealings with her child.

This is his view. One that he must never share, even though he is currently angry with Lexie. He knows though, and so does she. He sees it sometimes in her eyes when she watches him looking after Tash. Pride makes her pull her shoulders back and stand rigid, while her eyebrows pull tight with jealousy, and tears tumble from her lashes.

They are supposed to be on the same side, working together for their baby.

Tash needs feeding. This is still Lexie's territory. Cooper sniffs, – she needs changing first. He does the necessary, cleans everything up and carries his daughter downstairs, still crying, with the soiled nappy in a bag. When he reaches the kitchen, Lexie is sitting, arms folded, at the table.

'Hungry child incoming,' he says, with an attempt at levity. 'Over to you.'

He doesn't smile. His face muscles are unwilling to stretch into any sign of thawing emotions. Lexie's face is similarly rigid as her arms reach up to grab Tash.

'I've cleaned your laptop as best I can. It might be OK, I don't know.' She nuzzles her cheek against the baby's before eyeballing Cooper again. 'And for your information, I didn't leave the orange juice in a stupid place. You're making excuses, just like you always do. Looks more like tech rage to me. I'm going into the other room to feed Tash.'

Lexie is up and gone before Cooper has a chance to defend himself. 'Thanks for changing Tash, Cooper. Thanks for going and getting her. Thanks for being such a good dad,' Cooper mutters, he thinks, in a high voice imitating Lexie's.

'I heard that,' she shouts back, causing Tash to elevate the volume on her crying. 'Why do men always expect to be congratulated for doing what they should be doing anyway? Grow up, Cooper.'

Silenced by the verbal slap on the wrist, he listens to his daughter crying until it's punctuated by rustling and a note of anguish in his wife's voice. 'Come on, Tash, dammit. You're hungry, but if you keep crying, you won't be able to latch on. Shut up, damn you.'

Lexie never talks to her daughter like this. Lexie never raises her voice at all. What is happening to the two of them? Becoming parents was meant to weld them together, turn two individuals into a high-performing team. Recently, they seem to be morphing into combatants, deliberately inflating petty rivalries to gain favour with their new boss, young Tash. Or is that just him?

It shouldn't be like this.

They need to become a team, or their relationship will crash. The thought sends a chill through him. Lexie is everything that he lost before. Without her, who knows what would have happened to him?

Cooper picks the laptop up. It's sticky. He grabs a baby wipe and cleans the lid again, inside and out, and runs it carefully over the keys. Probably not the best approach, but it came easily to hand. Once it no longer feels like an uncleaned table in a cheap café, he carefully presses some keys. It still functions, even if it can no longer be trusted. Not wanting to disturb Lexie, but pleased to hear that she is no longer swearing at Tash, and her obvious tension appears to have dissipated, replaced by gentle sucking sounds, Cooper creeps out of the kitchen door into the back garden. He looks around for something pretty he can pick as a peace offering. A delicate purple plant looks appropriate, but there are only three blooms on it; he is reluctant to denude it. He moves towards a showy daisy-like plant in a pot. The same argument applies. Every flower you pick leaves fewer in the garden. In trying to bring Lexie round, he might make her even more angry.

Cooper has a brainwave.

Kneeling on the small lawn, which he has failed to mow this week, Cooper picks a lapful of daisies, pinching each one clear of its plant as close to the base as possible. Can he remember how his mother taught him to make a daisy chain? He made one for Lexie when they were first together, but that was years ago. He makes a hash of the first one, splitting the stem too low down, ending up with a fray rather than a buttonhole. The second one works better. He pushes a flower head through the opening he's made, the sharp green smell of sap bringing back both happy and painful memories. He's hunched over, adding more daisies to the chain. Sun beats down on his back, gentle but warm, as if the heat is stroking him. The tension between his shoulders eases with every flower added to the necklace. Smiling to himself, he tests the length and joins the circlet of flowers together. As he completes the exercise, the squeak of the hinge on the kitchen door makes it clear that Lexie has found him.

'What are you doing?'

Cooper stands, turns and moves towards Lexie. Her hands are on her hips. Tash is not with her.

Cooper raises the garland over her head and arranges it on her chest, which is rather larger than usual from the breastfeeding. The light breeze sends a suggestion of sweet milk towards his nostrils. He wants to reclaim her breasts, stroke them, squeeze them, suck them without worrying about causing her pain or discomfort. Without meaning to, his finger grazes her left breast as he arranges the necklace. Lexie doesn't flinch.

Cooper stands back, surveying his handiwork. Lexie's features have softened. She reaches down to touch the soft, damp flowers, already beginning to wilt in her hands. Bending her head, she examines the petals.

Cooper can't quite bring himself to say sorry.

Tears drop from the end of Lexie's lashes.

'I find everything so difficult at the moment.'

'I know. Me too.' Cooper walks close and folds her into his arms. She submits, resting her head on his shoulder, her hands, clenched into fists, pressed against his chest.

'It doesn't work when we fight.'

'I know that too,' he replies, speaking into her hair. 'I realised today that someone, my father, obviously, has hacked my computer. He knows everything I'm trying to do.'

Lexie looks up. She's wearing a bit of mascara, but it's smudged. 'How do you know?'

Cooper breathes out hard through his nose, sending a breeze through a tendril of Lexie's hair. 'It's no specific thing, but I realised why nothing I try works. I keep meeting brick walls or polite refusals. That shit of a father of mine is blocking everything I do.'

Lexie shifts a little further away from his chest. 'Did this realisation come at the time you had the accident with the laptop?'

'Round about the same time, yes.'

Lexie nods. She opens her mouth but doesn't speak immediately. Cooper breathes faster, trying to think of a way to stall the coming reprimand.

'Tash won't settle. She's in the pram. Let's go for a walk. I've got something to tell you.'

'You were going to say something when you came in. I remember now.'

'That's right. It should cheer you up.'

Soon, they're outside, passing Len's door. 'It's him,' Lexie says, nodding towards the front door.

'What's him?' Cooper says, jiggling the handle of the pram to settle Tash's grizzling.

'It was Len who started the X campaign.'

'No. Len?' The idea is laughable. Cooper finds himself looking at the front window, spotting a movement as Len dodges behind the curtain.

'I'm telling you, Len wrote the letter to The Daily Mail, and that was how it got tweeted and started a storm, and the Mail started the campaign. Keep walking and stop gawping at his house as if he's been unmasked as a secret agent.' Lexie adds her hand to the pram handle, increasing their forward momentum and getting them past their neighbour's house.

Once they're safely out of Len's line of vision, Cooper stops. 'I can't believe it, or get over that he owned up. He'd know I wouldn't like it.'

'He didn't mean to.' Lexie pushes her hair out of her eyes, giggling as she does so.' It just came out.'

Cooper shakes his head. 'I don't know what to say. His intentions are good, but he doesn't understand what he might unleash. He's an old fool.'

'Cooper!'

'Sorry, but he is. He's caused a shitshow when I was trying to keep it under my control.'

Lexie lets her eyes examine his face. She says nothing for a while, then takes his arm and pulls him forward. 'Let's push on, so Tash goes to sleep.'

Cooper keeps moving, but his feet are dragging. Thoughts are fighting in his brain. What does this mean for his project? What will happen to Len? What will happen to them? How can Cooper turn this to their advantage?'

Lexie pulls his arm closer to hers. 'Cooper?' she says, her tone gentle but coaxing. He knows he is about to receive a lesson, one that he probably won't like.

'Yes?'

'I know you've worked so hard trying to set up an investigation, and I'm really proud of your efforts.' She pauses. 'But, they're always one step ahead, aren't they? That's the whole point. It's an information society. We're the pawns, and the Government, institutions, whatever, they're the queen in the game. They have more ways of moving, and they control the outcome. However hard you try, it's not going to work.'

'Well, thanks very much.' Cooper stops again, puts the brake on the pram, and reties his lace that doesn't really need retying.

'Don't get all stroppy. I'm not criticising you, just stating a fact. They're in control.'

'What are you saying, then?'

'Len behaved in a way someone younger wouldn't, and it worked. He's done us a big favour and now they're on the back foot. We owe him.'

Cooper allows his mind to drift, considering the possibility that Lexie might be right, and that he's been outperformed by an old man.

'He's done us a big favour, and he was worried that he'd got us into trouble.'

'I need to think about the implications.' He slows his footsteps. There's a way forward here, he's sure.

'Don't think too much, Cooper. Just be grateful. He wrote to the Home Secretary, too, although that probably ended up in the shredder.'

'Hmm.'

'Have you noticed something?' Lexie's voice is so quiet it is barely above a whisper.

'What?' Cooper finds himself whispering, too.

'Tash is sleeping. Let's go home. It's been a long time.' She says no more but looks into his eyes with pupils dilated.

Cooper doesn't need telling twice. His pace accelerates.

They leave the pram downstairs and tiptoe towards their bedroom, as if creeping past suspicious parents when they were teenagers.

'What about freshening up?' Lexie whispers.

'Really?'

'Yes. Don't be long. I'll wait here.' Lexie lies down on the bed, stretching her arms above her head, her top tight against her breasts.

Cooper showers quickly and efficiently, drying himself and

splashing some rarely used aftershave on his jaw.

After emerging from the bathroom with a feeling of relief that the sex drought is over, he enters the bedroom to the sound of gentle breathing.

Lexie is fast asleep.

15.

Marilyn

All those meetings with Bruce flash past Marilyn's eyes. She thought he was the one hard done by, cursed with an ungrateful child. Now she's seen that 'child' in the flesh, he looks so different from her deluded imaginings. It's hard to see the malign character she has expected in that soft, cheerful face. There appears to be no evil in the way he hugs his mother and presents his wife and daughter.

What she sees is a gentle young man, one who is learning to be a father and husband.

One who has been deserted and banished by his own father.

And yet there is so much history here. Bruce's pain has shown for years on his face and in his actions. There must be something she is missing.

Marilyn's inclination is to throw herself under the next passing bus. She's always found it simple to hate Amy, and by extension Cooper. It's enabled her to love Bruce and keep an easy conscience.

The moral high ground is her favoured position.

She's not about to change her mind about the merits of the Programme but her confidence is wobbling.

Marilyn drags herself up, conscious of mud and loose grass sticking to her jeans. She can't face any more interference from strangers with good intentions, so she forces her feet to lift from the soggy ground, putting one in front of the other by dint of willpower alone.

The thought of going back to an empty flat increases her sense of overwhelming gloom. The location that usually lifts her spirits is the office.

Already she feels a little better. With every step away from Cooper, the painful influence of his face weakens.

Just because he has a baby doesn't make him a good person.

Marilyn remembers the pain in Bruce's face at his son's treachery.

She must try to see things clearly.

After jumping on a Central Line Tube at Ealing Broadway, Marilyn hears a sniff from another traveller, dressed in the type of office wear she usually favours. It reminds her that she needs to change. She gets off at Marble Arch and hurries down Oxford Street to Selfridges. Pulling her cap low to avoid being identified by the CCTV, she negotiates a way through the busy store and heads for the Ladies' toilets. This time, she remembers to wee. The cubicle is small, and she bashes her elbows in extricating herself from her unfamiliar outfit, replacing it with her office clothes. Her blouse, despite the careful folding, is slightly creased, but even with this disappointment, she feels immeasurably better for re-adopting her familiar persona. She stuffs the other clothes into the backpack. They don't fit as well this time and it is something of an effort to close the zip. It catches on a piece of fabric; she leaves it three-quarters zipped.

Marilyn scrubs at her hands in the washbasin, nearly rubbing them raw in the process.

'Oxford Street is filthy, isn't it?' a voice on her left says. Marilyn grunts in reply, not wanting to draw attention to herself, or turn her face to address the woman, in case her appearance is remembered. Instead, she pulls the scrunchy out of her hair and attempts to brush it into a more appealing style. When she looks up, the woman has gone.

Once outside, she joins the crowd of tourists and work escapees. Her stomach churns at the hot fatty smell of a passing burger in someone's hand. Street smells of urine and sweet vapes linger under the heavy cloud above her. Marilyn walks briskly up a side street and round another corner until she finds a half empty skip, walking past to make sure she is not being watched or followed and to check for cameras, and loops back, hurling the backpack in with a nifty underarm swing. She barely breaks pace.

Relieved of her burden, Marilyn trots back to Oxford Street and picks up the Central Line at Bond Street. Before long she hops off at Chancery Lane.

A short walk will clear her mind.

As she emerges from the station, her phone rings. She's going to leave it for later but her grandmother's name flashes up and she's reluctant to make personal calls at work.

'Granny?'

'Marry, something awful has happened.' Ivy's voice is breathless, tremulous.

Marilyn forgives the childhood pet name, which usually grates on her. She stops and ducks into a doorway. 'Tell me. Try to stay calm.'

'It's Gramps. He had the call. He's gone, Marry. He's gone.' Ivy breaks down into heart-rending sobs.

'Oh, Granny. I'm so sorry.' Marilyn crouches. Her legs tremble. 'I don't understand. He had years left.'

There is no answer, only choking sounds.

'Granny?'

'This bastard Government. He did have years. Then something happened. No explanation. He got the four-minute warning on his Life Counter. You know the one. *Get to a place of safety. Lie Down.* Luckily, we were at home. He was too stunned to do anything. I'm sure the Life Counter releases something when it issues the warning.'

It does. Marilyn knows, of course.

A sedative, like a pre-med.

'So, what happened?'

'He walked meekly, as if he was in a dream, into the bedroom and lay down. He even took his shoes off. He closed his eyes and prepared to die.

'I'm so sorry.'

'I grabbed his hand, held him as best I could. He wasn't really there, even then. He gave a tiny shudder. There was no pain. Then all his muscles relaxed. I watched as life drained from him. His face changed colour, gradually, from top to bottom, turning pasty, yellow.'

Marilyn tries to breathe slowly. She knows how the procedure works, how the Life Counters carry the seeds of their recipient's destruction. It's never felt this personal before.

'I hate the buggers. I want to go with him.'

'I know that, Granny, but you're in shock. This was unexpected.' Marilyn needs to be the grown-up here. 'You know what happens next, don't you? They'll come to pick up his body before long, now the claim has been triggered.'

'And I'll be waiting for them,' the elderly woman says. 'If I do something really bad, maybe they'll kill me too.'

Marilyn paces the pavement. A boy on an e-scooter nearly takes her out. 'Please don't be rash,' she says. 'I'll be there as soon as I can. I don't like to think of you alone with, you know.' She hesitates. 'Alone with him for any longer than necessary. I need to dash into the office to pick up some things, and I'll be with you soon. Hold up, Granny. I'm here for you.'

The call fails.

Marilyn had been looking forward to regaining the sanctuary of the Home Office and a return to her usual persona. After her recent exchange with her grandmother she now feels she is travelling to Mordor and Mount Doom.

Does Ivy blame her for what has happened? Marilyn certainly blames herself. Despite being intimately involved with the Programme, this is the first time she has personally witnessed a Life Counter Extinction.

She is incandescent, angry at the iniquity of the situation, furious with herself and mad as hell at Bruce.

Her intention is to slip into the office, pick up her things and escape immediately to comfort her grandmother. As she turns the corner to her door, she sees a shadow through the glass. The unmistakable shape of Bruce is standing, hunched, inside the room.

Marilyn's chest tightens. 'I didn't expect to see you here.'

'Why not?' he replies. 'I work here too, don't I?'

'Uh, yes. Sorry. My mind was elsewhere.' Too right it was. 'What are you doing in my office?' Marilyn's handbag shakes in her hand. Her eyes involuntarily dart to the key hidden under the plant. It doesn't look disturbed.

Bruce scratches his head. 'I was looking for you and then I remembered you were off on manoeuvres. So, what did you find?' He doesn't attempt a smile.

Nothing comes to mind that is interesting enough to satisfy him, while being sufficiently non-committal not to give the game away. It is an effort to turn her mind back to the question of Amy.

Marilyn places her bag underneath the desk, making this a slow and deliberate operation, while she plays for time. 'Would you like a coffee?'

A bronchial 'eugh' emerges from Bruce's throat. 'If I wanted a cup of coffee, I could have fixed one up myself in the hours you've been gone. What I want is some answers.'

Marilyn's gullet feels like sandpaper. 'Bruce, I won't be a minute. I do have results for you, but I'm gasping. I've been on my feet for half the day. Could you give me five minutes to grab something to drink? I'll be back before you know it. I can bring it into your office and brief you there if you'd rather.'

She would prefer to get him out of her domain. She would like to be anywhere else but here.

'I'll stay right here.' Bruce lowers himself heavily into her chair.

No escape.

'Won't be a minute.'

The need for speed doesn't allow Marilyn much time for thought on how to present her findings. After hurtling outside the office to grab a creamy latte with lashings of much-needed sugar, she returns, finding Bruce standing at the very window she had used as a thinking aid earlier today.

It seems so long ago, back in the time when she believed in the Programme. What a difference a day can make.

At least she can sit at her own desk again, and she beckons to him to sit opposite her.

She's going to tell him the truth. He needs to know the consequences of his plotting against Amy and their son. She would love to tell him what they have done to her only remaining family, but that would be too much information.

'Well? You've obviously discovered something. Am I not going to like what you have to say?' Bruce puts a hand through his hair in that distracted way that she has always found so heart-wrenching in the past.

No longer.

Her heart is hard.

What effect will the truth have on him? Who will suffer most from the situation becoming clear?

Marilyn needs time to think.

'Bruce. I have made some progress, but there is more to find out.'

Bruce jumps up out of his seat. 'Stop prevaricating, woman. Tell me what I need to know. Is Amy having an affair?'

So, he doesn't have an inkling of his real rival.

'I'm not sure. I did manage to follow her, and she met a man…'

'I knew it. I'll kill her. The deceitful bitch. After all I've done for her.'

'Hold on, Bruce.' Marilyn slips out from behind the desk and grabs his arm as he careers around the room. 'I'm not sure that she's having an affair.'

'I'll have it out with her tonight.' He picks up the jacket, which Marilyn now notices on the side of the chair. 'She's in trouble now.'

'No, Bruce.' He turns, surprised, at her tone. 'I told you. The body language wasn't right. I don't think it's an affair, and he was younger than her.'

'That means nothing.'

'She was wearing trainers.'

Bruce narrows his eyes and wrinkles his nose, a gesture he usually reserves for junior office staff who have messed up and to whom he is about to dish up a serious bollocking. He says nothing, leaving an invisible question mark in the air.

'What I mean is that a woman like Amy would dress up more if she were meeting a man she was having an affair with.' It doesn't sound satisfactory, even to her. It is difficult to focus on this, now trivial, matter.

Bruce stares at her, his eyes travelling across her features for an impossibly long time. He says nothing. The room is too quiet. Marilyn tries not to swallow, but the temptation is overwhelming.

'You're naive.' He moves over to the window and looks out over the unappealing vista. His fingers drum on the painted windowsill. 'I'm still going to have it out with her tonight. I need answers.'

'I'm not sure that's a good idea.' Marilyn stands beside him. Too close, nearer than she wants to be now; he hasn't put on deodorant this morning. 'If you really want to find out what's happening, don't let on that you're suspicious. She'll clam up, or she'll tell you any old lies that come to mind.'

'Hmm.' Bruce's eyes are fixed on the skyline. He used to pay more attention when Marilyn gave him advice.

'Give me time to find out more. I can keep surveillance on her, and soon I'll be able to fill you in. But you need to keep quiet about what I've told you, or she won't carry on behaving naturally.'

'Oh, for God's sake. It's like having a bloody nanny.' He wanders back across the room and slumps down in the chair, dropping the jacket on the floor. This is not the Bruce she knows, the man who sees a path, follows it and is confident in his direction – even when he's wrong.

This shadow of the dynamo she is used to doesn't even seem to take up as much space in the chair. He stares into the air, before reaching into his pocket and pulling out his phone. The finger that scrolls through his messages is red raw from chewing. This drawing away of confidence would usually alarm her. After her recent shock, she finds it a positive development.

'Jesus!'
'What is it?'
'This bloody thing on X.'

'What thing?' Marilyn has never seen the point of X.

'Apparently, some imbecile has sent a letter to the newspapers about the New Directive, and it's gone viral. You know how these things spread.'

'Yes.' Not really, but his attitude is leaving her with a vague sense of unease and déjà vu, to add to her other problems. 'Can I have a look?' She tries to keep her tone neutral, unhurried.

Bruce's phone is smeary, but nothing can disguise the words she saw only this morning, although on X they appear as a typed letter from the Daily Mail. The words jump out at her again: 'Once this is widely known, there will be an outcry.' So, it was a threat, after all.

'Aren't you going to say something?'

'It's not helpful, is it?'

Her grandmother's plight slips further to the back of her mind. Marilyn is in peril herself. She has muted Life Counter notifications for months because she thought she was untouchable. This top-tier Civil Service perk now seems ill-advised.

'Not helpful? That's an understatement. What do these people know of the issues we face? Some spotty teenager in a smelly bedroom, feeling important because they've gone viral.'

'I don't think it's a teenager…'

'Do you know something about this? If you do, and you've kept the information from me, there'll be trouble.' Bruce jumps up and advances towards her.

Marilyn backs away. Who is this man? She used to believe she had a handle on Bruce. His new incarnation is deranged. 'I don't have much to do with X.' Her voice is little louder than a whisper.

'Well, perhaps you should.' He's so close she can feel the heat from his body.

'Even if I did follow X, I've been busy, on your behalf, following Amy. Try to remember that.'

Bruce points at her with his reddened finger. 'I pay you to help me. Don't forget that. You need to be aware of where your loyalties lie.'

Marilyn stands a little taller. 'I have been unfailingly loyal to you, Bruce, through thick and thin, and it hasn't always done me much good. And it's not you who pays me, anyway, it's the taxpayer.'

For the first time today, Bruce's mouth breaks into a smile, but not a pleasant one. His eyes are unaffected, and his lips twitch in a lopsided manner. 'Put it whichever way you like, you depend on me for your job. Let's not forget that. There are things you don't know.'

'What do you mean?'

'Never mind. You're implicated, that's all that matters.'

Bruce turns to leave. Marilyn is surprised by the wave of relief that washes over her. As he reaches the door, he pivots to face her, grabbing the door frame with both hands.

'And get on top of fucking X, will you? It's bloody lethal. I don't want to be bothered with it. Sort it.'

He's gone. Marilyn opens the window, putting her head out as far as she can and taking long, slow breaths. With her back to the door, she fishes out the key from under the plant pot and turns to open her secret drawer. Sitting down, she holds the letter below the level of the desk and reads it again.

And again.

And again.

How on earth can she deal with this?

Bruce's words come back to her – 'There are things you don't know.' 'You're implicated, that's all that matters.'

How much she has done to assist him in his endeavours.

Written papers in her persuasive style to encourage the Home Secretary to adopt the New Directive.

Participated fully, enthusiastically in changes to the algorithms to alter the tone of the Programme. She still doesn't fully understand the effects that these would have. She knows for a fact that Bruce understands even less.

Encouraged Bruce in his vendetta, convinced that it was the right thing to do.

Hated Amy with a vengeance, and for what? Because she was

jealous.

Done what she thought were the right things, but without doubt for the wrong reasons.

Seen the world in generalities, without looking at the human beings involved.

Taken too long to realise what an evil thing she has done.

Is she as bad as him?

What is so hard to work out is what she should do. She recognises a threat when she sees one, from Bruce at least.

Something holds her back. Marilyn remembers the Bruce she fell in love with, the one who was hurt and disturbed by his thankless child and his ungrateful wife. Can he have changed so much?

Then she thinks of King Lear, a deluded man who spiralled into madness.

Marilyn has sacrificed so much for someone who doesn't appreciate her efforts or the opportunity cost.

What happened today to her grandfather has stopped her in her tracks, even without the evidence of Bruce's unravelling. It is clear to her now that the Life Counter Programme makes bad things happen to good people, and she has helped it on its way.

Her coffee sits untasted on her desk. The sight of the froth, cold now and unappetizing, makes her vaguely nauseous. She remembers that no food or drink has passed her lips since breakfast time. She feels too sick to eat.

Her mind is in a spin. Different versions of Bruce flash in front of her. Kind, considerate Bruce, when he wants something done. Something that perhaps he doesn't want to do himself. Angry, erratic Bruce, when what has been done does not meet with his approval. Teasing, flirtatious Bruce when he has been trying to pull Marilyn further into his web.

She's hopelessly caught.

Perhaps now she should tell him all she knows, but announce that she wants no more to do with the project.

Resign.

Leave.

Escape.

Where would she go?

'There are things you don't know.'

'You are implicated.'

The image of Bruce's face appears before her again; livid, in colour and manner; vindictive; dangerous. Her shoulders flinch as a shiver passes through her. Her hands, now resting on her knees, begin to shake. If he is prepared to cut himself and his wife off from his only son and destroy his future, what might he do to Marilyn? She pictures herself, a cold, mangled body in a black bag, shoved in the canal.

Marilyn has forgotten what it means to be part of a family. She has no parents left to turn to in times of trouble, to ask for advice. Thanks to her devotion to Bruce, she has no partner to tell her that it doesn't matter, that she can start again. Her grandparents were all she had. Now she has lost one of them.

Today she saw a family trying to reconnect, making a tentative attempt to rebuild what they have lost. She has been complicit in causing their pain. Marilyn finally sees that no family is good or bad. All parents begin by loving their children. Some fail to do the right thing but, for most of them, that is not their intention. They're merely not equipped to get it right.

Did Bruce ever believe in his plans?

Or was it all a way of punishing the son who had the temerity to see life differently?

What a shitshow.

Is the man completely mad?

Marilyn is trapped.

All she can think of at this moment is that the longest journey begins with a single step.

She'd better get up to speed on X.

But first, she must visit her grandmother to offer support and beg forgiveness.

She picks up her bag and takes a deep breath.

16.

Cooper

Cooper wants air. Lexie is in the sitting room, feeding Tash yet again, with the TV blasting out some celebrity rubbish that makes him want to kick the wall.

Cooper stands in the hall, pushing his arm into a light coat. Life is hard, and the joy of having their wonderful baby doesn't always outweigh the sheer burden of their present situation.

'I won't be long. Heading out for a walk.'

'Fine.' Lexie's voice is muffled by the wall between them, but her tone does not sound encouraging.

Cooper ties his laces with great care. There's so much more he wants to say but it will only make things worse. He says it in his head instead.

I need your support, to feel that you still love me.

I want to feel your touch, your body, to know that I still matter to you.

I must be more than just a dad.

Don't make me feel that this is all my fault.

Don't make me hate myself.

'I won't be long.'

'Good. I need to go out later.' Her voice is gruff. It sounds as if she's coming down with yet another cold.

'Bye.'

When was the last time they kissed, properly? It's hard to remember the sound of her pleasure.

Fuck.

Cooper tries not to slam the door.

He walks without thinking about where he's heading. His hood is up against the driving rain that still manages to get inside and trickle down his neck. Why is the weather always bad when he's feeling down?

Rain seeps through his trainers, causing his socks to rub on the heel. He's tempted to turn around and go home, but what's waiting for him there? More recriminations? A car speeds past, close to the kerb, and soaks his jeans. He hears another behind him and instinctively moves further from the edge. This one slows down. At least someone has some consideration. The engine idles. A car door opens with a strange creak. Needs oiling.

'Get in.' The voice is deep, raw, strangely familiar. Cooper doesn't place it immediately, but the hair on his arms tingles with dislike.

He turns. It's hard to see inside the car because of the dark interior, but he recognises the hand that is forcing the door open. How could he forget the limb that frequently belted him in anger?

'I said, get in. I want to talk to you.'

'Hello Dad. Great to see you too.' Cooper's mood lifts immediately. His father is the last person he wants to see, and yet, the fact that he has sought him out demonstrates something clearly.

Bruce has a problem.

'Come on. Do I have to wait all day?'

Cooper bends down to examine Bruce's face. It's a shock. It's years since they've met, but he could be a different man. Skin hangs off his haggard features. There is a yellow tinge to the bags under his eyes. It's almost enough to make Cooper feel sorry for him.

Not quite.

'Why would I want to get in a car with you after everything you've done?'

He's careful not to mention Lexie, although Bruce is bound to be well-informed.

'Because I expect you'd like to see your wife and child again.'

Cooper finds himself stuck in his stooped position. His mind works fast. He's only just left Lexie. The man is bluffing. But can he take the chance? Bruce clearly knows where he lives and has anticipated his movements.

His father still controls him.

Bruce revs the car. 'Of course, if you don't want to speak to me, you might prefer to risk the consequences.'

Cooper's Life Counter buzzes. It must be a coincidence. Shit, this man is good at turning him paranoid. He grasps the door handle and pulls the door open further, allowing him to get into the car. He says nothing, can't even bear to look at his father.

'Seat belt on.'

'I forgot how much you like to follow the rules, especially your own ones.'

'Grow up, Cooper. It's a perfectly reasonable request.'

Cooper grunts but does as he's told. He remembers what his father's driving is like.

Bruce revs the car hard and speeds away from the kerb. His hands grip the steering wheel as he drives, taking the corners fast and slowing down on the straights. He's watching his mirrors constantly, his eyes darting from the rear view and then to either side. Cooper pulls his hood down and turns in his seat, scanning the road behind before swivelling to stare at Bruce.

'You seem nervous, old man. Are you afraid of being followed or something?'

For the first time, Bruce turns and meets Cooper's eyes. 'I'm not afraid of anything, never have been. What could possibly be bothering me?'

Cooper holds his gaze; Bruce looks away, back to the road, just in time to notice a lorry that's pulled up in front. He slams the brakes on, before accelerating again and overtaking.

'A little matter of abduction, perhaps?'

'Don't be ridiculous. You got into the car of your own free will.'

'Free will. That's a joke.' His Life Counter buzzes again. He checks it and sees that Lexie is trying to contact him. Cooper reaches into his pocket for his phone.

'Don't reply if that's a text.'

'See what I mean.'

Cooper has lost track of where they are, which is a stupid

mistake on his part. He's been so irate at his father that he's failed to track their progress. He vows to do better. Trying to look sullen, which is easy in the circumstances, he scans the hinterland. They're in West Ealing, the tattier end. Carpet warehouses and vape shops vie with Indian takeaways. Bruce takes a sharp left and pulls up into a parking space, riding the kerb with his nearside wheel.

'Cooper, we're not going to get anywhere with this sniping. I want to talk to you, that's all, but I can't do it if you're going to be so aggressive.'

'You can't be surprised by my attitude.'

Bruce lays his head on the steering wheel, inadvertently setting the horn off. A cat jumps from its resting place under the car in front. 'I just want to talk, please. Is that too much to ask?'

It shouldn't be.

All these years, Cooper would have loved the chance to talk to his father, properly talk, to put his point of view across and persuade Bruce that their relationship could be mended. A tiny strand of hope flickers through his mind. His father's apparent vulnerability is a new thing for Cooper. He would love to believe it is real.

'What do you want to talk about?'

'Everything.' Bruce's head is still down, his voice raw with emotion.

'What's wrong, Dad?' Cooper's hand reaches out, as if it is unconnected with his mind. He pulls it back. He will not touch his father.

'I've always tried to do the right thing, by you, by the country.' Bruce raises his head and pushes his hair back with his left hand.

Cooper finds himself nodding.

'Sometimes there are unintended consequences.'

'You could say that.' Cooper thinks of his lost years, banished from his family, obstructed in his career. Is that what he's talking about, or does he have the Life Counter Programme in mind?

Bruce turns towards him. His eyes are swimming. 'I want to talk to you, man to man, but we can't have a proper conversation when

I'm driving and you're shouting at me. Can we sit down together and have an adult chat?'

'If you like.' Cooper checks the time. 'But I need to get back soon to look after the baby. You'll know all about that, I'm sure, in fact, you must do, since you threatened me with losing her and my wife. It wasn't a good place to start.'

'I know, but it was the only way I could think of to get you into the car.'

'How about "Hello Cooper, I'm sorry for everything. Can we talk about it?"'

'I don't think you'd have believed that.'

'True.'

'Well?'

'Whatever. Let's talk.' Cooper goes for the door handle, but Bruce's hand shoots across to stop him.

'This isn't a good place, be fair. I only stopped here because you were stressing. There's somewhere nearby we can go. OK by you?'

'Fine.' Cooper sighs and slumps a little further into his seat.

Bruce restarts the car, with less aggression than before, and pulls out of the space with more control than he entered it. After several twists and turns and one illegal journey down a one-way street, Bruce pulls up in front of a bay-fronted house in a row of identical red brick terraced properties. The house next door has chipboard panels over all the windows and a weed-strewn front garden. Something brown scuttles past as they approach the front door. Bruce pulls a key out of his trouser pocket and opens the door, ushering Cooper through in front of him. The air inside is close and stale, with a residual smell of cats.

'What's this then? Have you gone down in the world?'

Bruce turns to him with a tired smile. 'It's a safe house.'

Cooper laughs, a little hysterically. 'What? Are you working for MI5 now, then?'

'Very funny. It's somewhere I can come when I want to go off-grid.'

The word brings a twinge of unease to Cooper. 'Why off-grid?'

Bruce stands in front of him, throwing his hands wide. 'Nothing sinister. I just want to have a chat that can't be overheard, that's all. As you know, surveillance is everywhere.'

'Most of it installed by you.'

Bruce shrugs. 'Come and sit down. I'll see if I can find us something to drink.' He takes Cooper through the front room and a small dining area towards the kitchen at the back. It all has an unloved air. Bruce pats a chair in the dining area while moving through himself to the kitchen, opening cupboards and eventually finding cups and a jar of instant coffee.

Cooper grips the back of a chair, noticing a build-up of dust and grime on the wood, and casts his eyes towards the sitting room. This really isn't Bruce's style at all, unless he's changed dramatically in the years since they've last been together.

'No milk, I'm afraid. Is black OK?'

'Sure.' Cooper's throat is dry. He's not sure whether it is real thirst or the shock of his father turning up after all this time.

Bruce brings out two cups of foul-smelling coffee and puts one down on the dining table in front of Cooper. 'Let's sit here. You won't want to relax on the sofa with me, I'm sure.'

'You're right. I feel safer here.' Cooper takes a sip. 'God, that's rough.'

'Sorry.' Bruce takes a gulp of his. 'Probably been in the cupboard too long. Better than nothing, though.'

Cooper isn't sure about that, but at least it gives him a prop while he is obliged to talk to his father. He takes another sip. It burns his lips, but he's starting to get used to it. 'So, you wanted to talk. Let's talk. I need to get back.'

Bruce nods, stirs the liquid in his mug and watches the swirls as they spin round the surface. He looks up. 'Cooper, you need to stop your investigations. They're causing harm.'

Cooper is mid-gulp, and he gags, spitting a little out onto the table. 'Stop? I haven't been able to start. You've closed me down, haven't you?'

'Have I?'

'You know you have. Come on. My contacts all clam up as soon as I get in touch. I feel like Google's playing with me. Everything I try to do ends up in a blind alley.'

'I might have pulled a few levers.'

'Too right you have. What more can you do to me?'

'You'd be surprised.'

'Is that a threat?'

'Cooper, Cooper. Don't be so aggressive. I come in peace.' Bruce casts his arms wide, palms up.

'It's hard to believe that Dad.'

Bruce leans forward. He keeps his voice low, but the grit in his words is menacing: 'You are getting involved in things you don't understand.' He sits back, pushing a greasy lock of hair off his forehead. 'In fact, I don't fully understand them myself. These algorithms have a life of their own.'

'I think you'll find that is the point. Is that what you meant about unintended consequences earlier? Are you saying that you need my help?'

'What I am saying is that you need to stop interfering, for your own good. Are you feeling alright? You look a bit strange.'

Bruce's voice is booming, then retreating. His face is blurring. It's turning from a set of recognised features to a knobbly potato.

Cooper feels a hand on his forehead and another on his wrist.

'Cooper? What's wrong?'

The world turns black.

17.

Lexie

Lexie's phone rings shortly after she's put Tash down to sleep. Cooper usually texts first to avoid waking her. As she picks her phone up, she notices the number has been withheld. It's probably a scam but she'd better answer in case.

'Hello?'

'Am I speaking to Mrs Box?'

'Er, yes. Speaking.'

'Mrs Box. This is Inspector Drury here, from Central London Police. I'm sorry to bother you. I hope it isn't a bad time?'

Lexie's fingers grip the metal edge of her phone. The man's voice, soft and gentle, is struggling to reach her mind, blurred by a fear-induced fog.

'Police? Has something happened?'

Tash has started whimpering. The noise is magnified by the speaker on the baby monitor. Before the man can answer, the noise increases, as if someone has turned a dial on a volume control. For once, Lexie doesn't want to run to her. The usual desperation to soothe her is there, but the timing is dreadful. Lexie feels horribly torn.

'Don't concern yourself. It sounds as if you have your hands full there.'

'Has something happened to Cooper?' Her own voice is rising in volume. The final word comes out so breathy it is as if it has been expelled from a cannon.

'Your husband is perfectly safe. Let me assure you of that.' He pauses, coughs quietly. Lexie's insides turn to water. She crosses her legs, clenching her buttock muscles. *Get on with it*, she thinks. *You know his name. Tell me what's happening.* No words escape her lips.

'Don't distress yourself, but your husband is in custody.'

'In custody?' It's hard to speak. Breath rushes from her mouth in staccato bursts. 'Why?'

'We are investigating –' A strange noise on the line. It sounds as if he's sucking his teeth. 'We are investigating potentially illegal activities. Your husband is helping us with our enquiries.'

Lexie drops. Luckily, the sofa is immediately behind her, allowing her to fall with a heavy squat rather than collapse on the floor. Air is expelled from her seat with a noticeable whoosh. 'I'll be there straight away.' Please, Tash, wait a minute, she thinks. 'I'm sorry, my baby is becoming distressed. We'll come now. Tell me which station and I'll be there.'

'Please don't do that,' he says, his voice mellifluous, calming. 'We will be in touch shortly. I'm sure this will be sorted out in no time. Sit tight with your baby. This is purely a courtesy call. Goodnight now.'

Lexie continues cradling the phone long after the call is ended. She imagines the man on the other end of the line doing the same. Or will he go back to Cooper and tell him his wife is a weak and fretful woman? Worse still, will he return to Cooper and beat him senseless?

He doesn't sound like that type of man.

Panic rises in her, equalling Tash's cries in intensity. It's been a bad afternoon, with the baby fretful and frustrated, arching her little back and crying her lungs out. She thought that was all she had to worry about.

None of this makes sense. Cooper went out for a walk, not so long ago, and now he's been arrested. The Police knew her phone number. That must mean that Cooper gave it to them. Perhaps there is some connection with their recent complaint to the Police.

Her mind is spinning. The man sounded kind, sympathetic. Why would he be like that? Something niggles at the edges of her brain. Think, Lexie, think. Be like Cooper. Examine the evidence. In her experience, the police are either pleasant but patronising, if you report a crime, or box-ticking in their hostility if you are accused of something.

There was no hostility in his demeanour.

Should there be?

Not that Lexie has ever done anything wrong, but she's seen how they can be with other people.

This man was strange though. Almost avuncular, thoughtful about her parenting difficulties at the same time he was explaining to her that her husband had been arrested.

Lexie remembers her sharp intake of breath at the news. This is what she has been fearing for so long. Now it has happened, and it has landed in her brain, the panic has subsided. She is strangely calm.

Her superpower is connecting people and things, joining the dots so progress can be made. She must use these skills now.

Dropping the phone on the edge of the sofa, Lexie runs upstairs and brings Tash down, realising that it will be easier to decide what to do without a caterwauling baby rattling her nerves. Holding Tash against her shoulder, feeling hot little breaths tickling her ear, Lexie begins to breathe more easily.

He hasn't been charged. They will work this out.

Tash's desperate crying has stopped, now she is being held so close, but she is still wriggling. Something is wrong with her that feeding, changing and sleep will not solve.

She's missing her father. He's so good with her in the fractious early evenings.

Lexie paces. She will work out what to do. She can do this.

She must.

In her shock, she forgot to ask about a lawyer. Cooper would have had all the right questions at his fingertips if it were Lexie in this position.

Of course, Lexie would not have been caught out like this.

The man told her to stay home and wait. He would be in touch.

All those questions she omitted to ask.

Where was he arrested?

On what grounds?

Why is he being held?

Where?

What can she do to help?

Lexie stops at the window. It's getting dark. She moves back towards the kitchen. Tash nibbles at her shirt collar, sucking and drooling. Lexie keeps moving. The sucking becomes quieter and slower. Before long, as Lexie continues to think, while humming a gentle song, Tash is asleep. Lexie levers her gently onto the sofa, banks her up with cushions to stop her rolling off and sits down beside her.

If she does what they say and keeps quiet, will it help Cooper?

Like hell it will. All her life, Lexie has done the right thing, toed the line, ticked the right boxes, and this is what it has led to. She is on her own when she most needs support.

What if she does the opposite? It might make Cooper's situation even worse. In any case, she has no idea where he is.

Lexie picks up her phone, ready to phone her mum. Marika will know what to do. Before she knows it, she has dialled and her mother has answered.

'Darling. How is everything? When are you coming over to see us?'

'Oh Mum.' Lexie takes a slow breath. 'It's great to hear your voice. I need to ask you something.' She tries to keep her voice level, but she can hear the tremor. Her mother will certainly notice it.

'Of course. Why don't I pop over?'

'No.' She says it too loud. She so wants company but suddenly she knows that Marika is not the person to ask. 'Not yet.'

'Oh!'

'Sorry, Mum. I didn't mean it like that. There's something I need to do first. Could you come over later? Say eight, or nine? I know it's a big ask. I'm a bit rattled today. And, any tips on settling Tash? She's running me ragged.'

'Aah, no wonder you're stressed. I'm sure you've tried everything. Now and again, nothing works apart from carrying the baby around for hours. Try to keep her cool. I'll come over at 8.30

ish. Use my magic powers to soothe her.'

She can hear the pride in Marika's voice.

Lexie lets her eyes travel around the room, devoid of Cooper.

'Thanks, Mum. See you later. I'm looking forward to a big hug. I think she's waking up. I'd better go.'

'Bye darling.' Lexie can hear the sadness in her mother's voice at having to say goodbye. Later, she will think of what she must say to Marika.

Right now, she knows who she needs to talk to about Cooper. His Mum, who she only recently met but already feels she has known for a hundred years.

'Amy?'

'Lexie.' A short pause. 'How lovely to hear from you.'

'I'm afraid you might not like what I have to say.'

There is silence. Perhaps Cooper's mother has experience of this.

'I've just had a call from the police. Cooper's been arrested.'

Amy sighs. 'I knew this would happen, sooner or later. I'm willing to bet Bruce is behind this.'

'You don't sound surprised.' Lexie feels aggrieved on Cooper's behalf and is tempted to put the phone down. But she's so alone. 'Bruce could have him arrested?' she says instead.

'Not directly, but it will be because Cooper is stirring the waters. Bruce only needs to whisper in the right ear and the Government machinery cranks into action.'

'I don't know what to do.'

She hears Amy's breathing. It's loud, but it's calm. This makes Lexie feel a little better, but has she put her mother-in-law in an impossible position?

Lexie hears a strange clicking noise over the line, as if Amy is making clip-clop horse noises with her tongue. 'Stay where you are,' she says. 'I'll be over as soon as I can.'

'Won't that alert your husband?' Now Lexie feels very guilty.

'Bruce is away on a "mission of mercy" to some ailing relative up North, so he won't know. You shouldn't be on your own at a time like this.'

A gentle warmth presses through Lexie's veins at the thought that this kind and gentle woman will soon be with her. She hadn't realised how scared she was feeling until this moment.

While she waits, Lexie gently lifts Tash from the sofa, rocking her as she stirs, praying that she won't wake up properly. She is lucky. The baby must have worn herself out with all the crying earlier in the day. She does nothing more than whimper as Lexie carries her upstairs and lowers her into the cot. Holding her breath, she backs out of the room and creeps downstairs again. She searches Google Maps for nearby police stations, but nothing she finds gives her any conviction that she will find her husband there, even if she were allowed to visit him. The only benefit she has gained is in the time she has wasted while waiting for Amy.

What a wonderful sound an idling car engine is when you are waiting for someone to arrive. Of course, the revs and tyre squeals of a car parking might be the police, rather than Amy. Lexie peers through the curtains to see her mother-in-law almost running from the car. She hurtles to the door and throws herself into Amy's arms. That is when the tears start.

18.

Cooper

Cooper's eyes are tight, stuck together. He tries to subdue a wave of panic at not being able to open them. What is that pounding in his head? The worst hangover, and yet he doesn't remember drinking. He doesn't remember much, to be honest. His limbs feel heavy. When he tries to move them, they won't budge.

Fragments of memory return. His father. They were talking. Then what?

Cooper keeps trying to blink, willing his eyes to open. Eventually, they begin to loosen. He expects to see light as he forces his lids apart. Instead, he picks up nothing but gloom.

It all comes back to him. He's in the house that smells of cat piss. With his father. Or not.

Cooper's senses sharpen. He listens for sound. Is that the creak of floorboards from upstairs? A toilet flushes. He is not alone. Cooper flexes his limbs, wanting to be ready for whatever might happen, but they still won't move. As the mental fog lifts, he realises what he should have known all along, that he is tied up. He tugs at his arms, to no avail. His legs are the same. As he tries, he almost topples over. Now, his eyes are working again, and he peers through the murk, forcing his stiff neck down to check on his legs, which are tied with rough twine to the chair legs. His arms are held behind him. He works at the knots by rubbing his wrists together, but there is no give.

Footsteps coming down the stairs.

No time to escape or loosen his bonds.

This is ridiculous. Imprisoned by his own father.

He hears the door to the front room open and a shadowy figure emerges. A scratchy noise suggests the drawing of curtains, snagging as they close. A light-switch snaps. Bruce's figure comes closer, his features ghostly in the yellow artificial light. His face is drawn, giving nothing away about his mood. His eyes flick from Cooper's face to the captured arms and restrained legs. He allows himself a ghost of a smile.

Cooper keeps his face impassive. Inside, he rages. Of all the hurts, insults and iniquities Bruce has inflicted on him during his life, this is the worst. What has happened to this man he used to call a father?

A long time ago.

'Good, you're awake. If you've calmed down, we can talk.'

Bruce plants himself at the table, sitting opposite Cooper. He places his hands on the top, drumming his fingers on the wooden surface. Cooper wonders what imaginary tune is passing through his mind.

Cooper sits still. If his limbs were at his disposal, he would cross his arms in front of him. Instead, he looks away, apparently fascinated by specks of something unrecognisable and potentially unpleasant on the sticky floor.

'Coffee?'

Cooper's head snaps back to his father.

'No, thank you. After the last time, I think I'll pass.'

Bruce sniggers. 'Yes, I imagine it did taste a little off.

'What was in it?'

'I believe it's some type of date rape drug. I purchased it clandestinely, as you can imagine, so it's difficult to be sure.'

'Well, thanks, Dad. You could have finished me off with some dodgy, unregulated chemical. So this was always your intention, to abduct me and drug me? What is the point?'

Bruce leans forward. A toxic mix of unwashed clothes and stale sweat wafts towards him, competing rather successfully with the all-pervasive odour of cat urine. 'Cooper, do try to stay calm.' Bruce scratches the corner of his eye. 'The drug was a precaution, one that I found, sadly, was necessary. Do you think I wanted to drug my own son? All I wanted was a grown-up conversation. I hoped we could reconnect, become friends again.' His eyes trail towards the closed curtains. Blinking, he looks back at his son. 'But you were so hostile. I knew I would never be able to calm you down enough to talk about the issues we have to address.'

'Are you surprised?' Cooper finds his voice is croaky. He longs for water but will not ask this man for a favour. 'I know you think the ends justify the means. Well, news alert, they don't. Not in my universe. How could I even have a reasonable conversation, let alone be friends, with someone who's messing with people's life chances for his own mercenary reasons?'

'There you are, you see. Still so angry.' Bruce glances at Cooper's arms, pinned out of danger's way. 'You brought it on yourself. Your own stupid fault, as always.' A strange expression, perhaps regret, washes across his face. 'It shouldn't have to be this way.'

'Too right. It wouldn't, if you had anything resembling a moral compass.' Cooper is not about to weaken. He plants his feet hard on the floor, trying to move. His chair almost tips over backwards.

'I needed you neutralised, and here we are. Now we can talk.'

'Yeah, right.' Cooper has an urge to spit in his face. He gathers the saliva around his tongue. It's so tempting. Tempting, but pointless. He swallows. 'I must get back to Lexie. I should have been home hours ago. She'll be worried sick. She's probably reported me missing by now. They'll be out looking for me.'

'Hmm. A reasonable assumption.' Bruce looks to the ceiling, stroking his chin, then jumps up, walks into the kitchen and grabs a packet of Bourbons from a cupboard. He puts them on the table very close to Cooper and begins to eat one, dissecting it and nibbling round the outside. 'That would be very inconvenient for me, wouldn't it? Which is why Lexie received a call a few minutes ago to say that you'd been arrested on suspicion of sedition.'

Cooper laughs. 'You've been watching too many spy movies. I don't think Lexie even knows the meaning of sedition.' It's becoming a struggle to continue batting back Bruce's comments, but he's determined not to show weakness or fear.

'Ahh, maybe not, but she knows the sound of a policeman's voice, or what she thinks is a policeman's voice, and she's never heard me speak. Sounds like a lovely girl, by the way. The baby was bawling, but your wife sounded surprisingly calm, in the circumstances.' Bruce takes another biscuit. 'What you need to realise, Cooper, is that there is no other way. The Programme is running, it's been authorised by Parliament, it's legitimate. Nothing's going to change.'

The smell of sugar and cocoa makes Cooper nauseous, or perhaps it's the side effects of the sedative. Lexie will be beside herself with worry and anger. Will she immediately think the worst of him, or will she be moving heaven and earth to get him released?

Stay calm. Play him at his own game. Perhaps it's true that getting angry earlier has put him in this position.

'She will be calm. Lexie is so much cleverer than you imagine. She will have seen through your pathetic little subterfuge. She's probably tracking my phone as we speak. There sure as hell isn't a police station in this street, so she'll have the real police on it straight away.'

'Oh yes. About that,' Bruce nods towards a bucket of water sitting between the table and the kitchen. Rolling his sleeve up, he plunges his hand down into the water. 'Ouch. Still quite hot.' He raises his arm, brandishing a dripping phone.

Cooper makes a conscious decision to stop his shoulders slumping. He will not give Bruce the satisfaction. 'What a mastermind you are. Clearly in the wrong job.' He tries to wriggle his wrists without letting his shoulders and upper arms move. It's surprisingly difficult. 'OK. You have my full attention, unfortunately. You want to talk, so talk. What's this all about? Why have I been deprived of my freedom, and what do you think you are going to achieve?'

Bruce stands up and begins pacing in front of the table. 'It's all become very complicated.'

'You're not kidding.'

'Do shut up, Cooper. The point of this is for you to listen.'

Cooper emits a heavy sigh. This is going to take a long time.

'The New Directive hasn't gone entirely to plan.'

Cooper says nothing.

'To be honest, there's been a bit of a stink about it.'

Cooper hears a muffled shout of 'I fucking hate you' through the party wall with next door. He knows how they feel.

Bruce lowers his voice. 'Don't even think about shouting. The type of people who live around here don't get involved. Their lives are way outside your experience.'

'You might be surprised by what my experience has been.'

'Take the warning, Cooper. I mean it. If you want to see what's her name, Lexie, again.'

Cooper counts silently. It helps to calm his racing pulse. 'You were saying, about the New Directive.'

'This X campaign. It's making waves. It needs to be shut down.'

'Don't look at me. I've had nothing to do with that. You've closed my social media down, remember.'

'But you must know where it comes from.'

This is what fear looks like. Bruce is running scared. 'I repeat. I had nothing to do with it. I have no influence there. You're going to have to sort this one out for yourself.' That sounds clear and honest, even if it isn't strictly accurate.

For God's sake, Len, keep your head down. Cooper's mind whizzes through what might happen. What will Lexie do? Will she be convinced about the 'policeman'? Who will she talk to? Her next action might dictate whether Cooper makes it home or not.

'I don't believe you.' Bruce's lip is curling.

'That's your privilege.' Cooper shrugs his shoulders. 'But it's the truth. Imprisoning me will achieve nothing except make me hate you even more. If that's possible.'

Bruce's eyes seem to shrink into their sockets. He coughs in a way that suggests all is not well with his lungs.

'You look like shit, by the way, Dad. I'm sure I do, too, but I have the excuse of abduction. Is Mum not looking after you these days?'

Bruce blinks. 'What do you know about that?'

Cooper raises his eyebrows in a look of mock disbelief. 'It looks like I've touched a nerve. Has she seen the light and left you?'

'No, she hasn't, not that it's any of your business. I haven't been home. I'm officially out of town, seeing a sick relative. I forgot to pack a bag.'

Cooper smiles, meaning to do so internally, but it appears on his face. He thinks back to his meetings with Amy, looking better each time he sees her. She's regaining her vitality and health at Bruce's expense. How can her husband not know that they have reconnected and are plotting against him? He knows so much else about Cooper and his family. Surveillance can be a perfect idiot, fortunately, showing images without demonstrating what they mean.

'How is Mum, by the way?'

'None of your business.'

'Fair enough. You destroyed my relationship with her and kept me away from my family, after all.'

'You're getting on my nerves now.' Bruce swipes the packet of biscuits off the table. Cooper imagines shards of chocolate biscuit shearing off the cream inside.

'Let me go then. You've achieved something, I suppose,' he says, employing a deliberately more reasonable tone. 'Congratulations on demonstrating your power over me. You've shown that you know where I live, which was never a secret. You could have come to see us at any time. You've succeeded in plucking me off the street, scaring my wife witless and upsetting my baby. You've destroyed my phone, although that was pointless because I'll get another one. You've basically stamped on me, which is what you've done for most of my life. Of course, what you could have done, which I realise is beyond you, is build bridges.' Cooper has an unbearable itch on his nose. He wrinkles it repeatedly in an attempt to displace the irritation. 'If you think this project of yours has gone wrong,' he continues, 'you could have asked for my advice. We could have worked together. You must realise that I have everything to gain and nothing to lose by helping you unpick it. It's destroyed my life and that of my family, after all. Did you ever consider that?'

Bruce sits down heavily and buries his head in his hands. 'Of course, I thought about it. Why else do you think I contacted you?'

'Unusual method of contact.'

Bruce looks up. There's a strange thumping sound from next door. 'It's too late, isn't it? I realised that the minute you got into the car. I hoped for better things. I sought reconnection, perhaps even a family reunion.'

'No chance. The bad memories go too deep. You'd have to work very hard for a long time to get my respect again. I guess you wouldn't be up for that.' Cooper coughs. His throat is so dry it's hard to speak, although there is much he wants to say. 'So, are you going to let me go?' He examines his father's face more carefully. He's always been erratic, but there's something unhinged about his mood swings now. It's as if he's doing the good cop, bad cop routine as a one-person show.

A psychologist would have plenty to say about Bruce Box.

'I'll tell you what I'm going to do. I'm going to leave you here a little longer to make you more compliant. What I really want to see is if this social media rubbish stops while you're incapacitated.'

'I've told you the truth about that. It's nothing to do with me, as you'll find out soon enough.'

'Well, we'll see, won't we?' Bruce stands and tucks his shirt back into his trousers. 'I'll see you later, Cooper, quite a bit later.'

'You can't leave your own son without food and water.'

'Watch me. You're not my son. Not now. You tried to trash my project.'

'I didn't need to. You've done it yourself.'

Bruce reaches across to slap him, but checks his arm mid-flight. 'You're not worth it.'

He turns his back on Cooper. Bruce's shirt, drenched with sweat, sticks to his spine in places.

Cooper opens his mouth to call his father back, but what's the point? The man is demented. While he's thinking about it, the light flicks off, the front door closes, and Cooper is alone in the dark.

First, he shouts, yells, and screams, hoping that someone will hear and help. There is a brief lull in the argument next door, then it resumes.

Cooper examines the options. None of them is palatable. He wriggles his wrists again, but the bonds are sound. Could he topple the chair? What would that achieve?

He wonders what time it is, not that the knowledge will make much difference to his predicament.

He waits a few minutes, hoping that his eyes will adjust to the dark. This turns out to be helpful. Although the curtains are drawn, they are cheap and flimsy and the light from a streetlight outside delineates the outlines of furniture and doors. His long legs are an advantage. Although he is tied, his feet are flat on the floor. He attempts a little shuffle, seeing if he can move himself and the chair. It is possible, but very difficult to manoeuvre, and he has the table legs to negotiate. The floor layout is cramped and crowded with furniture. But it's his only chance and he has all the time in the world, unfortunately.

Cooper thinks of Lexie, imagining her fear and worry, stuck in the house alone with a screaming baby and believing that he has done something stupid. He hopes that her faith in him will prevail.

Cooper's target is the kitchen.

Shuffle. Shuffle. It's painfully slow, requiring huge effort from feet, legs and glutes, and one false step could topple him over, and then it's game over, because it would be impossible to right himself. He keeps going. At one point, he almost tips over, but manages to bounce off the back of another chair. He's upright again. His misstep helps him to realign himself. His direction is subtly altered; he is heading towards the shadowy area of the kitchen.

Cooper rests. His breathing is raw and throaty. He is so thirsty, not to mention exhausted. Thoughts of Lexie keep him going. He takes a long, slow breath, slowing down his heartbeat, and continues his snail-like progress. Eventually, he is inside. A stray knife has jammed the cutlery drawer open. Cooper's challenge is to move himself, arms behind him, and get out a knife.

It's a tough prospect, but his only chance.

After much pushing and shoving, he is in position, only to discover, which should have been obvious, that the drawer is too high for him to reach into with his arms trapped.

Cooper slumps forward. He is beaten, destroyed, and he's desperate for a piss. Sweat pours down his face. Hunching in defeat, his hands knock against the unit front. Something snags against his knuckle. He moves his fingers in the dark to try to establish what it is. The unit has split, or something, and there is a jagged edge.

Yes!

Cooper manages to lever the rope into position so it's up against the rough area; he begins to rub. It's impossible to tell if it's going to work. All he can do is persevere. It's not going to be quick, for sure. Cooper decides to work in five-minute bursts, or what he feels are five-minute bursts anyway. The first attempt seems to make no difference at all. He waits for a while, wondering if it is worth proceeding. He has nothing else to do, so he carries on. Is it his imagination, or is the weight becoming a little less? Five minutes is a long time. His biceps and triceps are complaining, but he's sure he's making progress. After the fifth go, he knows he is. He begins to rub for longer between rests. He is getting there. He works harder and harder, faster and faster. Yes. Nearly there. In a burst of energy, he rubs so hard that he loses concentration and before he knows it, he has toppled over.

Disaster. After all that effort. He wants to yell in frustration. Instead, he jiggles his wrists, which are now rubbed so raw that every movement is agony. He pushes and pulls. The rope is sufficiently frayed that with a little more effort, surely, it will break. It does. His arms are free. Injured but not constrained. From here, he can undo his legs and stand up.

He almost flops to the ground. His muscles have been cramped for so long that they don't want to work properly, but with some gentle massage and flexing, he is in business again.

Cooper pauses only to fill a glass with water and drink it down in one, then walks through to the front room, limping slightly. His hand is on the light switch, but he decides to leave the room dark, in case Bruce has surveillance on the house. Will he have cameras inside? This seems unlikely, since the footage could be used against him. Cooper is at the door, ready to turn the catch and escape.

It's double locked.

Think. Can he break a window? Better still, he searches for a back door. Their locks are often less secure. The door by the kitchen is locked. Obviously. There's a mat. Bruce wouldn't be so stupid as to leave a key under it.

He isn't.

Cooper slumps to the floor. If only he weren't so exhausted.

He forces himself to his feet. There must be a spare somewhere. Ransacking each drawer in the kitchen is unsuccessful. He races up the stairs, checks cupboards in every room without any luck. He even lifts up the top of the old-fashioned cistern in the bathroom just in case.

He is trapped.

A crumpled bed looks almost welcoming, but Lexie needs him. He will not give up.

Downstairs again, he tries all the windows but they are securely locked. In desperation, he finds a grubby towel in the kitchen and wraps it around his fist and forearm. There is a glass panel in the back door and it may be breakable. It looks worryingly sturdy. Not much point in smashing the glass if he bleeds out on the floor from an arterial cut.

Cooper tries kicking at the glass panel. It shudders a little but remains intact.

He's about to revert to his idea of smashing it with his fist when his eye rests on the catch of the window next to the door. The window is shut and the pane that opens is on the small side, but the handle is at half mast, as if it won't close, and therefore lock properly. He drags a chair over, steps up and jiggles the mechanism. It is well and truly jammed, but he can tell from the angle of the keyhole that it's not locked. After several attempts to free it, he returns to the floor.

There must be a way.

Cooper bangs his head against a wall cupboard in the kitchen. Every minute that passes is a longer period of anguish for Lexie. He opens the cupboard door and finds a half-full bottle of vegetable oil. Running some over his fingers, he returns to the matter in hand, working the greasy liquid into every angle of the window latch. After cleaning his fingers on the towel, he tries again. It feels a little looser. He perseveres and eventually, with a gentle squeak, the window opens.

Without waiting another second, Cooper squeezes his body through the narrow opening and jumps down into the back garden, expecting at any moment to see Bruce emerging from the shadows to grab him and force him back inside. He climbs over the flimsy fence, which almost collapses under his weight, into the garden of the derelict house next door. He noticed when they arrived, today, or was it yesterday, that there was a footpath running down the side of that property. The fence on this side has already collapsed, so it is no problem to gain the path and escape to the front.

Usually, he would have some reservations about climbing through gardens in rough areas at night-time, but after what he has just gone through, it seems no challenge at all. Besides, the dawn is breaking.

Now, where the hell is he and how does he get home with no money and no GPS?

On foot. Obviously.

19.

Marilyn

Marilyn lines up the coffee cup into the perfect position on the desk to provide calm and support as she works on her laptop, trying to educate herself in the ways of X. Much as she hates social media, it is a welcome distraction from her new reality. Last night her grandmother veered between agony and fury, clutching at Marilyn but, without doubt, blaming her too. This elderly lady is Marilyn's one remaining close relative, and she neither wants nor can afford to alienate her further. Hours spent comforting her and trying to give reassurance that there would be an investigation - fat chance - have left Marilyn wrung out and in a bleak state of mind. Lack of sleep hasn't helped. It was 2 am by the time the body had been removed, Marilyn extricated herself, and she laid her head on her own pillow. Sleep failed to come for most of the remaining hours.

This morning is no less bleak, made worse by gritty eyes and a thumping headache. She was worried that she wouldn't be able to find the offending X account, since Bruce hadn't given her much to go on, apart from waving his phone at her amid splutters of fury, but it's easier than she feared. A quick look at what's trending and she quickly finds @coffeeshopwarrior and his (she assumes the person is male, although there is nothing concrete to prove this) impressive and faithful following. Marilyn has made periodic and erratic attempts to engage on X, and her list of followers hovers infuriatingly around the one hundred mark. This person, who only started tweeting recently, has more than fifty thousand.

Astonishing.

On closer examination, it seems that @coffeeshopwarrior hasn't posted much at all, apart from the original tweet, replying to the woman who'd put the Daily Mail letter up on the platform.

Interesting.

Marilyn had assumed that he was the instigator, but perhaps he is merely riding the wave. It makes her think that he, like her, doesn't really know what he is doing on social media.

Perhaps he regrets what he started.

Marilyn certainly does.

If he isn't stoking the flames constantly, as she had assumed he would be doing, there is a chance this will die down. She is wondering what the Government could do to damp down the frenzy when she hears the irritating squeak of the hinge on her office door.

Bruce is standing in the door frame.

It takes a moment to register what is different about him. He is wearing the same clothes she saw him in last night. They looked lived-in yesterday, to put it politely, but today there is another level of degradation. His tie has gone, the shirt is no longer merely stale, but in a state way beyond grubby. Chocolate stains smear the front, and his collar is bent over inside the shirt on one side. Greasy tufts of hair are plastered to his scalp. Deep hollows have almost completely obliterated the whites of his eyes.

His appearance deserves a comment or even sympathy, but she's all out of positive feelings. In fact, she's livid.

She remains silent. It's not as if she wants to speak to him anyway. If she says nothing, perhaps he will go away. Marilyn manages a brief smile and looks back at her laptop.

'So, you're ignoring me this morning, are you?'

Marilyn fails to suppress a weary sigh. She raises her eyes to his exhausted face. 'On the contrary, Bruce. I am interrogating X, as you instructed me last night. A good night's sleep would have helped, but my evening took an unexpected turn.'

Bruce, unsurprisingly, fails to pick up on this.

She continues. 'If you don't mind my saying so, you look as if you could do with some rest too.'

She is aghast at her audacity and waits for a reaction. Bruce will not be used to his faithful acolyte venturing an opinion about his appearance. She averts her eyes while waiting for an explosion.

The room remains quiet. When she looks up, Bruce is

examining the chocolate stain on his shirt, licking a finger and rubbing at the mark. Without looking at her, he says, in a croaky voice, 'Come into my office now. There are things we need to speak about.' He turns away and walks towards his own space. Not so long ago, Marilyn would have longed to tuck in his crumpled shirt at the back. What if someone sees him in this state? He is usually the type of man who insists on standards being maintained. Today, she feels nothing but disdain. She raises herself from her desk, stuffing her feet into her shoes, closes her laptop and follows him.

This won't be good news.

Bruce is standing by the window. The light behind him makes his edges look hard. 'Bruce, before we start, I'm concerned for you. I can tell something is very wrong. Would it be best for you to go home and have some rest? It's hard to think straight when you're exhausted.' She wants to add that he looks a mess, and that she is also too tired for a serious conversation.

'Yes, yes,' he replies, making each word sound like an accusation. 'I am aware that I'm a tad rumpled. I'm going home to clean myself up shortly. There are matters we need to discuss first.' A ghastly smile flashes across his face. 'I've been having a little chat with my son.' Bruce drops this in as if he and Cooper are on the best of terms and catch up regularly.

'Cooper?'

'The very same. Such an interesting young man.'

Marilyn swallows. Bruce clearly wants her to ask the circumstances, so she won't. If he's been talking to Cooper, will he know that she's withheld information from him about Cooper and Amy?

Marilyn's phone beeps from inside her handbag. She reaches in and silences it.

'You said there were things we needed to discuss. Is this about your son?'

'Only indirectly.' Bruce shoves his hands into his suit trouser pockets and begins to pace around the room. One of the openings is ripped on the seam. 'Do you remember Rangan?' He turns to face her, his hands still encased, elbows out as if he is trying to do a silly elephant impression.

'Rangan? The IT expert we brought in to work on the Directive?'

'That's right. The man you found to work on the "special project."' Bruce makes quotation marks in the air.

'I only found him because you asked me to.' She swallows. 'To make the alterations to the algorithm, you mean?' Marilyn feels her face flushing. She experiences an urgent need to empty her bowels. Instead, she crosses her legs as tightly as they will go. 'I was following your direct instructions, Bruce.'

Why is he talking so freely?

'Of course, Marilyn. You followed my instructions. You could have challenged them, of course.' He smiles, as if this would have been possible.

'But we agreed that it was the right thing to do.'

Pictures of her grandfather's body flash through her mind.

'Exactly.' The awful smile is back, even more gruesome to Marilyn now. 'Only, it seems to be having unforeseen effects. Would you agree?'

'Umm.' Now she visualises the letter on X. 'Would you like me to see if I can locate Rangan and call him back in? He would be the best person to look at the code. Perhaps he could make alterations to…er…ameliorate any unfortunate consequences.'

Bruce makes a strange sound in his throat. It could be an attempt at a laugh, or rising panic. 'Rangan is no longer available.'

'You said he went to visit relatives in India, didn't you?'

'Is that what I said? I repeat, Rangan is no longer available. It was important that he was not able to speak about what we had done.'

Marilyn had been in the process of having positive thoughts about Rangan having an extended break in his ancestral home. She struggles to process what Bruce is saying and while she tries, her facial muscles spasm mid-movement. Did Bruce just say what she thought he said? Marilyn realises she is gripping her thighs with her fingers, digging hard into the muscles.

Today started badly, but it is heading precipitately downhill with every moment that passes.

'Let's just say he's staying in India indefinitely, shall we?' Bruce's skin has acquired an even pastier tone.

'Right.' Marilyn's voice is gruff, reverberating from deep in her throat. 'So, if Rangan can't sort this out?'

'I'll find someone, and you will work with them.'

'To do what, exactly?'

'To examine the changes and deal with any anomalies. It's important we can still offer improved numbers to the right people.'

Marilyn stands up, afraid that her muscles will contract so much she will be unable to move. 'You know I never agreed that we should do favours for your mates.'

Bruce moves towards her and presses his face close to hers. 'You are such a child. You know the way it works, the way the world turns. You just chose to pretend it wasn't happening. If you'd really objected, you should have said something earlier.'

She slumps back into the chair. He is right, of course. It was easy to follow Bruce's lead when she was blinded by adoration. In what twisted world had she ever felt like that? The man in front of her is not the one she fell in love with. She has not changed, but Bruce, once an appealing, driven man with a strong moral compass, has become erratic, corrupt, deranged.

She must make a stand before it's too late. Surely she, as a senior employee, would be less easy to neutralise than a freelance IT specialist? Marilyn is not at all sure of her safety but comes to a decision that this is crunch time.

She sits forward. Her legs feel as if they've given up on her, but, with a supreme effort, she stands and raises herself to her full height, which is still many inches shorter than her boss. 'I didn't bring this up before, but now I realise that was wrong. I will not condone what you're doing. I will certainly not help you. You're on your own now, Bruce. Take a look at yourself and pull back before it's too late.'

The office is deathly quiet. Bruce's window is shut; no traffic noise permeates the double glazing. There is none of the usual hubbub of busy people hurrying past his door. Marilyn waits for an explosion that never comes. Why is he not erupting with fury at her insubordination?

Bruce ambles to his door, which Marilyn has left open. He closes it. After the horse has bolted, she thinks. His hands are in his pockets again as he walks back to her. His legs have regained a jaunty stride.

'We've talked a lot about the Directive and what we've done to it over the last year, haven't we, Marilyn?'

'Yes, I suppose we have.'

Where is he going with this?

'And we've had plenty of meetings with Rangan too?'

'Yes.'

'Where have we had these meetings?'

'In here?'

'Quite. And you've had meetings with Rangan on your own, where you've discussed in detail what we wanted him to do?'

'Yes. I've passed on your requirements to him, of course.'

'And where have those meetings taken place?'

'In my office.'

Cold seeps into her stomach.

'Yes. Interesting, isn't it, that all the detailed meetings have taken place between you and Rangan alone and in one place?'

'What are you trying to tell me, Bruce?'

'You're being a bit slow here, but you never were the sharpest, were you?' He's walking around her now, round and round, making her dizzy. 'Your office is bugged. Mine isn't. If you fail to support me in this, I will release the recordings, which will show, surprise surprise, that you are the instigator of the whole corrupt enterprise.'

Marilyn wants to move, but her legs won't oblige. It feels as if she's stepped on a smudge of superglue and stood there while it set. She tries to think back through all the meetings. Surely, this can't be true. There must be times when Bruce has given himself away. How can she be sure? She can't. The only thing that is clear is that she is in a hole, not entirely of her own making, but she has helped to dig it.

She has no room for manoeuvre. No space to escape.

'So? Still want to stand up to me?'

Tears prick at her eyes; she will not show weakness. How could she ever have thought she loved this man? Disgust and fear fight within her. Marilyn tries to stand a little taller. 'Of course I want to stand up to you. You are not the man you were.' She wants to be strong and defiant, but her emotions threaten to defeat her. She turns away from him and walks to the window. Lifting her wrist, she wipes at her streaming eyes with a sleeve. 'You're a beast, Bruce.'

She won't look at him.

'You've corrupted me, scarred me.' Now she turns.

'You deserve to rot in hell.' Her breath is coming fast, unlike her words.

'What choice do I have?'

Bruce smirks, the effect gruesome on his battered face.

'None, I think you'll find. I'm glad we understand each other.' He brushes his hands together, looking more cheerful by the second. 'You'll see, it will all come good. Now, go and sort that stupid X rubbish out while I find a replacement for the dear departed Rangan. I have already identified a prime candidate.'

Marilyn imagines herself kneeing him in the balls, holding him tight and twisting her kneecap hard into his most vulnerable area.

Perhaps a golf club, swung between his legs, would be more effective.

Followed by a final stamp on his face when he was down. That one would be for Rangan, always kind and courteous and ignorant of the true purpose of the alterations he was being asked to make.

'Yes, we understand each other. I wish I'd realised before what a misguided and unpleasant individual I was working for.'

His expression hasn't changed.

'I will do what I must do on your behalf, but it's more than you deserve. I'm not surprised your son hates you, Bruce. Not much of a father, are you?'

Bruce winces. She's hit him where it hurts.

She hurries to the door, opens it and turns for a last glance at the object of her hate. Presumably thinking her back would remain turned, he is slumped on his desk chair, his head in his hands. He mutters, 'God, what have I done?'

This tiny intimation of humanity fails to soften her in any way.

Marilyn slams the door, but cannot maintain her composure when she reaches her own office. Raising her head from her desk, she casts her eyes around for where the recording device might be. A bit late now.

Bruce will learn, she thinks, that Machiavelli was wrong. It is not better to be feared than loved.

All projects end in failure eventually.

20.

Lexie

'I don't know what to do.' Lexie's head is buried in Amy's shoulder, although because of the difference in their heights, she is bending down and is pretty sure that her mother-in-law is on her tippy-toes.

It's reassuring to feel the warmth of another human being, an older adult, someone with more experience of life. Lexie imagines her own mother standing with hands on hips and shaking her head from side to side at her daughter's disloyalty in choosing another shoulder to cry on first. Guilt stabs at her like a bad case of indigestion, but something about Amy gives Lexie confidence that they will find a solution. Hard as it is to accept, Amy knew Cooper from birth and might have an inkling about what's happened.

Amy is close to Bruce.

Lexie pulls away gently. They're still standing by the door. 'Come inside properly. I don't want people to see.'

Lexie doesn't want Len to see, more specifically. She is under strict instructions from Cooper not to give Len any more information. He's a wonderful man, kind and generous, but he is inclined to go off-piste when he's struck by a brilliant idea. Lexie argued with Cooper about this. Len's intervention has moved mountains, but Cooper can't see it because he always needs to be in control of events himself.

They've got this far because Len stirred things up, started a social media bandwagon, even if that wasn't his intention.

Could this have been the cause of Cooper's arrest?

Best to keep him in the dark until they know more.

Amy is still holding Lexie's hand as they move into the sitting room. Her skin is soft against Lexie's, rough from constant washing and nappy changes. Insistent pressure from Amy's long, manicured nails cuts into her palms.

'Where's Tash?' Amy asks, keeping her voice down to a barely audible whisper.

'She's upstairs,' Lexie replies, equally quietly. 'She's been fractious. I'm hoping she'll sleep.' She lets Amy's hand go and holds up two sets of crossed fingers.

'I'm dying to see her, but let's leave her to sleep. We've got some talking to do, decisions to make.' Amy puts a warm arm around Lexie and pulls her in tight. The kindness is more than Lexie can take, and sobs punch through her chest. Amy strokes her hair. 'Try not to worry. I'm here to help. Together, we'll think of something.'

Lexie longs to believe this. She leans into Amy's embrace. This is the closest she can get to Cooper right now. Her longing to see him is intense, completely overpowering. Lexie deeply regrets every cross word, grumpy attitude and turned back she has shown Cooper since the baby was born. How could she ever have doubted him? She's been an idiot to underestimate his importance to her, the strength he brings and the love he offers.

Where is he, really, and is he suffering?

More urgently, can she trust Amy? In her heart, she knows she can. Lexie's brain reminds her that Amy is Bruce's wife. Her loyalties may be complicated and conflicted. It is possible that Bruce has put Amy up to the contact with Cooper and his family.

She longs for Amy to be for real, to be on her side.

'Lexie? You're very quiet. We need to believe we'll get him out.'

'Sorry. I was miles away.'

'Come and sit down.' Amy pats the cushion on the sofa, as if Lexie isn't in her own house. 'You're beside yourself with worry. Of course you are. So am I. We need to work together if we're going to have a chance of finding him.'

'I know.' Lexie lowers herself onto the seat cushion, noting, irrelevantly, that they need plumping and that the house is a mess. The only element of the room that still looks sleek is the painting on the wall. 'Only – '

Amy puts a hand on her knee. 'I understand. You called me because I'm Cooper's mum and I know him well, but now I'm here, you've remembered that I'm Bruce's wife and therefore suspect. Am I right?'

The relief that Amy has put into words what Lexie was agonising about but afraid to say washes over Lexie. Her hands, pulled tight into fists, begin to relax. Her shoulders lower infinitesimally. She manages a small smile, but it brings more tears with it. 'You're so wise, Amy. I realised that straightaway, even in the small time I've known you. I see where Cooper gets it from.'

Amy smiles, a lovely, natural reflex, and Lexie sees Cooper reflected in her face. Now she knows she can and must trust this woman. Cooper has sent her a secret message. 'I've never met your husband,' she continues, 'but, from what I've heard, he is a very complicated and difficult person. I hope you don't mind me saying that?'

Amy's smile changes to a laugh, and not a happy one. 'Tell me about it.' She looks down for a minute, tugging at a pulled thread on her trousers. After a while, she raises her eyes to Lexie, a resolute set to her lips. 'We need to decide what to do, but it's important that you understand some background. I know Cooper has been reticent in what he's told you, and there are many things that even he doesn't know. Bruce has become a monster, and you can be assured that I am completely alienated from him and am looking to leave the relationship. He's the only one that doesn't know that yet.'

Lexie opens her mouth to speak, a great weight lifted from her heart. Pictures flash across her mind of a possible future, with Amy being a constant presence in their lives, untarnished by the relationship with her obnoxious husband.

Amy holds up her hand. 'There's more I need to say, and it's important.'

Lexie nods. Her fantasy drifts away.

'It's only fair to say that he wasn't always like this. You know a little about me now. Do you think I would have married someone like that?'

Lexie shakes her head, knowing that she must let Amy have her say.

'When I met Bruce, he was a very different man, enthusiastic and idealistic.'

Lexie finds this a little difficult to believe, but parks her doubts.

'I know it seems unlikely, but it is the truth.' Amy tucks a strand of hair behind her ear. 'We met at university. He was campaigning against world poverty, and I got involved. He was so driven, enthused about things that most of the students only paid lip service to, and it wasn't long before –' She hesitates, looking at her feet for a moment. – before I realised that he really mattered to me. I thought I was passionate about his causes, but I think I just wanted to be near him.'

Lexie feels queasy. Amy's lovely, but it's not pleasant thinking about her feeling passionate about Cooper's Dad.

'It was more of a slow burn for him. I was a convenient helper, always ready to step in and do whatever he asked. Oh, and I was fiercely loyal, defending him from anyone who said a bad word about him. Loyalty has always been central to Bruce's demands. That's what attracted him. Then something changed. I don't even remember the circumstances, but it was as if he opened his eyes and realised that I was more than a fellow student. I'll spare you the details, but from the moment we got together, he was deeply committed.' Amy goes quiet for a minute, pushing at a loose piece of skin on the side of her nail. 'That's the thing with Bruce. He's committed. When something really matters to him, he gets so stuck in that he can't see any other way and will accept no opposition.'

'To the extent that he will arrest his own son?'

'If that is what's happened. I have this strange feeling that the situation is not exactly as you've been told.'

'Why?'

'I don't know. As I said, it's a feeling. The thing is, he's a civil servant. Very high-ranking, I know, but he's not a policeman. He'd have to have grounds to get him arrested, and what could those be? I think there's another answer to this.'

'Let's hope so. I still don't understand how him being so

committed could result in some of the awful things he seems to have done, if Cooper is to be believed.'

'Something changed, years ago, when Cooper was a child, after our daughter died.'

Lexie cannot stifle her sharp intake of breath.

'It was when this Life-Counter Programme was first mooted. It was his idea, although he had no idea initially about how it could be engineered. His idealism made him interested in nudge policies, where they encourage people to do the right thing. It was very benign when it started. I'm sure it began from a good place. His sense of loss was so massive, all-encompassing. Enhancing and saving lives must have seemed like a positive reaction to an unthinkable event.'

'So what changed?' Lexie tries to look at her watch without distracting Amy. Tash is quiet now, but who knows how long that will last? Once she's bawling again, it will be much harder to talk. Also, Cooper is rotting in a police cell. Lexie is inclined to believe this is the case, despite Amy's doubts.

'He met resistance from the establishment, the policy makers, the media, all sorts really. It made him angry. I think that's when he started to believe that the ends justify the means and turned crooked. It's also when he stopped talking to me about what he was doing.'

'I'm still a bit hazy on what he's been doing to "turn crooked" as you put it. Cooper hasn't told me that much.'

'He's probably trying to protect you. I don't know the details myself, but I've been trying to find out what I can. Bruce thinks he's very clever, but he does leave clues, and he's useless with his computer security.' Amy looks into Lexie's eyes. 'Once I tell you this, my life with Bruce is officially over. We can't come back from what I'm about to say. Are you happy for me to burden you with it?'

'Yes, I think so.' What Lexie really wants is for Amy to spit it out quickly before Tash wakes up.

'What I think has been happening is that he has been taking bribes to improve the data for important people. On the other side, he's been damaging the data for people he has it in for. That's what happened to Cooper and now Tash.'

'I don't understand how he'd be able to do that. It's a big, complex project, isn't it, with constant monitoring and checks and balances. How could one person corrupt it?'

Amy shrugs. 'I'm not sure I get it either. Certainly, he won't have been able to do it on his own. Bruce is a generalist, not an IT specialist. He must have had help, and that's his weakness. If we can find out who did his dirty work and how, there will be evidence.'

'That's what Cooper's trying to do.'

'Yes, and that's why Bruce is attempting to neutralise him, and that's why we have to find out more and get him out.'

Lexie shivers. This is becoming sinister. Until Tash was born, Lexie thought she lived in a reasonably benign environment. Governments could be incompetent, unfeeling, slow to react, but she had the idea that, most of the time, they were trying to do the right thing.

Cooper had never been so sure, hence his campaigning journalism. Lexie sometimes thought that he banged on too much about his beliefs, holding authority to impossible standards.

Now she knows he was right all along.

And look where it got him.

Lexie feels so alone without Cooper by her side. Thank goodness Amy is here.

'Lexie?'

'Sorry. I was thinking about Cooper. I wish I'd listened more closely to him. He was right, and I used to fob him off sometimes.'

'Don't worry about it. I know he can be a bit full on when he gets up a head of steam. The best thing we can do for him is to spring him from wherever he is.'

'But how can we do that? We have no idea where to start.' Lexie stands up. It all seems hopeless. What's worse, she can hear the first whimpers from Tash, little grumbles that will soon gain momentum and be impossible to ignore.

Amy gets up too and closes the plantation shutters, making the room immediately feel gentler and safer. 'I have an idea.' She straightens the cushions on the sofa, bashing the top ones as if she has a grudge against them. 'We don't know where he is, but we know who is responsible for his disappearance, whether that is imprisonment or something else.'

Lexie nods. This doesn't seem to be getting them anywhere.

'We are pretty sure that Bruce is responsible. Agreed?'

'I suppose so.' This is a big leap, but Amy reckons she has an idea, so Lexie is prepared to go with it.

'We can't go straight to Bruce. I don't want him to know that I'm on to him. I think he's got a pretty good idea that I'm not happy with him, but I don't intend to signpost my intentions yet.'

'Right.' Lexie's feeling desperate. Tash's cries are getting louder, in a pattern she recognises, and it makes her heart sink. She's been unable to settle all day. She's missing her Dad, and that in itself makes Lexie feel inadequate. 'You said you had an idea?' She can't stop her eyes from travelling upwards to the source of the cries.

'I do.' Amy looks upwards, too. 'We'll go and get Tash in a minute, but hear me out. Bruce has a number 2, a woman called Marilyn. I can't stand her, to be honest.' Amy's face lights up with the hint of a grin. 'She idolises Bruce and hates me. She'd probably like to marry Bruce herself. Well, she's welcome to him.'

'She won't be much help then.' Lexie checks her watch. Tash is overdue for a feed.

'I'm not so sure. Bruce has been behaving bizarrely recently. Marilyn is bound to have noticed, and she probably knows more than we do. I think she is basically honest, just blinded by her feelings for my husband. But she's a good civil servant. She may be beginning to have doubts about what he is doing. I told Cooper about her, and he wanted me to approach her and talk to her woman-to-woman, to appeal to her better nature. I wasn't sure before, but Cooper's disappearance or arrest or whatever it is makes me realise he was right all along. It's all we've got right now. Are you happy to give it a go?'

'I guess so. We don't have much choice. If it's what Cooper wants you to do, I guess we owe it to him to try.' Lexie feels her shoulders tensing. 'Sorry, I'd better get Tash now, before all hell lets loose.'

'Of course. Can I come too?'

Lexie smiles. 'Yes, please.' They climb the stairs one behind the other, and the burden feels a little lighter.

Half an hour later, Tash is changed, fed and calmed. Amy seems to have the same caring touch as her son. They sit together, refining the plan over tea and toast, and the world looks a little less bleak.

When Amy leaves, to get home and avoid arousing Bruce's suspicions, the house feels bleak and empty.

But there is hope. Marika is on her way. Thank goodness for real mums. Lexie has some explaining to do, but she is no longer alone.

*

Tash has miraculously calmed down and is upstairs sleeping peacefully, probably gone for the night. Is this Amy's doing, or have her calmness and maturity merely rubbed off on Lexie? Lexie still finds it hard to settle while she waits for Marika. She turns on the TV, keeping the volume low. The thought of waking the sleeping baby is terrifying. On the other hand, she wants to cuddle her, to feel her warmth, to find comfort in another human being who is fifty percent Cooper. Flicking through the channels, Lexie finds nothing that can engage her attention for more than a couple of minutes. She is surprised to notice that her hands are shaking. She didn't think she felt that bad. Suddenly, she starts to shiver, and her teeth chatter. What is happening?

Lexie fights the urge to panic. Come on, Mum. Hurry up.

In her confusion, she fails to notice the first ring of the doorbell. The second time it goes, it enters her consciousness. How can she answer when she's shaking all over? Why doesn't Mum use her key?

The noise will wake the baby.

Lexie hurries to the front door, trying to ignore the weakness and shaking in her legs.

She opens the door a crack, keeping the chain on. Her face meets Len's. He's peering through the small opening. Her anxiety turns to irritation. What is he doing here at this time of night? Lexie takes the chain off and opens the door to its full extent.

Len is in his pyjamas.

'Hello, Len, what can I do for you?' Lexie tries not to sigh but isn't entirely successful.

'Sorry. I know it's late.' Len's voice is very deep and always loud.

Lexie puts a finger gently to her lips. 'It's fine. My mum will be here soon. But could we whisper? Tash is sleeping.'

'Oh, sorry, love. I didn't think. If it's a difficult time—?'

It is, obviously, but Len looks forlorn; she doesn't have the heart to tell him.

'Is there a problem?'

'I've been a bit worried about this social media thing, you know. Could I have a word with Cooper? I see his car's there.'

'Oh, Len. Cooper isn't here.' She fully intends to make up some rational reason why he is absent, but instead she bursts into tears.

'Oh, dear.' Len fiddles with the buttons on his pyjama jacket. 'I have come at a bad time. What can I do to help?' Len looks behind him at the darkened shape of Cooper's car. 'I thought he must be here.'

Lexie tries to pull herself together. 'Come in for a minute.' She controls her sobs, but, in doing so, brings on an attack of hiccups. She and Len hover in the hall. Something about the fact that Len is in his pyjamas makes her hesitant to invite him in to sit down. Trying to keep her wits about her, Lexie remembers that she is under strict instructions not to tell Len more than is absolutely necessary.

'What have you been worrying about, Len? What you've done on social media has been amazing. It's made such a difference.'

'Yes, well, I've surprised myself really.' Len scratches his ear. 'What I wanted to talk to Cooper about is what I should do next. I don't want it to lose momentum, if you know what I mean.'

'It's probably best to let it lie for a bit.' Cooper's anguish about the likely results of Len's efforts is fresh in her mind. 'These things can be hard to control. They tend to get out of hand, if you aren't careful.'

'It did seem to be making a difference, though.'

She can hear the pride in his voice.

'Anyway, enough about me. What's this about Cooper not being here? His car is outside, and you seem upset.'

'Oh Len.' Lexie goes to steady herself with a hand on the console table in the hall, only to remember they moved it because it became an obstacle course when carrying the baby. She pushes a hand against the wall instead. 'I had a call earlier to say that Cooper has been arrested, but they didn't tell me much about why, or where they're holding him, or what I can do about it.' Her voice is wobbling, and she makes a big effort to keep it steady. 'I don't know what to do.'

Lexie feels a little stronger, but also guilty for burdening him with her problems, as Len braces his feet and pushes against the wall with a hand against each side. It seems an odd thing to do, until she notices that his legs are shaking.

'Dear God, is this my fault?' he says, his voice loud and reverberating in the enclosed space.

'No, of course not,' she says, putting an arm around his shoulders and guiding him back towards the door. 'I am working on a plan, but you caught me at a bad moment. That's the only reason I was upset. We will get Cooper back soon. I'm sure of it. You mustn't worry. The best thing for tonight is for you to go home and get some sleep. I am not going to be alone.'

'Everything will seem better in the morning,' he says. 'That's what my wife always used to say.'

'And she was right, I'm sure. Good night, Len. Get some rest.' She steers him through the front door.

'And you, dear.'

'I will. Good night.'

'Good night. We'll speak tomorrow.'

Len creeps down the front path. Lexie is concerned by the

thoughtful look on his face as he leaves. When Len thinks too much, things tend to happen.

21.

Marilyn

The office window is wide open, in a small act of defiance. Bruce hates draughts. Marilyn's door is fully closed, as an added deterrent. There is so much to do, but she has very little enthusiasm to carry out whatever might serve to aid her boss's interests or implicate herself further. After a sleepless night, Marilyn is devoid of ideas. Her only one so far today is that, if Bruce dares to enter her realm, she might trip him up in such a way that he would be catapulted out of the window and come to an untimely end. Since there is a flat roof outside, this is a forlorn hope.

It doesn't stop her fantasising about the possibility.

Marilyn's phone startles her out of her mental torpor. She picks it up, but, seeing Bruce's home phone number, she declines it swiftly. Bruce is here, slightly tidier and cleaner than of late, but as haggard as she has seen him recently. She knows he is here because she remembers glaring at him as he walked past only a few minutes ago.

It must be Amy, but why would she call?

Marilyn grabs her bag, stuffs her feet into the shoes under her desk and slips out of the office. It's not until she is clear of the building, has turned a corner and has checked for CCTV on the external walls of the adjacent facades that she ducks into an alleyway and delves into her handbag to find an ancient Nokia phone into which she has recently put a new pay-as-you-go SIM. Thank goodness she had at least thought to do that once she realised what Bruce was up to. Amy's called from a landline, so she can't text a reply. Holding her iPhone in one hand and Nokia in the other, Marilyn copies the number and hits the call button.

Come on, come on. Answer, why don't you? I'm like a sitting duck here in the street.

She's about to give up when, finally, the call is picked up.

'Hello? Who is this? Cooper?' The voice is echoey, anxious, with a breathlessness that masks Amy's usual voice. Marilyn is pretty sure it must be Amy, if only because of the phone number, although she has always seemed so self-assured in the past.

A lack of certainty rattles Marilyn. She won't give anything away.

'Not Cooper. You just called me.' Marilyn maintains surveillance on her surroundings as she talks. Her insides are in a knot.

'Marilyn?'

'That's right.' Abrupt. Don't help her. This could be a trick.

'But the number?'

'I'm on a burner phone. You called me on my personal number in the office. I can't answer there.'

'Oh hell. I didn't think.' Amy's voice is softening.

'It doesn't matter.' Marilyn can hear the tension in her own voice, taut and staccato. Not very friendly. 'What do you want?'

'Oh, God. This is a bad idea. Forget I phoned. Goodbye.'

She's overdone it.

'Stop, Amy. I want to hear what you have to say.' Marilyn pauses. 'Is this to do with someone known to us both?'

Amy lets out a slightly hysterical laugh. 'You could say that.'

'We shouldn't talk on this line. You're calling from home, aren't you?'

'Yes, stupidly.'

'Give me your mobile number and I'll text you a location for us to meet, where I know the CCTV is disabled.'

As soon as Amy has done so, Marilyn ends the call, then immediately sends a message:

Meet me at 'Nails and Brows' near Longacre. They have a room at the back we can use to talk. I'll bring coffee.

OK, comes the reply. *I'll be there as soon as I can. Thanks.*

Marilyn has committed herself. She is beginning to feel like a fugitive, hoping she hasn't made a mistake in letting Amy know of her secret space. This is a woman who has been her enemy. Why has she been so quick to assume that Amy has something helpful to say? Despite queasy misgivings, instinct tells her she has done the right thing. Her previous lassitude has disappeared, replaced with a spark of hope that something might be about to change. She does at least know that Amy has been deceiving her husband. When she had first become aware of this, she had hoped that Amy's and Bruce's falling out might leave space for her to take over. She shivers at the thought of this now.

There is no time to return to the office, but she will reach Covent Garden earlier than Amy. Marilyn does a little aimless window shopping and arrives, coffees in hand, surprised to see Amy standing outside the building, trying to look inconspicuous. She wouldn't make a spy. Marilyn nods to her, hands her a disposable cup without comment and gestures towards the door. As they enter, the receptionist is spooning mouthfuls of noodles into her mouth from a plastic container.

'Sorry', she says, as a pungent note of garlic and ginger wafts their way. She wipes the corner of her mouth with a vermilion fingernail. 'We're short-staffed. No time for lunch today. Did you have an appointment?'

Marilyn flashes a small business card in front of her, bending closer. 'We are here to borrow the back room for a while. OK?'

The receptionist's eyes swivel left to right and open wider. 'Sure, go ahead,' she says, swallowing a mouthful of food. Marilyn and Amy walk past her, feeling her eyes on their backs, head past the various beauty stations, through a door at the back, and up a set of stairs which could do with a good vacuum. Marilyn catches a heel on a rip in the carpet but keeps her balance. At the top of the stairs, she heads left and opens a door most noticeable for its scuffed paintwork and individual plastic lettering spelling out the word Manager, although the 'r' is peeling off from the bottom.

'This is a bit cloak and dagger,' says Amy, as Marilyn ushers her in.

'It is, isn't it?' Marilyn manages her first smile of the day. 'I did them a favour a while back, and this is what I asked in return. Even then, I was concerned about surveillance. I didn't know the half of it, unfortunately.'

There is a desk in the corner of the room, and an old sofa with cigarette burns on it. Marilyn gestures for Amy to sit there, while she settles herself on the swivel chair by the desk, twisting round to face her. In an elevated position, she feels she has a better chance of keeping the initiative.

'I had to guess with the coffee. I hope it's OK. Flat white, no sugar.' Marilyn takes a sip of her own and has to lick the froth off her lips.

'Perfect.'

'I'm assuming there's a problem, for you to phone me. I'm also speculating that it is something to do with the way your husband is behaving.'

Amy places the coffee cup carefully down by her feet; she rubs her hands together. 'I don't know where to start. I'm a little nervous about bothering you with this.'

'What you mean, I think, is we don't know each other, we don't necessarily like each other, and we certainly don't trust each other. Am I right?'

Amy blinks. 'It doesn't sound very nice when you say it like that. I'd rather put it that we don't know much about each other.'

'Whatever way you want to say it is fine by me, but we don't have much time. You contacted me. Now's the time to tell me what's up.' Marilyn is aware that this has come across as very brusque, more unfriendly than she intended. Amy won't know that Marilyn is in a desperate situation and her stomach is churning so badly that she's trying to remember where the loo is.

Amy picks up her coffee cup, takes the top off, and gently swirls the contents by swinging her hand in a circle. She stares at the moving liquid for some time before speaking. 'I'm not aware that I've ever done anything to upset you, but I am conscious, have always been conscious, of your hostility towards me. I apologise if I have inadvertently done anything wrong in your eyes.'

'You haven't.' Marilyn sighs. 'Not really. Let's say that Bruce painted a narrative that wasn't very positive about you. I've come to realise recently that I shouldn't believe anything he says.'

Amy's eyebrows rise, and her gaze travels over Marilyn's face. 'Have you two been having an affair?'

The room suddenly feels very hot. Marilyn clamps her mouth tight shut and takes two slow breaths. 'No, absolutely not. I would never do that, truly.' She coughs out the dryness in her throat and stands up. 'I used to have a high opinion of him. That's all. Now I don't.' Amy is still studying her carefully. 'I'm sorry if what I'm saying distresses you.'

Amy finally takes a swig of her drink. 'Distresses me? I'm relieved. It makes it easier for me to raise what I want to talk to you about.'

Marilyn sits down, nodding her head. 'Good. Let's hear it then.'

'From what Bruce has said in the past, I get the impression that you are fully involved with the Life Counter Programme.'

Marilyn swallows. Her saliva tastes bitter.

'Yes, I am, more's the pity.'

'And you know about our estrangement from our son, Cooper?'

'Yes, I do. The falling out happened before I started working on the project, but I have a rough idea of the history.'

Marilyn finds it impossible to maintain eye contact at this point and concentrates on swivelling her chair repeatedly from side to side. Where does the line fall between being economical with the truth and downright lying?

Amy is undeterred. 'And you know that Cooper suffered deficits in life expectancy from the Programme?' she continues.

Blood rushes to Marilyn's cheeks. She rubs her hands up and down her thighs. 'Yes, I do. Some adjustments were made to the algorithm, at Bruce's instructions. These had a negative impact on your son. I'm sorry.'

'And also now his daughter.'

'Yes.'

How do you feel about that, Marilyn? Do you think that was a just and reasonable thing to do?'

Marilyn puts her head in her hands, ducking it down so it bangs against her legs. 'No. I'm so sorry.' Her voice is muffled. 'None of it is right. It's all a terrible mess and I've been so misled.' She jumps up. 'There are things I need to tell you, quickly, before I lose my nerve.' She begins to pace around the small room while trying to keep her eyes on Amy. 'Bruce thought you were having an affair.'

'Me?' Amy laughs. 'And I thought it was the other way round. Until recently, that is, when his personal hygiene headed south. I realised I must be mistaken.'

Marilyn nods. They are seeing the same picture, it appears. 'Yes,' she continues. 'He thought you had changed and became less attentive to him. You were taking more care over your appearance, apparently, so I agreed to follow you, to try to find out.'

A small dimple appears at the side of Amy's mouth as she smiles. Marilyn begins to feel ridiculous. 'What did you discover?'

'Nothing bad.' The words jump out of Marilyn's mouth. 'I saw you meet Cooper, and his wife and baby. That was when I began to doubt Bruce. You looked so right together.'

'Have you continued with this…. surveillance?'

Marilyn stands up and begins to pace in the small space. 'No,' she says. 'I told Bruce I would, but I haven't. It didn't seem right. I also didn't tell him that you met up with your son. I told him some rubbish and said I didn't think you were having an affair.' She stops in front of Amy, who has her arms crossed. 'The thing is, the situation is getting out of hand now. This X campaign and the petition. The algorithm is coming up with unpredictable results, and the whole thing is a mess.'

Amy sits forward.

'Too right it is. And what effect do you think this is having on Bruce?'

Marilyn recognises a leading question when she hears one.

'He's unhinged. I don't recognise him. He's become a monster.' Marilyn wipes sweat from her forehead.

There's no point in holding back now.

'And he's blackmailing me.' Marilyn stares out of the small window at the vista of overflowing black bins. 'I've just discovered that he's been bugging my office all this time and has made me have all the meetings in there when I'm talking with the IT guys who were messing with the code. He's said that if I do anything or say anything against him, all the blame will lie with me. He'll deny it all. I don't know what to do.' This seems to be the point at which Marilyn should burst into tears, but her professionalism won't allow her to do so. Instead, she turns a stony face to Amy. 'So, what did you want to talk to me about? As you can see, I'm up shit creek so I don't know if I'll be able to help you.'

Amy nods, her lips closed tightly. After a pause, she opens them wide, before saying, 'We're both up shit creek.' Her eyes find Marilyn's. 'Perhaps we can paddle together.'

Marilyn lets out a slow breath. 'That's the best offer I've had all day. The only one, in fact.' She smiles, in spite of herself.

'God, he's a piece of work, isn't he?' Amy runs a hand through her hair. 'I thought I was going to have a torrid time trying to persuade you to help us. I didn't realise Bruce had done the work for me already.' She gives Marilyn a faint smile, but her eyes are haunted.

'Well, it would never have occurred to me to reach out to you, because, well, I always regarded you as Bruce's lap dog or guard dog, I'm not sure which.' Marilyn tries to return Amy's smile, but it's hard to put any true feeling behind the gesture.

'A very flattering image, I must say. That's rather how I thought of you.'

Marilyn can't help feeling that she's handling this badly. 'Sorry,' she says. 'Anyway, you said you were looking for help from me. I'm not sure I understand. If you want me to reverse Cooper's deficit, and the baby's, I'd love to, but right now I'm struggling to stay alive myself.'

Amy nods her head. 'So you don't know about Cooper?'

'What about him?'

'He's gone missing. Lexie had a call from a police officer to say that he'd been arrested, but the man wouldn't say where he was or what he was being charged with.'

The room is suddenly very quiet. A faint hum of chatter from downstairs becomes audible. A honking laugh makes it through the floorboards. Marilyn's head feels fuzzy around the edges. She sits down; the swivel chair swings from side to side. 'Arrested, you say?'

'Yes.'

'No details?'

'No.'

'When did this happen?'

'Yesterday.'

Bruce's image flashes in front of Marilyn, dishevelled, dirty, manic. 'Bruce is involved in this. There's no doubt in my mind. And I don't think he's playing by the rules.'

'So, what can we do?' Amy puts a desperate emphasis on the final word.

'First, we need to find Cooper, and I'm willing to bet he isn't in a Police Station, and then we need a plan to get his life back. Right now, I don't know where to start, but something will come to me. Our interests are aligned, Amy, let's do this.'

Marilyn drains her coffee. She feels so much better. She's not on her own anymore.

22.

Cooper

The thought of taking his shoes off and easing his blisters is the only thing keeping Cooper going as he approaches his own home. Without the sharp pain of the raw flesh rubbing the heel of his shoe with every step, he might have lain down in the gutter and gone to sleep. If he'd had his phone or any money on him, he would certainly have stopped for a rejuvenating cup of coffee and something to eat. Something with plenty of carbs. A pause to process what has happened to him. As it is, hunger, pain, and thirst are ganging up on him, pushing out thoughts of Lexie and the baby. His anxiety about what Lexie has been going through returns when he raises a bruised hand to bang on the front door.

He hears footsteps. Then a pause. Does she not realise it's him? Of course not. She would expect him to have keys, but Bruce has taken them.

She thinks he's in prison. Any caller will seem like a threat to her.

'It's me, Lexie.' He begins with a bellow, wanting to be heard, but has a vision of Tash waking and bawling, so lowers his voice.

A stifled sob from the other side of the door.

The sound of a drawer being opened and a clink of keys. So familiar but usually he is on the inside with her.

A creak as a gap appears between the door itself and the frame. Needs oiling.

Lexie's eyes are red-rimmed. Tash is in her arms.

'They released you.' This comes out in a gasp. She's staring at him. He feels even more dishevelled under her gaze. She stands back. 'Thank God. Come in, quick.'

Cooper walks inside, and stoops to remove his shoes without causing any more pain than necessary to his feet.

Lexie goes to hug him, but it's difficult with the baby between them. She settles for kissing his shoulder, leaning in as she does so.

'Didn't they give you your keys back? Where did they hold you? Oh, Cooper, I've been beside myself with worry. They didn't tell me where you were. I'd have come if I could.'

'Shh. Don't worry. I'm here now. Let me take Tash. Give you a break. You look all in.'

She moves as if to hold Tash towards him, then draws her back onto her shoulder. 'You must be exhausted. Why don't you wash and change first?'

'I'm guessing I need to?'

'Um. It'll make you feel better.'

'Fine.' When he thinks of what he's been through in the last few hours, it's no surprise he smells a bit ripe. Cooper trudges up the stairs. Not quite the homecoming he was expecting. Eight years ago, she'd have thrown herself into his arms, no matter what he smelled like. They were a couple. Now he's not sure what they are. He turns halfway up the stairs, throwing her a couple of sentences almost as an afterthought. 'I'd kill for coffee and toast, Lex. I've got lots to tell you, and the situation isn't what you've been told.'

'Oh, of course. Sorry. I guess you haven't had a good night's sleep.'

Cooper manages an exhausted chuckle as he heads into the bathroom and closes the door.

Fifteen minutes later, he's clean, the old clothes are on the bathroom floor, and he's downstairs, gulping coffee and ramming toast and peanut butter into his mouth.

'I've left the clothes on the floor. They're evidence.'

'Evidence?' Lexie sits opposite him, rocking Tash, who is making quiet, contented breathing sounds.

'You were told I'd been arrested?'

'Yes. I knew you were pushing it too much with your investigations.'

'On the contrary,' he says, licking butter off his thumb. 'My investigations were getting precisely nowhere. As you very well know. I wasn't arrested, I was kidnapped by my own father.'

He hears Lexie's sharp intake of breath. 'Kidnapped? So the

phone call I had....'

'Was from Bruce.'

'I've spoken to your father?' Lexie's mouth gapes. She runs her tongue over her teeth. 'Really? Your father? But he sounded, I don't know, kind and thoughtful.'

Cooper almost spits out a mouthful of coffee. 'Kind? He must have been putting that on. This is the man who forced me into his car, abducted me, drugged me and tied me up in a disgusting rotting house in some rat-infested street, then tried to force me to help him out of his self-inflicted mess.'

Lexie pulls her chair back. An ashen pallor spreads across her face. Cooper expects some kind of horrified shriek, but she remains quiet. She holds Tash up against her shoulder and gently kisses the top of her head. Eventually, she shakes her head and says, 'I had no idea. I'm so sorry. But I don't understand what he hoped to gain.'

'Nor me. Did he really think I'd come to heel after all he's done? Lex, I think he's losing it. He didn't seem right in the head.'

'What does he want you to do?'

'I think he's got himself in a mess with all the algorithms, and he was hoping I might help him unravel it all.'

'But if you did, wouldn't it help us?'

Cooper jumps up. She isn't getting it at all. 'That's not the point. He's made the mess. I'm not going to have anything to do with it.'

Lexie frowns. She's holding Tash tighter than ever. 'So he let you go?'

'No. He left me there, tied up, with no food or water. I managed to escape.' Cooper shows her the rope burns on his wrists. Now Lexie lays Tash gently in her lap and touches Cooper's bruised and damaged skin with soft finger strokes. Even this gentle pressure is painful. Cooper does his best not to wince.

'I'll get some arnica,' she says, handing Tash, who's now blowing bubbles, to Cooper. He raises her carefully onto his shoulder, trying not to put pressure on his weakened wrists. Tash proceeds to dribble remnants of her feed down the back of his fresh T-shirt.

Lexie returns, rubbing the greasy white cream onto one wrist while he holds the baby with the other, then repeating the process with his other hand. 'Any other injuries?'

'Cuts and bruises. Nothing bad. Sorry, I couldn't tell you. The bastard drowned my phone. Also, there's the little matter of me being tied up and unconscious.'

Lexie breathes so fast he sees her chest moving. Maybe the reality of the situation hasn't landed yet. 'You poor thing,' she says eventually. She strokes his hair and kisses the top of his head, almost as if he, too, is a baby. 'I was so worried. I've been talking to your mum.'

'Mum? Really? That's great. Is she happy to help further? Did you talk about my plan?'

'Yes, she's....' Lexie is stopped in mid-flow by the doorbell. It rings a second time, then a third. 'Who can that be now? Why do they keep ringing? I bet it's Len again.'

She moves towards the hall.

'Lex, wait. It might be...' Too late, she's gone, just like she always answers her phone on the first ring.

Cooper forces himself up. His hamstrings remind him what he's been through. Tash is getting heavier by the day.

'Alexandra Box?'

'Yes. Is something the matter?'

'Alexandra Box, you are under arrest, on suspicion of acting against the public interest in pursuing a social media campaign to propagate false information about the Life Counter Programme.'

Cooper rushes to the door. Lexie has wedged herself against the wall, while two police officers have forced their way inside. Cooper stands in front of Lexie, his face up against that of the male police officer. He moves even closer. The man doesn't flinch.

'She's done nothing,' Cooper says. His voice sounds loud in the enclosed space. 'You have no right to arrest her. Where is the evidence? Did my father put you up to this?'

The man, a pasty-faced individual with a double chin and a

substantial middle, blinks. He looks vaguely familiar. Cooper realises he is the same officer they spoke to when they made the complaint. At least this proves he isn't an impostor.

'It's Mr Box, isn't it?'

'Yes.'

'I don't know what you mean about your father.' The man fiddles with the Taser attached to his belt. 'I don't know who your father is. We received an anonymous tip-off from a member of the public that your wife was responsible for the false information on X.'

'That's rubbish. And you know it. My wife has never done anything wrong in her life. You only need to look at her ninety-seven years to see that. You need evidence. I know perfectly well who made the anonymous tip-off and he's not reliable. If it comes to that, I can make a counter-allegation. And I will. What right have you to arrest her on this basis? Are you mad?'

The policeman examines Cooper's face for a moment before saying, 'Hmm.' He pushes Cooper out of the way and addresses Lexie again. 'You have a right to remain silent. Anything you do say….'

Cooper grabs the man's arm. 'Stop. This is ridiculous. You can't do this.'

His hand drops back as the policeman shakes his arm away with surprising force. 'I hope you aren't thinking of obstructing a police officer, Sir? What will happen to the baby if you're both taken into custody?'

Cooper steps back.

'If there is anything you aren't happy with, please take it up with the Police Complaints Board.' He turns towards Lexie. 'The car is outside, Ms Box.'

Lexie grabs her handbag from beside the front door, sends a despairing look towards Cooper and Tash, and is shoved outside. A gust of wind catches the side of it and the door slams behind her.

Cooper runs to the downstairs loo and is copiously and noisily sick.

Bruce must have discovered his disappearance. He has

correctly surmised that Lexie is the best way to get Cooper's defences down.

He wipes his face, realising that he has put Tash down on the floor of the room. She seems surprisingly unconcerned by her unceremonious dumping on the cold surface. Cooper picks her up and hugs her. For the first time, he wishes there were someone he could leave her with so he could concentrate on helping Lexie. 'What now?' he says, staring at her but not really seeing her. 'We've got to save your mummy. She's done nothing to deserve this, and it's all my fault.'

23.

Len

Len's hand is shaking as he holds back the edge of the curtain and spots the police car edging out from the kerb. Lexie's face is visible in the back seat. Even from this distance, Len can see the tears streaking her cheeks and the redness around her eyes. He would like to believe that they are taking her to Cooper and that the whole thing has been a misunderstanding but it's not credible. The inescapable conclusion is that Lexie has been arrested as well.

Where is the baby?

This is all Len's fault. He's drawn attention to his neighbours, who are being punished for his misdeeds.

He was only trying to help.

Len lowers himself into a chair. In fact, it's more like a slow-motion collapse as his backside hits the cushion. Should he give himself up? Would that result in Cooper and Lexie being released? He doesn't think so. He has two courses of action. He could lie low and wait to see what happens, or he could crank up his online activities to create even more of a fuss.

Len is not one to take the easy option. He looks upward, thinking of his dead wife.

'What would you tell me to do, love?' He rubs the bristles on his jaw as he waits for her judgement. 'What, you think I should carry on, do you? I thought you'd say that. Brave girl.' Len levers himself upwards, putting a hand on the wall to help himself rise. 'The trouble is, I don't know what I'm doing. I need help. Do you think I should go up to the coffee shop to see if there's anyone to talk to? Yes, you're right. I'll do that.'

Len feels a little better for thinking the matter through. Action always beats passivity. It's not cold, but he puts on his light windcheater. You never know when it might rain or the wind blow cold. He feels a little frail today and takes his stick as a precaution.

His steps are slow and his thoughts ponderous as he trudges towards the place that always makes him feel better, provided there is someone there to talk to.

The wind does blow and brings a few spots of rain with it. He is glad when the door of the coffee shop is in reach. It seems to be moving further away with every week that passes. He pushes the door open with relief and moves inside. At the table nearest to the door, he is delighted to see Steve sitting with a very pregnant young lady. What was her name again? Len isn't sure that he's ever known.

'Len, my man. We've been talking about you.'

'You have?'

'We have. Come and join us.'

Len is more than happy to sink into the chair next to Steve. He hasn't forgotten that it was Steve who got him going on the social media lark, and he wonders if he can bring the conversation round to this subject without making it too obvious.

'You sit with Tracy for a minute, Len, and I'll get you your coffee. Usual?'

'Yes, please. Thank you very much. It'll be nice to sit down.'

'I thought you were looking a bit wobbly there.'

Steve has gone to the counter, and Len is at a loss as to conversational gambits.

'You look as if you're at the blooming stage now, dear,' he says, and then wonders if that isn't the sort of remark you should make these days.

'Blooming enormous,' she says, laughing, blowing bubbles into her coffee.

'As long as you're well, that's the important thing.'

Steve is back, plonking Len's coffee down so hard that some splashes into the saucer. As Len pours the spillage back into the cup, he notices that his hand is shaking. This is a new thing. Should he worry? 'Just what I needed. Thanks.' He takes a sip. It's good. 'Actually, I'm glad you're here. I fancied a chat.'

Tracy is nudging her boyfriend in the ribs. 'Yeah, we wanted to talk to you too.' When he doesn't say anything, she continues. 'I'm worried about this new thing you were telling Steve about. You know, when they take time off the baby's life.'

Now Len looks carefully at her, he notices the deep shadows under her eyes. He takes his hand away from his cup and pats her fingers. 'I remember my wife worried about everything when she was pregnant. It's natural to be anxious, but all your frightening thoughts will disappear once the baby is born. You take my word for it.'

Steve and Tracy exchange glances. 'There may be some things,' Steve says, stopping mid-sentence as if he's a vinyl record that has stuck.

Len holds his cup halfway to his mouth, giving Steve what he hopes is an encouraging look.

Steve clears his throat, scratching the skin on his neck. 'The thing is, a couple of things have happened — you don't need to know what they are — that have affected our scores, and we're afraid that now, with these changes you were talking about, the baby will be penalised.'

'Oh dear. I'm sorry. It's not just my friends, then.'

'No, mate. If you read some of the comments on your account, you'd see that it's becoming widespread.'

Len is quiet for a moment, clasping his hands together. He wants to consult his wife again, but knows that wouldn't be appropriate in public. 'Right. I've been in a quandary myself. That's what I wanted to talk to you about.'

'Fire away,' Steve says, jumping up to help a woman trying to open the door with a buggy and a toddler on her hip. 'There you go, love.'

She gives him a harassed smile and a whispered 'Thanks.'

Len waits until he has Steve's attention again. 'Well, I was really pleased with the splash when that lady tweeted my letter.' He squeezes the fingers on one hand with their opposite numbers. 'Only, they drew the authorities' attention to my friends, my neighbours. So, I was in two minds about whether it had been a good idea at all.'

Steve nods. 'I can understand that. But it's a good thing, yes, making a noise, making those tossers uncomfortable?'

'That's what I thought, on balance. Lexie, my friend and neighbour, thought so. Her husband, Cooper, wasn't so sure.' Len doesn't know if he should use their names, but it seems the right thing to do. The worst has happened; he needs to make it public.

'Right. You're using the past tense. Has something changed?'

'That's what's been worrying me,' Len continues, slightly annoyed that Steve has broken his train of thought. 'Last night, I popped over, and Lexie was in tears. She'd been told that Cooper had been arrested.'

Tracy sucks air between her teeth and claps her hands across her face. 'And was it about the campaign?' she asks.

'I don't think they said. Lexie was all over the place to start with, but she told me to go home and not worry.'

'So, of course, you worried like mad?' This is Steve. He does seem to get it.

'I didn't sleep all night. Then, this morning, the police came and took Lexie away.' Len feels his voice wobble. Len does not cry. Not often, anyway, and not now, when other people will see.

Tracy is peeping out at him from behind her hands. 'That's terrible.'

'I keep thinking about the baby. What's happened to her?'

'And you don't know if Cooper's been released?' Steve asks.

'I don't see that he could have been. Not since last night.'

'No, I guess not.'

'So now I don't know what to do. I've been keeping quiet, but I can't do that anymore. I must act.'

Steve blows air out through his mouth. 'You're right. You've got to do something now. Too much has happened.'

'But what? I've been racking my brains on my way up here, but I can't think of anything that would make a difference.'

Steve's phone goes off. He pulls it out and declines the call. Staring at his phone for a minute, he texts fast and furiously, before putting his mobile on the table. 'This is the answer,' he says, pointing at it. 'It worked before, and it will work again, but we need to go large now. Do something more.'

'Really?' Len says. They seem to be going round and round in circles. Was it really a good idea to come up here to talk to them?

'Let me think a minute.' Steve drums his fingers on the table. 'Something more. Bigger exposure. I'm up against the limits of my expertise here.'

Tracy tugs on his sleeve. 'Easy. Shoot a video. I do it all the time,' she says to Len, 'about how to do special make-up and things. Everyone does it.'

'Not me,' Steve says. 'But it could work.' He rubs his stubble. 'What do you think, Len? It would mean coming out of the closet, showing your face. You might get arrested yourself, but it will sure make a stink.'

Len manages a weak smile. 'I could speak out about the terrible injustice of it all.'

'You could get yourself in trouble, though,' Tracy reminds him.

'I don't care. I've had my life. They can throw me in prison, for all the difference it would make. If I could just get Cooper and Lexie their lives back first. They've been arrested because of me, and I must put that right.'

The more Len thinks about it, the more the idea appeals to him. He isn't a vain man, but he's always wanted to do something brave, something that will make a difference, and this could be it. No one depends on him. He can take the risk. 'I like it. Let's do it.' Len pushes his hands on the table as if he is about to stand up and make a speech there and then. Almost immediately, he lowers himself back. 'I don't know how.'

Steve throws his head back and laughs, showing an impressive set of fillings. 'It's a piece of cake. We can do it with my phone. Hell, why don't we do it right now, before we change our minds?'

'Don't you need to be back at work?' Len feels an uncomfortable rumble in his gut.

Steve checks his phone for the time. 'I should, but let's do this first. It shouldn't take long. Kathy, do you mind if we do a quick video, free advertising?' I'd like to have other people on it, as witnesses.'

Kathy wipes her hands on her apron, walking towards them. 'What's it about?'

Steve pauses. 'Do you remember that thing with Len, when that lady tweeted his letter and it went viral, and we set up an account for him?'

'The thing about the Life Counter rubbish?'

'That's right.'

Kathy rubs her forehead. She looks tired again. Glancing at Tracy's impressive bump, she smiles. 'Let's do it. Got to stand up for my regulars, right? What harm can it do?'

Steve claps her on the back. 'That's the attitude.'

'There's lots of people in here. Try to get them in shot if they don't mind.' Kathy slips two fingers in her mouth and emits an ear-piercing whistle. 'Listen up, everyone. My friend Len here,' she says, draping an arm around his shoulder, 'would like to make a video of himself making a statement about something that is important to him. I'd like you all to listen and, if you agree with what he has to say, give him a good cheer at the end. Free hot drinks on the house. If you don't like what he has to say, we'll edit you out. Is everyone happy?'

No one complains, and a few desultory cheers break the silence. Several thumbs up appear, but the level of interest is muted.

'I don't have a clue how to edit people out, but let's hope it's not necessary,' Kathy says, speaking behind her hand to Steve.

'Right, Len,' Steve says, 'do you want to prepare something to say?'

Len thinks for a moment. 'No. I'm going to speak from the heart. It will work better that way.'

Steve chews his lip. 'OK. If you reckon you're prepared, let's go. You sit in Tracy's seat, then we can see everyone, and Kathy, behind you.' Steve sets the phone ready to record. 'And speak up, so people can hear you.'

Len nods. His throat feels dry. The cup of coffee is in front of him, barely touched.

'Go.'

'Hello.' The first word comes out too quiet. 'My name is Len,' he continues, at a deafening volume. 'I'm not important, not a political person, but sometimes you have to stand up and be counted when bad things happen.'

Len pauses for a moment, looking straight at the phone but seeing Steve behind it mouthing 'Get to the point.'

Len nods, then realises that the gesture won't make sense on the video. Perhaps they can edit that out. 'I'm not experienced with social media, in fact I'm very new to it, but I wrote a letter to a newspaper about how the Life Counter Programme has affected some friends of mine, and it seemed to take off online. That is why I am now speaking out and showing my face, because things are getting worse.

'People need to know.

'The Government needs to stop this nonsense.'

Len feels that he is getting into his stride, but Tracy is making winding motions with her hand, which isn't entirely encouraging.

'Everyone knows how the Life Counter Programme started. We were sold this promised land where the Government would help us to live a better and longer life by encouraging us to be healthy in body and mind. It seemed very simple, a no-lose situation. If we kept our side of the bargain by paying attention to official guidance and being kind in word and deed, the future would be ours. All we had to do was let them harvest our data through phones and computers, and they'd do the rest.

'It hasn't quite worked out like that, has it?

'They never mentioned the downside of the Digital ID, which is so very useful, or the constant tracking through CCTV and facial recognition technology. I never knew about any of those things back in the day. A good idea can soon turn bad if the wrong people get hold of it.

'Now we've reached the state where my two friends have had decades of their baby's life stolen, yes stolen, because of something which the Life Counter Programme thinks they have done wrong in the past. My friends are lovely people. They are not the sort to do bad things. This is politically motivated.

'I was angry about this, which was why I wrote my letter. By making a splash, I seem to have made things worse. Yesterday, one of my friends was arrested. Today, his wife was also taken into custody.

'They have done nothing wrong.

'If anyone is at fault, it is me, for embarrassing the Government. If someone should be arrested, arrest me. You know where I am now, and who I am. I am an old man with nothing to lose. Let my friends go so they can look after their baby.

'This is an appeal to everyone in the country. Stand up against this evil Life Counter Programme. Stand up for the rights of babies and children.

'Spread this video.'

Tracy holds up a paper napkin with 'Retweet' scribbled on it.

'Yes,' Len continues. 'Retweet it. Get the word out. Let everyone know what the Government is doing.

'Join me in my campaign.

'Please.

'Thank you for listening, I mean watching.'

Len takes a breath. A huge cheer goes up from around all parts of the coffee shop. A woman holds her baby up to camera as Steve pans the screen around the room. The baby, an initially cheerful, flush-cheeked little soul, seems alarmed by the extended roar of support and begins to bellow.

The video is still rolling. Steve begins to film himself. 'Even the babies here could be affected by what is happening.' He swings the camera around the café before focussing on Tracy. 'Another baby will soon be born who may face the same issues.' He regains centre stage. 'Babies are being born every minute. Who knows how many of them are suffering in the same way? Don't be a bystander.

Even if you aren't personally affected, stand up for those who are. Share this far and wide on X, Facebook, Instagram and TikTok.

'Make it happen, folks.'

Steve stops the video and finally notices the death stare directed at him by Tracy.

'What?' he says.

'This is Len's thing. We shouldn't be in it.'

He rubs his head with the flat of his hand. 'I know. Sorry. I got carried away.'

'We'll get into trouble ourselves.'

'I'm sorry, Tracy,' Len says. 'I know it was a risk, but it was helpful. Steve added all the things I forgot to say or didn't know how to put properly. It will make a difference.'

'I suppose,' Tracy says, sinking lower into her chair. 'But I've got no make-up on!'

Steve laughs. 'Now we have it. I was thinking I'd have to edit us out, but now I realise I should have got hair and beauty in.'

'Thank you both,' Len says, putting his hand on Tracy's shoulder. 'What do we do now?'

'We'll watch it through. Check it's OK. Then put it up on the X account. But Len, mate, we need to get you a smartphone and set up all the social media accounts for you, then you can post on your own. You need to keep the momentum going.'

Len swallows. Every day that passes, his intervention is becoming more complicated. He looks upward. 'What do you think, love?' he whispers. 'Can I do this? Have I given you a surprise?'

He feels a smile growing. It's quite enjoyable taking a risk.

24.

Cooper

The incessant drizzle has fizzled out, and Cooper feels the warmth of watery sun touching his back as he sits on his front step near the car. Tash is in her pram, jammed between the front of the house and the low wall by the pavement. Their front garden is more an apology than an actual space. He hopes she is sleeping, but doesn't dare look. She's too young to understand the trauma of her mother being arrested and her father abducted, but she seems to have picked up on something. It has been a mission to settle her. Now she is quieter, Cooper himself feels worse. He and Lexie had so little time to talk before she was swept away by the police.

Escaping from his father seemed such an achievement at the time. He had hope in his heart as he arrived home, only to have Lexie snatched away from him before he had even filled her in on the complexities of the situation. The coincidence of the arrival of the police officers is too great. They may have been real, but Bruce must be responsible for their appearance.

Cooper keeps reliving the look of anguish on Lexie's face as they dragged her away. In that desperate, frozen expression, he saw misery, fear and yes, he can't escape it, blame.

She's in trouble, and he isn't with her. She's at the mercy of the authorities, and it's all his fault.

Again.

His phone is in a bucket of water in a dingy house in West London.

Bruce has taken his wife away, and her whereabouts are unknown.

He is tethered to his adorable but dependent daughter and cannot abandon her to rescue Lexie.

Cooper stands and fishes a sudsy sponge out of his bucket of hot water; he begins, without enthusiasm, to wipe it across the bonnet of his car. It's not one of his favourite jobs, which is why the ingrained and dried mud is overlaid with a light film of sticky pollen. There's something about mindless tasks, though, that always helps him sort priorities and issues in his mind. He follows a flitting trail of possibilities. If he stays quiet, they might let Lexie go. Of course, Cooper could retrace his steps to Bruce's grungy torture chamber and give himself up. He's rubbing at a tenacious, squashed insect while debating the options with himself.

'Cooper?'

He swings round, sending a trail of suds in an arc from his hand to the front of Len's windcheater.

'Len! You startled me. Sorry. I've splashed you.'

Len rubs a hand over his damp coat. 'It's not a problem. I got wet earlier anyway. But what are you doing here?'

Cooper gives him a sideways look. 'I live here.'

Len's eyebrows are drawn together so hard they meet in the middle. He licks his lower lip. 'I talked to Lexie last night. She said you'd been arrested. She was so worried.'

Cooper feels a sinking sensation in his stomach. He lays the sponge on the roof of his car and glances towards the pram. All is quiet. 'Yes, well. It's complicated. I was, how can I put it, detained, but I'm free now.'

Len scratches his head. 'Then I saw Lexie leaving in a police car. I thought she'd been arrested too.'

'She has.' A huge sigh escapes the bellows of Cooper's lungs.

'And you're washing your car? What are you thinking of? You should be up there with her, man.'

'Come on, Len!' Cooper's hands are wet and wrinkled from the water; it doesn't stop him pushing his hair back with his right hand. 'It's such a shitshow. Sit down for a minute.' He gestures to the step.

Len stares at the concrete slab. 'I get down there, I'll never get up again. I'll stay standing while you give me an explanation.' Usually, Len would make a joke about something like this, but today, nothing is as it should be.

'OK.' Cooper pauses and rubs his middle with a damp hand.

'My father abducted me last night from just up the road.'

Len lets out a low whistle.

'He knows where I live. I escape. Lexie is arrested. Coincidence? I don't think so.'

Len nods. His eyebrows have lost their angry look, but his eyes are opaque.

'I have no desire to wash my car. I came out here to check it over for listening devices, because that's the sort of thing my father would do to try to control me. I didn't find anything, but Tash seems settled out here; I didn't want to move her. I couldn't sit there and do nothing; I thought it might help me think to wash the car.'

Len graces him with a nod. 'I see, and has it?'

'I haven't got far!'

'Do you want a hand?'

'No, it's OK. It won't make a difference anyway. I might just take the car out and buy a new phone.' He wishes Len wouldn't keep giving him long and possibly hostile stares. 'It's a complicated story, OK. Where are you coming back from, anyway?'

Len jangles his keys in his pocket. 'I've been down the coffee shop.' He swallows. 'Cooper, you know the little bit of bother when I wrote that letter to the newspaper?'

'Yes?'

'Well, the thing is…' Len has taken the keys out of his pocket and is rubbing the jagged edge of the front door key against his thumb. 'You see, I thought you'd been arrested, and then Lexie and what have you, and I was worried sick. I thought the baby might be on her own, and I couldn't stop thinking about it.'

'Did you call Social Services?' Cooper can hear an edge of panic in his own voice. He moves a little closer to Len, whose eyebrows shoot upwards.

'Social services? Those busy bodies? Of course not. Who do you take me for?' He steps backwards. 'No, it's nothing like that. Only, I thought you were in desperate straits, so I decided to disregard what you said before about not doing anything else.'

'Right.' Time seems to have frozen. 'Spit it out, Len. What have you done this time?'

'Well.' There is now an anxious smile on Len's face. 'With the help of my friends, I've uploaded a video onto...' He blinks. 'Now, was it X, or Facebook. Do you know, I'm not sure. They did that bit.'

'A video? What sort of video?' Save him from people who try to help.

'It was a statement. A call to arms, if you like, asking everybody to share what has happened to you across the internet. You know, the arrests, the stealing of the baby's years, that sort of thing.'

'Shit, shit, shit.' Cooper shakes his head wildly, so much that the breeze is catching his hair. 'What have you done?'

Len stands a little taller. 'What I've done is tried to help. Look at the state you're in. This might make it better. I don't see how it can make it much worse. I'm not ashamed, and if my video goes viral, like the last post, it might do some good, mightn't it?'

Cooper wants to be angry. He'd been so clear that Len should keep out of it unless given clear instructions to the contrary. There again, this could be good. He has the ghost of an idea sparking in his synapses. He must harness Len's enthusiasm.

Right now, he needs to lie down in a dark room to let the idea grow.

Surprising himself, he advances towards Len and throws his arms around the old man.

'Thank you. I know you're trying to help. We sure as hell need it.'

Len wriggles out of the unexpected embrace but pulls his shoulders back and beams. 'Not many people touch me these days.'

'Len, could we have a look at your video? Do you have a phone on you?'

'Ah.' Len scratches the inside of his ear. 'I don't have a phone, currently. We recorded it on Steve's phone, and he put it up there.'

'Steve?'

'He's my friend. He's on the video too. And Tracy. She's his girlfriend. They're going to have a baby soon.'

It's all starting to make sense. 'So Steve and Tracy are worried about their baby, too?'

'Yes, that's what I meant about a call to arms. Everyone with a new baby or a soon-to-be new baby is at risk. This could take off.'

Cooper's mind is working fast. 'Len, you could be a genius. I'm not sure yet. But we need to see this video.'

'Steve is getting me a mobile phone, so I can reply to people and put up more things. And set up accounts on the other social media thingies.'

'Right. That's good, up to a point. But, Len, we need to work together on this. I'll need to use your phone and accounts, once we have them, because I'm blocked from social media by my pain in the arse father, but I can do things through you.'

'So, I've done a good thing?'

Cooper laughs, something he thought he would never do again. 'Maybe,' he says. 'I'm not sure yet. You've certainly done something, in a way I can't at the moment because I'm blocked, and you've given me an idea. But Len?'

'Yes?'

'This could be dangerous. You've seen what my father is like. Are you sure you're up for this?'

Len pulls his body up a little taller. 'I certainly am. Like I said in the video, I'm an old man. What do I have to lose?'

Cooper claps him on the back. 'Come in and have a beer. We can talk it through. You've given me an idea.'

Together, they lift the pram over the step and take Tash inside.

25.

Marilyn

Marilyn creeps down the corridor towards her office. Cognizant of the cameras in every corner and other places besides, she fixes a determined neutrality to her features. Her intended demeanour is serious, professional, downhearted but not beaten. It is important that Bruce, who will undoubtedly be keeping tabs on her, sees that she is dejected but expecting to persevere with a project she now hates.

He's such an idiot that he might believe it.

It's a difficult tightrope to walk but she feels a new lightness in her heart, knowing that she has seen through her so-called 'superior' and is no longer alone in working on her fightback.

The thought that Bruce's own wife is helping her has brought an unaccustomed warmth to her feelings. A smile plays behind her features but there it must stay, unseen, until she is ready.

Marilyn opens the door to her office, keeping her shoulders deliberately hunched. Once inside, it is annoying that she must keep up the pretence, but she is fighting for her survival.

Sitting at her desk and kicking her shoes off, she wonders if he has eyes on her or merely ears. She must assume the worst and act accordingly. Marilyn thinks of her mother's deathbed; this is her successful formula for achieving a sad but resilient expression. After powering up her system and navigating the laborious password routine, she casts her eye carefully and she hopes unobtrusively around the room, returning her gaze soon to her desk and the small sensor at the top centre of her screen. Of course, he doesn't need a camera when there is one built into her laptop. Bloody virtual meetings.

Of course, with the inbuilt camera and microphone available, he might not feel the need for other visual surveillance. She is always in front of her screen. Keeping her face determinedly neutral, Marilyn slips one hand under her desk and gives the underside of the table top the middle finger – several times. She feels like she did when stealing sweets she didn't want as a teenager.

Better.

More positive.

Clueless as to what to do next.

Determined to do something.

Her phone goes. It's Bruce. 'Please come in here. Now.'

Marilyn doesn't reply but raises herself out of her seat and slips her shoes back on. He will expect her to be sulky and she mustn't alert him to her change in mood.

The door to his office is open. As she enters, she sees that the chair opposite him, the one she usually sits in, is occupied by a younger woman. Bruce doesn't look up but points vaguely with his pen at another chair, set a little way off, at an obtuse angle to his desk.

Marilyn sits down gingerly and risks a look at the other woman. Is this her replacement? Her long, luxuriant black hair cascades over her shoulder, hiding her face partially from view. A suggestion of vermilion lipstick peeps out from behind the curtain of hair.

Marilyn hates her on sight.

Bruce looks up. He is clean again, at least. His shirt is fresh but deep hollows sit under his eyes. His look is piercing. 'This is Ayeesha.' He waves in her direction. 'She is Rangan's replacement. You will remember our conversation about his return to India and our need to keep the code up to date.' Bruce is rubbing his nose.

'I remember it very well, Bruce.'

That was quick.

'Hello Ayeesha.' Marilyn turns towards her and stands, extending a hand. Ayeesha doesn't get up but clasps the offered limb with a distinct lack of enthusiasm. Generally, one would smile on introduction to someone new. Marilyn has attempted to extend this courtesy even though her face doesn't want to oblige. Ayeesha's look is guarded, but she does eventually reciprocate, although her eyes remain untouched by the gesture. It's difficult to tell if there is hostility there. They both resettle and turn towards Bruce.

'Well,' he says, scowling. 'Off you two go. I'm a busy man. You know what to do, Marilyn. Brief her and get on with it.'

Marilyn nods. If Bruce has romantic intentions towards this young woman, he is hiding it well. 'Right, Ayeesha, I don't know how much you know already, but the changes that Rangan made to the code...'

'My predecessor?' Ayeesha glances at Bruce.

He coughs, his eyes darting here and there before resting briefly on Ayeesha.

'Yes,' Marilyn continues. 'The changes he made have had unexpected results.'

'Not in here.' Bruce's voice is penetrating, unpleasant. 'I have things to do. In your office, now.'

Damn. She was determined to get something said in here, but he would be bound to sweep his office frequently for bugs anyway.

'This way, Ayeesha,' she says, motioning her towards the door. 'When do you want me to report back, Bruce?'

'Just get on with it,' he says, his concentration already shifted back to his screen.

They are soon in Marilyn's office. She seats Ayeesha opposite her desk and is about to return to her usual position. She glances at the other woman, who remains silent.

What is going on here? It's not hostility Marilyn sees, but something else, and she isn't sure what yet.

On an impulse, Marilyn pulls her chair out from behind the desk and places it on the other side, nearer her guest. Pulling a pad of paper out from a drawer and picking up a pen, she sits opposite her and studies her carefully.

Friend or foe?

'So, I'm sure you're excited about working on the Life Counter Programme. It will look good on your CV.'

'Yes, of course.' Ayeesha nods her head. 'I've heard so much about it.'

'Really? I thought we'd been keeping it under the radar. I assume you mean in general terms.' Marilyn's heart thumps in her chest. This girl has turned up so quickly. It unnerves her. 'I'm sure Bruce has checked out your experience carefully. It is a complex project.'

'I am perfectly qualified, have no fear.' Ayeesha's eyes are huge. She is blinking more than seems normal and clenching and releasing her fingers repeatedly.

'Did you know Bruce already?'

Ayeesha tucks her hair behind one ear. 'I met him for the first time just now, but I knew of him before. I already work in the Department, you see. He put out an advert on our intranet for experienced coders with specific skills. I've been thoroughly vetted. You need not worry.'

I bet you have, thinks Marilyn. But such a risk. He doesn't know her. Bruce must be rattled, desperate to rescue his darling project.

He is becoming rash.

Maybe it's time for Marilyn to take a punt too. Instinct tells her Ayeesha is not all she seems. Her instinct is never wrong. Well, maybe sometimes. Marilyn pulls out her pad, catches Ayeesha's eye and writes in large letters:

This office is bugged. Do you know what you are getting into?

Marilyn puts the pen down and Ayeesha takes it. She pauses, looks at Marilyn and then begins to write.

I assumed that would be the case. I've heard talk about this man. The word is he's a psychopath.

Her hair slips down and brushes the page.

Marilyn snatches the pen from the top of the paper. This girl is unexpected. But it could be a complicated double bluff.

Why are you doing this?

Ayeesha looks deep into Marilyn's eyes and picks up the pen.

Why should I trust you? You are his number two.

I could say the same to you, Marilyn replies. *You've just taken on a critical project for him.*

Marilyn returns Ayeesha's gaze as if eye contact alone will help them to understand and trust each other. She continues:

I used to believe in him. Now I hate him. He is blackmailing me to do this work. I think he's going mad.

Pointing to the paper, she adds:

We need to say something or he will become suspicious.

Marilyn puts the pen down and pushes the pad across. 'I'm sorry,' she says, 'It took me ages to find my backup notes. Sometimes my security measures defeat even me.' She gives a little insincere laugh. 'Have you been briefed on what Bruce wants?'

'Not in any level of detail,' Ayeesha replies, while writing – *You can trust me because Rangan was my friend.*

Was? Marilyn scribbles.

Was. I know what happened to him. I need to be here to find out more. I owe it to him. We have a history, Rangan and me.

'I see,' Marilyn says. Her heart is racing. 'Basically, the code that Rangan put in needs some adjustments, to make it, how shall we say, appropriate to changing circumstances.'

Let's get out of here,' she writes.*' I have a place we can go where we can talk. Can you come now?*

Sure thing. Ayeesha writes.

I'm so relieved. I thought you were going to be on his side. Marilyn smiles, hoping that Bruce doesn't have another camera on them, or they are royally screwed.

That's what I thought about you. Ayeesha's expression has softened. There is no longer an unreadable look in her eyes.

Marilyn hands her another piece of paper, on which she has scribbled an address. 'Here is a brief list of issues with the current code, as far as I understand it now. Obviously, I am not an expert. I assume you will need some time to assess the situation and decide on changes. We can then speak again.'

'I'm sure it won't be simple,' Ayeesha replies, arching an eyebrow.

'I will arrange your security clearance and access to the code and data. I know you already work in the Department, but we'll need to jump through additional hoops for you to be able to have sight of the code itself. You can let me know of anything else you require. Are you happy to proceed?'

Ayeesha makes a great play of examining the piece of paper. 'I am indeed. It looks like a fascinating project.'

'Is it achievable?'

'Everything is achievable, if you put enough effort into it.'

Marilyn smiles. 'I look forward to working with you.'

Sooner than Bruce realises, Ayeesha writes. 'Goodbye Marilyn. I'll keep in touch.'

Ayeesha leaves the room and Marilyn slumps into her seat. What just happened? Her brains are scrambled. It occurs to her that she has believed everything Ayeesha has told her. This might be a mistake.

Having said that, she is all out of options and time is not on her side.

Marilyn picks up her papers and puts them through the shredder, which, luckily, is out of camera range. She sits down at her desk and pretends to work at her screen for a few minutes before heading out to meet her interesting new colleague on safer territory.

26.

Cooper

She picks up on the first ring.

'Mum? It's me.'

'Cooper.' He holds the phone a little further from his ear. 'Where have you been? I've been trying to get hold of you, and Lexie. Lexie's phone is ringing out and yours comes up as unavailable. I've been out of my mind with worry.'

'Sorry. It's a long story, Mum. I couldn't call.'

'Lexie thought you'd been arrested.'

'Not quite.' Cooper counts to five while he wonders how much to say. Now he thinks about it, his hands start shaking. Time to stay calm.

'It's a long story. Basically, Dad kidnapped me, and I escaped. He's now had Lexie arrested to punish me.'

Amy gasps on the other end of the phone. 'I'm so sorry.' The line goes quiet. 'I know he's been erratic,' she continues, 'but I didn't think he'd be capable of this. Are you all right?'

'As good as I can be under the circumstances, I guess.' Cooper glances upstairs. He's chosen this moment because Tash is sleeping. Who knows how long that will last? 'Look, Mum? We need to talk, but not on the phone. I've got a new one now but it's the same number. Dad chucked my old one in a bucket of water.'

There's a crackle on the line.

'Are you laughing?' he asks. 'It doesn't seem funny to me.'

'Sorry, it's not. Put it down to shock. The phone in the bucket sounds like the sort of thing Bruce used to do when you exasperated him as a child. He always did believe in low-tech solutions. That's the only thing that was amusing.'

'Hmm. Not amusing, believe me. Mum, can you come over? We can walk and talk. I know there are developments.'

'Yes. I saw…'

'Tell me later. Come now if you can.'

'I'll be there. Sorry, I'm not used to being secretive.'

The call is gone.

Cooper spends the waiting time tidying up and googling Len's name, but nothing comes up. No surprise really. Bruce will be blocking Cooper's access to searches. He wants to see the video. He needs to understand what new craziness Len has started. Waiting is so frustrating.

An hour later, Cooper and his mother are lifting the buggy over the front doorstep. Cooper thanks all his lucky stars that Lexie has supplemented breastfeeding with a bottle. He's given Tash a formula feast in the hope that she will sleep while they talk. Amy is making eyes at her and chatting away to her little granddaughter in an inconsequential way.

'Best let her go to sleep, Mum.'

'If I have to.' Amy gives him a warm smile. 'I never thought I'd have this joy. I'm so sorry Bruce is ruining it for you.'

'You and me both.' Cooper pushes the buggy forward and Amy follows, still keeping her eyes glued to Tash, who is blowing milky bubbles. 'We have to assume that he's watching everything we do,' he says, rearranging the blanket covering the baby. 'He can probably predict where we're going to go before we know ourselves.'

'I've been very careful,' Amy says, frowning and biting her lip. 'Only, I did phone you, didn't I, and I also called Marilyn, Bruce's number two, as per your plan, before you disappeared.'

Cooper stops looking where he's walking as his head swings round to look at his mother. The buggy hits a bump in the pavement and the carriage judders. Tash grizzles and he is forced to reassure her before he continues. 'You didn't waste your time, did you? How did it go?'

Amy stops for a moment and stares at him, forcing him to slow down too. A football arrives from nowhere, hitting the wheels of the buggy. The scuffing sound of a trainer on tarmac lets Cooper know where it's coming from; he kicks it back not very elegantly towards the red-faced child who is running towards them.

'Sorry mister.'

'No worries.'

Amy hasn't answered his question but is still standing there in a rigid posture. He returns her gaze and raises his eyebrows.

'Sorry. You were about to tell me….'

Amy pushes her hair out of her eyes. 'We agreed that I was going to get involved and do what I could to help. We'd talked about this.'

'Yep. It's great,' he replies, 'I'd forgotten how quick you are at getting on with things. I guess I feel a bit left out. Keep walking. We're conspicuous here. I'd like to get to the park. Cameras everywhere.' The houses are close to the pavement and he imagines multiple sets of eyes watching, filming, noticing their movements.

Amy strides on, moving fast to keep up. 'You weren't here. I came over to see Lexie because she was beside herself when you disappeared. We had to do something, so we thought we'd activate the plan. Damn.' Amy stops and lifts one shoe. 'Filthy dog mess.' She wipes the side of her shoe on a patch of tufty grass at the side of the pavement, giving Cooper time to realise he's being unfair. He kicks a buckled Coke can into the gutter.

'Sorry. You're right. How were you supposed to know?' They walk on, soon reaching the gate to the park. 'So tell me how it went. My expectations haven't been high. Her tongue is so far up Dad's backside I'm surprised she met you.'

'Cooper! That's disgusting.' Amy takes the handles of the buggy from him and starts pushing. Tash's eyelids are dropping. 'She's a woman, and Bruce has been so erratic recently that I knew even she'd be having second thoughts. I was planning to appeal to her female values.'

'And?'

'I was right. I had all my arguments to hand and thought I'd be in for a long slog, but it turned out I was pushing at an open door. Bruce has stitched her up. He's basically blackmailing her to continue his work and has been recording all the things he's made her do. He's done it in such a way that there's no evidence against him.'

'The bastard.'

'Exactly. She hates his guts now. He thinks she'll do what he says, grudgingly, but she's out to get him, or at least to pervert the whole thing, to turn it back to what it was supposed to be.'

'That's good.' His mind is buzzing. 'Let's sit down here for a minute.' He moves the buggy a little to the side as they lower themselves onto a bench, so he can continue to jiggle the handle if Tash grumbles. 'Mum.' He takes her hands in his and looks into her eyes. 'Can you trust her? This might be some complicated double-bluff.'

Amy gives his hands a squeeze and then frees her own. She fiddles with her beaded necklace. 'I believe her. She wants to help. She needs to, for her own sake as well. It's more a case of can she actually do anything to stop it? The juggernaut is accelerating.'

'So we aren't any further forward?'

'I think we are. We have a safe space where we can meet. I met her yesterday and she messaged me today to say there have been positive developments and she wants to meet tomorrow.'

'Can you keep the messages secure?'

'Telegram. End to end encrypted.'

Cooper laughs. 'You've changed, Mum.'

'The circumstances have changed, so I've changed with them. If I'd stayed with Bruce…'

'Have you left him?' Cooper can hear the hope in his voice.

'Not yet. Not officially. In my heart though.'

'Go on.'

'If I'd stayed with him, and he hadn't gone completely haywire, I would have convinced myself to stay quiet. But then you turned up, and Lexie, and little Tash.' Her voice softens. 'How could I possibly choose him over all of you?'

Cooper gives her a hug. 'It means the world to me that we've reconnected. It's been lonely since I was kicked out. Then I met

Lexie and couldn't tell her anything about what had happened.' Amy leans into his embrace, stroking his back with her hand. 'She had no background on why I'd lost years on my Life Counter, and I couldn't tell her, so she was thinking all sorts.'

'Like?'

'Like I was a criminal or a drug addict or something like that. I'm so relieved that she stuck with me, that she knew that the numbers didn't add up with the man I am, and she chose to believe in me.'

'I'm relieved too. I don't think you would have reached out to me if the crisis with Tash's birth and the life deficit hadn't happened.'

He nods. 'You're probably right. Isn't that sad though?'

'In some ways, yes, but the important thing is that we're together now.'

Amy wipes a rogue tear off Cooper's cheek. 'So here we are, but Lexie is in custody. What can we do to change that?'

'That's the problem, isn't it? I had a text, just before I called you, saying – *Don't attempt to secure your wife's freedom. She is safe and well but anything untoward you do will lengthen incarceration.*'

'Can he do that?'

'Can he do any of this?'

'Cooper, we can't do nothing, can't sit and let her rot in prison.'

'I know, but we also can't do anything that is obviously us, if you see what I mean.'

'Sort of.' Amy stands up. 'Well, I'll keep talking to Marilyn. See what these positive developments are. I wonder if she could do something to help?'

Cooper gets up too and peeps into the buggy. Tash is out for the count. 'Whatever happens, Mum, remember that she might not be for real. Bruce might still be controlling her.'

Amy shakes her head vigorously. 'You didn't see her. That woman hates him.'

'Anyway, we can't rely on her entirely. We need another front.' Cooper lets out a deep sigh and stares across the grass towards a patch of trees. An elderly man is sitting on a bench under an oak tree, staring into the distance. 'Well, our wild card is Len, my neighbour.'

'I think Lexie might have mentioned him.' Amy threads her arm through the sleeve of her lightweight jacket.

The breeze is also shivering the hairs on Cooper's arms. He rubs them warm with his hands. 'Len is a loose cannon. He's very sympathetic, and he loves Lexie to bits, but he tends to stir things up accidentally, by trying to help but not really understanding what he's getting into.'

'So, what are you saying? Are you going to give him something to do?'

Cooper lets out an exasperated laugh. 'I don't need to. He keeps doing things himself. He's got friendly with some keyboard warrior and set up social media profiles, highlighting our case. It's got us into all sorts of trouble so far.'

'Aah, yes, I heard about this. It was that letter that went viral, wasn't it?'

'That's right, only now he's gone further. He thought we'd both been arrested, and he was beside himself. He's now done a video, apparently. He told me about it, but I can't find out what it's about because Dad has blocked all my social media access. I'm going to be reliant on Len and he hasn't got a clue what he's doing.' Cooper puts both hands on his head and rubs his hair vigorously, causing his T-shirt to ride up and expose a hairy navel.

'I don't do much on social media, otherwise I'd look for you.'

'No, not you, Mum. Dad would spot that straight away. Apparently, Len's "friends" are setting up accounts for him on several platforms so he can reply to things himself. God knows how that will turn out!'

'I'm not sure that's going to help us,' Amy says, catching hold of the buggy. 'It could do more harm than good.'

Cooper pushes air through his teeth. 'We don't have many options. The way it's looking now, almost anything is better than doing nothing. I'm going to try to direct Len more from now on. I've worked out a strategy.'

Amy pulls her jacket tighter. She opens her mouth to speak but pauses as a middle-aged man with an earpiece passes close by. He glances at Amy before walking on. Cooper's and Amy's eyes meet. 'Let's walk back,' she says, nodding towards a path in the opposite direction to the one the man is following. They increase their pace. 'Let's see what tomorrow brings, shall we?' she says. 'This is getting increasingly sinister. I have no idea what Bruce thinks about me now, but I'd probably better get back, and not give him any more cause to doubt me.'

At Cooper's door, they part. 'Keep me posted. Tomorrow, or whenever you've met Marilyn,' Cooper says, 'text me and we'll meet.'

'Same with you,' Amy replies. 'Let's see if Len can serve up a storm, with your guidance.'

27.

Len

The house feels particularly bleak and empty this morning. Len doesn't know what to make of his chat with Cooper yesterday. He always used to think that Cooper was a straightforward man who loved his life, his wife and now his baby. Recent events have complicated Len's view of his next-door neighbour. He's seen an erratic and volatile side to this apparently kind and gentle man.

Someone who calmly washes his car when his wife is in prison.

Besides this, Len feels uncomfortable about the instruction not to act on his own account. After all, what he's done so far has had beneficial effects.

Unless Lexie's arrest is down to him.

He decides not to dwell on that.

What has been weighing on his mind is the video he and Steve have done.

It's no good. Len stares out of the front window and sees that Cooper's car isn't there. He glances around the front room, at the dingy light on this cloudy day, the cracked leather settee that seemed so up to the minute when they bought it, the ingrained dirt on the arms where he pushes himself up, and the rug that's never straight. So different from Cooper's and Lexie's modernised little palace next door.

When in doubt, do something. When in doubt, seek out other people, to subdue the fog of solitude.

Len puts on his coat and immediately feels a little more resolute. When he arrives at the coffee shop, however, it is less than half-full. Of course, it is relatively early, but after what he hopes was his triumph with the video, there is a part of him that expects a standing ovation.

How stupid.

Len shuffles to a seat and looks around, in the hope that Steve and Tracy are hiding around a corner. Kathy, clearly not as pushed for time as is often the case, wanders over and lays a hand on his shoulder.

'The usual, Len love?'

'Yes, please, Kathy. You're quiet this morning?

Kathy checks her watch. 'It's early yet. Couldn't keep away, eh, after your moment of celebrity?'

Len looks down at the table and shuffles his feet. "It wasn't my idea, you know,' he says, raising his eyes to Kathy's face. 'I got pushed into it by Steve and Tracy. I didn't want to let them down when they were so worried about what's happening.'

Kathy smiles, bends down to put her arm around his shoulders and gives them a squeeze. 'You did a good thing. Let's see what effect it has.' She glances over towards the counter. 'That reminds me. Steve left me an envelope for you on his way to work. I'll bring it over with your coffee.' She gives his shoulder a final pat and heads off to the counter.

It makes such a difference to feel the touch of another human being.

Len looks at the envelope for some time before opening it. He sips his coffee, enjoying the biscuit on the side, and notes the scribbled 'Lenny' on the front. 'Lenny?' What would his wife say? There is a perfect fingerprint of grease on the top left-hand corner.

Is Steve too embarrassed to see him in person?

Perhaps he's had second thoughts and decided the video is too dangerous to put up online. That would get Len out of Cooper's bad books. He's surprised at the heavy cloud of disappointment that descends on him at the thought of this eventuality.

Finally, the coffee is finished; he has run out of excuses to avoid seeing what Steve has to say. He tears open the envelope to find a scrappy piece of lined paper with a rough edge, torn from a larger sheet.

Len, what a star. Wait till you see how your video is going. We've got you a phone and set up some accounts. I'll come to your house at 1ish to show you how to use it. My current job is quite chilled and I'm 'going to the dentist!' See you later, Steve.

Len's hand, holding the paper, is shaking. This is going too fast for comfort. He shuffles up to the counter, where Kathy is cleaning the espresso machine with a wet cloth.

'Thanks, love,' she says, taking his dirty cup. 'I'd have picked that up.'

'Wanted to save you a job,' he replies. He clears his throat.

Kathy waits, his cup in her hand.

'Steve says he's coming to my house with a new phone.'

'Well, that's exciting. There'll be no stopping you now. We'd all better watch out for the new social media phenomenon.'

Len doesn't think he can hear sarcasm in her words.

'But how will he find my house?'

'Len, dear. We all know where you live. Don't you remember the time when Steve drove you home after you had that funny turn last year?'

Oh yes. Len has blocked the embarrassing incident out of his mind, the time when his legs went from under him and he ended up in a heap on the floor with no knowledge of how he got there. They'd insisted on taking him to A&E but nothing untoward was found.

Len doesn't like reminders of his increasing frailty.

'Oh yes,' he says. 'I'd completely forgotten. How silly of me.'

Kathy pats his hand. 'This is all very exciting, Len. Make sure you get Steve to write everything down for you. The steps to log on and the passwords, and everything. New phones and accounts can be very confusing.'

Len smiles. She thinks he's stupid and old. It makes him more determined to make a success of this. 'Cooper will help me,' he says. 'He wants us to work together.' He moves towards the door.

'That sounds like a good idea,' she says, as he moves out into the street. 'Keep us posted, won't you?'

Once Len arrives home, the time drags. Perhaps Cooper will

get back before Steve turns up. That would be helpful because he can be involved from the start. On the other hand, Len would love to have some time to acclimatise himself to the new medium before he talks to Cooper.

He needs to make sure they don't upload the video without Cooper's say-so.

Len sits in his favourite chair for just a minute and puts the sport on TV. There's no racing on, which is a disappointment, and the cricket is delayed by rain. He leaves it on, and, it seems, a minute later, the doorbell goes. Len blinks and checks the time. It's past one and he's wasted his opportunity to organise his thoughts.

Steve is all smiles as he comes in, brandishing a battered plastic bag that says *Every Little Helps*.

'You got my note, Len?'

'I did.' Len stands back for Steve to come in and pass him in the hall. 'The thing is, Steve, I've been talking to Cooper and...'

Steve is past him and heading through the door into the sitting room. He turns his head back to face Len. 'Cooper? I thought he was in custody.' He carries on walking and dumps the bag on the dining area table.

'Well, that's the thing,' Len continues. 'I thought he was, but it turns out he'd been kidnapped by his father, but he escaped. So, he's back.'

Steve stands facing Len, with the bag behind him. He nods his head vaguely. 'Right, I see,' he says. 'I'm trying to work out whether that's good or bad. He's back, but he was kidnapped. A bit of a shocker. And by his own father, at that.'

'I know. But at least he's here.'

'Yes. So, what about Lexie then? Are you going to tell me she was abducted by aliens and everything we said in the video was wrong?'

Len swallows. 'No, she has been arrested. Cooper confirmed that yesterday. She is in custody and Cooper has been told that he mustn't do anything that might jeopardise her chance of getting released.'

'Well, that's OK, isn't it?' Steve is moving from one foot to the other. 'This has nothing to do with Cooper, so to speak. This is your stand, not his.'

Len rubs his hands together, feeling the friction of over dry skin on his palms. 'Cooper has insisted that he and I should work together from now on. That I shouldn't do anything without his say-so. That he wants to see what we've done so far and use my social media accounts, when I have them, because his dad has blocked him from all his profiles.'

'Too late, mate,' Steve licks his lips, delving with his tongue into the corners. 'It's all up there. You're live.' He shoves his hand into the plastic bag and pulls out a smartphone. 'This is you, Len. You're a social media presence. Cooper can't do a thing about it, nor can we.'

Len sinks into his armchair. 'Cooper's going to kill me. I didn't think it would happen this quickly.' His head feels too heavy for his body.

Steve sits down in one of the hard dining chairs, holding the phone closer to Len. 'I'm sorry if you think we've gone too fast, Len, but social media is immediate. That's its power. There would be no point in making that video and not putting it on, because the moment would be gone. We weren't to know that the information we had on Cooper at the time was wrong. Anyway, I reckon that being abducted by your own Dad, who is right in the thick of it all, is way worse than being arrested by the police, who do at least have to observe the formalities.'

'I suppose so, but I promised.'

Steve leans forward. 'Let me show you what we've done. The response has been epic, believe me. Cooper will be stoked.'

Len bites his lip. 'Show me then.' He remembers what Kathy said. 'While you're there, open that drawer. There's paper and a pen in there. I need to have everything written down so I can keep up with it all.

'Sure thing.' Steve finds the requisite articles and places them on the table. 'Come and sit here. It will be easier.' He helps Len up and pulls out a second chair for him. Once Len is seated, he begins to explain. 'So, we've got you this phone.' He holds it up, his fingertips cradling it as if it might explode.

Len rifles in his pocket, bringing out a ten-pound note. 'How much do I owe you?'

Steve waves his other hand. 'Not a thing. It's Tracy's old one. I've put a new SIM in.'

'But, don't you have to pay for a contract? I'm forever seeing adverts on the TV.'

'Look, don't worry about it. Let's concentrate on finding out how it works and see what's happened, shall we?'

Len nods. His gut is grumbling in an alarming way.

'So, you have a password to open the phone, right? We've stuck with the four-digit one. Keep it simple. It's this.' Steve scribbles onto the paper, 9876. 'OK so far?'

'Yes, as long as I don't lose that piece of paper.' He laughs, but the sound seems to echo around the room.

'Once you're in,' Steve continues, 'this screen comes up with all the apps. See these icons?'

Len examines the screen, taking off his glasses, rubbing them on his trousers, and returning them to his nose. The coloured square boxes, like everything else to do with this phone, look unfamiliar. 'Yes,' he says, his voice quieter than normal.

'To find things, you swipe like this.' Steve runs his finger across the screen, then engages eye contact with Len, saying nothing.

Len nods.

'Forget about most of the icons. You won't need them for now. Just concentrate on these.' He stabs the screen. 'I've grouped them together so they're easy to find.'

A rock forms in Len's throat. He swallows it. No reply seems necessary at this point.

'So, X first. This is what started the ball rolling. You're logged in, so, for now, all you need to do is press the icon. Try it now.'

Len taps the screen. Writing and photos jump out at him. 'Oh.'

'Now, look at the little bar at the bottom. Do you see the

magnifying glass? Tap that.'

Len does so, and a slightly different screen comes up.

'Go down a bit, after that headline, and you'll see what's trending on X .'

'I remember that from before, when you said the letter was trending.'

'That's right. Now, see what's trending. See that #Lennythelion?'

Len looks closer and nods.

'That's you, mate. Your video is trending, big time, and we only put it up first thing this morning. You're a big noise, like it or not.'

Len's mouth twitches at the corners. Is he proud, or is it indigestion? There's certainly a grumbling in his gut that is becoming more insistent. Steve is going through things so fast, and it's hard to focus. His mind feels fuzzy at the edges.

'Look at these thousands of likes and comments, Len. You can reply to the comments. You can post new things. You can do anything you like.' Steve goes through the steps to do these things and writes them down as well, but Len knows that he needs time to try it out for himself, with no one watching.

'And this is Facebook and Instagram. We've put it up there as well, and it's massive.'

'Thank you. I don't know what to say. I don't mind telling you that I'm stunned.'

Steve checks his watch. 'Enough for one day, I think. Why don't you digest all this and let Cooper know what we've done? If he isn't pleased, when he thinks about it, then he's an ungrateful bastard.'

Len forces himself up. 'Lots for me to look at,' he says.

Steve grins. 'I'd better get back. That "dental visit" took a while.' His smile turns into a chuckle. 'Call me if you have any problems. I've put my number in your contacts, but here it is again.' He scribbles a number down. 'Enjoy basking in your fame.'

Len sees him to the door and returns to his armchair, holding the phone in his hand.

What a turn-up.

Len casts his eyes at the ceiling. *Who'd have thought it, love?*

28.

Marilyn

Marilyn is waiting at the nail salon; Ayeesha has been delayed. This isn't suspicious. There has been so much for her to do and astonishing pressure for her to come up to speed quickly. She's also having to interact with Bruce and the Life Counter team to ensure that she doesn't arouse suspicion.

To allay charges of wasting time and to calm her nerves, Marilyn has her nails done. They never look like the ones in the adverts, being short and stubby and often bitten. They are a big improvement, though, Marilyn thinks, as she holds her hand at a distance to admire the result. She's gone for a glittery metallic blue, not what she would have chosen a few weeks ago. They give her a little added confidence.

Finally, Ayeesha arrives in the secret upstairs room, her beautiful hair frizzing a little on her forehead.

'Sorry,' she says, banging her laptop bag down on the table. 'So much to do, and then Bruce turned up out of the blue. Scared the life out of me.' She slumps down in the seat next to Marilyn's.

'What did he want?' Marilyn swivels her chair to face Ayeesha. If she examines her features carefully during their conversation, will she be able to detect any subterfuge?

Ayeesha sighs. 'Checking up on me, I guess. He wanted to know if I'd got on top of the existing code, and he had a list of changes he wanted made.'

Marilyn leans forward. 'Did he come to where you're working?'

'He did, but he insisted we go into your office to discuss it, and gave me a handwritten list, saying that you'd worked out the changes and that he didn't understand them, but he was under the impression they would correct any anomalies. I'm supposed to leave the list in your office.'

Marilyn stands up and throws her empty cup in the bin. A

dribble of cold coffee hits the smudged and shabby wall. 'He's such a shit. He's told me the opposite. He doesn't want the iniquitous bits changed, merely hidden. His main concern is the social media campaign. He wants it neutralised. God knows how I'm supposed to do that. I'm hoping to do the opposite. It might finish him off.'

'Exactly. People in the office are talking about it. Apparently, there's a video now. I haven't had time to watch it yet, with Bruce breathing down my neck.'

'But back to the code for now, yes?' Marilyn says, glancing at her watch.

'Of course. There's lots to tell you.'

'Does his list amount to much?'

'Not really. It's what you said. He wants to hide the corrupting bits in clear sight, to ensure that no one can work out what he's been authorising. He doesn't want to correct it at all.'

'It makes no sense, though,' Marilyn says. 'The results are becoming clearer by the day.'

'True, for the babies, but it's not obvious, unless it's publicised, that some people have unfairly been given extra years, and others have been penalised.' Ayeesha delves into her bag and pulls out her laptop, swiping a biscuit crumb off its surface.

'Still, you'd think he'd at least be trying to row back a bit. It's bound to come to light eventually.'

'It's funny,' Ayeesha says, sipping the coffee that Marilyn bought for her, 'sometimes the most calculating and apparently clever people can make very stupid mistakes, and I think it's because they're convinced they're brilliant and can't see their own inadequacies.'

Marilyn can't stop a little smile ghosting across her face. 'And he's rattled,' she says. 'People make mistakes when they're panicking.'

'True. That's what we have to hope for. Anyway, how much do you know about the Programme as it began?'

'I know what the original spec was.' Marilyn sighs and slumps back in her seat. 'I understood,' she continues, 'and was complicit in the corrupting changes that Bruce ordered. I believed in his good intentions in those days, you see.'

Ayeesha nods. Her lips are set in a tight line. 'Well, Bruce wants things hidden, but he doesn't know how Rangan works, worked, I mean.'

'I need to ask you about Rangan.'

'OK. Code first, though. Rangan always had a policy of clarity in his programmes. He annotated everything meticulously, so anyone who had to amend them could clearly see how things worked and what needed to be changed.'

Ayeesha scribbles in a notebook, but the words aren't immediately understandable.

'That sounds like the Rangan I remember,' Marilyn says.

'Yes, and he also has an audit trail of exactly what was changed and when. And why? More scribbles from Ayeesha.

'Do you think Bruce knows that?'

'I very much doubt it.' Ayeesha sits back and smiles. 'He wouldn't know where to look. The notes are written in a way that they only make sense to people who know what they're doing. You have to click into the code to reveal the comments, and there are several levels of them. They also state the date of change and who authorised them. Mostly, he's put that down as Bruce.' Ayeesha writes a large B and circles it.

Marilyn raises an eyebrow. 'But it was me he dealt with. He barely knew Bruce.'

'I'm sure. But Bruce was the big cheese who brought him in. It might annoy you, but think about it, it's in your interests for Bruce to be named, not you.'

Marilyn nods. Ayeesha's right, but it still seems unfair. Unfair but lucky, as it turns out.

'Anyway, forget about your wounded pride. Let's crack on. The point is, it's impossible to go back in and change the notes.'

'Impossible? Really?'

'Well, I could do it, if I wanted to, with some difficulty, but why would I?'

'Quite,' Marilyn says, feeling a little better.

'So, you see. That's why he's dependent on people like me.'

'What I don't understand is why he has so much faith in you, that you will blindly do what he says.' There's something here that still doesn't make sense to Marilyn. It's nibbling at her nerves.

Ayeesha chews the inside of her cheek. 'I've wondered that myself, but I guess he's desperate. And I come very well recommended, by some people in high places.' She crosses her legs.

'So, Rangan?'

'In a minute. First, I need to go through the corruptions, to check you're aware of them.'

Marilyn shifts in her chair. Her nose is itching like mad, but she sits on her hands. Is Ayeesha trying to punish her, or does she always rub salt in wounds like this?

'So, on the plus side,' Ayeesha continues, apparently oblivious to Marilyn's discomfort, 'credits were given to members of the Government, civil servants, celebrities and anyone who put their hands into their very deep pockets.'

'That much I knew.' Marilyn kicks at a crumb on the floor.

'I'd be interested to know how you justified it to yourself.'

Marilyn continues to look at her feet. 'I don't know.' She pauses, and, deciding to be brave, regains eye contact with her colleague. 'Bruce told me that each individual had done good things for society, that their genes were somehow superior to other people's and that they deserved to have more time to live and procreate.' Marilyn no longer worries that Ayeesha might be on Bruce's side. The look in her eyes could cut through steel. 'I was blinded by admiration, OK? I'm not proud of it.'

Ayeesha leans forward. 'And the debits?'

Marilyn gulps. 'Criminals, drug takers, alcoholics, um people who make bad choices, have too many children.' She takes a couple of slow breaths.

'And?'

'And now, anyone Bruce takes a dislike to, including his own son and grandchild.' Marilyn hides her head in her hands. 'Especially his own son and grandchild. That's what turned me,' she says, conscious that her reply is muffled. 'And Bruce's behaviour has become so erratic. It's impossible to admire him now.' There's a painful stinging behind her eyeballs. 'And there has been a deeply unfair effect on a close family member of mine.' She raises her head. 'How could I have been so stupid?'

Ayeesha's eyes soften, finally. 'You're not the only person to be taken in, believe me. It all seemed such a good idea to begin with, to encourage people to improve their behaviour. It had popular support, didn't it? But who judges? Any system is only as reliable as the people who control it.'

'And that's Bruce.'

'Precisely.'

Marilyn sits forward. 'And he's tried to stifle public debate. I think that boat has sailed now, though.' There's no point in beating herself up any further. 'I told Rangan what Bruce wanted, but I never really understood how it was achieved.'

'Right, well, that's probably you and everyone else in the country. That's how he's got away with it for so long. To oversimplify, it's a bit like posting adjustments to a set of accounts. Each alteration has a code, which governs how much extra time is given or what is taken away. The population is on a massive database, and the code increments or decrements, as appropriate. The algorithms are constantly interrogating the database, so group changes can be executed with a specific code, and sometimes, now, the algorithm is making its own decisions without reference to a human being. That's where Bruce is beginning to lose control, but I don't think he understands that properly.'

'God. What a mess. So, when you say the algorithm is making its own decisions? What do you mean exactly?' Her feet are rocking, as if she is teetering on the edge of a cliff, trying not to look at the sea raging against rocks, so many hundreds of metres below.

'Well, say Bruce takes against someone and has their life shortened, the AI will look for other individuals with similar characteristics and do the same thing. This is new, and I'm sure Bruce didn't intend it to work that way.'

'So, it's going to become even more of a shit show than it is at the moment?'

Ayeesha nods. 'Wait till the people affected hook into the existing X campaign. Oh boy. It will be carnage.'

'Wait a minute.' Marilyn is blinking hard. She wants to do her lip pull thing that helps her think, but she's in company. 'This is bound to hit some of the people Bruce has given extra time to, unless they are treated separately on the database and ring fenced against alterations.'

'Indeed, it will. No one is safe now.'

'I don't understand how it could have been written in such a way that the AI could go rogue.' Marilyn wishes she weren't so far out of her comfort zone.

Ayeesha shrugs her shoulders. 'The people making the decisions don't understand the reach of AI. It operates so fast, learns so quickly, but it doesn't always learn the lessons its creators want. This system is out of control.' She sits back, crossing her arms. She doesn't look as alarmed as Marilyn feels.

'The whole thing needs closing down, straight away.' Marilyn is on her feet again. She pulls at her dress, which has ridden up.

'Of course, but he will never authorise that. He'd have to pay all that money back to his benefactors. I wonder what he's done with his ill-gotten gains? Does he have a mega yacht or something?' Ayeesha leans forward and scrolls through something on her laptop.

Marilyn frowns. 'No. He spends all his time working. I can't think why he's doing it.' Connecting with Ayeesha had seemed such a good idea, a way to end the madness. Now Marilyn feels she's trying to untangle a huge mound of threads. Every time she pulls a loose end, she only succeeds in tightening a knot in the middle.

'My guess is that he's channelling the funds into some tax haven or other, ready to escape from the inevitable. That's what I'd do in his position.' Ayeesha bites her lip. 'I'm afraid he's trying to set you up as the fall guy. He must realise, on some level, that it's all going to collapse around him.'

The room feels very cold. The perspiration collecting in Marilyn's armpits is joined by a cold sweat on her forehead and the back of her neck. She grips her hands together to stop them shaking.

'The only way to stop it is to make it public,' she says.

'That might not save you, though.'

'I know that.' The future life Marilyn has been hoping for flashes before her eyes. What does it amount to, really? 'But this matters, doesn't it? The whole country could collapse if we don't do something radical. I must push my own fears aside and do the right thing, mustn't I?'

Ayeesha says nothing. Her eyes are seeking Marilyn's, examining her face. She blinks. For the first time, Marilyn notices the dark shadows under her eyes and the tension between her eyebrows. Her gaze is gentle, perhaps pitying.

Marilyn swallows.

'You're right, of course,' the other woman says, finally. 'But I don't have the first idea of how we should do it. It isn't simple, and if we do it wrong, we could make everything worse, if that's possible.'

It is Marilyn's turn to nod. Her pile of imaginary thread is becoming more knotted by the minute. 'Cautious approach, I guess.'

Ayeesha places a hand on Marilyn's. 'One step at a time. I needed you to understand, though, that you, personally, are in great jeopardy.'

The door downstairs bangs shut.

'Shall I tell you about Rangan now?'

Changing the subject is a good idea.

Ayeesha looks into the distance. 'We've been friends since University. Really good friends. Same course. Same Masters. Same company for our first jobs.' She looks at Marilyn. Her eyes seem even larger. Tears are collecting in the corners. 'We did have a fling at one stage, but soon realised we were best as friends. He told me when he started working for Bruce. He was excited at first, because it was such a challenging project, but he soon started to doubt Bruce's intentions. Rangan is, was, very straight, honest. Aware of the dangers IT manipulation can produce. So, he kept me in the loop, let me know how he was annotating things in case of problems, and got my name up on a list of approved contractors, just in case. Put my name right at the top.'

Her mouth twitches into a momentary smile.

'What did he expect you to do?'

Ayeesha's mouth hardens again. 'Investigate if he disappeared, which he did, shortly afterwards. My guess is that he confronted Bruce and paid the ultimate price.'

Shivers run up and down the hairs on Marilyn's arms. 'I don't think he is a murderer.' Even saying the word seems ridiculous. 'This is Bruce we're talking about. He's a civil servant.'

Ayeesha snaps her laptop open. 'You never know what people are capable of until they're in danger. I know Rangan is dead. I would have heard from him otherwise. I'm out to get even, regardless of what you decide to do.'

'You know where I stand, and what I have to lose.'

'Then let's get to work, shall we?'

29.

Cooper

Sitting in Len's house, at his slightly grimy computer, is supposed to be a distraction for Cooper, but, despite surges of enthusiasm when he sees how well Len's video is trending, he can't get Lexie's predicament out of his head. Several times an hour, he jumps up, determined to make a nuisance of himself at the police station. Equally frequently, he sits back down, knowing that interfering will only make her situation worse.

Or so he has been told.

There is no doubt in his mind that this is Bruce's doing. Lexie is imprisoned precisely because he has escaped.

So why doesn't Bruce have him picked up again?

Nothing is making sense.

'Len, there's no point standing at that window all morning. It won't make Lexie come home any sooner.' Len's looming presence is blocking light from the window. It's hard to believe this is the same structure as their house. Mahogany furniture, heavy curtains and busy wallpaper give the feel of a period sitcom. Len moves from his viewing station but paces around the room instead, adding to the churning feeling in Cooper's own gut and mind.

'Makes me feel better. I can't do nothing.' Len puts the emphasis on 'I'.

'I'm not asking you to do nothing. Come and see this. Your video is exploding all over the internet.'

'It is?' Len shuffles over. It would be an exaggeration to say that he's smiling, but there is a slight lift to the edges of his previously downcast lips.

'Yes, come and see.' Cooper drags a second chair closer to his and pushes away a half-drunk cup of coffee, in which specks of curdling milk are floating. Len settles himself down and removes his glasses to see the screen more clearly, rubbing at the increasingly bulgy bags under his eyes.

'See here,' Cooper says, jabbing a finger at the screen. 'Nearly two million views now on X and half a million retweets. That will make even more people follow you. It's unbelievable. Look at all the comments.' Cooper opens up Len's tweet so the streams of comments become visible. Len's angry face stares out at him from the screen.

'It's strange seeing myself there,' Len says. Cooper hears the pride in his voice. How does he explain to him how much danger he is in now? The old man's head is well and truly over the parapet. Either the media or the police could be at the door any minute. All the more reason to keep Len's face away from the window.

'I've heard you tapping away at the computer. What have you been doing?'

'Mainly, I've been replying to some of the comments. It helps to raise visibility and keep it trending.'

'So, you've been replying as me? Shouldn't I have seen what you've been saying?'

Cooper bites at the edge of his nail. 'Sorry, Len. I didn't realise you wanted to vet everything.'

'I don't really.' Len sits there for a while, not saying anything further, but, strangely, his lips are working as if he's talking without words.

'It's a matter of speed. I want to spread this as fast as we can before the thought police catch up with us. So I'm replying quickly, linking to other places, trying to build up a spider's web the algorithms can't block.'

'I understand all that. I know I'm slow.' Len sits back and rubs at his lower back. He bites at his dry, cracked lips. 'I'm happy for you to reply. Could you think about your grammar, though? I'm very particular about getting the sentences right when I'm writing, and this is going out in my name, isn't it?' Len's eyes are red and rheumy, more so without the protection of his glasses. Cooper feels a wave of protectiveness sweep through him, as if Len is his child rather than a neighbour. The first smile of the day spreads across his face.

'So let me get this right,' Cooper says, pleased to feel some mirth but not wanting to laugh at Len. 'You don't care what I say as long as I put it correctly?'

Len nods. 'Is that silly?'

Cooper scratches his head. 'Not silly, but this is X, not an essay competition. If you look at how other people write things, you'll see that they use abbreviations, fragments rather than sentences, shorthand explanations, total garbage sometimes. Hardly any punctuation either!'

'Hmm,' Len replies. 'Perhaps you could bear my wishes in mind, though, if you're pretending to be me.' His eyebrows raise into perfect arches.

'Point taken. I'll try harder.' Cooper feels the urge to salute. With Len watching, he tries hard to put the next reply in a way Len will be happy with, but is relieved when Len pushes himself up and wanders towards the window again.

'There's a police car pulling up,' Len says.

Cooper jerks his head up. 'Away from the window, now.' Len moves himself into the shadows behind the curtain but still maintains his sentry duty.

'Are they coming in here?' Cooper jumps up and stands behind Len. He towers over the older man so it's easy to view the road from this vantage point.

'They've found a spot near your house.'

Cooper tweaks the curtain. 'I'm guessing it's not good news.' His hand on the fabric begins to shake as he sees one of the police officers open the back door of the car to help someone out. 'Lexie!' Cooper exhales heavily. 'Oh my God. It's Lexie. She's back!'

Cooper sprints away from the window, but Len grabs his shirt before he's got anywhere near the door. 'Wait a minute. Do you want them to know you're here?'

'But I've got to see how she is. She looks exhausted.' They both return to the window, still hiding. Lexie's hair is tangled and dull. She's still wearing the clothes she had on when she was taken away so abruptly.

'Think for a minute, Cooper. They've brought her back. That means she's been released. They might be planning to replace her with you, or me, perhaps. Don't give them the opportunity to do that.'

Cooper is rubbing his nose so hard it's warming up. 'You might be right. But I wanted to be there when she got back.'

Len gives him a long look.

'I didn't think she'd come back like this. I thought I'd need to make some kind of intervention, do something dramatic. I can't think what it can mean.'

Len continues to stare at him but doesn't say anything to help him decide what to do.

'All right. You're right. I'll wait here until they've gone, as long as they let her inside.'

'I would give her five minutes to brush her hair and tidy herself up before you go in. That sort of thing is important to women, you know.'

Cooper steps back from the window. 'Come on, Len. Nobody thinks about that stuff now. That's sexist rubbish.'

Len raises an eyebrow.

'OK. Five minutes then.'

'Once they've gone.'

'Once they've gone,' he repeats.

Len moves back towards the laptop. 'Is there anything else I need to know about this?' He points to the screen.

'Well,' Cooper says, thinking on his feet but desperate to get next door. 'You could read through the comments I've made on your behalf. See what you think. Start replying yourself, now you're all set up. Then you'll be happier with the grammar.'

What harm can it do?

'Are you happy for me to do that?'

'Well, you're the one that has made such a difference, aren't you? I've been a bit tied up, literally.'

Len smiles. 'I might do that. I've got the time, after all.'

'That's right. You have. I need to find out what the situation is with Lexie. It might be a while before I can come back, but when I do, we need to do more.'

'More? Haven't we done a lot already?'

'We have, but it's not enough. Social media has its limits. We need to make more of a splash. I'll keep thinking about it.'

'The police have gone, look,' Len says, nodding his head towards the window. The police car is heading down the street.

'I'm off, Len. Make lots of comments, but don't do anything crazy, will you?'

Len smiles. Cooper sees a twinkle in his eyes behind his glasses. 'Of course not, Cooper. You can be sure of that.'

30.

Lexie

Turning the key in their front door has never felt so good. No pram in the hall or the living room. The house smells indefinably different. She sniffs. Enclosed. Stale, as if the windows haven't been opened since she was dragged away. She opens the small window in the front room, then heads through to the kitchen and opens the bifold doors, breathing in the relatively fresh air from outside. The through draught helps to clear the odour.

The pram is in the garden, empty.

'Cooper?'

No answer. Her voice reverberates through the house.

'I'm home. They let me out.'

Still no answer. If he were here, he'd be bounding down the stairs by now, two steps at a time. Where is he? The terrible thought crosses her mind that he has been taken into custody in her place. Or that his father has bundled him into a car again and dragged him away to some secret place. Where's Tash? Although she knows that the baby won't be here without Cooper, she can't help herself from running upstairs to check. The nursery is empty. Reasonably tidy, although a couple of babygrows are draped over the edge of the cot. One of them has baby sick down the front, so she bungs it straight in the laundry basket.

Their bedroom next. The bed is unmade, the duvet scrunched into a ball in the middle of the bed, but apart from that, the room is tidy. No clothes on the floor. No clues as to where he might be, either. Perhaps he is doing something innocuous like walking Tash in the park. Her intuition tells her otherwise.

Lexie's excitement at being home is beginning to dampen. What is home if the people who matter to you aren't here? She heads downstairs to the kitchen and starts loading dirty cups into the dishwasher.

Where is he?

As the last piece of dirty crockery is tidied away and she closes the door of the appliance, she hears a key in the door. Lexie pushes her fingers through her hair and lifts her arm, sniffing experimentally. She's left it too late to get clean, and she's desperate to see them both. As she rushes into the hall, Cooper is turning the latch with one hand while balancing Tash with the other. Lexie hurries to take the baby from him, holding her close, breathing in that incomparable sweet, soft baby smell. 'Cooper,' she says, trying to add him to the cuddle. She sighs. It's so good to be back.

He engulfs her in his arms. 'Lex. I'm so sorry. This is all my fault.'

She eases herself away. 'Not your fault. Your father's.'

'Even so. I escaped, and you were taken.' He holds her away from him. 'Let me look at you. How are you? Did they let you go?' He pulls her closer again.

Lexie holds Tash, balancing her on one hip while raking through the tousled chunks of her own hair with her other hand. 'I'm fine, filthy but fine. I wanted to shower before you saw me.'

'No need for that,' he says, stroking a stray lock away from her face. 'Although Len did say you'd want to tidy yourself up.'

'Is that where you've been?'

'Yes, Len's excelled himself again with his gung-ho activism.'

Lexie raises her eyebrows, opening her eyes wide. They feel tight.

'No really, he has. You wouldn't believe it. I'll tell you all about it in a minute.'

'But first of all,' he says, taking her free hand and pulling her towards the kitchen, 'you need to sit down and recover.'

Cooper's hands are clammy.

'I'm fine.'

'Of course you aren't. Your hand is shaking, for a start.' Cooper lifts Tash gently off Lexie's hip just in time. Lexie feels her entire body begin to shake, and her vision darkens. Cooper manoeuvres her over the chair and pushes her down. 'Delayed shock,' he says.

'Sit quietly while I get you some water.'

'I feel a bit –'

A bowl appears in front of Lexie, and she retches, but nothing comes up. 'Sorry. I'll be better now.' Tash is examining her with wide, enquiring eyes. She seems older already. 'Let me have her back, please. I've missed her so much.'

Cooper holds onto Tash a little longer. Does he believe she's OK? Eventually, he nods and places the baby in her lap. Lexie can see properly again and breathes in deeply, desperate for the infant smell she has been deprived of. She luxuriates in Tash's hot little breaths against her cheek.

'So,' she says, once she's ready, Tash in her lap, and a steaming cup of tea in front of her. 'I never felt they knew what to do with me. Sure, they asked me lots of questions about the social media campaign, but I was completely honest about that. I had nothing to do with it, and I made sure they knew that.' She pulls the string of the tea bag, swirling it around the mug. 'Obviously, I didn't say anything about Len.'

Cooper rubs the skin between his eyebrows. 'Don't worry. Len's outed himself now. He's not under the radar anymore.' He gesticulates with his hand, almost as if he's waving at an imaginary crowd. 'But carry on.'

'Ooh, you lovely little darling,' Lexie continues, brushing tears from her cheek and trying to hide the gesture by rubbing her nose against her daughter's. 'I signed a statement to say I wasn't involved, and I got the impression that they believed me, but then I was taken straight back to a police cell.'

Cooper's forehead tightens, as if the reality of what his wife has been through has only just dawned on him. He's fidgeting like mad. 'The police told me not to come, and I had a message from my father to say that if I didn't stay well out of it, it would be worse for you.'

Lexie leans across the table and places her hand on his. 'Don't worry. I know. You're the sort who would be battering on the police station door, but it wouldn't have helped.' She takes a sip of her tea. Her vocal cords feel raw, unused. 'I felt like I was in the way. They avoided my eyes when they brought me food, and were evasive when I asked what was happening. And when I asked to see a lawyer, they looked distinctly uncomfortable. That's when I realised they'd broken the law, or procedure at least, by arresting me.'

Cooper nods. 'They had no evidence at all,' he murmurs.

'I knew I was getting somewhere then, so I kept demanding to see a lawyer, pestered them again and again, made a nuisance of myself, and they suddenly brought my things to me and said I was free to go. They even gave me a lift home.'

'Len and I saw you arriving a few minutes ago. He made me wait until the police had gone.'

Lexie nods. 'Sensible. So, what do we do now? I'm free, but I wouldn't want to push it too much. I don't want to repeat that experience, that's for sure.' Tash has fallen asleep in her arms. Lexie holds her a little tighter, feeling the baby's warmth tickling her own skin. 'You said Len had been up to something? I distinctly remember asking him not to do anything silly when I told you'd gone missing.'

'Yeah, well. That's Len for you.' Cooper stands up and reaches for her phone, which is lying flat on the kitchen table. 'Surprise, surprise, he didn't listen to you. What he's done is brilliant, though. It's opened another front for us.' He pushes it towards her. 'Go on, X. You'll see in a minute why you didn't need to worry about incriminating Len.'

It's low on battery, but still working. Lexie does as Cooper asks and passes the phone back to him. After a little swiping and stabbing, Cooper holds the screen up to her while she watches the entire video, becoming more astonished with every sentence. At the end, she sits there for ages, shaking her head, before saying, 'I didn't know he had it in him. Surely, I'm not that good an IT teacher? I mean, how did he do it? The video, the production, getting it up there? I can't believe it.'

Cooper is moving from foot to foot. 'He had some help. Some

guy he chats to at the coffee shop. Obviously knows what he's doing.'

'So, it's all out in the open now?'

'Better than that. Look at this.' Cooper holds the original tweet out to her.

Lexie squints. 'Nearly four million likes?'

'It's pretty much doubled since I last looked at it. I'll fill you in on it all later.'

'Amazing,' Lexie laughs. 'Good old Len, but will it be enough?'

Cooper sits down heavily. 'No. I don't think so. It's certainly working in a promotional way, but…'

'Your dad will double down on what he's been doing.'

Cooper nods. 'That's my fear. He'll get Len closed down. That's why I need to move as fast as possible.'

'He can't close everyone down. He doesn't own X.'

Cooper rubs his hand backwards and forwards across his jaw. 'No, but he'll find Len soon enough. I must do more.'

'There is no time, by the sounds of it.'

'There isn't. I have the germ of an idea, but it hasn't crystallised yet. I can only do it through Len's account, but I need to work out the best way to go about it and do it as soon as possible, before he's down and out.'

'What is it?' Lexie's concentration is going, but this is obviously important to her husband.

Cooper holds a hand up to his mouth, sucks in a breath through his teeth and exhales heavily. 'Work in progress,' he says. 'I'll tell you more when I've thought it through, if that's OK?'

That is more than fine.

'I want nothing more than a hot shower and some time to settle down,' Lexie says. 'Why don't you go back over there and do whatever you have to do?'

'Are you sure?'

'Positive. Off you go, before it's too late.'

31.

Len

The house is quiet in Cooper's absence, and Len doesn't like it. He stares at the computer and forces himself to focus. The thread of comments on his post is massive. Cooper said it was better to work on the computer, so it would be easier to type the replies. Len is terrified he'll press the wrong key, lose the page and not be able to navigate his way back. Worse still, what if he writes something stupid and can't take it back? It takes him a little while to settle his nerves and feel even slightly competent. Strangely, the longer he spends on the site, the easier it is becoming.

First, he reads through all Cooper's comments, to get a feel for what he is supposed to be saying. It becomes clear that part of the point in replying is giving some sort of validation to the people who have taken the time to comment and showing that he is a genuine human being who is worth interacting with.

The whole process is fascinating.

He is talking to people from all around the country. All around the world, in fact, even if those elsewhere are astonished that people in Britain are suffering in this way. How could this happen, they say, in the modern world? In a democracy? How could people's rights be cancelled in this draconian way?

Do they feel smug, or worry that evil will be contagious and the same could happen in their country?

To start with, Len tries to echo Cooper's replies, but with better grammar. After a while, he understands why people use a more colloquial tone. Damn it, he's starting to adopt it himself. Every *Sick, dude* makes him sit a little taller, while *thank you so much for all you are doing for us* makes him think, sadly but proudly, of how Sylvia would have nodded and brought him a glass of beer from the cupboard under the stairs. She was not one for fulsome praise, but he always knew when he'd earned her approval.

He replies, quicker than he would have been able even last week, *I hope I can make a difference. Please share this as widely as possible. Together we can change the Programme.*

The first negative comment hits him like a punch in the gut. *Fuck off back to your swamp, you old git. The world's changed. Get over it.*

Cooper has warned him about this, so, after the initial shock, he is able to treat it with a certain amount of equanimity. It helps that several other people have already replied, castigating the individual. Cooper has told him that some of the more vicious replies might be coming from a troll factory, but Len imagines a pasty-faced youth with long greasy hair bearing down on him with menace.

He moves on.

After replying to a few more people in a slightly generic way, he scrolls down to find a long comment. The profile picture shows an attractive young woman with long blonde hair. *I'm really impressed with what you have achieved so far, Len. I'm working on the story here at Sky News. I'd love to learn more about what has happened to your friends and how and why you have become involved. DM me your number, and we can set up an interview. Don't delay, please.*

Len sits back. Is this a scam? Cooper has spoken to him severely about the risks of being taken in by people online. He clicks on her profile, and she seems genuine. She has a lot of followers. In fact, now he looks more closely, he recognizes her.

Wow.

Len drums his fingers on the dining table. He looks towards the hall, half imagining that Cooper is at this very moment walking with his long, gangly stride up to the front door. Really, he should consult him about this.

And yet.

She said *don't delay*.

He might be on the news, today's news. Tomorrow might be too late. Cooper said that himself.

Len casts his mind back to his tuition from Cooper to remember how to do a direct message and is delighted that he remembers. He texts the number of his new mobile phone to the woman, expecting to get no answer, and continues with his task of replying to comments. Now that he has been approached by someone from Sky, the comments feel a little dull and workaday.

In no time at all, his mobile rings, and he picks it up gingerly and answers. It is her. She wants to film an interview right now.

Len is nervous. This is too fast.

It's so easy, she says, just a simple chat, one person to another. She will send a link to his email address, which he happily supplies, and they can talk over Zoom. It will be just like talking in person, much easier than his earlier video.

She makes it seem like no effort at all.

In fact, she is right.

Before long, he is staring at this rather beautiful woman, and it is almost as if they are in the same room.

'Len,' she says. 'Thank you so much for talking to me today. I am Anna, and I am especially interested in what you have to say because I am pregnant myself. I am invested in pushing for a satisfactory solution to this problem. I hope you understand that I will not misrepresent you in any way.'

Len nods at the screen. There is something about her that reminds him of Lexie, and this makes her seem trustworthy. 'I'm happy with that,' he says.

'OK,' Anna says. 'Let's just chat, and I'll cut the interview to fit the segment.'

Len nods his assent, even though this doesn't make much sense to him.

'So Len, what has made you stick your neck out to get involved in something like this?'

'Well.' Len hesitates, wondering how much he should say. He feels Cooper sitting on his shoulder, metaphorically speaking. 'I saw the distress that this has caused my friends, my very good friends,' he continues, 'and I couldn't bear the injustice of it.'

'The injustice? Would you like to tell me a little more about what you mean by that?'

Hearing the word a second time increases his anger at the situation. 'They are good people,' he says. 'If they have ever done anything to warrant having their lives shortened, I have never seen it. And now, their baby, a true innocent, has suffered. What could she possibly have done wrong in her short life?' He tries to slow his breathing. A pulse is racing in his ears. 'Whoever thought up this *New Directive*,' he says, hearing the sneer in his voice,' is either bad or mad. There is no other explanation for it.'

Anna blinks, a slight smile playing at the corners of her mouth. 'So, Len. Do you worry that taking a stand will cause you problems, personally?'

Len sits up straight. 'I imagine so, but I'm ready for it.' He hesitates. He has promised to be careful. On the other hand, being careful means sitting in a chair and letting the world go on without you. He takes a long, slow breath. That's being careful, isn't it? 'So far,' he says, 'my friends have been harassed and treated badly, illegally, I'm sure, by the authorities. Cooper,–' Oh dear, he didn't mean to use his name. Oh well. 'He has been pulled off the street and abducted, by his own father, no less, for trying to investigate what happened, and Lexie was arrested. I believe she is home now.'

Anna's mouth is a perfect 'O' of shock. After a quick blink, she lowers her eyes and appears to be writing something down.

'If that happens to them,' Len ploughs on, 'I'm sure something similar will be done to me, but I don't care. I feel so strongly about this.' He wants to stand up but settles for gripping the edges of the dining table with both hands. 'They can do what they want with me. I've had my life. There were tough times when I was growing up, but they were nothing compared to what's happening now. It's totalitarian. That's what it is. We're getting back to the Nazis here.'

'Thank you, Len. I can see that your feelings about this are very genuine.'

'They are.' Len stabs a finger at the screen. 'Soon, they will silence me. I know that. I must get my message out to as many people as possible before that time comes.'

'Well, this is your moment. The social media campaign is good, great even, but we have a broader reach. You can be on the primetime news. It will put you at risk. I need you to know that, but it will give you a platform, a big one. So, what would you like to say to your audience? What should people do?'

Words want to tumble out of Len's mouth, but he must think this through. This is a call to arms. He takes a deep breath and pulls his body up as tall as possible. 'Be aware, firstly. Think how many people you know who could be affected by this. Think of your family and friends and how they might suffer, not to mention the ones that come after them.' He pauses. 'Can anyone listening say that they have never done anything wrong? I doubt it. We all do our best, but we don't always get it right. I know I don't. But some people don't have as many chances as others, have never been shown as kids what's right and wrong. We need to recognise that before we start doling out punishment.'

'That's good, Len, but what should people do?'

'Oh, right.' He's been on his soapbox. Settle down. 'Spread the message far and wide. I might be imprisoned, but they can't throw everyone in jail, can they? Tell everyone, go on social media, write to the newspapers, email the news programmes, the Government, anyone you can think of. Demonstrate on the streets. That's still allowed, isn't it?'

Anna smiles. 'Currently, yes. Who knows, in the future?'

'And put Bruce Box back in his box. That's what I say!'

Tiny lines appear between Anna's perfectly shaped eyebrows. 'Mr Box has a profile of sorts,' she says, after a brief pause. 'We might have to cut that, for your own sake.'

'You know best, I suppose.'

'That's a wonderful interview. Thank you so much. Look out for yourself on the news.'

'There's one thing I don't understand,' Len says, worrying that he is going to look stupid.

'Yes?'

'Well, you've been all on my side. You haven't really asked me anything difficult. And, you've told people that you might be affected yourself? Aren't you supposed to show both sides?'

'Hmm,' Anna says. 'It's hard to see another side to this, isn't it? And don't worry about me. As I said, we'll cut the interview to fit. We will cover all the bases. Lovely to meet you. Bye.'

Anna ends the call. Len feels a little flat, and for the first time worries about how well he controlled it, and what Cooper will say. Speaking of which, the doorbell is ringing, and something tells Len that this will be Cooper returning.

It is.

How much should he tell him?

Cooper is smiling. The anxieties of the previous days seem to have been assuaged by having Lexie back.

'Cooper. I didn't expect to see you back so soon.' Len leans slightly back, rocking his feet onto the heels of his slippers. 'Shouldn't you be staying with Lexie? How is she?' He moves away from the door, allowing Cooper to come in.

'She's fine, amazingly.' It's true. He does look amazed, his eyes wide and a happier look on his face than Len has seen for some time. 'She's tired, though. I don't think she got much sleep. She suggested she'd take it easy and I should come back over here.'

Len rolls his tongue around inside his mouth. 'Surely your place is there with her, even so?'

Cooper's boyish happiness subsides. 'I know. But I told her what you'd been up to.'

Len coughs.

'Don't worry. I let her know what a success it's been. She's really impressed with what you've achieved.'

Len shuffles back a few more steps.

'But she knows we need to go with the momentum, to maximise what we can do before they, er, catch up with you.' Cooper runs his hand through his hair, leaving a tuft sticking up at the front.

'So, have you done some more work on it while I've been gone?'

'Um, yes, I have. I've answered more comments.' Len is moving towards the laptop. 'And, er, I found a comment from a journalist who wanted me to contact her.'

Cooper has gone extremely quiet. Len avoids his eyes.

'So, I did contact her, and I've done an interview with her.'

Cooper's mouth is hanging open. He shuts it in time to say, 'You've done all that, already? I haven't been gone long.' Cooper is rubbing his fingers with some vigour over his dry lips.

'Yes, well, it was only a short interview. She wants to get it on the news today.'

Len is hoping to see a look of amazed congratulation on Cooper's face. Instead, Cooper marches over to the laptop, hovers over it and hunches, with his hands gripping the table and his arms braced.

He speaks very slowly. 'I thought we agreed not to do anything precipitately,' he says, turning his head to glare at Len.

Len's gullet feels tight, as if he has a golf ball stuck. 'I know that, but this was Anna from Sky News. She's on our side.'

Cooper is still looking at him with an unblinking stare.

'She's pregnant,' he says, in a quieter voice.

'OK,' Cooper says, slumping into a chair and putting his head in his hands, 'What did you say?'

Len has the advantage now since he's still standing. He puts one hand on his hip, keeping the other one resting on the table. He's feeling a little light-headed, and Cooper's attitude isn't helping. 'I was very careful and measured in what I said,' he replies, hoping that this is, in fact, the case. It's hard to remember what he said in the heat of the moment. 'She was very encouraging. I felt very safe talking to her.'

Cooper sighs, but he lifts his head to look at Len. 'Well, it's done now. We'd better wait to see the interview,' he says. 'But these journalists can be very manipulative. I should know.'

'Cooper, I know you've had a terrible time lately, but I think you're getting this out of proportion.'

'Oh yes?' Cooper replies, cocking one eyebrow.

'I know I'm not as clever as you, but I have got things moving, you have to admit.' Len sits down, annoyed that his brilliant coup is not gaining much, if any, gratitude.

Cooper's eyes are red. It's the first time Len has noticed the physical degradation of this poor man.

'I know.' Cooper sighs again. 'I'm sorry. I am grateful. Honestly. I was only saying to Lexie that you've achieved what I failed to.'

Len sits up straighter.

Cooper hasn't finished. 'It's just it's such a fine line between publicising the problem and exacerbating it,' he says.

Len chews the inside of his cheek.

'Or even becoming it.'

'Let's wait and see, shall we?' Len replies. 'She said it would be on the news today and, as I'm sure you said earlier, they could come for me any minute. Tomorrow could be too late. I think we should do more twittering, don't you?'

'Tweeting,' Cooper says, with a rueful smile. 'I don't even know if it's called that anymore. Come on then, let's get on with it, before they haul you off and clap you in irons!'

32.

Marilyn

Marilyn is fast asleep when her phone rings, the safe one that she only uses for things Bruce wouldn't like. Her sleep has been so disturbed recently that she is fully awake in an instant.

'Marilyn. It's Amy. Have you seen the news?'

Marilyn squeezes her eyes tight and then open, trying to release the tired, gritty feeling. 'News? What time is it?'

'5.30 in the morning. Sorry.'

'That's OK.' Marilyn pulls on a sweatshirt over her pyjamas. 'I was struggling a bit last night. Had some wine and went to bed. Stayed away from my phone.'

'When you say struggling?'

'Basically, panicking about getting the blame for the shitshow that is Bruce's project.' Marilyn gets out of bed and rakes her fingers through her hair. It's dried out and frizzy as hell. She leans down to check her appearance in the mirror and wishes she hadn't bothered. 'I couldn't sleep,' she adds, as if this is surprising, 'and then I heard the phone, so I must have dropped off at some stage. I was dreaming that I was a message in a bottle, bobbing on the sea. The tide would go out, and I thought I was safe, that I would escape the people chasing me and wash up on another beach far away. Then, high tide would approach, and I would return to the original piece of sand, with a crowd of people standing there, waiting to capture me.'

'I'm so sorry, Marilyn. This is all Bruce's fault, but you've become caught up in it.'

'Don't be too sorry for me, Amy. I bought into it all initially. I'm complicit, no doubt about it. Anyway, I'm digressing. You said there was news. I'm guessing it isn't good.'

'I'm not really sure,' Amy says, after a short silence. 'Do you remember the old guy who started the X storm?'

A laugh catches in Marilyn's throat. 'How could I forget? Life was almost ticking along normally before that.' Fear grips her. There is no way she's on top of the social media battle, as Bruce commanded. Progress is being made with Ayeesha, but she should at least have something to show Bruce about X to lull him into a false sense of security that she's working to help him. 'What about it?'

'It's gone crazy over the last twenty-four hours. He released a video, you must have seen it?'

'I've had my head down with the IT specialist. We're concentrating on that side of things. Every time I go on social media, I feel physically sick, so I've been avoiding it.'

'I don't think you can afford to do that.'

'I know.' Marilyn leaves the phone outside her ensuite for a minute and tries to wee quietly. When she returns, Amy is babbling, something about an interview. 'Sorry, I missed some of that. Can you rewind to when you told me I shouldn't ignore social media?'

Amy sighs. 'You don't make it easy to get to the point, do you?'

'Sorry.' Marilyn creeps down the stairs with the phone pinned to her ear and fills a glass of water at the kitchen sink, putting the phone down while she glugs the entire contents. 'Carry on.'

'Right, first the video, which really took off. He seems to be interacting more now.'

'OK. So, that's good, I guess, if it puts Bruce under pressure.'

'Yes.' Amy sounds breathless, excited. 'Then, there was an interview on Sky News. I caught it on the app, but it was on the main bulletin too.'

'An interview with the old guy?'

'Yes. It's dynamite. He says, and I quote: "Whoever thought up this *New Directive* is either bad or mad. There is no other explanation."'

'That's bold,' Marilyn says, although it occurs to her that what he says is nothing more than common sense.

Amy lowers her voice. 'Then he names Bruce.'

'Oh.' Now Marilyn understands the early phone call. Bruce has always liked to stay under the radar, to leave other people, like herself, to carry the can if things go wrong. That's why he went into the Civil Service rather than Politics. 'Does he name anyone else?' she asks.

'No, you're safe there, for now. But the Home Secretary is going to be livid.' Amy is quiet for a moment. Marilyn's mind races. How much difference will this make? Is the situation spinning out of control too fast for her plans with Ayeesha to come to fruition?

'Bruce is going to go ape,' Marilyn says, as if he hasn't already.

'That's what I'm coming to,' Amy says. 'Bruce didn't come home last night. I know he's been erratic recently and has lied his guts out, but he always gives me advance notice if he isn't going to be there. I wondered if you'd seen him?'

'No. Ayeesha did, very recently.' But was that yesterday, or the day before, or the day before that? The days are merging into a continuous nightmare. 'No, I haven't seen him. He'll be around somewhere, though.'

'His car's gone, and some of his clothes. He's even taken a toothbrush and shaving things.'

Marilyn stares out of the kitchen window. A pigeon is sitting on the windowsill, pecking at the glass and fixing her with its beady eye.

Where can Bruce have gone?

'The thing is, Marilyn, if he's disappeared, it probably means that he's got some extra grenade he plans to throw into the dugout, or he's departing the scene to leave you to take the blame.

The pigeon craps on the windowsill and flies away.

33.

Cooper

Cooper is over at Len's house again, feeling guilty that he is spending so much time here when he should be with Lexie. She insisted, saying there's no time to waste.

Ironic, really, when their time is being stolen all the time.

Cooper no longer looks at his Life Counter. It's too depressing. Last time he checked, he only had five years left, and the worry about getting the four-minute warning to find a safe place when he has a wife and child to protect is chilling. Easier to ignore it. Constant buzzes on his palm indicate that everything he is doing is having a negative effect on his life length and acceptability profile, but why would he want to know that what he is doing now is damaging his status? If he doesn't do what he can, there will be no future for anyone.

Lexie is onside. Despite doing nothing wrong herself, she's accumulating guilt by association with, they both assume, frequent hits to the length of her life. She isn't checking any more either.

So, here he is, more or less camping out in Len's house, happy when Len is asleep, less so when the old man is looking over his shoulder. Fortunately, Len is conked out in the chair right now, snoring heartily. There's a limit to how much damage he can do when he's unconscious.

Cooper has watched Len's interview several times now. He can't believe that Len has voiced the name of Cooper's father to millions, bringing the shadowy string-puller into the light of day, exposing his misdeeds.

His feelings are complicated. The journalist in him is breathless at what Len, unschooled in the ways of the media, has achieved. Surely, this can't be beginner's luck? Not knowing the accepted way of dealing with something like this, Len has jumped straight in, feet first, and blazed a trail across mainstream and social media.

Cooper tries to reassure himself that he could have achieved more if his own father hadn't been tracking him and blocking his path.

As a neighbour and friend, Cooper fears what the consequences of his bravery will be for Len. He hasn't just put his head over the parapet; he's put a rifle in Bruce's hands. Len looks peaceful sleeping in his armchair, his backside slipping so low that the cushion is teetering on the edge of the frame, and the old man is nearly horizontal. He can't have any idea of the danger he has put himself in by naming Bruce in his interview. The hairs on Cooper's arms rise and shiver.

Surprisingly, the last vestiges of filial love make him worry for his father, too. What a situation he is in. And what about his mum? Will she suffer for her close association with Bruce?

Cooper must act. Amy's number is busy, which is infuriating. She's been keeping him in the loop about her work with Marilyn and the IT consultant. He wants to know what progress they've made. At least Cooper managed to set that up.

More importantly, he wants to talk through his latest idea. Len won't understand, and Lexie will be distrustful of the potential fallout. Amy is the one he wants to talk to.

He tries again. Still busy.

Cooper stands and begins pacing. He'll wait till her line is free and talk to her about it. He doesn't want to be precipitate and make things worse. He stands at the front window and looks out into the street. Stretching, he puts his hands high above his head, until his T-shirt rides up, exposing a small amount of untanned, hairy flesh. He watches as a police car crawls down the road. What are they looking for? After two passes through the area, the car disappears.

Cooper tries Amy's number one more time. Still busy. Who the hell is she talking to? He feels jittery now. There's no time to waste. Instinct tells him his idea is sound.

His fingers hover over the keys for a moment before he opens another tab and loads Instagram. Fortunately, Len is already set up on the platform, courtesy of his friend at the coffee shop, but most of Cooper's effort has gone into X so far. That's about to change.

Using Len's profile, or coffeeshopwarrior as he is known, Cooper loads the video of Len's interview with Anna at Sky as a reel. He hesitates at the search bar. First, he types "influencers", chews his lip for a while and refines that to "pregnant influencers" and finally settles on "pregnant influencers UK". It's hard not to laugh when his screen fills with a gallery of bumps of various sizes, sported by women with impressive hair and make-up but very few clothes. Perfect! There are so many of them. Gathering their Instagram names, he adds a large handful of them to the post. After some reflection, he types, "Don't let your baby's life be compromised. The New Directive is stealing years from innocent newborns. Like and share." He adds a few hashtags and posts it.

It's done, for good or bad. No sense in going for half measures. Cooper checks how many followers Len has: 55,000. That's not enough. Cooper loads Len's original video and shares it again, naming many more of the influencers. He does this again and again, varying his post a little each time, until he is happy that he has saturated this rather specific market. With the final few posts, he asks readers to consider what they or their partner might have done to upset the authorities and shorten their future baby's life.

Enough.

Cooper sits back and rolls his stiff shoulders. Strange clicks and crunches emanate from his upper back.

Part of him wants to delete his Instagram posts immediately. Has he gone too far? He takes another look and realises it's too late to retreat. Likes and messages are coming constantly. Len's number of followers is rising geometrically.

He needs something to distract him.

Right on cue, his phone rings and Amy's name comes up.

'Mum. I've been trying to get through to you. I wanted to talk to you about something, but I've gone and done it anyway.'

There is silence on the line.

'Mum, that is you, isn't it?' What if Bruce has her phone?

'Yes, it's me,' she says. Her voice is wavering.

'Is everything OK?'

'What do you think?' He can hear her blowing out breath noisily. 'Your father's gone missing. I think he's done a bunk.'

'Oh shit,' Cooper says, as he feels his body slump.

Len shifts in his seat and opens one eye cautiously.

34.

Marilyn

Checking what is trending on X, Marilyn is unsurprised but alarmed to see #newdirective #BruceBox #notinourname and #HandmaidsTaleUK at the top of the list. It is not until she scrolls down repeatedly that she comes to #climateemergency, a subject that has been dominating the headlines.

A snag of skin on the edge of her fingernail gains her attention, and Marilyn nibbles at it like a not very hungry hamster. She feels the familiar acceleration in her heartbeat as anxiety builds about what Bruce will have to say. She sits back. Bruce isn't here. He has abandoned his home and taken his possessions with him. This much she knows from Amy. Perhaps he really has gone for good. In which case, she no longer needs to worry.

It's a wonderful idea.

Certainly, there's no point in chasing the X angle or social media generally.

A great weight seems to lift from her broken shoulders.

Bruce is the Programme. Without him, it will fail; she will be saved.

Or will she? This is so unlike Bruce that she feels sure he has something else up his sleeve.

Marilyn calls Amy, not bothering to absent herself from her office. She does, however, use her secret phone.

'Yes?' Amy is breathless when she answers.

'Have you seen him?'

'No, still no sign. I keep hoping he's gone for good.'

'Me too.' Marilyn risks a brief laugh. 'Only, I'm scared about booby traps. I can't believe he's disappeared off the face of the earth.'

Amy is quiet for a moment; Marilyn hears the faint sound of a car revving in the distance. 'Me neither. It's a great fantasy, though.'

'Where do you think he's gone?' Marilyn asks, not expecting a sensible answer.

Amy makes a low humming sound in her throat, almost as if she is meditating. Odd metallic clinks and clatters disturb the line. 'What are you doing?' Marilyn asks.

'Sorry,' Amy says. 'I was putting things away in the kitchen while I was thinking. This is so unlike Bruce that I'm floored. I couldn't even hazard a guess about where he might be. Could it be that dive where he took Cooper and imprisoned him? Or maybe he's gone abroad. I can't find his passport, but to be fair, I haven't seen that for ages. He's very secretive with things like that.'

'So we don't have a clue, basically.'

'No, I guess not.' There is a pause on the line. 'Hang on, Marilyn. Something's breaking on the news. Let me turn the volume up a minute.'

While she's waiting, Marilyn brings up the news on her laptop. The forbidding face of the Home Secretary fills the screen. She is making a statement to journalists outside the Home Office.

'There's something about Bruce,' Amy shouts over the phone.

'I know. I'll try and catch it this end. Speak to you later.' She kills the call.

She's missed the statement itself, which must have been brief, but the Secretary of State is submitting herself to journalists' questions.

'What effect will this have on the future of the Life Counter Programme, Home Secretary?' Marilyn recognises the woman from Sky News.

'As I have said,' the politician replies, her weariness evident from her slow, deliberate delivery, 'The Life Counter Programme is an important part of the Government's mission. However, a review will now take place to address certain –' she hesitates to find the right word '– inconsistencies that have been alleged in recent days on social media and elsewhere.'

The camera pans to the journalist, who nods in thanks.

'Where is Bruce Box? Will he be held to account?' The Home

Secretary looks around, apparently trying to identify the questioner. Her eyes settle with disapproval on a dishevelled writer from the Guardian. 'Bruce Box is on sick leave. It is my understanding that he has been admitted to hospital. I have no further details for you at this time.'

'Home Secretary?'

'I'm sorry, that is all for now. I will answer further questions in due course.' She packs up her prepared statement and marches off.

The camera returns to the news anchor, who has her head to one side, a finger pressed to her earpiece. 'Well, a developing story there. The Life Counter Programme is under review, and its chief architect is missing and presumed sick. This must be a great embarrassment for the Home Secretary. I'm going to turn now to the Shadow Home Secretary. Thank you for joining us today, Alec. What do you make of all this?'

Marilyn minimises the window. She's seen enough. What is happening is impossibly good, but potentially, impossibly bad. What does 'under review' mean? If they do genuinely review what has been done, who will get the blame, Bruce or her?

How far has Ayeesha got, and will it be enough?

Marilyn sits back in the chair and eases her shoes off. Her toes are throbbing. Bruce is the one who has been named in the media, so he is the one who should bear the responsibility.

She might be in the clear.

But that all depends on where Bruce is and how effectively he can be silenced.

Marilyn forces her shoes back on and stuffs her phone into her bag. It's time to check on progress with Ayeesha. The building is an enormous maze, but within ten minutes, she is in Ayeesha's office.

Her hair is tied into a high ponytail, and she barely looks up when Marilyn enters.

'Hi Marilyn, I'll be with you in a minute.'

'How did you know it was me?'

Ayeesha looks at her now. Dark circles mar her warm complexion. 'No one else comes in here.'

'Right. I brought coffee.'

'Thank you. I could do with that, for sure.'

'You've been overworking, haven't you?'

'Probably,' Ayeesha says. 'I get engrossed. Anyway, given how crazy Bruce is getting, I thought I'd better get on with it.'

'So you haven't heard the news, then?'

Ayeesha looks up, picks up the cup and takes a long drink. 'News?'

'Bruce has done a bunk.'

Ayeesha's eyes widen.

'The Home Secretary has announced a review of the Programme.'

'Fuck me! Sorry,' she says, squirming in her chair. 'That just came out.'

Marilyn smiles. It's nice to see this beautiful woman behaving in a less-than-perfect way.

'So where does this leave us, and what are we doing?' Ayeesha twiddles a loose lock of hair, making herself look, for a moment, like a teenage schoolgirl.

'We need to get it done, and live, and quickly as possible, so the bad stuff all has Bruce's fingerprints on, not ours.'

'Yours, you mean.'

Marilyn swallows. 'So where are we on that?'

'Pretty much done, believe it or not. I might not have slept recently, but I've been working hard.'

'That's brilliant.' Marilyn gets up and throws her cup in the bin. 'Make the changes live as soon as they're done. I'd better get back to my office and check everything's in order there. Keep me in the loop, will you?'

'Of course.' Ayeesha gives Marilyn a long, slow look. 'Where do you think he is?'

'According to the party line, he's on sick leave, in hospital.'

'Do you believe that?'

'Not for a minute. He's cleared his clothes out of his home. Why would he do that to go into hospital?'

Ayeesha nods.

Despite the uncertainty they're under, Marilyn feels a distinct lightening of her spirits as she makes her way back to her own office. The work environment without Bruce in it is a huge improvement. She hums lightly as she returns to her own room, then walks softly to Bruce's office to look for clues. She can't resist sitting in his chair and having a brief swivel, noticing the marks on the carpet where he has done the same. The air is still redolent of the Bruce of the last few days, stale and despairing. She tries a few drawers in his desk, but they are all empty or locked. It is clear of anything, even a laptop.

Marilyn stands, walks to the door and has almost reached the handle when she hears a commotion in the corridor. The door opens towards her. In front of her are two police officers in stab-proof vests, accompanied by her anxious assistant.

'This is her?' asks the older policeman, his stomach straining against his stab vest.

Marilyn's assistant nods while mouthing 'Sorry' at her boss.

'Marilyn Newman, you are under arrest and charged with wilful corruption of the Life Counter Programme. Anything you say…'

'Hang on a minute. What are you doing, arresting *me*? This is the responsibility of my superior, Bruce Box, as I'm sure you well know.'

The police officer brandishes a thick A4 envelope. Marilyn spots the address of Scotland Yard in Bruce's handwriting. Trust Bruce to corrupt the technology but to be unable to use it himself, resorting to the most old-fashioned approach.

'We have in our possession a comprehensive set of evidence that the corruptions to the Programme were actually instigated by you.' He continues to read Marilyn her rights while brandishing a set of handcuffs.

'There's no need for that,' Marilyn says. 'I won't resist arrest, being confident of my innocence. Do you really believe these accusations, made by a man who has disappeared on sick leave, apparently going into hospital? I don't believe that story for a minute, and I don't suppose you do either. My understanding is that he has run away.'

The policeman ushers her through the door. 'You can explain all that to us in your statement,' he says, 'but I must insist that you come with us.'

As they leave, Marilyn's phone buzzes, and she manages to catch a glimpse of the message.

'We're live. Going for a sleep now. Ayeesha x'

35.

Lexie

Cooper's voice is indistinct, but the familiar cadences travel through the ceiling to where Lexie sits on the rug upstairs, changing Tash's nappy. Exciting new baby stages seem to happen every day now. Tash's little limbs flail as Lexie wields the wet wipe to repair the ravages of a particularly evil nappy. The baby's eyes are sparkling; her gurgles suggest incipient speech; a wicked grin is spread across a face that is shaking from side to side. Lexie smiles back, whispering words of love and tickling her daughter's tummy. She is becoming a little person now, and when she grins like this, she looks just like her father.

But what a world she has been born into.

Tash's Life Counter is flashing and bleeping as if in time with her movements. An ominous sound emerges from her rear end and Lexie gets a clean nappy under her just in time before another poo emerges.

Tash giggles again, and it's impossible to feel annoyed when she's so happy. Lexie feels a connection she has struggled to establish so far. She blows a raspberry on Tash's tummy and continues to clean her up.

How can Tash be so wonderful when the world is such a terrible place?

The Life Counter flashes again. Lexie is afraid to look. In fact, she and Cooper have had a pact over the last couple of weeks that they will not check their own or their baby's device. It's the only way to remain sane.

And yet she wants to know.

Lexie can no longer hear Cooper's voice. Tash tips her head as if she, too, were trying to catch the familiar tones. Before Lexie has too much time to think about it, she hears the thundering sound of her husband taking the stairs at least two at a time.

'Lexie?' He bursts into the room.

'Was that your mum?' Lexie asks, looking up as he looms in the doorway.

'Yes.' She doesn't like the way his eyes are huge like fried eggs, and the lower half of his face frozen.

'Any developments?'

'Yes.' Cooper kneels beside her and brings his face near Tash's. 'Hello gorgeous,' he says, staring into his daughter's eyes and grabbing a waving arm and kissing it.

Lexie tries not to feel jealous.

Cooper holds one of his daughter's hands in each of his, turning to face Lexie. 'No sign of Bruce still, but Amy has heard through the grapevine that Marilyn was arrested yesterday.'

'Oh no.' Lexie sits back on her heels and puts a hand over her mouth. She feels the moisture in her exhalation. 'That's the end if she's gone. She was the only one who was on our side.'

'Yes,' he says, his tongue ticking against his teeth. 'Recently, anyway.'

There's something he's not saying.

Lexie waits.

'Although she did have someone helping her.' Cooper grabs Tash, fastens a new nappy and picks her up, pulling himself to a standing position. He twirls a few times with his daughter in his arms. The shock has gone from his face. He looks surprisingly happy, given the circumstances. Tash has that effect on him.

'Bring her here,' Lexie says. 'I need to redress her.'

Cooper gently places her back on the mat. Lexie sits forward but slumps over her knees. 'What's the point?' she says. 'It's going from bad to worse. She'll have no life at all soon. Marilyn was our last hope. If she gets the blame and Bruce is still around, who knows what will happen?'

An arm slips round her shoulders, and Lexie leans into it. 'Sorry,' she says. 'It just gets to me sometimes.'

'I know,' Cooper replies. 'Me too, but we mustn't give up. This might not be bad news.'

'Really? Why?'

'I don't know. We know my dad is to blame, and maybe that will become clear if they have an investigation, as they said on the news. The fact that they're reviewing it shows they know there's an issue. If the media clamour continues, and I'm doing everything I can to make that happen, who knows what the outcome might be?'

'I'd love to believe you're right,' Lexie says, pushing a strand of hair away from her face. 'By the way, Tash's Life Counter has been going crazy. I've been afraid to look at it.'

Cooper frowns. He fiddles with Tash's toes for so long that Lexie wonders if he's heard. She clears her throat, ready to repeat her words, but notices that he's flexing his hand, using it to pick up Tash's plump arm. As he does so, the device flashes through the skin on her palm. He examines it with great concentration. He taps the baby's flesh a couple of times.

'What's the damage, Cooper? Is it a lot worse?'

He doesn't answer for some time, instead blowing air through his teeth, a habit that has always irritated Lexie.

'Well?'

Cooper bites the inside of his cheek, creating a noticeable indentation in the skin. 'I don't understand this,' he says, scratching his head. 'Her Life Counter's gone back up to 100.'

'What?' Lexie's heart is pounding. 'Let me see.' She snatches Tash's wrist, bringing a laser look from her daughter. Cooper's silence is unsettling. 'You're right,' she says, as soon as she examines the baby's palm. 'What's going on?'

Cooper blinks hard. 'Could it be that it's gone into reverse, that Marilyn's plans are working?' He is breathless, his voice cracked.

'Quick, check yours,' she says, grabbing his wrist.

'It has been going off a lot,' he says, 'but mine always does. I've been ignoring it.'

'Don't ignore it now. Look, please. We've got to know.'

'I've got to tell you, Lexie. Mine has been going down regularly over the last few weeks. I didn't want to worry you even more. That's why I said we shouldn't look.' Cooper gently touches Tash's hand again.

'Now's the time to check,' Lexie says. 'However bad it is. We need to know.'

Cooper takes his time, looking aimlessly at his palm for several seconds before tapping it. Even then, he doesn't speak, merely blinks rapidly.

Lexie pushes his arm. 'Tell me, now.'

Cooper clears his throat. 'Mine's gone back too. My numbers have gone back up to ninety.' He continues to stare at the illuminated patch of skin, then finally looks at Lexie. He's still blinking. 'This can only mean one thing, that Marilyn managed to get something through before she was arrested. I can't believe it.'

'How can we be sure?'

Cooper pulls out his phone from his jeans pocket. 'Let's see if there's anything online.'

Lexie almost forgets to breathe as he swipes and stabs at his phone, muttering and tutting as he stares at it with narrowed eyes.

'So?' she says, when she realises that he is off in his own little dream world.

Cooper shakes his head, less in a negative way, more as if he's trying to clear the fuzziness of his brain. 'Loads of people are posting. Their babies' lives have lengthened, their own have lengthened. Others are complaining that nothing has changed for them yet. It seems as if it's a work in progress.'

'That makes sense, doesn't it?' Lexie asks. 'I'm guessing that if they've put a patch in, it's got to interrogate the entire database, and that will take time.'

Cooper looks at her, eyebrows raised. 'Ooh,' he says, in a high-pitched voice. 'Get you. I didn't think you knew much about how these things work.'

Lexie laughs. 'I don't. It just sounded like the way it might go.'

'I can't be sure, because I don't know how the system has been built, but something's certainly changed, and it's going in the right direction.' He sweeps Lexie up in his arms with Tash between them.

This is how parenthood is meant to be.

36.

Len

Len is having a quiet snooze when Cooper flies through his front door. It takes a minute or two for him to come to; it's hard to make sense of what his friend is babbling.

'It's worked, Len. We've done it.'

'Worked? What?' Len shifts his frame in the chair. He's been sitting awkwardly, and one leg has gone to sleep. He tries to get up; the leg stubbornly refuses to move.

Cooper runs over to the laptop on the dining table and furiously taps the keyboard. 'Look,' he says, gesticulating at the screen. 'It's started.'

Len rubs sleep from his eyes and manages to get himself upright. He moves towards the table, trying not to put too much weight on his bad leg.

X is open on the screen. #LifeCounter is trending, along with #gettingmylifeback and other hashtags in a similar vein.

Len blinks. Does this prove anything at all?

'You're going to have to tell me more, Cooper. I don't understand what's changed so suddenly. Is this something to do with that father of yours going off sick and the other woman being arrested? I saw it on the news last night.'

Cooper is hopping around as if the floor is too hot to stand on. Len has never seen him look this excited. 'It's definitely helped that my father is out of action,' Cooper says, 'although there's more to it than that.' Cooper sweeps a hand down his face, pinching his cheeks, and finishes off by tweaking his own nose. 'There are some things I haven't told you.'

Len dips his chin and gives Cooper a hard look. 'You've been keeping me out of things,' he says, and his stomach does a little dip. It's not nice to be kept in the dark. 'I thought you trusted me. You've got to admit what I've done has got results.'

Cooper has the grace to look a little embarrassed, or so it seems to Len. 'You've done brilliantly, Len. But the last few days there have been some secret things going on, in Bruce's office, and it was essential that nothing got out about it.' Cooper's pushing the hair on the back of his head up, stretching it against the way it naturally lies. Yes, he's being shifty all right.

'Can you tell me now, then?' He does his best to look disapproving, but the grumpy expression militates against his personality.

'Umm.' Cooper hesitates. 'Yes, I think I can. We've been working with "that woman" as you call her, and a tech expert, to make changes to the software. It had been corrupted by Bruce for his own ends, and they were trying to restore it. Bruce's final act, from his hiding place, wherever that is, was to send the Police a dossier about Marilyn, and that's what got her arrested. But she was trying to put things right. I'm hoping Bruce doesn't know what she's been up to. I think he's just trying to shift the blame.'

Len's brain is whirring. He doesn't feel he has the full picture. 'If Marilyn's been arrested, and is getting the blame for the Programme, what's trending now?' He's pleased that he manages to use the right jargon. How he's grown in the last few weeks.

'Of course, you haven't seen any of the posts.' Cooper pulls up several, all giving a similar story, that their Life Counters have begun to restore years to their lives, and even more about babies that have had injustice reversed. 'See?' he says, settling down now that he has something functional to do with his limbs.

'I still don't understand.'

'I'm very surprised myself. Ay —the tech expert, must have managed to put the changes through before Marilyn was arrested. It's great news, but how sustainable is it?'

'And what's going to happen to Marilyn? It sounds to me as if she's the heroine here.'

Cooper rocks back on his heels. 'Not initially. She seems to have bought into his way of looking at things and was his willing slave for years. But even she realised he was becoming deranged and through my mum, we've managed to turn her round.'

Len nods. 'That's good.'

'Yes, although Bruce helped us, inadvertently. She was beginning to want to stop helping him, but when she said so, he blackmailed her. That's when her attitude really shifted.'

Len stumbles back to his chair and flops down. This leg is still troubling him. 'And now she's getting the blame.'

'Yes, and the improvements she's made could all be reversed.' Cooper slumps onto the chair in front of the computer. Seeing him lose his enthusiasm gives Len a burst of energy. He rubs his hands along the arms of his chair before pushing himself to a standing position. Moving closer to Cooper, he puts a hand on his shoulder. 'I know,' he says. 'We need to do more of the same. Perhaps we can save her.'

Cooper looks up. 'You're right. But what can we do?'

'Another interview?' Len quite likes this celebrity lark now that he's getting used to it.

Cooper starts pacing. 'We need something new. Let me think for a minute.' He's moving fast around the room, stubs his toe on the table leg and settles for cracking his knuckles. 'I know. It's obvious, isn't it?'

'It is?'

'Yes. The power of social media. Let's start a #FreeMarilyn campaign. That will play well.'

'You're right. You're a genius. Why didn't I think of that?'

Cooper stares at him, and Len wonders if he's done something wrong, until he realises that Cooper is thinking his idea through. After a few more seconds, he starts moving around the room again, all the desolation leaving him as suddenly as it arrived.

'Well,' Len says, waggling his head from side to side, 'we all know how good I am at this social media campaigning. What do we do?'

'So you are. Let's get started.' Cooper pulls up a chair and settles Len down in front of the screen, before sitting beside him. He clicks the add button on Len's profile. 'What shall we say?'

'You know the details. You'd better do it.' Len feels that familiar fear, that he is on the edge of a cliff and is afraid of slipping.

Cooper sits in front of the screen, humming quietly to himself and rubbing the flesh of his forefinger backwards and forwards across his lips. He squares his shoulders and allows his fingers to hover above the keyboard.

Come on, Len thinks. It's not like Cooper to hesitate. He gives Cooper's elbow a nudge. 'You're best when you're sure of yourself, Cooper. Best get on with it.'

Cooper nods and allows his fingers to begin. *Our campaign is working*, he writes. *My friend's daughter's years have been restored. It's not over yet. Bruce Box has escaped, and Marilyn Newman has been arrested. She is innocent. Spread the word.* #FreeMarilyn #LifeCounter #PeoplePower #FightInjustice

'What do you think?' he asks Len.

'Good.' Len says. What does he know?

'It's going out in your name. You need to be happy.'

Len nods. 'Let's go for it.'

Cooper hits 'post' and sits back to wait. 'This will spread quickly, I'm willing to bet.'

He is right. Len watches in awe as the like counter increments steadily, and most of these people are also retweeting. It's frightening, really, he thinks, that something that has been said in his name spreads so fast, even though he has had no say in the content, and the people reading it may have little understanding of the issues involved. Social media is a tinderbox with limited responsibility. He's lucky to have lived most of his life without its dangerous interference. He hears Sylvia's ghostly voice in his head, telling him that he's loving every minute of it and it's brought him a new lease of life, not to mention a lovely circle of people who care about him and look out for him.

Not all bad then.

'What else should we do?' he asks.

Cooper springs to life. 'I'll copy this onto the other platforms and see what happens,' he says, typing furiously.

'Do you think you'll be able to go online yourself soon?' Len asks. It is beginning to feel as if Cooper is invading his sense of self, and there is something rather disconcerting about that.

'That's an interesting thought,' Cooper says, his eyes fixed on the screen. 'Probably not.' He looks at Len, and a gentle smile lightens his features. 'It's refreshing writing as someone else. Makes me feel quite free.'

'While I,' Len says, 'feel as if my strings are being pulled. I would be pleased if you could investigate recovering your own accounts.'

Cooper nods. 'Will do. In the meantime, think about the profile you've gained. When this is all over, you can use your newfound fame for whatever you like.'

Len thinks this over for quite some time after Cooper has gone back to his own house and family; while he mulls over possibilities for the future, the like counter clicks inexorably upwards.

37.

Cooper

Tash is asleep in Cooper's arms. She has been fractious this morning, and her rosy cheeks and constant dribbling suggest that teething is the issue. Now she has finally settled, he's reluctant to put her to bed and risk her waking. Besides, the weight of her is comforting, her softness against his body, the warmth of her steady breath.

The knowledge that she has her life back.

What is still niggling furiously at the edges of Cooper's brain is the confusion about what's really happening with the Programme. His #FreeMarilyn campaign is gaining traction, but the Government is being worryingly tight-lipped about the outcome. The last time he looked, Marilyn was still in custody, and no statement had been made about the developing situation.

Cooper has no confidence that the future is secure. While the Life Counter Programme is operating, what has been regained could easily be snatched away again.

More to the point, where is Bruce, and what is he up to?

Still holding Tash tight in his arms, Cooper edges a hand down to the arm of the sofa from where he manages to grab the remote control and switch the TV on. BBC news fires up, the presenter attempting a half grin as she articulates some time-filling human interest story while the minutes creep up to the hourly news bulletin. The biting surfaces of Cooper's teeth grind together as he consciously tries to keep his arms, holding Tash, relaxed, lest she might sense the tension and begin to cry. He needs news, and yet he fears it. What good has news done him recently?

The weather presenter is on, visibly pregnant as she narrates a familiar story of wind, rain and unseasonal temperatures. Has her mind been set at ease by the campaign to rescue the life chances of babies, or has she been sailing along confident that her baby will not be affected? From the expression on her face, the viewer would think that no concerns ever troubled her thoughts, as she manages a gentle smile even when describing pestilence to come.

Through the open window, Cooper catches the sound of rubber on tarmac. Looking up, he sees his mother's car. After trying to pull into a tiny space, Amy seems to give up and double-parks. She emerges in a hurry and runs up to the door. Stupidly, he doesn't rush to open it, and the insistent din of the bell being pushed repeatedly makes Tash stir and begin to squirm in his arms. Amy is not one to rush like this.

Unless.

Cooper's feet stick as if held by powerful magnets to the floor. A cold coil of fear fills his insides. His mind slips out of his body and observes his frozen form from somewhere near the ceiling. He hears but doesn't react to the fast light footsteps of his wife as she hurries down the stairs to let Amy in. While Tash wriggles furiously and begins to cry in earnest, he hears a whispered conversation. Amy runs into the room, glances at him, snatches the remote from his hand and switches the TV off just before the news bulletin begins.

A suggestion of lavender hand cream as Lexie gently lifts their daughter from his arms. He senses the softness in her gaze but feels unable to meet her eyes. Amy rushes towards him, wrapping her arms around his back. He automatically hugs her, too. Unable to avoid looking at her, he notes that her face is blotchy, her eyes bloodshot and red-rimmed.

Cooper regains his senses. He knew this would happen. 'He's dead, isn't he?'

Damp seeps through his T-shirt onto his skin as Amy rests her face against his chest. 'The police came this morning,' she says, her voice muffled by the fabric against her lips.

Cooper gently pushes her body away from his. 'We'd better sit down, Mum.' He hands her a tissue from the box beside the sofa. Amy sits, dabbing at her watery eyes and rubbing her nose.

'I don't even know why I'm upset. I've hated the bastard for years.' She attempts a laugh; it turns to a gurgle in her throat.

Cooper sits beside her, putting an arm around her shoulders. He feels fully present again. His hand, resting on her arm, is shaking. If she shouldn't be upset, he ought to be jubilant, after all that has happened between him and his father.

Shock is a strange thing, hitting you with a physical punch when your brain is least expecting it.

'Tell me what they said,' he says. 'Take your time.'

Amy closes her eyes, taking several slow, even breaths, an open palm placed firmly against the top of her ribcage.

Cooper waits. Lexie is in a chair in the corner of the room, feeding Tash. He would know this without looking because Tash has recently started making strange gulping noises as she sucks. There's something very reassuring about this everyday sound.

'There were two of them who came to the door, a man and a woman. I knew it was bad news straight away from the sympathetic looks on their faces. They asked if I had anyone they could call. I thought of you straight away, but it didn't seem fair, and I couldn't wait. I needed to know what they had to say at once.'

Cooper feels much the same about needing to know immediately, but knows he shouldn't say so. The story will come out when she's ready.

His patience pays off. Amy looks directly at him. Already, her eyes are a little clearer, and the blotchiness of her skin is subsiding. 'They found his car, parked on a building site in West London. It had been torched.'

Cooper is ashamed of the disappointment he feels. 'That doesn't prove anything,' he says.

'Cooper,' she says, taking his hand in hers. 'There was a body inside.'

'Oh.' The hairs on the back of his neck stand to attention.

Amy releases his hand, rubbing both palms down her thighs. She swallows. 'There wasn't much left of the car. It must have been quite a fire, but they managed to get ownership from the chassis number, which was still readable.'

'And the body?'

'Burnt beyond recognition. Even dental records will be no help.'

'It might not be him, then.'

'It's him, Cooper,' she says, stroking his arm. 'You know your dad. It's the sort of thing he'd do, faced with this situation. He wouldn't want to have to argue his case. Also, he sent a message to the Home Secretary before it happened.'

Cooper feels Lexie on his other side, the baby in one arm, while she hugs him with the other. She hasn't had time to adjust her clothing. A couple of drips of milk land on his arm. He looks at them, thinking nothing, absolutely nothing.

Maybe something. Hate. Loss. Loneliness. Relief. Now the thoughts crush in. Why has Bruce done this, disappeared into the night without facing the consequences? Who and what has he left in limbo? How can his machinations be disentangled?

What a mess.

Tash is gurgling, bubbles of milk on her lips. Lexie squeezes Cooper tight, her breathing calm and controlled. Amy, too, seems to have moved beyond her own sense of shock.

Cooper pulls away from them both, standing up as he does so.

It's over.

They are free of the megalomaniac who tried to destroy them.

Cooper is now the only man in the family.

It is a lonely thought.

He feels tears at the back of his eyes. The emotion is not for his father, but for the relationship they didn't have. 'It's better this way,' he says, noting with dispassion the slight tremor in his voice. 'I suppose he feels he has taken an honourable step, but it's the coward's way out really. He's left the mess for others to fix, but at least he can't hurt us anymore.'

Cooper still feels blank, unable to access any genuine emotion. Both his wife and mother are staring at him, as if wanting him to show something that either isn't there or is so deeply buried that it won't come out until later, much later. He wipes his eyes with the back of his hand. The beginnings of tears haven't really developed but he needs to show them something.

'I feel flat, more than anything,' he says, walking over to the window and watching a small bird disappearing into a hole in the fascia board of the house opposite.

'Do you think there'll be anything on the news?' Lexie asks. 'It might give us a little context.'

What a very strange way of putting it.

'Let's see.' He looks around for the remote. It's on the floor where Amy must have chucked it after her intervention. Cooper picks it up and turns on the TV. He's amazed to see that it's almost time for the next hourly bulletin. Can it really be an hour since their world changed?

The red breaking news banner states the bald facts – Body found in burnt-out car in West London. Seeing the words has a chilling effect.

It makes it real.

The presenter comes on screen, her expression severe. 'A body has been found in the search for missing senior civil servant, Bruce Box. It had previously been reported by Government sources that he was in hospital. The human remains were found in Mr Box's burnt-out car. A time embargoed press release from Mr Box was received by the Home Secretary this morning. It stated his intentions and took full responsibility for the failings in the controversial Life Counter Programme. His family has been informed.' The newsreader pauses. 'In related news, Marilyn Newman, Mr Box's deputy at the Home Office, has been released from police custody. A spokesperson for the Metropolitan Police has said it is expected that all charges against her will be dropped in the light of Mr Box's statement and untimely death. A further statement about the future of the Life Counter Programme is expected in due course.'

Cooper breathes out slowly. No mention has been made of the #FreeMarilyn campaign, but it's clearly played its part. Cooper's mind is spinning as he tries to think through, in logical steps, the implications of this news.

Marilyn is to be released, pending further investigations.

The theft of babies' years is being reversed, as evidenced by all the posts on social media so Marilyn's tech expert must have succeeded in what she was trying to do, but will this get Marilyn in trouble when the investigation looks at the Programme? It's all down to whether they genuinely investigate everything that happened or merely throw the whole project into a huge hole and hope the bad smell goes away when the next crisis arrives.

It's lucky for the Government that it's a long time till the next General Election.

As if on cue, the voice of the Leader of the Opposition breaks into Cooper's thoughts.

Lexie turns the volume up.

'Frankly, I'm astonished by the daily revelations about this iniquitous Programme. We always knew that the Government was incompetent, but the extent of the information that has come out about the social engineering involved is quite appalling. They are either mad or bad, and probably both. The Public is disgusted by the lot of them. They should stand down and call a General Election.'

'May I ask what your party would do with the Life Counter Programme if you won an election?'

Cooper gives the politician his attention. The Leader of the Opposition is sweating under the studio lights. Her usually hairdresser-fresh, shiny hair has lost some of its curl. 'We would cancel it, of course. The whole thing is a can of worms.' She stops speaking abruptly and appears to be listening to her earpiece. 'Of course,' she continues, 'it's important not to rush to judgement. There must be a cross-party consultation to consider the future of the Programme.'

'I see.' The presenter sucks her lip. 'I seem to remember there was a degree of cross-party support when the Programme came into being.'

Juliet Knight opens her eyes extremely wide, as if the news anchor has pulled her mic off and started shouting abuse at her.

'That, Rachel, was before my time as leader, as you well know. I did express doubts in the early stages, which is on record. Anyway, the Programme as originally envisaged appeared to be a sensible way to support people into a healthy old age in these times of increased longevity. How could we possibly have known that a madman would take it into his own hands and pervert it according to his peculiar and evil way of looking at things?'

'How indeed. Thank you, Juliet Knight, for being with us today. I'm sure we will have much more to divulge as further information becomes available, in particular details of those individuals who benefited from Mr Box's corruption.' She gives a crooked smile. 'And now onto other news.'

Cooper flicks the TV off.

'What interesting times we live in,' he says, picking Tash out of Lexie's arms and swinging her from side to side. 'It looks like you've got your years back, little one, and that's all I care about.'

'Gently,' Lexie says, putting a hand against his arm. 'Remember, she's just had a feed. We don't want it all coming up again, do we?'

'Practical as ever, my darling,' Cooper says. 'Group hug to celebrate?' He puts his spare arm around his mother and directs his gaze at Lexie, who hugs them both, with Tash enclosed happily between the three of them.

Lexie is the first to detach. 'We'd better tell Len. He'll be thrilled.'

'You're right. I bet he knows already. He's a news fiend these days. He's probably conducting an interview as we speak.' The words could seem harsh, he realises and hopes his happy smile softens them. Before any of them has a chance to move, the doorbell rings, followed by a persistent knocking.

'That will be him!'

38.

Cooper

Three weeks later

It is a balmy day, gentle sun bathing their skin as they walk in the park with Tash in her buggy. In the last three weeks, they have made love six times, which is a big improvement on the previous weeks and months since Tash was born. The huge weight that has been pressing on Cooper's head and shoulders is slowly lifting.

Having a small baby still presents considerable challenges, but Cooper no longer feels that everything is his fault or that Lexie believes he is to blame. The joint project to fight the Life Counter Programme has been successful, although the future is still in doubt. The Government has announced an inquiry, and in the meantime, all data analysis and updates have been frozen. Marilyn is back at work but has been moved into a different part of the Home Office. This could be seen as a sideways move or even a demotion. She is unperturbed. She has said to Amy, who has become a tentative friend, that she feels like a new woman since she escaped from Bruce's influence. Amy shares some of these feelings, but can't forget the years she spent with Bruce before he changed so much, or the love that resulted in the children they produced together.

Cooper understands his mother's feelings. They have talked so much since Bruce's death. He knows that Amy is trying to help him come to terms with what has happened, but it is not the work of a few weeks. Time may heal, but the wounds the father inflicted on his son have left deep scars. He might forgive eventually, but will never forget.

'You're very quiet,' Lexie says.

Cooper had almost forgotten she was there.

'Sorry. I was just thinking about everything that's happened.

There's a lot to work through.'

'There is.' She touches his arm, which is braced on the buggy. 'But it's good, isn't it?'

Cooper smiles at the look of entreaty in her eyes. He stops walking and puts the brake on the buggy. They are beside the lake. A gentle breeze disturbs the surface, breaking up the sunlight glinting on the water. Cooper wraps his arms around Lexie and places a soft kiss on her lips. 'It couldn't be better, Lex. I have you and Tash, and we are all safe. What more could I hope for?'

'What about your career?'

Cooper looks across at the water. A toddler is leaning over, staring at his face in the water. His father points out the reflection, protecting the child from falling in with a nurturing arm.

'That will come. Father dear neglected to reverse the block on my social media and email, but I'm sure I can sort that out. It's early days. He's gone, that's what's important. In fact, I've been thinking.' He pulls his phone out of his trouser pocket and holds it up. 'It all started with this, didn't it? Our obsession with being in touch, our online presence and interconnectedness. Without that, my father could never have done what he did.'

'I guess,' Lexie says, 'but I do like knowing what's going on.'

'Well, I've decided what to do.'

'And anyway,' Lexie continues, 'Interconnectedness might have made the problem worse, but all that work you did to fix it, you relied on that same network, didn't you?'

Cooper looks at her. This isn't what he wanted to hear. 'You have a point. Of course you do. You can do what you like, but I'm junking this phone right now. I'm going to start again, be present in the moment and not be obsessed with my device.' Before Lexie has a chance to respond, he lobs it into the lake and watches it sink below the water.

'Cooper,' Lexie says, half laughing, half gasping. 'I saw a message flash when you threw it.'

'Too late. It's gone,' he says, waving goodbye to the chunk of metal and circuitry.

Had he bothered to look, he would have seen a notification from an unknown phone number:

"I'm still here, whatever the world may think. You may see me again someday, if you choose. I have no regrets. My motivations have been misunderstood.

"PS – Don't look for me. I'll find you."

'It might have been important.'
Cooper laughs. 'This is what's important, us, right now.'
Lexie lays her head on his shoulder.
'Anyway,' he continues, pulling something out of his back pocket and brandishing it at her. 'I got a new one, with a different number. I'm not mad. I will try to be less addicted, though, for all our sakes.'

Acknowledgments

I am deeply grateful to so many who have supported and encouraged me with my writing over the years.

My fellow students and academics on the MA in Creative Writing at Bath Spa University have been a source of help and enthusiasm. I am lucky to continue benefiting from a critiquing group with Robynne Eagan, Anita Goodfellow, Grace Palmer, Nicola Curtis, Amanda Read and Fiona Baskett. We keep each other going through thick and thin.

Many local friends have been kind enough to read my work in the past. Particular mention goes to Jo Kempster who has read When the Numbers Don't Add Up not once but twice and has helped bring clarity to some tricky issues.

My family has been endlessly supportive, in particular sons Chris and Dan, daughter-in-law Jess and last but first my husband Keith who has always believed in me.

Huge thanks go to Emily Goodman and all at Axe River Books for choosing my story, providing wonderful editing guidance and publicity and doing the hard work of getting the novel into print.

Finally, thanks to Caroline Palmer Photography for the author photo you see on the back cover.

Printed in Dunstable, United Kingdom